PENGUIN

treading on dreams

Kristin Williamson is the author of *The Last Bastion*, a political history of World War Two, *Princess Kate*, a novel for young adults, the bestselling novels *Tanglewood* and *The Jacaranda Years*, and a biography of anti-apartheid activists, the Watson brothers, *Brothers to Us*. She has an academic background in history, education and theatre, and spent many years as a teacher and journalist.

Kristin Williamson and her playwright husband, David, now divide their time between Sydney and the Queensland coast. They have five grown children.

OTHER BOOKS BY KRISTIN WILLIAMSON

The Last Bastion
Princess Kate
Tanglewood
The Jacaranda Years
Brothers to Us

treading on dreams

on

dreams

KRISTIN WILLIAMSON

PENGUIN BOOKS

Penguin Books Australia Ltd
487 Maroondah Highway, PO Box 257
Ringwood, Victoria 3134, Australia
Penguin Books Ltd
Harmondsworth, Middlesex, England
Penguin Putnam Inc.
375 Hudson Street, New York, New York 10014, USA
Penguin Books Canada Limited
10 Alcorn Avenue, Toronto, Ontario, Canada M4V 3B2
Penguin Books (NZ) Ltd
Cnr Rosedale and Airborne Roads, Albany, Auckland, New Zealand
Penguin Books (South Africa) (Pty) Ltd
4 Pallinghurst Road, Parktown 2193, South Africa

First published by Penguin Books Australia Ltd 1998

1 3 5 7 9 10 8 6 4 2

Designed by Nikki Townsend, Penguin Design Studio
Typeset in 11.25/14 pt Apollo MT by Post Pre-press Group
Brisbane, Queensland
Made and printed in Australia by Australian Print Group
Maryborough, Victoria

National Library of Australia
Cataloguing-in-Publication data:

Williamson, Kristin, 1940–.
Treading on dreams.

ISBN 0 14 027932 6.

I. Title.

A823.3

For Hope, Karen and Christopher
and in memory of my father, Harry

I have spread my dreams under your feet;
Tread softly because you tread on my dreams.

'He Wishes for the Cloths of Heaven'
W. B. Yeats

prologue

It is an afternoon in summer and a sea breeze blows in through the open window drying my tears. I wipe my face quickly before my sister, Charlotte, can make fun of me. I am almost five. She is eight and she is going to a birthday party to which I have not been invited. I know it isn't *my* friend who is having the party so there is no reason why I should have been invited, but as I watch Charlotte race from the house and skip out the front gate in her party dress, carrying her present of a Little Golden Book, an egg cup and a Violet Crumble bar, I can't help feeling sad.

It is before our father has come home from the war, so I am alone in the house with Mother. I can hear her humming to herself in the next room and I know that any minute she will open the piano. Dear God, don't let her start to play. If she does she will never stop. Not for hours. She will play Chopin or Schubert or Debussy, one of her favourites that goes on forever, and she will forget that I am alive.

Mother swishes past the door on her way to the piano. She is wearing a long skirt and a soft scarf tied at the throat which floats behind her like seaweed caught in the gills of some rare fish. Her hair is looped up into a golden knot. When she plays the piano she closes her eyes as if she is dreaming. If I shout to make her notice me, she opens her eyes very wide and looks startled, like a bird that has crashed into a window.

But she is not opening the piano. She has gone into the kitchen and she's banging cupboard doors. She sticks her head round the corner and smiles at me.

'Anna, would you like to go for a picnic?'

Thank you, God.

We set off along the track that runs beside the Merlin River not far from our house, each with a small haversack on our back. Here the river is hardly a river at all, but a deep winding creek. The afternoon is hot and windy and the mud on the creek bank has a dry crust on it, broken into jigsaw pieces that curl up at the edges. It looks hard but when we walk on it our feet sink down to the ankles and grey mud clings like plasticine to our legs. We like the feeling of mud oozing between our toes and laugh at the rude suction noises when we haul one foot out and plonk the next one in, leaving footsteps like a giant's.

In the mud live river crabs, tiny blue and pink creatures that scuttle sideways to escape our feet. A flock of birds – white-eyes, Mother calls them – are nesting in the saltbush and when they hear us, the giants, squelching towards them, they dart out of the dry bush and swoop away into the heat haze.

We sit down under a tree and unpack our haversacks. We drink our lemon cordial and eat our hard-boiled eggs and Uneeda biscuits with sultanas, Kraft cheese and celery. Mother hums to herself and smiles vaguely, her thoughts far away. Suddenly she turns to me and says, 'Why don't you jump on my back?'

I am pleased. The offer to be close to her is rare. She doesn't believe in cuddling children, or perhaps she just hasn't thought we might need it.

'We'll leave our haversacks here,' she says and dumps them in the bushes.

I clamber onto her slender back and cling to her shoulders. I smell her hair, which looks like honey in the sunlight, and close my eyes, nestling my head on her neck. When we reach the white sandy beach, Mother begins to canter like a horse, and I laugh.

'We're going to have an adventure. Do you want an adventure?' she calls excitedly.

'Yes!' I shout back.

'Hang on, then.' She wades into the river, which is no longer a creek, but wide and blue like the sea. 'You remember the fox and the gingerbread man?'

'Yes.' I am uneasy going in so deep but holding Mother tight I try to be brave like she is.

In the story the gingerbread man runs away from home because people are chasing him, trying to eat him. 'Run, run, as fast as you can, you can't catch me, I'm the ginger-bread man!' he yells cheekily. He runs and runs until he comes to a river. A kind fox says, 'Jump on my back. I'll carry you across.' So the gingerbread man does. 'My feet are getting wet,' moans the gingerbread man. 'Then jump on my neck,' says the wily fox. 'They're *still* getting wet.' 'Then jump on my head.' The gingerbread man does so, and in one gulp the fox has eaten him all up . . .

Mother has been swimming strongly for about ten minutes now. The water is deep but calm. Her skirt billows out around us like a parachute. I imagine that I am riding on the back of a mermaid, not a fox. Soon we are level with the tall, slimy pylons of the Merlin Heads Bridge. A delivery van rumbles across it over our heads, rattling the wooden planks. They sound much louder from down here in the water.

'Are we swimming all the way across the river, Mummy?' I am anxious. There is still a long way to go.

'Why not? It's an adventure! No one will believe we did it.' Mother is breathing hard. I cannot see the bank on the other side. My clothes are heavy with salt water. The river is alive with huge leathery hunks of brown seaweed that float around us like monsters. I am starting to feel frightened but I know I mustn't let Mother know in case she panics and loses her strength. 'An adventure!' she gasps, her head low in the water.

Suddenly the wind whips up and little white-crested waves appear all around us. Mother begins to gag on the water and to splutter. Her head disappears beneath the waves. I keep clinging to her disappearing head and sob. I don't cry out or flail about in panic, but just cling.

For years after, I wake damp with perspiration and gulping great mouthfuls of air, clutching my pillow or the bedpost. The terror of drowning still billows in my sub-conscious mind like wind filling the belly of a sail.

Mother rests now, hugging a bridge pylon. It is slimy and green, encrusted with barnacles and stinks of mus-sels, but it is our salvation. After a few minutes Mother's arms start to ache and the waves send us both crashing against the pylon so the barnacles cut our arms and legs.

Mother pushes off, back into the deep. We are now more than halfway across the river. I look hopefully for a fishing boat but it is a blustery day and there isn't one in sight.

We are making fair progress towards the township of Merlin Heads when we hit the tidal wash that drags the surf into the river from the sea. We swirl and twist and allow ourselves to be taken fast by the current for what seems a long way. 'We must go with the sea. The sea is our friend!' Mother shouts. My arms grip her neck, almost choking her, and I whisper over and over the only prayer I can remember, 'Dear Father God to Thee we pray, Please send the food we need today, Remember those who may have none, And please provide for everyone, Amen.' Even today, whenever I am in distress, I find myself mouthing this same inappropriate but comforting little prayer.

Suddenly we stop travelling at such speed. The water feels warmer. Mother staggers forward and falls. Her feet have touched the bottom. When we reach the opposite bank we collapse in the thick grey mud and lie still for a long time with the river lapping at our feet. We rest our heads on the saltbush and breathe in its warmth. When we have the strength to look around, we see that we have been washed a long way down river. Merlin Heads is not there, only paddocks and a dirt road. After a while we get up, wash the mud from our clothes and faces and walk back along the road towards the bridge. The mailman comes along in his van and Mother hails him. He gives us a lift back across the bridge to where we left our haver-sacks. When Mother tells him how we got there he does not believe her.

'You swam across the Merlin, nearly a mile, with a kiddie on your back? Nah! Get out of it! A surf lifesaver could hardly do it. He wouldn't, anyway. Not when the tide's comin' in and there's sharks around. Grey nurses. They caught an eight footer near the co-op last weekend. Just there,' he points.

Mother doesn't try to persuade him that what she has told him is the truth. She just smiles to herself and strokes her shoulder where the barnacles have made it bleed and asks him polite questions about his family and grey nurse sharks.

But the story gets around and Mother becomes something of a legend.

chapter one

$\mathcal{I}$t is the spring of 1954, almost ten years after my
mother swam the Merlin River with me on her back,
and I am sitting in the same chair by the window of our
house above the sea as I did that day. I am pretending to
read *Pride and Prejudice* but at the same time I'm watching Mother altering one of her dresses for Charlotte.
Charlotte is standing on the wooden piano stool and
Mother is on her knees, pinning up the hem. Mother has
pins in her mouth so she can't speak. When she wants
Charlotte to turn slowly so she can see if the hem is
straight, she makes humming noises and gestures with
her hands.

Charlotte is seventeen and by far the prettiest girl in
this district. Our mother, Katharine, is always saying
what a pity it is that we can't afford to buy Charlotte the
clothes that would make her shimmer. Shimmer is an odd
way to put it, but that's what she says. Mother was once
a beauty herself and understands the importance of
clothes. She has cut down a great many of her own for
Charlotte, but having a cleverly remade dress is not the
same as having a new one, as Charlotte often reminds her.

Mother is long-necked and elegant. Her beauty is a little faded now but she still wears her hair looped up into a flaxen knot and her scarves trailing absent-mindedly behind her. She walks and sits and even sleeps with a natural grace she seems unaware of. She is often vague and smiles with a faraway expression, as if watching some amusing play performed by actors who are invisible to everyone but her. Our mother is Anglo-Irish, and she looks frail but has a will of iron.

When Charlotte wants to upset me she tells me I am becoming exactly like Mother – not in appearance, of course (I am not beautiful), but in temperament. I don't know why I should be so afraid of this. I admire Mother. She is an exceptional woman, but her passions and moods are extreme. Yesterday she gave a terrible deep sigh, and said, 'By the end of this summer I know I will have become either bankrupt or mad.' Then she went off to practise her Schubert as if nothing had happened. I find that sort of behaviour disturbing.

Charlotte is disturbing in a different way. When she's sitting quite still by the fire and leaning towards it to dry her hair she looks like an angel. Her skin glows and her hair falls forward like a rosy fleece, but in an instant she can change into a harridan, scowling and ranting. If only she didn't have such a foul temper. She is so full of grand ideas and spends so much time locked in her room sulking about never being able to make her dreams come true.

Charlotte is feeling bitter at present, which makes it harder than usual to live with her. Her great ambition has always been to become an opera singer, and she certainly has the voice for it. Mother says she has a 'true ear' and 'absolute pitch', which none of the rest of us have. Charlotte began singing solos in church at the age of seven. Our family has always joked that she would sing Mimi in *La Bohème* at La Scala one day and – foolishly, I see now – we have made poor Charlotte believe it. It is not enough just to have a fine voice. She needs professional lessons, and suddenly we can't even afford the local singing teacher any more, let alone sending Charlotte to the Conservatorium of Music in Melbourne. So her hopes have been dashed.

Now Charlotte jumps down from the piano stool and swirls around in front of the mirror in her pinned-up blue dress. Mother stands back to admire her handiwork. She is not good at sewing and does it under sufferance, but I can tell she is pleased with the effect of this dress.

Charlotte twirls in the full, rustling skirt and then sighs rather tragically. 'I've decided to marry the first rich man who asks me,' she says to Mother. 'If he is fat, bald and ancient, so much the better. He'll be dead in a few years and then I'll have all the money I need to get to Europe and study.'

Mother smiles vaguely. 'Why not, dear?' she says.

Charlotte looks furious. She'd wanted Mother to protest, to beg her not to be so foolish, to say that she deserves much more than a fat, ugly old man and that a handsome suitor who appreciates her talent will be sure to show up very soon.

I look up from my book and make a suggestion that is not quite serious. 'While you're waiting for the rich man to turn up, Charlotte, you could sell flowers on the steps of the Melbourne Town Hall like Eliza Doolittle did on the steps of the Opera House at Covent Garden. If you sang a bit you might even get discovered.'

'Don't be such a moron,' says Charlotte bitterly.

Lately she has even lost her sense of humour.

There are five of us in the family – Katharine, our mother; Charlotte; Jonathan; Eliza (named after our maternal grandmother, not the Shaw character); and me, Anna. We have a father, Frank Danielssen, who is of Norwegian descent, but his whereabouts are a mystery. We're not even allowed to mention his name. He left us just after the war, when I was six, but I still remember him fondly. In fact I miss him very much, although Charlotte often says he is 'no great loss'.

The one good thing we know about our father is that he left us our 'albatross', the house we have lived in all our lives. We call it The Tower House, and we love it dearly, even though it is a bit of a wreck. It's set on a steep red cliff, high above the sea. To people who don't appreciate it, our house must appear bedraggled, intimidating and solitary.

When it's lit up at night it looks like a pirate ship. It juts out over the sea at a much more daring angle than the other conventionally constructed little ships. The neat fibro cottages with painted white verandahs give our big house a wide berth, as if they know that one day it might crash and break up on the rocks and they don't want any part of it.

At night The Tower House creaks and groans in the wind as if it has confessions it needs to make. Inside it is dark, the walls panelled with cedar like an old sailing vessel. It has hatchways and decks and balconies jutting out towards the ocean and the sky. When the wind blows, the house shudders and seems to roll. It is filled with things that we always tell people have been salvaged from shipwrecks, though I'm not sure this is true. There are ships' bunks, fold-out china washbasins, ladders, trunks, captains' chairs and even a bell.

The dining room is the only room that looks normal; it has the family silver on the chiffonier and framed portraits of our Irish ancestors hanging above a long Victorian oak dining table with balloon-backed chairs. At one end of the room is Mother's pride and joy – her grand piano.

There are three twisting staircases that lead to little bedrooms in our house. Mine is the smallest and highest. We call it the Crow's Nest. The windows are caked with salt and in high winds I swear the room creaks and then moves. I love living in such a strange, original old house and hope that we never have to live anywhere else in our whole lives.

Below the house an acre of overgrown garden slopes down towards the sea. There are winding stone pathways edged with climbing daisies and blue agapanthus. Grey, twisted tea-tree bushes clutch like bony hands at the wash-house and stables, threatening to crush them. The garage is a damp cave that has already fallen in at one end under the weight of red mud, but it doesn't matter because we've had no car for years. At the bottom of the garden is a vegetable patch, an enclosure with climbing ramps for our pet goats, Meckerli and Tabitha, a stable, a hen-house for the bantams and a flat expanse of grass that was once a croquet lawn.

Whenever Mother is particularly depressed about money she tells us we might have to sell The Tower House, but I know she couldn't bear to do it. She has always found a way of getting through our financial difficulties before. It's just that I notice she seems a bit frailer lately and gives those heart-rending sighs more often. Sometimes when Jonathan and Eliza are being noisy and quarrelsome she doesn't try to stop them but just walks away humming to herself. Even they watch her with puzzled looks.

For the past six years, until I moved into the Crow's Nest, I shared a bedroom with Jonathan, who is nine, and Eliza, who is seven. Charlotte is closer to my age than they are, but she has always preferred a room of her own. Until recently, I enjoyed being in with the little ones. Their room is long and high-ceilinged with rafters, like a country hall. At one end there is a raised platform which we have made into a stage with curtains. On either side of the stage are ladders leading to more platforms where chairs have been placed for the audience to sit. There are hand-painted billboards advertising 'The Grandest Circus Ever Seen' and 'Rose Red in the Magic Forest'. We performed these shows last year. Jonathan wrote them and painted the scenery, I directed, and Eliza invited her friends to take small parts while she took the leads. 'I was born to act!' Eliza announced to the family when she was about three, and we have more or less allowed her to act ever since. She has a dressing-room made of packing cases with a large gold star painted on the door and her name underneath.

There are sea chests full of props and costumes, and along the shelves are a mass of masks we've made – lions, devils, cats, witches with hair of straw – and a lot of grinning papier-mâché puppets. Dolls and teddy bears dressed as circus performers dangle by their legs from a tightrope strung between the rafters. There is a hammock draped in fishnet in which Eliza sometimes sleeps when she wants to dream about being a mermaid. On the wall above the hammock bed is an unfinished mural of fish and sea monsters. There is a large 'sea environment' created last summer from real rocks, sand, shells, crabs and a fish tank full of seaweed, which has now become rather smelly. At night a lamp covered in green cellophane transforms this section of the vast room into an eerie underwater cave.

We have always been allowed to use our bedrooms as we wish, and we don't see anything unusual about this. Our rooms are our creations. We are proud of them.

But recently the room I shared with Eliza and Jon began to feel uncomfortable. Cluttered. Chaotic. Claustrophobic. I wanted somewhere private with a door that could be locked and my own desk and a mirror. I felt embarrassed about telling Eliza and Jon all this because I knew they'd be hurt, so I tried to be tactful.

'I have a lot more homework to do this year.'

'We'll be quiet. We'll creep about like this.' Eliza walked on tiptoes, distorting her face to demonstrate the effort of being silent. She's a natural comedian.

I laughed. 'I won't be far away. You can come and visit, when I'm not too busy.'

'Who'll read to us before bed?' asked Jonathan.

'Who'll turn out the light?'

'Who'll think up the ideas for plays and tell us them in the middle of the night?'

'We'll be lonely. Scared. *Please* don't leave us. *Please*,' Eliza wailed.

'Don't be so dramatic. I won't be far away.'

And so I moved myself into the room beneath the tower. It is a small room, and I painted it blinding white – I loved its whiteness. Stark and light. I furnished it like a cell with nothing but a bed, a desk and chair, my books, and a pale rag rug. I pressed the narrow bed hard up against the window so that when I fall asleep reading books like Thor Heyerdahl's *The Kon-Tiki Expedition*, I can feel the rain on the glass and dream I am sleeping on a raft at sea. On windy nights I stare down at the cliff that supports our house, hold my breath and wait to feel the room move.

My favourite part of the house is the tower at the top. It is imitation neoclassic and very elegant. Our father built it himself. No one goes up there any more because it isn't quite safe. If it was I would sleep there.

There are a number of things that aren't safe about our house. The worst thing is the cliff that it stands on, which is crumbling into the sea. No one knows what to do about it so they try not to mention it. I have been planting creeper there and binding it with chicken wire, but in high winds the wire blows away.

Sometimes, locked away in my new, private room, I indulge in a daydream. Just as the cliff is dissolving into red mud and oozing down into the waves and the house is toppling perilously forward and we are all clinging to our favourite possessions and praying for a miracle, our father appears on a gigantic machine which drags the house and cliff back into position and sprays them with some invisible cement-like substance he has invented. He dismounts from his machine and embraces first me and then all the others in turn. Even Mother and Charlotte are moved to tears. He vows never to leave us again.

It is a foolish fantasy and quite childish, I know, but it keeps returning, even occasionally in dreams at night. Our father is always in his air-force uniform, which is what he was wearing when I last saw him just after the war ended.

The Tower House is just a building but it was a gift from our father. What I feel for it is not attachment. It is love. I find this hard to explain, even to myself.

Apart from our house almost falling into the sea, and apart from having no money or a father, ours is a fortunate family. There are plenty in the district who are worse off. Some have fathers who get drunk and are violent. Others have mothers with consumption or brothers and sisters with polio. A few have no houses at all and have to rent small shacks on the beach which are only meant for holidays. Whole families of New Australians live like that.

Mother tries to make friends with the New Australians. They used to be called Displaced Persons or Migrants but these names were changed to make them feel more welcome. The first New Australians came from the Baltic regions and the Ukraine, but now there are Dutch, Italians, Germans, Poles and British pouring in – even a few Irish, although Mother says none of these could be even slightly related to us. Mother is the granddaughter of Anglo-Irish landowners, who bred horses and seem to have been rather miserable, because they were unacceptable to the English upper class and despised by the Irish Catholics. They came here for the Gold Rush so I expect they were greedy as well as miserable. Mother says they came here because they were adventurous and wanted to escape 'The Troubles', but the Fitzsimons family didn't have much luck in their new country. They found no gold so they spent their savings on horses, but the horses were not fine stock and failed even to gain a place, let alone win the races they were bred for. Some of them died in the drought. My great-grandparents were bitterly disappointed, yet they didn't seem to realise they were running out of money. They still entertained, played music and gave generously to the people in their community they believed were 'needy'. They sold a lot of paintings and some valuable furniture to buy more horses; unfortunately these fared no better. They should have given up but they didn't. They were very stubborn people with perfect Victorian manners, which even Mother thought was embarrassing when you lived in a small country town and were deeply in debt.

You would think Mother might have learned something from all this, but I'm afraid she is very like her grandmother, who rode side-saddle in an elegant velvet habit, carrying cranberry jellies to the poor who lived in bark huts with dirt floors. I expect 'the poor' made fun of Great-grandmother behind her back, as the local people here do to Mother sometimes.

The New Australians treat mother differently. There are a lot of them living here in Skinners Bluff, probably because of the cheap holiday shacks. Mother thinks it's wicked to charge high rent for these places but some of the real estate agents do. The other day Mother carried a pitcher of homemade lemon juice to a group of men digging a drain on the road outside our house. It was a hot day and they wore handkerchiefs knotted on their heads to protect them from the sun. One of them was so grateful, he kissed Mother's hand. I must say she seemed to be communicating with them quite well, even though she doesn't speak a word of Italian or German or Yugoslav or whatever it is they speak.

This evening she has invited some Polish women to our place to hear her concert. She gives these little 'soirees' once a month. It's one of the few pleasures she indulges in, playing for the local people. Not many of them appreciate the music as she would like them to, of course, but she doesn't give up. She has been practising Schubert for days and days. Sometimes Charlotte sings an accompaniment, but probably not tonight.

'Charlotte's been in a bad mood all afternoon,' Eliza announced when I came into their room to see if she and Jon had clean clothes to wear for the concert.

'Does that mean she won't even pass round the tea and sandwiches afterwards, and that *we'll* have to dress up and do it?' asked Jonathan.

I nodded. 'Mother likes you to come. I'll help with the tea.'

'Will all the sandwiches be made of stuff like watercress and parsley and cucumber from the garden?' moaned Eliza.

I grinned. 'You know Mother likes to make *unusual* sandwiches.'

They screwed up their faces.

'I think I'll go for a ride on Grayling before people start arriving,' I told them.

'Good idea. A gallop along the beach will help clear your head before the long evening of listening politely,' said Jonathan, which I thought was quite perceptive of him.

He surprises me sometimes.

chapter two

On my ride this afternoon I saw something in the sand-hills that gave me quite a shock. It's not that I am a prudish person. I've read plenty of books that include the act of love, and I recognised immediately that this was what it was.

I'd been riding along the beach at low tide towards the bluff. The sand was hard and wide with a watery sheen on it like skin. Because of the cold wind there was nobody on the beach at all. Perfect. I crouched low on Grayling's neck and urged him into a gallop. The wind was behind us and our hair and mane mingled. My eyes were streaming and the sea water splashing up from his flying hooves half blinded me so that green waves and red cliffs and the forest of ghostly driftwood up ahead were blurred into one. I felt exhilarated. Wild. Powerful. As if I could do anything I really wanted to.

I turned the pony up into the sand dunes, out of the wind. Marram grass swished against my legs in a comforting, familiar way. I felt the warmth and closeness of the sand and smelt the saltbush. We would go home through the deserted camping ground where there were tea-tree logs to jump. Grayling enjoyed that. He was spirited and sure-footed in spite of being old. I dug my heels in and he careered off across the sandhills. Not a soul in sight. Just the gulls and a sea eagle. So I played a game that I sometimes do when I think no one is looking. I stretched myself flat on Grayling's neck and charged into a tunnel of thick tea-tree. It's a game of dare, in which I could be scraped off the horse by an overhanging branch or have an eye gouged out by a pointed stick.

I make myself do dangerous things sometimes to test my courage. I have a motto: courage and confidence. I would never tell anyone this, particularly not Charlotte. She would ridicule me or accuse me of getting like Mother.

Grayling was trembling with excitement as he plunged into the thicket. His body sank deep into the tunnel and we both disappeared. I clung on, squeezing my eyes shut tightly to protect them and bracing my body to withstand the scratches. After half a minute or so we emerged on the other side and I opened my mouth to yell in triumph.

That was when we almost trampled on them. They were naked. I pulled up sharply and stared down. I had not expected the act of love to look like this. I'd imagined something beautiful. The man had very white buttocks which didn't stop pounding even though we'd nearly galloped over them. The couple's clothes were flung on the sand around them like rags. They were grunting and heaving like animals. I should have looked away but I couldn't.

The woman's eyes were closed but her mouth was wide open, gasping like a fish out of water. She had pale skin and her hair clung to her head in long, damp tendrils. The man's body kept pounding into her. His neck was red and streaked with sweat. The woman turned her head to one side and looked at me. We stared at each other for what seemed a long time. Perhaps she was in some sort of trance. Then she realised I was watching and she looked worried. The man saw nothing. I fled.

The light was fading as we cantered through the camping ground on the way home, but I put Grayling over the most difficult jumps just the same – fallen trees half obscured by creeper, logs wide apart. It was stupid, but I felt angry about those people. Didn't they feel ashamed of behaving like that? Surely that was not the way normal couples made love.

I was angry at myself too. I had stared at them and been fascinated.

As I came close to home I thought about telling Charlotte what I'd seen but just the idea of having to describe it made me feel sick. She would probably think I was exaggerating. Or she might think I'd made the whole thing up just to disturb her. Charlotte dislikes anything ugly.

When I got home, just in case Charlotte's bad mood had changed for the better while I was out, I thought I would go and ask her whether she'd sing tonight. Mother likes her to take part in the soirees. I knocked on her door. She opened it a crack and then without much grace let me in. As Mother is fond of saying, Charlotte's room looks 'like a mad woman's breakfast'. She is as messy as I am fastidiously tidy. Clothes, manuscript paper, shoes, borrowed magazines, make-up, pots of opened face cream, old programmes, and dirty cups and plates were not just all over the floor but perched on shelves, mantel-piece and dressing-table. Every drawer was open and overflowing with more clothing and so was the wardrobe. There were dead flowers in vases of discoloured water, and peacock feathers, celluloid dollies on sticks and paper streamers from school parties she went to years ago with partners she can no longer remember. I often wonder how she finds anything but she seems to know where everything is.

She was brushing her hair so vigorously in front of the mirror that I could hear it crackling. She looked like a fiery angel.

I meant to ask tactfully about the singing but instead I burst out, 'Guess what I saw in the sandhills just now!'

She shrugged indifferently.

'A couple. Naked. It was disgusting!'

'What were they doing?'

'I think they were . . .' I couldn't say it.

'Rooting,' Charlotte said bluntly.

I blushed. I'd never heard my sister use such language.

'Who were they?' she asked without much interest.

'I've no idea,' I replied, and for some reason I felt that I might cry.

Charlotte looked at me very directly and said, 'Don't look so shocked, Anna. It's what couples *do*.'

'But it looked so . . . primitive, like animals. You wouldn't have liked to see it!'

'Every couple does it. Even Mr Darcy and Elizabeth Bennet!' She was poking fun at me for reading so much Jane Austen. I had once made the mistake of telling her that Mr Darcy and Elizabeth Bennet were the most romantic characters I'd ever read.

'Don't talk rubbish!' I said.

'They are described as "violently in love", Anna. What do you *think* they'd do?' She began stuffing clothes into a small suitcase.

'Where are you off to?'

'Uncle Martin's. I'm staying the weekend. Can't stand one single more of Mother's dreary little musical evenings.'

I must have looked upset because she said crossly, 'Don't pretend *you* enjoy them.'

'I don't particularly but they make her happy.'

'Why are you always trying so hard to make *her* happy? She doesn't try to make *us* happy. She's totally selfish, she doesn't fit into this world and she should never have become a mother!'

'Shut up! Why are you saying all this? She isn't selfish. She cut down her Alice Blue Gown for you.'

'What!' Charlotte looked at me as if I was an imbecile. 'What Alice Blue Gown?'

'It's what she calls it. From the song she sings, "In My Sweet Little Alice Blue Gown". It was one of her favourite dresses and she cut it all up for you.'

Charlotte tossed her head in disgust. 'It was far too young for her. She's thirty-seven, Anna!'

'Well, she still loved that dress, and you shouldn't say she's not fit to be a mother. People admire her, Charlotte.'

'They don't. Just watch them tonight while she's playing. Watch them sniggering.' She snapped the case shut and swung it onto the floor.

'They *never* snigger. You're wrong, and I think you're very selfish to go off and leave me alone to cope with her for another weekend. This is the third one in a row!'

Charlotte threw her hands up in the air. 'See! You admit it. She's impossible to cope with. She's utterly neurotic and irresponsible and I'm not sticking around to look after her. If you had any sense, you'd get out of this family too.'

She marched out the door and I followed, keeping step with her as she hurried down the steep path to the road.

'Don't go, Charlotte! Look, things will be all right if you'll just help me with the daily chores, like bills and housekeeping, looking after the little ones and the animals . . .' I trailed off because Charlotte was shaking her head vehemently.

'Anna, you know nothing about what's going on, or else you've deliberately closed your eyes to it.' She stopped walking and turned to me seriously. 'By the end of the year Mother will be forced to sell this house to pay the debts, and Eliza and Jonathan will be sent to St Augustine's Orphanage in Geronga. By then, I hope, I'll be living with Uncle Martin and Aunt Ursula. You'd better start thinking about what *you're* going to do.'

'You're mad. She'd never sell The Tower House. The orphanage?' I laughed to cover my alarm. 'Where would Mother go if we sold the house?'

'To Kew, the lunatic asylum in Melbourne.'

As she stalked off down the muddy red road to catch the bus, I shouted after her, 'Coward! Liar! Coward, coward, liar, liar!'

The wind was blowing so hard she probably couldn't hear, but it made me feel better. I was furious. Charlotte might be miserable about her own unpromising future but there was no need to make up horrible stories about what might happen to the rest of us. Our little family has survived so far and if Mother was getting tired of coping then I would just have to take over. I would do anything to keep the family from being broken up and The Tower House from being sold – with or without Charlotte.

As I rushed off to put Grayling in the stable in our lower garden I noticed that the chicken wire binding the cliff had fallen away in several places so I scrambled up to fix it. Mother does not seem particularly concerned that the cliff has been crumbling for years. It makes bits of our steep garden jut out unexpectedly like bizarre little balconies in a building that has partly survived an earthquake. Clumps of yellow jonquils wave innocently above the void. The Parapets, Mother calls them. Or sometimes, the Suicide Balconies. It's only a joke.

Our family has lots of jokes. Mother is a clever mimic and can make us cry with laughter when she takes off the prissy, judgemental postmistress handing us our final notice bills from the electricity department.

The local people don't approve of our house. It's 'a blot on the landscape', I've heard them say. 'It should be done up and turned into a school or a guesthouse, or pulled down to make way for a new block of holiday flats,' we hear them muttering as they tramp past on their way to the lookout at weekends.

From the lookout you can see the Heads. A lot of tankers go by and passenger liners from the P & O Line on their way 'home' to Britain and Ireland. (Mother still calls it home, even though she's never been there.) Sometimes she sits up at the lookout for hours just watching the ships pass by. Other people show their children the white ships in the distance, too, and tell them how it takes six weeks to get to England. Then they let them climb on the rusty cannon that they say has protected us all from the Japanese invasion, and show them how to carve their initials on the gun barrel. On the way home they point at our ramshackle house on the cliff and tell their children the names they've made up for it – Mad Hatter's Castle and The Haunted Mansion.

Our mother is amused by these names but we children are a bit ashamed. We've become used to being treated as odd in our own township. We pretend we don't care. We have a wild garden to play in, the sea and the beach just beyond the back gate and a house that's different from anyone else's. Although we have almost no money at all our mother has given us a sense of entitlement. This is rather inconvenient in our poverty-stricken state. I think this comes from her ancestors, who all seem to have been arrogant, daring and a bit mad.

'Did you know that your great-great-grandfather was an Irish politician who once rode his horse into the parliament as a protest?' She first proudly told me this story when I was about eight.

'What was he protesting about?'

'Well, he himself was a staunch Protestant but he believed it was unfair that Catholics were debarred from sitting in parliament. He supported the Emancipation Bill.'

'What was that?'

'It was to grant citizen rights to Catholics in their own country, but it was fiercely opposed in the House of Lords. Fiercely!' Mother always told stories dramatically. 'Eventually it was passed. Great-great-grandfather was delighted but unfortunately many other Anglo-Irish thought he was a traitor and he lost the seat of County

Clare which his family had held for generations, and guess who he lost it to?'

'Who?'

'The first Catholic candidate ever to stand in Ireland!'

'But wasn't that what he wanted? To have Catholics in parliament?' I asked.

'Oh, yes, yes, yes, but the irony of it. Don't you see? Poor Great-great-grandfather,' Mother sighed. 'He put up a fight for justice and I believe he did the right thing, even though the rest of the family thought he was mad!' She always finished this story triumphantly.

I think Mother admires her great-grandfather so much because she rebels against the ideas of her family, just as he did.

The most rebellious thing Mother ever did was to marry a Norwegian, and years ago I overheard her brother, Uncle Martin, telling her that it was the worst mistake she ever made. Our father wasn't there, so he couldn't defend himself. He'd been at the war and when he came home there'd been arguments for a year or so and then he'd gone away again. Probably forever. Uncle Martin had said this was a good thing. Mother had told him to mind his own business.

Mother often seemed to do things that upset Uncle Martin. A month after our father left us she invited his Norwegian aunts to come and stay with us. They had travelled all the way from Western Australia, which is as far away as Singapore where Uncle Martin fought the great battle against the Japanese and lost it when Singapore fell.

The great-aunts were called Ingeborg and Hedda. They were tall, with big bones and powerful faces like masks, and they had deep voices. They wore long dresses which almost touched the ground and their hair was white and drawn back in tight buns. They had strong brown arms and stood very straight and tall. In my memory they always stood. They did not sit. They scared me a little at the time but I liked them. They had strange accents. Aunt Ingeborg did not say, like other old ladies, 'Come and sit on my knee, dear, and have a chocolate.' She said, 'Und whoot are your interests, young lady?' as if she really wanted to know.

I stared at her with foolish, bulging eyes. 'Aunt Ingeborg, my interests are stories and dancing.'

She looked at Hedda and together they sighed. Then they smiled at me. They saw that Charlotte was like our mother. She was the dainty Anglo-Irish daughter with pouting lips and a wicked smile. She was deceptive and clever and extremely pretty. They looked at me and saw the serious, introspective Norwegian.

Mother was polite to the great-aunts. They stayed with us for a week. Perhaps they'd come to see why our father wasn't there, what the problem was between him and our mother, but they didn't ask questions or make judgements. They weren't that type. They merely visited and observed. They were solid and reliable, like two pylons holding up a bridge.

Before they left, Aunt Ingeborg and Aunt Hedda gave me a book of Norse legends and Charlotte a pretty seal-skin cap that had come all the way from Oslo. I wondered whether they had originally planned to give the cap to me and the book to Charlotte because she was older, but had changed their minds once they'd met us. Charlotte had immediately put on her cap and begun twirling like a skater and bowing to the imaginary admiring crowd, and I had gone off into a corner to read my book. The aunts had exchanged smiles and nodded wisely.

To Jonathan, who was not yet two, they gave a beautifully carved wooden engine, and for the baby, not yet born, they left a knitted shawl. They gave Mother a dozen bottles of red wine from their vineyards on the Margaret River. They told her it was young wine and was not to be drunk for at least five years. In ten years it would be very fine wine indeed. Mother thanked them and put it away in the dusty hole we called a cellar.

I missed the great-aunts when they left us. I asked Mother if we could write to them, but she said, 'I don't think they left their address.'

I never saw the aunts again, which was sad because they were kind and sensible and knew what to think. No one would ever dream of calling them mad. I felt relieved to know that I had relations like them, because the other side of the family was slightly unhinged.

I suppose people going past our house this afternoon might have thought I was unhinged, trying to bind the cliff together with the purple pigface. The forces of wind and sea are probably stronger than anything I can do to stop the cliff being undermined, but where the pigface is spreading, the cliff has actually stopped crumbling, so it must be having some effect. As I struggled to replant it I thought of Aunt Ingeborg and Aunt Hedda digging trenches in the hot sun to plant their grapevines by the Margaret River.

The wind had been blowing hard ever since I got back from my ride on the beach this afternoon and I was so absorbed in plaiting pigface between the chicken wire that I didn't hear Albert Marsden until he was standing close behind me on the cliff. His long silk scarf suddenly whipped across my face and I could smell his leather jacket. He laughed when I jumped.

'Sorry. I thought you must have heard the bike.'

He put out his hand to steady me. He was standing very close, smiling that wickedly playful smile that makes his eyes crinkle up and my heart thump in my chest. He looked pleased to have startled me. I glanced down and there was his gleaming motorbike parked by our gate.

'May I offer you some help?' he said intimately. My heart stopped pounding. I was improving, I told myself.

'No thanks.' I looked down at his hand still holding mine and covered in red clay. I was breathing too fast. 'Sorry, I've put mud on you,' I said awkwardly.

He shrugged and laughed.

We both looked up towards the house. Schubert's *Wanderer Fantasy* was just beginning.

'You're not coming in?' he asked.

'Later,' I said.

We grinned at each other rather sheepishly. I think he could guess that I wasn't particularly looking forward to the elegant evening that lay ahead and I sensed that he was only going because it was his duty.

He clambered backwards down the cliff and waved his scarf flamboyantly at me. He was twenty-seven years old and far too handsome for an Anglican minister. I laughed to cover the fact that I was blushing. I had just had a shockingly inappropriate thought about the Reverend Albert Marsden.

chapter three

*A*fter I had scrubbed my nails to get the red clay out and changed out of my jodhpurs into the only dress I own that is presentable, I crept into the far end of the dining room behind the piano, hoping that Mother would not notice I was late. Thankfully she had just finished the allegro part of the *Wanderer Fantasy*. It is rather thumpy and showy, as if Schubert is trying to bully people into listening. I love the adagio section which comes immediately after. I watched Mother's hands move like lightning up and down the keyboard, creating cascades of water trickling over a waterfall into a quiet pool. I imagined a forest. Then in came the main theme. So haunting. I wished I could play like that. I saw myself dancing. I was a nymph reflected in the pool. Then there was a rumbling in the forest. Thunder. And trolls approaching.

I tore myself away from the ballet I was choreographing in my head to look at the audience. There was a good crowd this evening, about fifteen people, seated in rows on our dining-room chairs. They always wear their best clothes and sit rather stiffly for Mother's performances. I recognised almost all of them. There were the regulars – our doctor and his wife, the two old Miss Bells who run the haberdashery store, Miss Bryant (the prissy one) from the post office, Mrs Lorimer and her two daughters, Shirley and Joan (they are my age and resent being dragged along but their mother wants them to have 'a musical education', which is a waste of effort anyway because they're both tone deaf). The bank manager and his wife were also here, which was unusual. I wondered if this was a good sign or a bad one. We owe the bank a lot of money. I decided to be especially charming to them afterwards. There were also the two Polish women Mother met on the bus to Geronga. They work at the Pelaco shirt factory, and she'd invited them because they know nobody else in the district. They both wore their hair in long plaits wound round and round the tops of their heads, which must have taken hours to do. Reverend Marsden was here, looking slightly less attractive in his stiff white clerical collar, without his flowing scarf, motorcycle goggles and jacket. That was a relief. Still, I looked quickly away in case I should have another shocking fantasy. Mrs Mooney, our neighbour, was here too with her oldest girl, Wilma, who was squirming in her seat. Wilma only comes to see my sister Eliza, who is her best friend.

Apart from the obviously bored Wilma, everyone sat staring at Mother with awe. When she plays, she is transformed. She's no longer tired or shabby. She comes alive. I feel proud of her, almost as if I might cry, but of course I wouldn't dare. Mother hates sentimentality. I looked across at Jonathan and Eliza, standing waiting to pass the sandwiches and make polite conversation with the audience afterwards, and I could tell that they were proud of her too. For a short time, while she is playing, we know that we don't have to worry about our mother. She is ful-filled. She looks radiant.

When the piece finished there was enthusiastic applause. Mother rose and bowed to everyone. The applause became stronger. She bowed again, being careful neither to look too humble nor too condescending.

'Your mother is not a professional musician, although she has the air of one,' Uncle Martin told me once. He had sneered a little and added, 'She's a good amateur and that's all she'll ever be.' I have hated him ever since.

Uncle Martin is our mother's only brother. She worships him and thinks all other men pale into insignificance beside him. When our father left us, Uncle Martin became a sort of surrogate father, although he has a family of his own. We don't need Uncle Martin; he's bossy and arrogant, although he means well, I suppose. Charlotte doesn't mind him, but then she's in the mood to accept charity from absolutely anyone. It's embarrassing that she spends so many weekends at their house. Aunt Ursula is completely dominated by Uncle Martin, which is odd because Mother says she's a very capable woman, although so conservative. When Uncle Martin was away at the war and no one was sure whether he was alive or dead, she taught high school for five years and looked after their two young children at the same time. Our cousins, Tom and Sarah, are now sixteen and fifteen. Tom is away at boarding school most of the time, which is a pity because I really like him. Sarah is about to become a boarder too. She is only six months older than I am but far more sophisticated. She has travelled overseas twice on the *Orsova*, stopping at Colombo, Aden and Port Said before spending months in London. She has also been to

France (her French is fluent and the pronunciation so much better than mine). She has her own horse, whereas I only borrow Grayling from wealthy Mrs Armitage who needs to have him exercised. Sarah and I ride together in school holidays when she's not too busy, which isn't that often since she goes to a private school and has friends who invite her to parties and dances all the time. I go to the local girls' high school. It's quite a good school, but we only have one dance a year and it's certainly nothing like the ones Sarah goes to.

I was daydreaming about dances when Reverend Marsden appeared at my elbow, motioning in the direction of Mother, who was accepting congratulations from Mrs Hill. She came in even later than I did, so she couldn't have heard much. Mrs Hill is a real 'gusher' and not at all sincere, but I don't think Mother realises this. She was smiling happily and thanking Mrs Hill and her friend, Mrs Barry, who was nodding in agreement with every false compliment being made.

Reverend Marsden raised his eyebrows at the little group. 'Your mother is a genius. She plays superbly and she's charming to her enemies.'

I couldn't help laughing. For a minister of God he is really quite clever. I felt like squeezing his hand, but of course I didn't. I love being with Reverend Marsden. We communicate without having to say much at all. I think he knows that I feel awkward at evenings like this. I wish he were a relative; a brother, perhaps. Then the thoughts I keep having wouldn't be inappropriate at all. It would be perfectly acceptable to roll down a steep sandhill with your older brother and then hug him close afterwards because you were both laughing so much. Or to ride on the back of his motorbike holding on tightly round his waist and snuggling your head into his leather jacket to protect yourself from the wind. You could even kiss him on the neck for giving you such an exhilarating ride, if he were your brother.

He gave me a look as if he almost knew what I was thinking, then smiled and walked off to be charming to others. I went to help pass the tea. Eliza and Jonathan were managing the sandwiches well enough. Eliza enjoys being a hostess. She has Charlotte's good looks, although she's chubbier, but at her age being plump doesn't matter. People think it's cute. Unfortunately Eliza already realises how pretty she is and has begun to expect compliments. When her baby front teeth fell out recently, Reverend Marsden said jokingly, 'Oh, Eliza, you've lost all your beauty!' She was devastated. She went straight to her room to change into her best dress to make up for the loss of the teeth. She was cross with him for days about that remark. Eliza is very confident in company and likes attention. She played the role of a wind-up doll in a school production of *The Toyshop* this year, and when she came onstage walking stiffly and saying 'Mama, Mama', the audience all went 'Ahhh!'

Jonathan, by contrast, hates to be noticed. He is an introvert, has a vivid imagination and is very sensitive. If he could have he would have escaped to his room tonight to get on with his current obsession, which is film-making. He has an ancient eight-millimetre movie camera which belonged to our father and he is making an animated short film about Tarzan, using a brown-painted doll wearing a leopard skin, and lots of stuffed animals. He films them in our garden which is a bit like a jungle and has constructed miniature swing bridges across the fishpond and has even made a fake crocodile. He is really quite clever because he's never made a film before and just learns how to do it from books. Sometimes, when things go wrong, like the film getting jammed because the camera is old, and all his weeks and weeks of patient work are ruined, he'll have a fit of rage, howling and banging his head on the floor, blaming himself for being stupid. It's terrible to watch, and all I can do is offer to buy him another roll of film with the pocket money I have saved for Christmas presents. I try to persuade him to give up for a while, or to wait until we can get advice from some expert, although that's pretty difficult since we don't know any. But he is very determined. He has written to the Victorian Filmmakers Club in Melbourne and they have accepted his application to join. They don't know he's only nine.

Jonathan is pale, with lank brown hair that hangs over his forehead. His eyes are green as deep sea water and very wide with long dark lashes, so it's a pity they are covered by hair.

Tonight he was looking miserable wearing his neat tweed jacket, a hand-me-down from cousin Tom, and passing the sandwiches but I know he was doing it for Mother. She expects it. Mother smiled down at Jonathan and pushed his hair out of his eyes as she asked the two New Australians about their children. Next, I suppose, she'll invite them all for dinner, although we've hardly enough food for ourselves.

Uncle Martin is always lecturing Mother about money. He's exasperated by her generosity, which he calls reck-lessness, so I don't like to burden her with more advice, but I do wish she'd restrain herself. At least she's agreed to me taking over the management of the household accounts. I'd been afraid to ask but last week I caught her in a serene mood after she'd been practising and when I suggested it she said, 'What a good idea! You're the only practical person in this family so of course you should be the housekeeper.' I hope she remembers she said that. She can be very vague when she's at the piano. When I was little I used to think that she went deaf every time she played.

I don't think of myself as a practical person – Charlotte says I'm a dreamer – but I do worry about our debts. I used to think that Mother was being considerate not telling us just how much we owed, but since I overheard Uncle Martin ranting at her for neglecting to pay even the most urgent bills, like the electricity, which has been cut off three times this year, I've begun to realise that she just doesn't think paying bills is important. When I try to discuss this with Charlotte she throws up her hands and says, 'Haven't you realised yet that our mother is eccentric, vague and absolutely *incompetent* with money? I'm getting out of this family before they put us all in some debtor's prison!' Charlotte is exaggerating because she's unhappy, I know, but it would be nice if I had *someone* to discuss the problem with.

There's plenty of gossip about Mother in our town. As the guests were leaving this evening I overheard Mrs Barry talking to her friend, Mrs Hill.

'Marvellous, isn't she?'

'A virtuoso.'

'She's had a hard life, but she'd never show it. Such a lady. A credit to the district.'

'A credit? I wouldn't say that exactly,' said Mrs Hill.

What on earth could she have meant? I wish Mother wouldn't invite such mean-minded old women to our house.

Sometimes I think she regrets these musical evenings herself. When the last guest had gone and we are all in the kitchen about to start cleaning up, Mother collapsed into a chair and became another person.

She sighed deeply and said, 'Why do I do it?'

I gave her an encouraging little smile and began stacking up dishes. I've become used to this sudden personality change once Mother is no longer on display. Jonathan and Eliza looked at her anxiously. They don't like her mood changes. It makes them nervous.

'What's that lovely tune you've just played, Mrs Danielssen?' Mother said in a nasal Australian accent.

'Schubert's *Wanderer Fantasy*, Mrs Barry. Did you enjoy it?' she replied in her own cultured voice.

'Yeeeahs, but could we have something we could all sing along to in the second half? Do you know that nice old song called "Peggy O'Neill"?'

Eliza jumped up enthusiastically and started singing 'Peggy O'Neill' in a sweet voice. Jonathan, relieved to hear Mother disapproving of the people he'd had to endure all evening, joined in, changing it into a comedy routine by miming a very bad piano player and putting in trombone-like 'oompapas'.

I grinned at them both.

Suddenly Mother sprang out of her chair. 'That's enough!'

The children stopped dead. They looked to me for reassurance but I continued washing the dishes; they took up tea towels and wiped them, looking subdued. I was fuming. When Mother is in this mood she requires an audience, not other performers. She is so selfish.

She flopped back into her chair and leant her head on one hand, looking tragic.

'The Reverend Marsden didn't mind your Schubert,' I said brightly. I try to ignore her bad behaviour.

She gave a wan smile. 'No, he didn't, did he?' There was a pause. 'They're always so poor, those young Anglican ministers.' Then she sighed deeply, a sound that chills me. 'Oh, I'm so bored, so dreadfully bored.'

Eliza said seriously, 'Jenny's mum was bored, but now she's got a shop.'

Mother laughed bitterly. 'That's what I should do! Go into business like everyone else in this money-grubbing town. Open a tea room. Paint shells. Start a bazaar selling grass mats and raffia serviette rings!'

Jonathan turned to her excitedly. 'Start a milk bar like the Doo Duck Inn!'

Mother laughed with an edge of sarcasm which the children didn't notice. 'Yes, darling. You could make the chocolate milkshakes. Eliza could put the ice-cream in the lime spiders, and Anna and I would do hamburgers with the lot.'

Jonathan and Eliza cheered and jumped up and down. I gave Mother an angry look and said quietly to the children, 'She doesn't mean it.'

They stopped jumping and stared at us both in confusion. Mother gave me a look that said, 'How can you be such a killjoy?' and gathered the two young ones close to her. 'Do you know what I think?' she said conspiratorially.

'What?' said Eliza, intrigued and instantly forgiving.

Jonathan was still doubtful.

'We've done such a good job entertaining those bores that we all deserve a good scream.'

My heart plummeted. Screaming is an embarrassing ritual that Mother encourages when she thinks we need to let off steam. We've been doing it for years. You can see why some people think she's mad.

'Me first!' said Eliza.

Mother nodded. Eliza turned her face up to the ceiling, opened her small mouth wide and let out a long, piercing yell. Her face went pink. She turned to Mother for approval. Jonathan's scream was more of a croaky shout, explosive and quickly over, but he seemed to feel satisfied afterwards. Next I had to do it. Mother knew I could not refuse or it would spoil things for the little ones. Dear God, don't let me hate her for making me do this, I thought. My scream came out rather strangled. Then it was Mother's turn. She screamed, dramatically, like someone discovering some horror in a Greek tragedy, not that I've ever seen a Greek tragedy. She was enjoying this infantile game. It seemed to draw her closer to Eliza and Jonathan. She hugged them, one under each arm, and they all laughed. I watched them from the sink, feeling utterly excluded.

I try not to feel jealous or hurt or disturbed by Mother's little games. I try to think only of her good times. When she is quite well she bakes cheese scones split down the middle with golden butter melting inside, and delicious gooseberry tartlets, shockingly sour, with pastry as light as cirrus clouds. The kitchen is fragrant with her cooking and she sings 'In My Sweet Little Alice Blue Gown'. It is easy to love her then.

She's not really ill, just mildly eccentric, Uncle Martin says. He understands her restlessness and boredom with life. He's affectionate to her and seems almost fond of her eccentricity. Whenever he comes to visit, once a fortnight or so, he seems to expect her odd behaviour, and he hardly notices her sudden mood changes. He's not at all alarmed when she suddenly hurls her afternoon teacup across the room, flings herself down on the sofa and bursts into tears. While she sobs he will gaze out the window, looking bemused. After a while he will suggest they take a walk, so off they will go together along the wild beach, arm in arm like lovers, and when they come back she will be laughing. It is such a relief. For an hour or so someone else has been responsible for our mother, has even made her happy. As they come back in the door she is sometimes teasing him affectionately by reciting a bit of Oliver Goldsmith's *The Traveller*, which he imagines is about him.

'Where'er I roam, whatever realms to see,
My heart untravell'd fondly turns to thee;
Still to my Brother turns, with ceaseless pain,
And drags at each remove a lengthening chain.'

They both love Irish poetry.

Although I don't really like Uncle Martin, I wish he would come and take her out more often. When I asked once if he would come every week he shrugged as if this was a foolish idea and said he was busy with his own family. I felt ashamed, as if I had intruded.

Uncle Martin is a solicitor in Geronga, a town fifteen miles from Skinners Bluff. He and Aunt Ursula and our cousins live in a new house that is immaculately tidy. Except for Charlotte, none of us feels welcome on the rare occasions that we visit them. They approve of Charlotte because she is always on her very best behaviour with them. They also quite like to show her off, I think. She was invited to sing 'Oh, My Beloved Father' at their wedding anniversary party last month, which she performed with such 'sweetness' that it brought tears to the eyes of their friends. It's an absolutely soppy song about some Italian girl who says she'll throw herself off the bridge into the river if her father doesn't allow her to go to her lover. It's not exactly appropriate for Charlotte to sing, considering her feelings for our father. She would never dream of asking him before she dashed off with her lover. I think Charlotte is hoping that Uncle Martin and Aunt Ursula will invite her on their next trip to London on the *Orsova*. If they do that, they might as well adopt her and be done with it.

Recently I have realised two important things. The first is that my body, which I've pretty much ignored until now, is becoming womanly. This embarrassed me at first but now I find myself using it to act out the different types of women I imagine I could be. A few weeks ago I placed a full-length mirror in my room, pushed away the copy of *The Kon-Tiki Expedition* (I read it partly because it's about adventurous Norwegians and one of them is called Danielsson whom I like to believe is a distant relation), and began my own voyage of discovery. I posed in different positions, using all kinds of props and costumes. Draped in a blue head shawl wearing a pious expression and holding a white bundle I became the Virgin Mary. Then I dashed the bundle to the floor, flung off the shawl and, with my legs wide apart, gun twirling in my holster, a tough grin on my face and wearing nothing but a cowboy hat, riding boots and a short, shiny petticoat, I was a shameless out-law. Parting my red hair in the middle and teasing it out wide on either side of my face, draped in strings of beads, dangling earrings and a paisley dressing-gown belonging to my mother, I was transformed into a Pre-Raphaelite beauty. I perfected a superior sneer, painted my lips and held a blue agapanthus flower from the garden at my throat. (We don't have any lilies.) Every novel I read lately reveals new characters for me to become. *Tess of the D'Urbervilles* is my favourite right now. Poor Tess deterio-rates so completely. Sometimes I pose standing demurely naked in a large shell, like Botticelli's virgin in *The Birth of Venus*, or I transform myself into a Parisian slut, painted by Toulouse-Lautrec, with hair all over her eyes and her hand on one hip sticking out at an angle.

Of course I lock the door before I do any of this. Once I heard Jonathan smothering giggles outside. He said he was filming me through the keyhole, which was almost certainly a lie, but I still felt mortified.

The second thing I realised only tonight. Perhaps it was a result of my confrontation with Charlotte and her horri-ble fantasy about what might happen to our family. Although I would never admit it to Charlotte, I'm afraid that she is partly right about Mother. Maybe she is a little crazier than it is safe to be. This makes my dream of keep-ing the family together in The Tower House much harder to realise. If I stay here and take care of Mother and the two younger children, I will risk becoming just like her. The alternative is for me to escape, like Charlotte, leave school and go away to the city to earn money to send home. Which choice should I make? It is a difficult decision. I have given myself four months, until Christmas, to decide.

chapter four

There were almost no men in my life until I was five. Because of the war there just weren't any about. The only man I ever saw, apart from our family doctor, the bank manager and the Anglican minister, was the ice man who came with a gigantic block of ice wrapped in a hessian bag which he carried on his shoulder and plonked inside our ice chest twice a week. The general store, post office, guesthouse and tea rooms were all run by women. Even the butcher was a woman. She was big with red cheeks and she wore a blue and white striped apron and wielded the chopper so fast that bits of fat flew off the carcass into the sawdust all over the floor.

So when I started school at Skinners Bluff State, a one-roomed rural school with a water tank at one end and a porch where we hung our schoolbags at the other, I was pleased to discover that our teacher was a man.

His name was Mr Delaney but we never called him anything but 'Sir'.

It was Sir who suggested I could start school early, before I was five. Perhaps he'd heard about my mother's daring swim across the Merlin River with me on her back and thought I needed protecting. He could have heard about it from the mailman who gave us a lift across the bridge, or from the fishermen at the co-op who embellished the story every time they retold it in the Merlin Heads pub, but I think that most likely he heard it from the ladies from the Church of England Guild, who made it their business to interfere when they judged that a child in the community was at risk.

The day after our adventurous swim two well-meaning ladies, whom we had never seen before, came to our house to visit. They brought gifts of lavender bags for the linen cupboard and Polly Waffles for the 'little girl'. They were both wearing hats with net across their faces and white gloves. They sat on the edge of their bentwood chairs in our huge ramshackle kitchen and did not mention the river incident but stared in dismay at the pots and pans dangling from the rafters, and the indoor jungle of honeysuckle and grapevines that climbed in through the ceiling and made a lattice of green from wall to wall. There is no doubt about it, they must have been thinking, poor young Mrs Danielssen was letting her standards of housekeeping drop. Was she losing her grip because of the war? Sick with worry about her husband away up north defending his country? It happened to women who'd been left alone too long. Was that why she'd swum across the Merlin River with the little girl on her back? They cast sidelong sympathetic glances at me, sitting politely, waiting to pass the tea. This poor young woman needed help, they seemed to be thinking. She was far too superior to put her head down on someone's kitchen table and have a good howl, but she was letting her household go. Just look at the cobwebs! Didn't she notice the cobwebs in her kitchen? They were filthy and blocking out the light. The ladies did not offer one word of recrimination, but Mother knew what they were thinking and smiled to reassure them.

'The cobwebs, Miss Hudson-Bell, are made by the tarantulas. They're quite harmless and very good at catching flies. We would never disturb them, would we, Anna?' I shook my head. 'It takes months to spin a web like that. Years.'

Mother smiled at the anxious ladies and offered them tea.

'We have a blue-tongue lizard in the bread crock and a family of bush rats lives behind that armchair you're sitting on, Mrs Merton. Would you like to see them? They're quite affectionate if you don't show fear.'

The ladies declined and left soon after.

As their solid, wounded backs retreated down the steep path to the gate Mother started to laugh very softly, making a chortling noise in the back of her throat. Once they were out of hearing she screwed up her eyes, opened her mouth and laughed louder, until she was helpless with laughter and had to wipe tears from her eyes. 'Poor old biddies,' she murmured. 'Poor, dear old things.'

Had she swum the Merlin River with me on her back just to shock the people of the town, to give them all something to gossip over?

I didn't know, but even at not quite five I sensed that this was the reason, and I dreaded the day when I too would have to perform daring feats to prove my courage. I felt the burden of this responsibility like a haversack of rocks on my scrawny shoulders. How could I explain to Mother that I did not feel brave like her? I did not believe that nothing could hurt me.

'Did you ever think that God might let us drown in the Merlin River?' I asked her, a few weeks after our 'adventure'.

'Yes, but he didn't, did he?' she replied, smiling. She had been calm and quite serenely happy ever since the river crossing.

'What would you and Charlotte and I do if the Japanese came?' I asked, determined to know the worst.

'We would walk out to the middle of the Merlin Heads Bridge, tie weights round our necks and jump off,' she replied without hesitation.

I considered this. 'Could God stop us?'

'Not if we had made up our minds to do it.'

'Are our minds stronger than God?'

Mother was pleased by this question. 'I believe so, though many people don't. When you are older, Anna, you can decide for yourself whether you want to follow God or your mind.'

I imagined a crossroads with a signpost, one sign pointing towards God, the other to Your Mind. How would I know when it was time to choose, and who would help me decide?

'Couldn't we just share our house with the Japanese instead of jumping off the bridge?' I asked hopefully.

'No. The Japanese are very different from us.'

'How do you know?'

'I've read the newspapers, and Uncle Martin has had letters smuggled out about the atrocities in the prison camps. They are cruel people, I'm afraid. He says we can't imagine how cruel.'

I tried to imagine cruelty. A week after I'd started school at Skinners Bluff State, a boy had deliberately

46

slammed a desk lid on a girl's fingers. The girl had cried from morning playtime until lunch, even after her fingers were bandaged. Sir had called that boy cruel and given him the strap but he didn't seem sorry. He had smirked. I imagined masses of Japanese soldiers smirking as they deliberately slammed desk lids down on the fingers of people I loved.

It was Sir who first taught me about making your dreams come true, or 'achieving goals' as he put it. He was fanatical about sport. He was a conscientious teacher and covered the blackboard with our tables, arithmetic, grammar and spelling for the whole day, promising that if we raced through all this by lunchtime, we could spend the afternoon training for the athletics. Sir's goal was to make Skinners Bluff State School come first in the combined sports against all the other schools on the Bellarine Peninsula and win the shield every year. We had won it for five years in succession. Every afternoon we closed up the classroom and went outside to practise sprints, distance running, hurdles, sack race, egg and spoon, relay races and broad and high jumps. The most spectacular and popular event was the high jump. Only the big boys were allowed to compete in this. The rest of us would stand around watching in awe. They looked like men to me. Some of them had broken voices and stubble on their chins. The law said they had to stay at school until they turned fourteen. High jumping was very tense, and we weren't allowed to make a sound when a big boy ran at the jump. If he made it over the bar we applauded. If he tipped it or failed to get over we sighed in sympathy. The most vital piece of equipment was the bamboo rod. If one was broken during training I would be sent home to get another. This was a great honour. Ours was the only garden where bamboo grew.

If the Japanese were as dreadful as Mother said they were, I couldn't understand why she had planted a 'Japanese garden' around our fishpond. It was pretty, with white pebbles, a tiny Buddhist shrine and a mass of bamboo. During the war years the bamboo had grown thick and strong enough to make me something of a celebrity at my school of twenty-seven pupils. I would run all the way home and Mother would have to drop whatever she was doing to come and saw down the straightest bamboo rod she could find. Once, when I arrived gasping for breath, she was listening to her favourite serial, *Blue Hills*, on the ABC. It was a particularly exciting episode which she didn't want to miss, but I was desperate not to keep the big boys waiting. As she bent double hacking away with her little saw in the Japanese jungle garden she turned to me and said meaningfully, 'Would *you* do this for *me*, Anna?'

'Yes,' I said without hesitation, while thinking I probably wouldn't. Even then I felt morally inadequate in the presence of my mother. I had lied to her so that Sir could achieve his goal, and the cheers I received as I trotted into the sports paddock with the brand new bamboo rod made it all worthwhile.

'Good on you, Anna!' said Sir, and held my hand aloft while he waved the bamboo in the other. The boys applauded and yelled my name in their manly broken voices. Sir had made me a heroine.

The champion high jumper was a boy named Bobbie Cook. He was going to join the airforce as soon as he left school. I had a crush on Bobbie Cook. One afternoon as he crammed himself into my 'little kid's' desk to correct my dictation, my friend, Marlene, dared me to kiss him. I thought this was as good a chance as I would get so I leaned up and gently kissed him on the shoulder of his maroon pullover. He put up his hand and said, 'Please, sir, Anna Danielssen's spittin' on my jumper.' I was deeply hurt. Sir was tactful enough to shrug off this complaint from the school's sporting champion.

Sir was not a sporting champion himself. He was short, stout and red-faced, with a hacking smoker's cough, but he could coach teams like no one else. Because the smoking had reduced his voice to a rasping croak, he controlled us with a whistle that he kept in his back pocket. A short sharp blast meant stop, a long low one, get ready, and a deafening long blast meant he was fed up with the lot of us and was giving us one last chance to pay attention before he took us all back inside to do schoolwork like normal kids.

As well as blackboard work and sport our school learned civics. Every Friday morning the whole school would be divided into four groups – gardening, sewing, cleaning and library. The big boys worked in the vegetable garden with Sir, growing onions and potatoes which were donated to St Augustine's Orphanage, the big girls did sewing with a special sewing mistress who came to show them how to knit socks on four needles for soldiers in hospital, and the little kids had a choice of cleaning out the washbasins and inkwells or reading the three children's encyclopaedias and the five Gould League of Bird Lovers books that made up the school library. Almost everyone wanted cleaning because the monitor let you flick ink at each other and sometimes have a water fight. Library was definitely the worst thing you could be stuck with, but someone had to do it because there weren't enough inkwells and washbasins to keep nine small children busy for two hours. I loved library but had to pretend I wanted cleaning. I would whine pitifully along with the other poor outcasts who were relegated to the back of the classroom to read books. By the end of the first term I knew the encyclopaedias and bird books almost by heart. I remember feeling cross with the kids who licked their fingers and turned the pages too fast, damaging the books and only looking at the pictures.

The one time Sir insisted that we stay inside the classroom all day was when the District Inspector was coming. The annual visit of the school Inspector filled us all with dread. Sir told us that if we did not perform 'with excellence' the Inspector would make us all go down a grade. He drilled us with tables and spelling, gave us rapid-fire tests in oral arithmetic which he called 'Speed and Accuracy', inspected our hair for lice and made us promise never, never to mention that we did sport every afternoon or the Inspector would send him away to teach thieves and murderers in Pentridge Prison. This we did not want.

Sir's full name was Claudius Scipio Delaney, and I'm ashamed to say that when we first heard his two Christian names, the whole school burst into uncontrolled laughter. We howled. One girl even wet her pants. Sir blushed deeper crimson than usual, but he smiled a bit too. He let us go on laughing for a good few minutes before he took out his whistle.

Once I was walking home out the school gate when a magpie swooped me and bit my ear so that it bled. I fled back inside the schoolroom with my hands over my head. Sir was writing up the next day's work on the blackboard.

He bathed my bleeding ear with Dettol and told me I was brave not to cry. He said, 'You like stories, don't you, Anna?'

'Yes, Sir.'

'Have you read about Romulus and Remus?'

'No, Sir.'

'Roman history. My passion, and Greek history too.' He took down from a high shelf some books I had never seen before. 'I can see you're fed up reading those kids' encyclopaedias. Have a go at these.'

'Thank you, Sir.' The books looked quite difficult for a five-year-old.

'You know who Scipio was, Anna?'

'No, Sir.'

'But you're interested, aren't you? I can see that.' He grinned. 'Not many of the other kids want to know about Scipio Emilianus so I'll tell you. He brought the Greek ideals to Rome.'

I wondered what ideals were. I imagined they might be bronze discs.

'The Greeks believed in a balanced life between mind, spirit and body.' He pointed to the blackboard. 'At this school we do the work of the mind in the mornings, the work of the spirit when we salute the flag at assembly and —'

'We do the work of the body every afternoon because we love sport!' I exclaimed.

Sir looked astonished. 'You are a clever little girl, Anna.' I loved Sir.

I wasn't sure that I loved Uncle Martin when he came home from the war later that year. My father was in hospital in Melbourne so Uncle Martin was the only other man in my life at that time. I couldn't remember ever having met Uncle Martin before he went away, but Mother had told us so many stories about him that I imagined I must have. While he'd been a prisoner of the Japanese for years and no one had known exactly where he was or even whether he was still alive, Mother had talked with such pride and longing of her brother that I'd grown tired of hearing about him. She must have mentioned our father, the airman, too, but I couldn't remember any details. All she said was that he was recovering well in hospital and would be home soon.

When Uncle Martin came home from being a prisoner of war he brought presents for us of gasmasks and coolie hats. I remember thinking he was thinner than anyone I'd ever seen and that his eyes were so bright and scary they could probably see inside your head and know what you were thinking. He stood very straight and spoke too loudly. Mother told me he was partly deaf because of the beatings.

Although Mother loved Uncle Martin dearly they clashed on several issues. He admired the royal family and had portraits of them all over his house. He was always giving presents of these portraits to Mother but she refused to hang them anywhere but in the lavatory. Whenever he came to visit we would all wait excitedly until he went to the lavatory and then try to smother our laughter at his shouts of indignation.

Mother supported an Anglican bishop known as the 'Red Dean' who claimed to be a communist. Whenever she mentioned him to Uncle Martin he would be outraged and she would shout back that he was 'conservative' and 'a capitalist'.

Mother was tolerant of Roman Catholics but Uncle Martin was rabidly anti-Papist. Once, when I was about six, he told my cousin Sarah and me that we should spit whenever we passed the local Roman Catholic church. We had thought this was an odd thing for a grownup to tell us to do, but we'd done it anyway. Mother was furious when she caught us spitting at the gate.

For a sister and brother Mother and Uncle Martin are not much alike. She gives away money she doesn't have to anyone 'needy' whereas he, who is quite well off, keeps his money to himself. She has a love of beautiful things that is, to Uncle Martin, quite impractical. 'Katharine, if you were down to your last sixpence you would eat the cheese out of the mousetrap and spend your money on one perfect rose,' he told her once. Sometimes I wonder if she behaves in this contrary manner just to infuriate him.

Mother enjoys taunting Uncle Martin but that's just playfulness. She loves him dearly underneath. However there are some men in the district she despises and she's not afraid of standing up to them.

chapter five

One night recently I was woken by a scream. I sat bolt upright, thinking I must have dreamt it. Then the scream came again. It was more of a wail and seemed to be coming from our lower garden. It was a woman's voice and she sounded as if she was being attacked. At first I thought it might be Charlotte, but she was away at Uncle Martin's place. I leapt out of bed, threw on my dressing-gown and ran barefoot down the narrow stairs to Mother's room. Her bed was empty. I raced to the fireplace to grab the poker. It had gone. My heart was beating high up in my chest as I raced back upstairs to find the only other weapon I could think of, my riding crop. Just then I heard another wail. I crashed open the back door and saw our mother alone in the moonlight. She stood at the top of the garden steps in her long cream dressing-gown, calm, statuesque and gripping the fire poker. She was looking down at the Mooneys' cottage which backs onto our lower garden. There was a light on in the kitchen.

'Are you all right, Mrs Mooney?' Mother called. The wailing stopped. There was no answer.

I looked questioningly at Mother, who motioned to me

to go back inside. I didn't want to so I moved out of sight into the shadows.

'Are you *all right*, Mrs Mooney?' she called again. She expected an answer.

There was silence. Mother walked purposefully down the steps, opened the small garden gate that led to the cottage, and went inside. I watched, feeling frightened, then followed her down. I hid in the bushes outside the kitchen and looked in the open window.

The room was in disarray. Chairs were turned over, a clothes horse drying children's socks and singlets lay in a heap on the floor, and pots and pans had been heaved in all directions. Ernie Mooney, a large, burly man, leant heavily against the fireplace, staring at our mother. There was a beer bottle dangling from one hand and blood trickling down his arm. Mrs Mooney was nowhere to be seen.

Mother turned on him angrily.

'Where is she?'

'None of your damn business,' he said sullenly.

I wished she would take care. He was sneering, and looked as if he might hit her with the bottle. Suddenly she lifted the poker and waved it at him fiercely. Ernie drew back in alarm.

'You cowardly great brute!' She brandished the poker close to his face. 'Tell me where she is!'

He cringed away from her and pointed towards the old brown leather sofa in the corner. 'Over there.' His speech was slurred.

Mrs Mooney crawled out from behind the sofa. She had cuts on her neck and one eye was badly swollen. She is a pretty woman and still quite young. She was dressed nicely, as if she'd been getting ready to go out, wearing bright-red lipstick, a floral dress and a smart little mati-nee jacket that was now torn at the sleeve. One of her high-heeled shoes had fallen off and she limped when she tried to stand up.

Mother marched across the room to help her up. Then she turned back to Ernie and pointed the poker at him.

'You animal! You should be locked up!'

Mrs Mooney said anxiously, 'No! No, Mrs Danielssen. I'm all right. Honest.'

Ernie held out his gashed and bleeding arm. 'Look what she done to me!' he said self-pityingly.

Mrs Mooney turned on him. 'You done it to yourself with your own bloody beer bottle!' Then she said sadly to Mother, 'Nice way to take me out for my birthday, eh? Promises to come home early and sober, and instead he's blind drunk and belts me up . . .'

'Out!' Mother told Ernie fiercely, pointing to the door. 'Just get out!'

'It's my bloody house,' Ernie protested half-heartedly and started to shuffle towards the sofa as if he might lie down on it. Mother lunged at him with the poker. He dropped the beer bottle and suddenly shaped up to her with his fists. Mrs Mooney let out a loud wail. I froze. I imagined our mother lying bloody and unconscious on the Mooneys' kitchen floor. Mother stared imperiously at Ernie for what seemed a long time. Slowly he dropped his fists, hung his head and walked towards the door. I shrank back into the bushes and watched as he went out the gate and headed down towards the beach. I supposed he would sleep off his drunkenness in the sand dunes.

Through the kitchen window I could see Mother bathing Mrs Mooney's swollen eye.

I waited for her in the shadows at the top of our garden steps. She didn't seem surprised to see me still there.

'Weren't you scared?' I asked.

'He's just a bully. Bullies are cowards underneath.'

'Why does she stay with him?'

'God knows.' She sighed.

After school the next day I went down to the Mooneys' place to collect Eliza, who had gone there to play with Wilma. Mother didn't know she was there so I thought I'd better rescue her before it was discovered that she wasn't at the piano, practising. Mother was having a sleep, as she often does in the afternoons. When she takes a Relaxatab she is dead to the world for a couple of hours.

I could hear the voices of children chattering and laughing and Burl Ives singing 'Jimmy Crack Corn' on the wind-up gramophone that had been Mrs Mooney's birthday present from Ernie last year, so everything seemed to be back to normal. I knocked on the door but nobody heard me above the din so I just pushed it open and went in. Mrs Mooney was ironing on the kitchen table and humming along to Burl Ives. A line of clothes was drying above the wood stove. The two youngest children, Wilma and Carol, were sitting with Eliza on the battered horsehair sofa which had been pulled close to the stove and were deftly picking potato chips out of a frying pan with their fingers. The two oldest, Raymond and Lorraine, were sitting at the opposite end of the kitchen table doing their homework and eating huge slabs of white bread and jam. As soon as Mrs Mooney saw me she stopped humming and put her hand up to try to conceal her black eye.

She nodded towards Eliza, who was finishing off the last fat chip, and smiled apologetically.

'She's fine, love. Tell your mum she probably won't want any tea.'

I nodded and smiled back. Our mother would be furious if Eliza couldn't eat her nourishing meal at home but I knew she'd much rather have chips fried in dripping. They smelt delicious. Mrs Mooney noticed me looking at them. 'Greedy little things have eaten every one. Never mind, love, have a piece and jam.' She was already slicing a thick chunk off the fresh white loaf.

'No, no, thanks, Mrs Mooney. I just had afternoon tea.' We were only allowed healthy wholemeal bread at home, dry and unappetising. I stood self-consciously by the door, feeling sure that Mrs Mooney knew I had heard the beating.

'Come on, Eliza. Mummy doesn't know where you are.'

Eliza looked up. It was obvious she didn't want to leave. Unlike our own kitchen, the atmosphere in the Mooneys' was cosy and friendly. She sat tight. Then she said by way of diversion, 'Anna's in the school ballet, Mrs Mooney.'

The other children all stared at me. 'Come on, Eliza, you have to finish your music practice,' I said, feeling uneasy.

Mrs Mooney looked up from her ironing, genuinely pleased. 'Oh, Anna. That's lovely! Your mum must be that proud.'

'Anna wants to be a ballerina,' Eliza announced.

'I don't. No, I don't.' I shook my head in embarrassment and laughed at the absurdity of the idea before anyone else could. 'I'm far too tall. I know that.'

'Well, you've got the grace for it.' Mrs Mooney put the iron back on the stove and picked up the heavy black kettle with a piece of thick rag. 'Cup of tea, love?'

Eliza was pleased that she had captured everyone's attention. She decided to go further. 'Anna likes . . .' She paused because she was about to reveal an important secret. 'Reverend Marsden!'

I felt the colour rising up my neck like mercury and turning my face bright crimson. The Mooney children fell about giggling. Eliza looked slightly appalled at what she had done.

'We *all* like Reverend Marsden. He's the handsomest vicar we've ever had in this town,' said Mrs Mooney, saving the situation, 'and Anna's got a better chance than most of us of getting him, so there.'

The kids laughed good-naturedly and Raymond let out a cheer. I managed a smile in spite of my shame. I felt so grateful to Mrs Mooney. She deserved something better in life than a husband who beat her. Her eye looked terrible, all purple and swollen. She noticed me looking and came across to the door where I was still standing awkwardly.

She passed me a mug of strong tea with lots of sugar, just the way I like it. Very quietly, so the children didn't hear, she said, 'He's not always like that.'

I looked at her, not comprehending for a second, then I nodded slowly. I mustn't have looked convinced because in the same quiet voice she explained, 'He lost his job yesterday. The Balts. They're all coming here from Poland and Yugoslavia and everywhere and pinching our men's jobs.' She paused to see if the significance of this had sunk in. 'Ernie's a good man, really.'

Wilma, who had overheard part of this conversation, looked up from peeling a thin strip of leather off the sofa and said, 'We had a new kid at school today and she was a Balt. Her name's Rocks Anne. She's got awful brown stockings made of thick wool and a short dress up to her bum and she stinks of garlic.'

All the little Mooneys and Eliza fell about in fits of laughter again.

'That'll be enough of your cheek, Wilma,' Mrs Mooney said sharply. 'Raymond, get outside and chop that wood before –'

The door creaked open and everyone turned to look. Ernie appeared, clutching his Gladstone bag. He stood quite still and peered around at the children, who stared at him in silence. He seemed entirely different from the bully of the night before – subdued and harmless. He smiled sheepishly at Mrs Mooney, who turned her head proudly the other way. The children watched intently, their eyes moving from one parent to the other. Ernie walked slowly across the room to where his wife had resumed her ironing. He bent down, opened the bag and presented her humbly with a newspaper parcel. She continued ironing. Ernie opened the parcel and produced a dead grey rabbit. Mrs Mooney refused to look at the present. Ernie held the rabbit up in front of the children, put his hand inside the back of its head to make its jaws move and its furry ears waggle. It looked like a grotesque puppet.

'Make me into a bunny stew, Rene,' said Ernie in a squeaky rabbit voice.

The younger children began to laugh. The older two looked uncomfortable, waiting for their mother to react. Mrs Mooney looked at Ernie coldly.

Ernie turned the engaging rabbit to talk to her. 'Go on, Rene. Make me into a lovely stew for Ernie's tea. I'll give you a kiss if you do.'

The rabbit hopped across the ironing, jumped up in the air and kissed Mrs Mooney on the cheek. She pulled away, laughing. All the children laughed too, the older ones with relief. Ernie gave Mrs Mooney a very gentle, rather humble kiss. She smiled. He was forgiven.

Suddenly there was a howl of pain from baby Carol, who was still sitting by the stove. She had accidentally touched the fat in the frying pan. Ernie lunged towards her and scooped her up in his arms.

'Oooh, love, show me!' Carol held up one pinkish finger. 'Daddy kiss it better?'

She nodded tearfully. Ernie stuck her finger in his mouth and sucked it. Then he pulled silly faces to cheer her up. She started laughing through her tears.

Then Ernie wound up the gramophone, put on another record and, bowing with mock gallantry to Mrs Mooney, he waltzed her round and round the kitchen to 'Irene Goodnight'. He was actually quite handsome when he wasn't drunk, and Mrs Mooney looked like a pretty young girl. This must have been her theme song or a family ritual of some kind because all the Mooney children knew the words and joined in singing, 'Goodnight Irene, Goodnight Irene, I'll see you in my dreams,' as they swayed in time to their parents' dance.

chapter six

'She's taken him back,' I told Mother as we were preparing the dinner in silence that evening.

'She's a fool.'

'He's not always like that.'

'She doesn't know any better.'

'What else can she do?'

'Leave him!'

'She loves him,' I said defiantly.

Mother turned and gave me a withering look. Then she noticed the khaki shirt I was wearing, which is far too big for me.

'Do you have to wear that shirt? Whose is it? Tom's?'

'No, it's mine. I like it.'

It wasn't mine and she knew it.

I had memories of my father. Were they memories or dreams? I couldn't be sure. They seemed too vivid for dreams, and they recurred often. I saw myself riding on his shoulders in hot sunshine. I was wearing a white cotton sunbonnet tied under the chin. There was a smell of sweat. Dragonflies were swooping through the air too close to me. One of them flew, crunch, into my face and I lurched backwards dizzily so that my stomach dropped and I clutched the air. My father's hand came up to support my back and I heard him laugh and felt great relief. Then he lifted me down and we started building a castle in the sand. We often built castles together. Or did I always dream of the same one? I couldn't remember. But what I did remember is that he wore a khaki shirt.

'When he flew at night he went over and over the same piece of ocean for hours. It was peaceful up there, just looking for Japs. Sometimes he saw the sun rise like a great big orange egg. He thought it was beautiful. One morning, flying into the sun, he thought of a plan. When the war was over he would build a tower on his house on the red cliff . . .'

'Was the tower to keep his children safe, so they could escape up there if the tide came too far in?' Eliza asked urgently.

'Yes, that might have been the reason, or maybe he just wanted to build them a beautiful tower to watch the sunset from.' I had been telling them one of their favourite bedtime stories, 'The Brave Airman', which was a way of letting them know we'd had a father once. Unlike me they had no memories of him at all.

I moved away to turn out the light.

'Is Mummy coming in to say good night?' asked Jonathan.

'She might. I'll see. Good night.'

I gently closed the door.

'Anna!' Eliza called. I put my head back round the door. 'Is the cliff really crumbling?'

'Only a little bit.'

'Uncle Martin says if there's one more big storm the whole house could fall into the sea!' she said dramatically.

'He's lying,' said Jonathan, 'Trying to scare us.'

'I don't think the house will fall into the sea,' I said, trying to sound amused, like an adult does when a child says something foolish.

'I'm not leaving this house even if there is a storm. I'll stay and float out to sea with it,' Jonathan said vaguely.

'So will I,' Eliza said, then thought better of it. 'Or else I'll go and live with the Mooneys.'

I had just taken the dry washing off the line and was carrying it upstairs in a wicker basket when I overheard Uncle Martin holding forth to Mother. I had noticed his car arrive and seeing that neither Charlotte nor my cousin Sarah was with him I'd decided to stay out of sight.

Uncle Martin is forty, three years older than Mother, but he behaves almost as if he were her father. He is tall and slim and carries himself like a military officer, even though the war finished nine years ago. He was a war hero, twice decorated, though I've never seen his famous medals. He still has boundless energy and, in his own way, he is just as eccentric as Mother, but I think he has less of her talent. He gets bored easily and likes a dare. The gate in his driveway is too narrow but he won't widen it; he drives at it really fast to see if he can get through without damaging the car. He is arrogant too, which runs in the family. He is very fond of Mother but far too critical.

I crept back downstairs and looked through the wooden Venetian blinds to see that he'd spread papers all over our dining-room table and was pacing up and down, gesticulating while she sat with her head in her hands.

He thrust an official-looking letter at her and said, 'Seven months unopened! Katharine, it's insane.'

'I know, I know.'

'God, what a mess!' He drew himself up, then said importantly, 'You're going to have to sell it, Kate. Put the whole rotting mansion up for auction – stables, rock gardens, decaying wash-house, bloody leaning tower, the lot.'

'Martin, don't be cruel. It might be a bit run-down but –'

'It's a bloody wreck!'

'I know. That's how I like it,' she said defiantly.

I grinned to myself in spite of my anxiety and put the washing basket down on the stairs to listen more attentively.

'I'm serious,' he threatened. 'You're in deep debt and you haven't paid the mortgage for so long it's a wonder you haven't been evicted.'

'The bank manager's a pleasant man,' said Mother, trying to sound practical. 'He wouldn't mind extending the loan.'

Uncle Martin stormed off to the other end of the room. 'I just can't seem to make you understand. The bank is *taking* this house, *forcing* the sale because the house belongs to it.' He thrust a document under her nose. 'It's all here in black and white. It's not my decision. It's that "pleasant" bank manager's.'

Mother turned her head away from the offensive document and raised her chin in the air to think. Then she turned back to Martin brightly. 'Look, you're a man, you understand the way they think. Go and see him. Tell him

I'm deeply sorry for forgetting to pay the instalments. I'll start doing it immediately. I've still got a bit of my inheritance money stashed away and when that's all gone I can take on a few more piano students.'

Uncle Martin stared back at her. She looked dreadfully vulnerable in spite of the brave front.

'Please, Martin. I don't want to lose the wretched house. Falling down or not, it's all I've got left.'

I couldn't bear to watch any more so I turned away and started folding a sheet. Surely Uncle Martin would offer us some help now. He could well afford it.

'Father was right,' I heard him say in a sneering, amused sort of voice. 'You're completely incapable of understanding anything to do with money. Why did you buy such an albatross in the first place? Because of some romantic dream you shared with a man who –'

'Be quiet!' Mother said angrily. 'If I make mistakes in my life I'll pay for them, but I don't want a lecture from you.'

'Then don't ask me to do ridiculous favours.' He paused, then said quietly, 'I'm sorry. I shouldn't have said that. He was a fine man.'

'Liar!' She was smiling at him, beaming. 'You detested him.'

He shrugged. 'At least you had the courage to marry for love.'

'And now I'm a burden to you, and so are my children. And this house. Poor Martin,' she said playfully. Then her mood changed abruptly. 'I wish to God I'd been educated!'

'Why?' he teased. 'You're a beautiful woman.'

'If our mother had lived, it would have been me who was sent to study law, not you,' she said grimly. 'I had a far better brain.'

'You weren't well.'

'I was perfectly well. I had bouts of melancholy, that's all.'

'You could have married any of a dozen charming rich young chaps on the land,' he said sorrowfully.

'What a brilliant career, to marry a moron,' she mocked.

'Better a rich moron than a penniless radical with no moral fibre.'

'Ha! So that's what you really think of him, is it? Go home, Martin. Leave me alone.'

There was a pause. She had won that round.

'Look, I don't blame you for what you did. I'm just sorry he spent all your inheritance and left you with this.' He gestured at the ceiling. 'Why do you think I've helped you all these years?'

'I don't *want* your charity.'

'I know. Look at you, as arrogant and rebellious as when you were eighteen,' he said admiringly. 'Poor as a sparrow and proud as a peacock.' He tried to soften her, to cajole. 'I could find you a job.'

'What as?'

'Gentlewoman's companion. I've found a rich old lady who loves music but hates noise. Bed-ridden. Grand old house. One of my most valuable clients. You'd have to live in.'

'And who'd take care of my children?'

I held my breath, and peered back in the window. 'Ursula. For a short time, until you can make other arrangements. She's already offered. You'd see them at least once a week.'

'No, Martin. I couldn't.'

'You were in boarding school before you were nine.'

'And cried myself to sleep every night for two years.'

'Didn't do you any harm in the long run though, did it?' he teased. 'Gave you strength of character. Guts. Moral fibre.'

Mother began to laugh. 'You're starting to sound just like Father.' Then she said, 'Seriously, Martin, you mustn't tempt me with suggestions like that.'

'Why not?'

'Sometimes I feel like the children's prisoner. I love them but they suffocate me,' she confessed. 'Once – and I've never told anyone this – when Eliza and Jonathan were very young, I did a dreadful thing. I was walking on the beach with them. The sun was setting, a glorious ocean of red, and I just started running. Away from them. Towards the sun. I could hear them screaming, "Mummy! Mummy!" But I couldn't stop. I must have run for a mile at least. When I stopped they just were little black specks against the dunes. I ran back, so ashamed. Jonathan couldn't catch his breath he was crying so hard. And Eliza just stared at me with a face that looked old and hard as a nut. She was two.'

'You'd been deserted by their father. Of course you felt like running away.' I watched Martin move across and put his arm around Mother's shoulders. She leaned on him gratefully.

I felt sick at hearing this story and angry at Uncle Martin's reply. I turned, intending to go upstairs and escape, but stopped when I heard Uncle Martin say, 'Listen, Kate, another thing. You can't keep on giving money away. You won't survive. I would never have survived in Burma if I'd shared what I had. I could never understand why they did it. Dividing food among fifteen prisoners meant they got virtually nothing themselves. They nearly all died. I never shared.'

Mother said affectionately, 'You wouldn't.'

I couldn't stand it any longer. I threw down the washing basket, crashed open the dining-room door, turned angrily to Uncle Martin and said, 'I think you're one of the most selfish people I have ever met!' Then I dashed out again, before either of them could say a word.

chapter seven

I was sitting in the kitchen reading this afternoon. It was a cold, blustery Saturday at the beginning of September and this was the warmest room in the house. Eliza and Wilma Mooney were making gingerbread men.

Wilma looked up from sticking raisin buttons on her man and said matter-of-factly to Eliza, 'Your mum's a loony.'

'Why do you say that?'

'I dunno. Everyone says. Isn't she?'

Eliza shrugged disdainfully. Then her eyes grew round and she whispered dramatically, 'She's got a disease. She's going to die. Soon we'll be orphans.'

Wilma was silenced.

Later I had a word to Eliza about making up shocking stories.

'Well, we don't know. She *might* have a disease,' was all she would say. Eliza almost believes her own stories. I suppose it's a way of hiding her fears about Mother, making up stories that are worse than reality. Eliza is a tough little thing. I think she'll survive. I'm more concerned about Jonathan, who shows very little reaction to anything.

If Mother has a fit of rage or weeping, he just goes quietly into his room and starts working on his film. Lately he's started 'filming' us all the time. At the dinner table when we are just talking amongst ourselves he will suddenly curl his hands up into the shape of a camera lens and 'zoom in' on us as if we're not real people at all, just actors he's directing. When we ask him to stop he takes no notice, just films that as well.

I followed him into his room last night to see if he wanted to talk.

'Jon, I think we should clean up this room a bit, don't you?' I gestured at the mess and laughed. 'It's a wonder you and Eliza don't get lost finding your way to bed.'

He looked around the room as if there was nothing unusual about it whatsoever. 'It's fine. We like it. Anyway, it's all set up for filming.'

I nodded. It was.

'Have you had any more letters from the Victorian Filmmakers Club?'

'Yes, they've accepted my application to join but there's a fee of ten shillings so I'll have to wait.' He rummaged in a drawer and brought out a typed letter which he thrust at me proudly.

I read the letter, which was addressed to Mr Jonathan Danielssen. They obviously believed he was an adult. He'd been invited to attend the next meeting in Melbourne.

'Perhaps I'll be able to lend you the money before the meeting, but it'll be hard to get there, won't it?'

'I'm thinking of ringing them up and asking if any of the members live down this way. Maybe I could get a lift,' he said seriously.

I stared at him. Sometimes I think he's not a little boy

at all but a dwarf aged thirty-five. 'Jonathan, it takes over three hours to drive there. The meetings are at night. Where would you stay?'

'I'll have to think about that,' he said gravely.

Ever since he was very young, I have felt responsible for Jon. When he was two and a half and Eliza was a baby of ten months our mother employed a local girl called Elsie Binch to help every evening for two hours with bathing and feeding, so that she could practise the piano.

Elsie hated children. I knew this because she had told me so on her first day in the job.

Jonathan was, Mother had explained to Elsie on her first day, an 'anti-social' child, rather shy and full of phobias. He was especially afraid of getting water on his head, but Elsie hadn't seemed to understand. I watched, appalled, while she forced him to sit in the tub and let the shower drench him. He had screamed and kicked in absolute terror, believing he was going to drown. Although he was only two, I knew his fear was real. I had seen him scream, gasp for air and then, if he wasn't taken out of the bath in an instant, vomit a huge spurt, like a projectile. I had warned Elsie not to put him under the shower but she had snapped back, 'Your brother is a sook.' I watched his face go very red as he screamed to be taken out of the shower. Elsie was deliberately looking the other way, bent over, pretending to look for the plug. He gasped. Then it happened. He vomited a stream of lamb's fry and bacon, carrots, peas and potatoes all over Elsie's starched floral apron and up into her hair. She screeched out, 'Shiiit!' It was the first time I'd ever heard anyone swear. I decided then that it would be better to try and look after Jonathan and Eliza myself while Mother was practising.

And so, at the age of almost nine, I had offered to take over the bathing, and Mother had accepted. Later I took on the storytelling and feeding as well. Sometimes I combined all three, sitting the two babies at either end of the tub and making up games for them, creating waterfalls and dams and bubbles to distract them from protesting while I washed their ears and hair. I floated their bears and golliwogs around them and made up stories while I spooned coddled egg and mashed banana into their unresisting mouths.

Eliza and Jonathan would sit smiling contentedly in their sea of soggy companions until their skin went white and wrinkled as tripe and Mother had played the whole of Chopin's D flat Nocturne, Opus 27 No. 2 through twice without a mistake.

I quite enjoyed this evening ritual. Although they were only babies I told my brother and sister bits from the Norse legends I had read in Great-aunt Ingeborg and Great-aunt Hedda's book. I told them about Thor, the huge red-bearded hungry god who had a bad temper and a chariot with wheels that made thunder. I told them about Loki, the son of two giants, who could change himself into anything and led monsters into battle against the gods. They smiled and asked for more as they ate up their supper. I wondered why all mothers didn't feed, bathe and tell their children stories at the same time. It seemed such a sensible thing to do. Mother was pleased with me and I felt grateful.

Ever since my outburst against Uncle Martin, I have started confronting Mother about not facing up to reality. It's part of my four-month plan to get her to be a normal, responsible parent. The first thing I did was to ask her what happened about Uncle Martin's threat to force her to sell the house, which I had to admit I'd overheard.

'We have a little more time,' she said vaguely.

'Exactly how much time?'

She didn't answer.

'Four months?'

She looked at me in surprise. 'About that.'

'So you'll handle the bank repayments yourself, or would you like me to do it?'

'I can manage them, Anna.'

'Good.'

While she was still looking startled by my directness, I said, 'One more thing. I heard you tell Uncle Martin you still had some of your inheritance money left. Is that true?'

'Of course it isn't,' she sighed.

'And you can't take any more students, can you?'

'I have more than I can handle already.'

'Do they all pay their fees?'

'Those who can afford to pay me, of course.' She sounded defensive.

'The Polish woman's children don't pay, do they?'

'No, but they're both quite talented.'

'I think you're very foolish to take on pupils who can't pay,' I said seriously. 'But at least you've been honest with me.'

Mother looked at me as if I'd suddenly turned into Uncle Martin.

Later I felt ashamed of having to interrogate her like that, but unless I know what's going on, how can I possibly help her?

Sometimes I think it would be simpler to do what Charlotte threatens to do and just run away to the city and not care whether the family is broken up or not, but when I think about it I know I couldn't bear to leave them.

The other night I confronted Mother about pretending we have more money than we do. I hate being the one to point out that she's deceiving herself. I don't exactly call her a liar, but even so she doesn't like it.

I was helping her prepare dinner while Jonathan and Eliza listened to 'The Argonauts' on the wireless. *The Muddle-Headed Wombat* was being acted out and they were both grinning at the squeaky, silly voice of the mouse character, who is clever, and the slow, thoughtful voice of Wombat, who loves Mouse, even though she bosses him around a lot. Then Eliza looked up and noticed what Mother was cooking.

'Oh, no! Not scrambled eggs. We had scrambled eggs last night. We have them nearly every night!' she wailed, sounding a bit like Mouse.

'Are we having silver beet again too?' asked Jonathan in disbelief.

'Yes, lovely silver beet from the garden and scrambled eggs from our very own bantam hens,' Mother said breezily.

Eliza and Jonathan exchanged looks of dismay.

'Why don't we ever have meat any more?' Eliza asked.

'It's just that I didn't get to the butcher, that's all.'

I lowered my voice. 'You ought to tell them the truth,' I said adamantly.

Mother stared at me with a look of hurt in her eyes, but didn't say anything further.

The following night she baked an egg and silver beet

pie with some scraps of bacon in it, which was a varia-
tion, at least. I can't remember the last time we had pure
meat. I think it was at Christmas when we slaughtered
one of the bantams.

Mother has apparently been doing some thinking
about my outburst at Uncle Martin. She took me aside one
evening and said, 'Anna, don't be too hard on my brother.
He suffered more as a prisoner than he will ever admit.
He makes jokes to hide the pain. He pretends he kept food
for himself, and maybe he did once or twice, but that isn't
what I've heard from the men who were with him over
there. He stole medical supplies from the Japanese to treat
those with malaria, and mangoes for the ones with
beriberi, and when morale was at its lowest, he played
tricks on the guards to lift the spirits of his men.'

'What sort of tricks?'

'I've been told he put white ants into the sleepers of
the Burma Railroad they were being forced to build so
that it wouldn't last long.'

I grinned.

'Unfortunately, though, it backfired because the
British took over the railroad straight after the war,' she
said with a smile. 'You may not know it but the prisoners
who survived with Uncle Martin admire him a great deal.'

I nodded, but I was still puzzled.

'Why is he like that, so daring and reckless?'

'He was like it as a boy. We grew up on a property
where Grandfather bred horses, and Martin would always
be the first to ride the horse we were breaking in. Sometimes they threw him, but he'd just get up and try again.'

I understood that. I often put Grayling over difficult
jumps and if I was thrown I would get straight back on.

'When he was about fifteen he brought a friend home from boarding school in the holidays and I distinctly remember them shooting at each other with rifles.'

'What?' I exclaimed.

Mother shrugged. 'It was a dare. They used to shoot across a gully, playing games of courage. They pushed themselves to the edge of physical danger.'

'Why didn't Grandfather stop them?'

'He did, eventually, but I also think he understood their motives.'

'Are all the Anglo-Irish mad?'

Mother looked thoughtful. 'I wouldn't say mad,' she said carefully, 'but there's a need to prove yourself as invulnerable. When you grow up in a country where you're hated by the Irish and despised by the English, what do you have to lose by being outrageous? It makes you feel better if you know you can endure almost anything.'

'But Uncle Martin grew up in Australia!' I protested. 'And so did you.'

'Quite true, but the values we were taught were those of the imperial nations. Show no pain, no fear and you will triumph. It was always an important thing for the Anglo-Irish to face the world and not reveal that they were hurting.'

'You don't have to do it any more, Mother. We're Australians!' I felt a mixture of sympathy for her and rage at the crazy beliefs of her family.

'You might not believe it, Anna, but I am trying to break away from the old beliefs.' She smiled wearily as if it was hard work.

'I'll help you,' I said enthusiastically. 'You'll be all

right, but Uncle Martin really worries me. Why is he still so determined to be daring now?'

'I think he finds it dull being a solicitor in a small town. He'd much rather be doing something physical and exciting – searching for minerals in the outback or diving for pearls in Broome. Even farming. But he feels he owes it to Ursula to settle down in a steady job and have the sort of conservative friends she likes. He admires her, you see.'

'Why?'

'For coping so well with the children and her job while he was away, and for keeping a home for him when he came back. She did cope well, I suppose,' said Mother unwillingly. 'So he'll do anything to please her now.'

'But he dominates her!' I protested.

'Ah, no. That's just the surface bluster. She's the one who calls the shots in that marriage. Look a little closer.'

I realised I didn't understand married people at all.

Charlotte is coming home from Uncle Martin's this evening and I must say I'm looking forward to seeing her. She managed to have the weekend invitation extended to a week, which I think is quite shameless, but she'll tell funny stories about Uncle Martin's stuffy friends and she'll bring us some leftovers from their lavish dinners. I hope she brings cold roast lamb or some steak and kidney pie.

'Seen any more couples rooting?' Charlotte asked as I helped carry the pile of American magazines she'd borrowed from Aunt Ursula up the steep path from the front gate.

I drew a sharp breath. 'Haven't been looking.' This

wasn't quite true. The image of the couple grunting and heaving had been haunting me. I even dreamt about them last night. They were underwater, still doing it. I was trying to warn them they were drowning but they didn't hear.

She laughed. 'You're sure it wasn't anyone we know?'

'Positive.'

'Not the handsome Reverend Albert M. perchance?' she said wickedly.

'Don't be disgusting!'

'Well, he does have rather a shocking reputation in this town. But you knew *that*, Anna.'

'He hasn't! I don't believe it,' I said, blushing crimson. 'It's malicious gossip.' Then, recovering my dignity, I asked, 'Did you bring us any leftovers?'

Charlotte looked blank.

'From Uncle Martin's place?'

'They didn't offer any.'

'You could've asked! You got some last time.'

'Well, this time I didn't. Do you expect me to beg them for scraps?'

'Why not? They throw away whole chops, give them to the dog!' I was beside myself with rage.

Charlotte looked at me critically. 'Calm down, Anna. Next time, *you* go and visit them. Then you can stuff yourself with chops for a week.' She sauntered off to her bedroom. I wanted to run after her and slap her.

'I'd rather starve than eat their bloody chops!' I yelled.

Charlotte did not deign to answer.

chapter eight

Charlotte left school last year and since we can't afford to send her to study in Melbourne she spends as much time as possible away from us. As well as staying with Uncle Martin's family she stays with the Hendersons, parents of her school friend Beverley, who wants to become an actress. Charlotte and Beverley have both joined GAMA, the Geronga Association of Music and Art. They're hoping to be cast in their next production, which is a Gilbert and Sullivan opera, *The Gondoliers*. Charlotte is trying out for Tessa and Beverley for Gianetta. These are the two gondoliers' girlfriends who are supposed to be flirtatious and pretty. I have no doubt that Charlotte will get Tessa, but poor Beverley can barely sing in tune. Maybe her acting will save her. I really do hope Beverley gets a role of some sort, otherwise it will be embarrassing for Charlotte to have to ask to stay with Beverley's family in town for the whole month of rehearsals and performance.

Beverley works as a salesgirl in the menswear department of Bright and Hitchcocks. Because of this she gets paid the same wage as a man. Charlotte could do this too but she says she's not interested in being a shopgirl. She has too much singing practice to do while she's waiting to be 'discovered'. Mother found her a couple of local children to tutor in piano, but she only does that when she's at home, which isn't often. Mother ends up teaching them herself, which I know she dislikes. She has too many pupils already and she has no patience, particularly with children who have no talent.

When I was seven she took my hands in hers and said, 'What giant paws. I really don't think there's much point in continuing our piano lessons, Anna. Would you rather have a pony?'

Of course I'd said I would, as I hadn't progressed far beyond *The Dance of the Gnomes*. My hands were so clumsy and Mother let out dreadful sighs of disappointment so often that the lessons were a nightmare, so I gave up the piano but unfortunately there wasn't enough money to buy a pony. Later, when I was older, I found Grayling to borrow, and I still ride him every weekend in return for grooming and feeding.

I borrowed a horse for Charlotte once too. He was a very quiet horse but she fell off nonetheless and vowed she'd never ride again. Poor Charlotte. I do feel sorry for her sometimes. I listen to her singing scales by herself in her bedroom and I don't know whether to dash in and hug her or beat her over the head with the music stand.

This morning I was singing 'Salley Gardens' while I was doing the washing up when Charlotte came into the kitchen. I was pleased when she picked up a tea towel and joined in. Her voice is much purer than mine but I can hold a tune. 'Salley Gardens' is from an old Yeats poem that Mother used to sing to us when we were young.

We sang it right through once and then a second time with Charlotte improvising a harmony.

'Down by the salley gardens my love and I did meet;
She passed the salley gardens with little snow-white feet.
She bid me take love easy, as the leaves grow on the tree;
But I, being young and foolish, with her would not agree.
In a field by the river my love and I did stand,
And on my leaning shoulder she laid her snow-white hand.
She bid me take life easy, as the grass grows on the weirs;
But I was young and foolish, and now am full of tears.'

As we were singing I thought that if any man could hear Charlotte singing 'Salley Gardens' he'd fall in love with her at once. I wish there was someone kind and a bit wealthy to look after her. She's too young and silly to choose the right husband herself, but I'm afraid that if something exciting doesn't happen soon in her life she'll go off with just anyone.

There is one local boy who really dotes on her and I think he'd be a fine choice. His name is Dougie Devlin. He's tall, kind, quite good looking and very shy. He doesn't have much money but he's smart and his father owns a timber yard and builds houses, so that would be a start. I sometimes go over to the yard and help out with loading timber onto the trucks to earn a bit of pocket money. (At least my 'giant hands' are useful for something.) The Devlins have two sons. Warren, the younger one, is a bit wild because his mother died when he was only ten, but Dougie is gentle and polite. He rides a big black horse on the beach sometimes and waves to me if he sees me on Grayling. While I work at the timber yard he comes over and makes conversation that always leads to the subject of Charlotte. Whenever he mentions her name he blushes. He's the kind of boy who'd worship Charlotte, which is the least she'd expect. He'd probably work himself half to death for her and get the money to pay for her trip to Europe and her singing lessons. The trouble is I don't think she'd find him interesting enough. She is planning to make her debut at the Lady Mayoress's Ball at the Palais in Geronga before Christmas and she hasn't decided who to ask to be her partner. I'm trying to think of a subtle way to suggest Dougie.

Unfortunately Mother doesn't like the Devlins at all. I don't know why. When I go over to the Devlins' timber yard to work I have to pretend that I'm out riding Grayling. Mother is particularly rude to Mr Devlin, perhaps because he calls her Kate instead of Mrs Danielssen. He's always politely friendly to her, never too familiar, but he refuses to pretend she is the Queen of Sheba, which a lot of other people do.

On Saturday night something alarming but quite fortunate happened. It gave Dougie Devlin the chance to behave like a hero and Charlotte at last not only noticed him but was favourably impressed.

Charlotte was away in town auditioning for *The Gondoliers*. I was sitting at the kitchen table helping Jonathan and Eliza with their homework and Mother was out on the balcony 'enjoying the evening' as she calls it when she sits alone staring into the dark. Suddenly she gave an excited shout.

'Come! Come quickly and see!' She grabbed the binoculars from their hook on the wall and held them up to her eyes. Eliza, Jonathan and I scrambled up and ran to see what she was looking at.

'Fire! There's a bushfire. A real one!'

Mother's eyes were bright with excitement.

I focused the binoculars on the scrub by the river half a mile away and saw smoke, burning bush, and men fighting a fire with what looked like hessian bags. Jonathan and Eliza took turns to look too.

'Come on, we'll have to hurry!' Mother said.

'Where?' I asked.

'To the fire!'

'What? It looks dangerous down there.'

'Oh, Anna. The firefighters need help. We'll take thermoses of tea, and more bags. Yes, wet hessian bags.'

She raced out the door and we had no time to protest. She came back with an armful of hessian bags we'd been saving for the sack race at the school sports, loaded them into Eliza's old cream wicker pram and hurried back to the kitchen. 'Anna, come and help me make tea. Lots of tea!' She seemed to have sudden manic energy. In no time we were off, hurrying along the dirt road towards the smoke.

As we came closer the sky turned red and we could hear the sound of flames crackling and trees bursting. I could tell that Eliza and Jonathan were scared but trying not to show it.

'Oooh look! What a sky,' said Mother in awe. 'Like Guy Fawkes Night.'

'Will it be hot, Mummy?' asked Eliza.

'Oooh yes, very hot. Come on! We're nearly there.' Mother was breathless with excitement. 'It's an adventure.'

'I hate adventures,' muttered Jonathan.

We parked the pram on a rise above the smoke and peered down at the fire raging below. The firefighters were blackened silhouettes, beating the flames with bags. There were a few men with water tanks on their backs.

We were the only women and children around. We stared in fascination.

'Do you think it's safe to be so close?' I asked Mother.

She threw back her head and laughed. 'Safe? Of course it is. Quite safe, quite safe.' She began unpacking the wet bags and the teacups. She poured strong black tea from the thermos flask and thrust two cups at Eliza. 'Here, darling, take those down to the men.'

Eliza's jaw dropped. 'Down near the fire?'

'I'll do it,' I said.

Now the fire was spreading towards two small houses and the men were pursuing it, shouting to each other in weary, hoarse voices. I climbed quickly down the slope to the first silhouettes and offered the tea. The men looked up, surprised and pleased. One of them was Dougie Devlin. They gulped the tea down thirstily. 'We've brought wet bags if you need more,' I said tentatively.

'Yeah, we do.' Then they looked up, recognised Mother and waved their gratitude. Even in this bizarre situation she returned their waves regally.

I ran back up the slope for more tea to find Jonathan coughing from the smoke. I shepherded the children away from the fire to a sheltered clump of tea-tree where I told them to wait. Then I ran back for more supplies for the men. It was quite exciting, being part of the fire-fighting drama.

Once all the tea was gone I grabbed a bag of my own and started helping them beat out the flames. We seemed to be defeating it because the flames were getting lower. After a few minutes I heard a shout. 'Anna. The kids!' It was Dougie Devlin running up the slope behind me and pointing to the tea-tree where Jonathan and Eliza were sheltering. The wind had suddenly changed direction and the fire was heading away from the houses and straight towards the trees. Mother was packing up the tea things and hadn't noticed. I raced after Dougie but he'd already reached them. He picked up Eliza, grabbed Jonathan by the hand and was running back down the slope towards me.

'Thanks, Dougie, thanks,' I said, clutching the children tightly.

'Maybe they'd be better off at home.' He looked up towards Mother, who was now staring out at the night full of flying sparks and apparently enjoying the spectacle. 'The Geronga Fire Brigade's on the way. You've been a great help. Tell your mum thanks.'

I nodded uncertainly.

'No, really. Thanks a lot.'

'Dougie Devlin saved our lives!' Eliza announced as soon as Charlotte came in from her audition. For once I didn't contradict her.

'He was very brave,' I said.

Eliza told the story in great detail with just a few embellishments. 'The tea-tree was on fire even before Dougie got to us but he dashed through the flames, and whoosh, picked us up in his big strong arms and *flew* down the hill to where it was safe.'

I screwed my face up at Eliza to indicate that she'd gone too far.

'Well, not really flew, but it felt like flying.'

Charlotte was feeling positive towards the family this evening, having just got the role of Tessa. 'Dougie sounds like quite a hero,' she said.

'He is. It might be nice if you thanked him for us, Charlotte, being the oldest,' I suggested. 'You know Mother won't visit the Devlins, in spite of Dougie's heroic deed.'

Mother had retired to bed after all the excitement.

'Yes, I should do that,' said Charlotte, much to my surprise. 'Maybe I'll go over there tomorrow morning.' And she skipped off singing, 'Hail gallant gondolieri.'

'Did Beverley get Gianetta?' I called after her.

'Yes. Amazing, isn't it?' We laughed because it was.

chapter nine

Things are going well for Charlotte at last. When she came back from visiting the Devlins this morning she was smiling rather secretively. Of course I was dying to know whether she'd asked Dougie to partner her in her debut at the Lady Mayoress's Ball. I followed her out to the garden where she started to pick the climbing daisies on the bank. She was humming one of the love songs Tessa sings to her gondolier, Guiseppe or Marco, I don't remember which.

I sat down on a rock and threaded a few daisies into a chain. 'Did Dougie blush when you thanked him?' I asked, trying to sound casual.

'No. Why?'

I shrugged. 'He does that sometimes. He's shy. He's rather good looking, don't you think?' I waited a while before adding, 'I think he likes you.'

Charlotte looked straight at me, raised her eyebrows and said, 'Does he just?' and went on picking daisies.

I sat down with my back to her. If she wanted to be haughty, what did I care? I felt like kicking her.

'I hope he can dance,' she said half to herself.

I swung around to face her. 'Why?'

She grinned.

'You asked him!'

She nodded.

'And he blushed?'

'Up to here.' She put her finger on her forehead. 'He's very sweet, actually. I'm quite glad I thought of going over there to thank him.'

Mother seems more peaceful after the excitement of the bushfire. Tonight she read to us, which she only does when she's feeling really well. She baked delicious cheese scones in the afternoon and she didn't even mind when we ate the lot before they'd had time to cool. All we'd needed for dinner was a boiled egg each and some toast and Vegemite. As soon as the meal was over Charlotte had jumped up, cleared the table, washed the dishes in a huge lather of soap and dashed off to her room to practise Tessa. Mother had smiled after her and sighed contentedly. We're all relieved when Charlotte's happy.

Mother put another log on the fire, took down her old copy of *Wuthering Heights* and seated herself in the rocking chair. This is the signal for us to come and sit at her feet. We grabbed cushions and made ourselves comfortable, the two younger ones wriggling close to see who could be first to put a head on her lap.

Mother reads well and obviously identifies with the drama. She picked up the story exactly where she left off last time, even though it had been weeks ago. We would never dream of asking her to go back over the parts we had forgotten.

'. . . my fingers closed on the fingers of a little, ice-cold

hand! The intense horror of the nightmare came over me:
I tried to draw back my arm, but the hand clung to it, and
a most melancholy voice sobbed, "Let me in – let me in!"

' "Who are you?" I asked, struggling meanwhile to
disengage myself.

' "Catherine Linton," it replied shiveringly. "I'm come
home, I'd lost my way on the moor!" '

I have read *Wuthering Heights* several times but I
always like to hear Mother reading it aloud. I know that
it frightens Eliza and Jonathan because I've had to wake
them up to stop them screaming when they have nightmares after being read to, but they wouldn't miss this rare
opportunity to get close to Mother and to share what she
is thinking.

Mother read on. Eliza soon fell asleep and Jonathan's
eyelids fluttered as he struggled to keep awake.

'. . . "I require to be let alone!" exclaimed Catherine
furiously. "I demand it! Don't you see I can scarcely
stand?" '

I touched Mother's sleeve and nodded at the children.
She stopped reading, looked at them lovingly, gave each
one a kiss and got up carefully so as not to disturb them.
I helped them into bed.

When I came back Mother was staring into the fire. I sat
down close to her. The atmosphere was warm and intimate.

'It *was* an adventure, helping those men fight the fire,'
I said quietly.

She looked pleased. 'I thought so.'

'A bit much for Eliza and Jon.' I tried to sound like a
friend, an adult, not a critical older child.

'Perhaps. But they'll never forget it.'

I waited. The fire crackled peacefully.

'You know our school ballet club?'

'Mmm.'

'I got selected to be in the troupe. To represent the school. They only picked twelve.'

'Really?'

'We're all getting white tulle dresses made by the needlework department. We dance to a piece called *Moment Musical*.'

'*Moments Musicaux*? Ah, Schubert.'

'Yes, I think so.' I got up in my shapeless pyjamas and danced a few steps, humming the music.

Mother smiled at me. Then she joined in humming the tune. 'Number three in F minor. Very pretty piece. You dance gracefully, Anna.'

For a minute I thought she might leap up and play it on the piano, but she just smiled vaguely and kept on humming. When I sat down she said, 'You always did love dancing. When you were little you'd ask me to put on the music to *Coppelia* or *Swan Lake* and you'd dance for hours all by yourself. You called it "dancing a story". Do you remember?'

I shook my head.

'You were quite an imaginative little thing, but I'm afraid you've grown too tall for a ballerina now.'

I blushed with indignation. 'I'm not the tallest in the troupe,' I said. 'I know I'm not as good as the others but at least I got in. I've got to have proper ballet shoes. They cost three pounds, seven and six. I know we can't really —'

'I haven't had a new pair of *walking* shoes for three years. How do you think we can afford shoes for dancing?' Mother was no longer smiling. She looked angry. I had broken the mood of serenity. 'The only money I have

91

in the world apart from the piano students, which barely pays for our food, is the child endowment money that's paid into my savings account each fortnight. It's only a few shillings but it mounts up, and when there's enough, do you know what I do with it, Anna? I take all of our shoes to the bootmaker's to be repaired. If there's anything left over after that I keep it in the account and save up to pay for your school uniforms and books.'

She was being a responsible, normal parent, just as I'd always hoped she would be. I had no argument whatsoever. But I had to say something. 'All right. All right,' I said miserably. 'But how can we afford to give money away to people like Mrs Mooney?'

'Because she's worse off than we are. We still have a duty to give to the poor.' She pronounced it 'puuer' like the English upper class.

'We *are* the bloody poor!' I yelled.

'Don't be vulgar,' she said icily, making it clear that the subject was closed.

Mrs Mooney has offered to make Charlotte's dress for the ball. She used to be a dressmaker and made wedding gowns. One of the brides cancelled her wedding because her fiancé ran off with her sister. The bride never came back for the half-finished dress, even though she'd paid for the material, so Mrs Mooney is remaking it for Charlotte's debut and giving it to her for nothing. (It's a pity she can't make ballet shoes.) I've seen the pattern for the dress and I must say it's very elaborate. Charlotte will look like Cinderella and everyone else like the ugly stepsisters. The skirt is so full that she'll need a dozen rope petticoats to make it stick out, and the dress has a plunging neckline, which seems to be the latest thing. I hope Dougie isn't too embarrassed to escort her.

I worked hard in the timber yard all afternoon on Saturday and made ten shillings. I know it will be impossible to earn enough for the ballet shoes in time, but I'm praying that the shop will let me put ten shillings down as a deposit and then pay them off gradually.

It was awfully embarrassing at the weekly ballet rehearsal yesterday. I was the only girl in the troupe still wearing the wrong shoes. They are cheap and so stiff that you can't bend your feet properly. Our ballet mistress, Mrs Krantz, who is German, lost patience with me and shouted, 'Bend your toe, Anna! Vot iss the matter with you? Agh, those shoes! Ven are you getting rid of those shoes, girl?'

I keep telling her the shoes have been ordered but they haven't arrived yet, which I think she knows isn't true because none of the other girls had trouble finding shoes. I'm terrified she'll replace me if I don't have the shoes soon. I'm only the second tallest in the troupe but the tallest girl is one of her best dancers, who has private lessons with her outside school hours. Mrs Krantz said, 'I haff plenty of my private students vaiting to get into this troupe if you are not so keen, Anna.' I almost cried when she said that but she isn't the sort of person who would understand my predicament even if I told her the truth. She has no patience with girls who don't live for their ballet. She wouldn't think it's enough that I've always loved dancing, even though I've never had a lesson outside the school ballet club, and I'd adore to wear a white tulle dress and dance on the stage in the school concert at the Regent Theatre. Even Charlotte would be impressed if she saw me dance there.

I had to do something to save the situation so at the end of the lesson I went up to her and said, 'Mrs Krantz, I really do want to be in the troupe, but if I haven't got the shoes within four weeks, I will understand if you decide to replace me.'

She looked at me sternly and said, 'Four veeks is a long time, Anna.' But then she nodded as if she knew there was more to this than a delay at the shoe shop. 'Very well,' she replied. 'Haff your shoes ready by October twenty-first. Zat gives you five veeks, vhich should be more zan enough.'

I didn't see Dougie on Saturday. He was out doing training with the Volunteer Fire Brigade (he'd been invited to join after his daring dash at the bushfire the other night, which was quite an honour). But Mr Devlin came out to help me work and when we'd stacked half a truckload he offered me a lemonade. He's always been friendly to me. As we were sitting down under the peppercorn tree he said, 'You're a hard worker, young Anna. Chip off the old block.' I wondered what he meant. Mother is hardly what anyone would call a hard worker or an old block. I looked at him questioningly but he got up all of a sudden and said, 'Back to the truck, eh, mate.'

Now that it's mid-September and the weather's getting warmer we have a new problem at The Tower House. Unwanted guests. Weekends are the worst time. Because we are close to one of the loveliest beaches in the district, people we hardly know drive out here from Geronga and 'just pop in'. Of course they expect to stay for lunch or afternoon tea. (They have no idea that we can't afford it except on special occasions.) Some of them even drop hints about staying the entire weekend. Occasionally we give in and let them. One dreadful afternoon last summer we had no less than twelve groups of uninvited guests. Since then we've developed 'tactics'.

This Sunday was sunny. I was stirring barley broth for lunch on the stove and gazing out the window, thinking about going riding and then for my first swim since last summer, when I heard a car door slam and the unmistakable voices of invaders. 'Quick! It's the McIntoshes!'

I switched off the wireless, took the saucepan off the stove and closed the windows. Mother hurriedly drew the kitchen blinds. Jonathan and Eliza flung themselves flat on the floor.

'Where's Charlotte?' whispered Eliza.

'At the Mooneys'. Getting fitted.'

'The doors to the balcony – they're wide open!' said Jonathan.

'Shhh. They won't see them. Too high,' Mother whispered. She lowered herself gently and lay on the floor too.

'That's where they climbed in last time,' I whispered urgently.

'All right. Close them,' she said. I leapt up. 'Be careful.'

I could hear footsteps on the path outside and the sound of about six people approaching – adults, children, even a dog. I crept silently along the passage towards the balcony. I lowered myself to the floor and crawled to the open door, reached up for the handle and slowly closed it, hoping they wouldn't look up and see the phantom arm. I locked it from inside and raced back to the kitchen. There was a loud knock at the door. Excited voices were clamouring outside the kitchen where we lay on the floor like corpses.

'What if they're not home?'

'They're *always* home.'

'Can I sleep in Jonathan's bunk like I did last time?'

Jonathan pulled a face and shook his head.

There was another deafening knock.

'Quick, Daddy, make them open the door. I've got to go to the lav.'

Eliza got a fit of nervous giggles. I stuffed a tea towel in her mouth.

The knocking became louder and more urgent.

'Yoohooo. Katharine! Anyone home?' The McIntoshes began to prowl round the house looking for a way to get in.

Then someone rattled the kitchen window, terrifyingly close. 'Bunk me up, Sheila. I think I can wrench it open,' said a masculine voice. We lay still, frozen with fear.

'They must be home,' said Sheila. 'I can smell something cooking.' There was more rattling. Then another male voice called, 'I've tried all the back doors, even the balcony. They really are away.'

'Wretched nuisance. Where else are we going to stay?'

'We could try Cathken Guesthouse. Might not be booked out.'

'Too expensive. What a blow.'

We heard footsteps retreating, whining children, the dog yapping and at last the sound of a large car driving off. Cautiously we peered out the window. 'Gone,' I breathed.

We all leapt up and performed a spontaneous dance of victory, waving tea towels, brooms and saucepans.

chapter ten

The warm weather lasted only a few days, then back came cold winds and wintry rain. It is often erratic like this in September, before the summer has really started. Mother gets moody when the weather changes.

The following Saturday afternoon was wet. Charlotte was in town rehearsing for *The Gondoliers*. Jonathan and Eliza had been allowed to play in the living room because their bedroom had a leak. They were building a cubby-house out of the dining-room chairs and some blankets and cushions, and doing it quietly enough, except for the occasional giggle. I was reading *Tess of the D'Urbervilles* because it was too wet to work at the Devlins' timber yard, and Mother was settling herself comfortably by the wireless ready to listen to a concert on the ABC. This is a weekly event and something she looks forward to.

The ABC announcer had just begun to introduce the concert when there was a yell from Eliza, who'd collided with Jonathan in the tunnel of chairs.

Mother sprang up, looking absolutely furious.

'Out! Get out! Both of you!'

They stared at her blankly.

Mother pointed to the door. 'I said get outside.'

'It's raining, Mummy,' Eliza protested.

'Out! Can't I have one hour's peace to listen to my concert? Noise. Always noise.' She covered her ears with both hands.

I put my book down.

'Take them for a walk!' she begged.

I stood up and went to fetch our raincoats. I handed one each to the children and gave Mother a reproachful look. She had already settled herself back by the wireless. The concert was beginning.

Outside, as we passed by the living-room window, Eliza pressed her wet nose to the glass and looked in at Mother appealingly. Mother pretended not to see her. The music rose to a crescendo. Mother leaned back in her chair and closed her eyes in bliss. I pulled Eliza gently away.

We trudged through the red mud and steady rain to the shops. There was no one much about and we had no money to spend, but we peered in the window of the Doo Duck Inn, which is the smartest milk bar in the township. It has a picture of Donald Duck painted on the front window, just like the comic strip. There are four-seater booths to sit in with padded vinyl seats and a jukebox that plays your favourite hit song if you have sixpence to put in it. When I earned my very first money at the timber yard I took Charlotte to the Doo Duck Inn and shouted her a spider. (I couldn't take Eliza and Jon as well or they'd have asked where I got the money; Charlotte, I trusted not to tell.) We sat in the first booth. Charlotte ordered passionfruit and I had lime. A lime spider is my idea of heaven. We had to leave quite soon because some rough-looking boys called bodgies, wearing black leather jackets and ripple-soled shoes and their hair slicked back with Brylcreem, were making remarks about Charlotte. She pretended to be furious but I think she didn't mind all that much. They were quite flattering remarks. One of the bodgies was Warren Devlin, Dougie's younger brother, but Charlotte didn't recognise him.

After we'd looked in the shop windows for a while Jonathan, Eliza and I stood outside Cathken Guesthouse where there is a row of thick pine trees that makes quite a good shelter from the rain. We settled down on a floor of fallen pine-needles which smelt clean and dry. When I was small I called these thick brown pine-needles 'fur-bob' and built cubbies out of it.

Once Uncle Martin took us all to have dinner at Cathken Guesthouse. It was Mother's birthday and we ordered the set menu – pea soup, Chicken Maryland with lots of crumbed pineapple and banana around it, and chocolate blancmange with tinned peaches for dessert. We thought it was a grand meal. I remember the dining room had a strange smell, a mixture of floor polish, beer and frying fat. There was a vase of poppies on the table which occasionally dropped petals into our soup. We thought this was funny and added to the novelty of being taken out to dinner. Uncle Martin ordered the waitress to take the vase away. She was an old woman with a black dress and white starched cap, and she looked quite hurt – no other table had flowers. Maybe she'd put them there for Mother's birthday. Apart from that incident it was a happy evening. We'd all brought Mother little surprise presents. Jonathan had made her a wooden matchbox holder with the word 'Mother' painted on it. Eliza gave her a comb in a case. Charlotte's present was a brooch that unfolded with views of London Bridge, and I had sewn together a 1952 pocket diary. That dinner seems a long time ago but it was only two years.

I wondered if Jonathan and Eliza were remembering the same thing as they crouched mournfully under the pine trees.

'Hey, let's go to the big sandhill!' I said suddenly.

They looked up from their dripping rain hoods.

'The really huge one?'

'Yep.' I grabbed them by their cold red hands and started running down the muddy road to the beach.

At the top of the spectacular sandhill we looked out along the beach and could see all the way to Merlin Heads. The tide was coming in and the waves were rough. There was hardly any beach left at all.

The sun was beginning to come out from behind the clouds. 'Look! God's peeping out,' said Eliza.

'How high up are we? Ten storeys?' yelled Jonathan, his voice almost disappearing in the wind.

'About seven,' I yelled back. I didn't really have a clue but Jonathan feels reassured by facts.

We looked down the steep white dune, which was rippled finely by the wind. There was not another mark on it – not a blade of grass, a tree, a seagull, a footprint.

We were about to desecrate it.

'Who's first?' I yelled.

'Me!' screeched Eliza, and she was off. Her red hood flew back and her cape soared behind her as her small legs raced madly, leaving big footprints in the pristine sand. Jon and I laughed at her ungainly flapping. It seemed to take ages for her to reach the bottom. She landed in a heap and turned to wave at us triumphantly.

Jonathan set off with his arms out like a bird, but he lost balance and fell sideways, rolling down the last section of the dune. At the bottom he sat up, laughing and covered in sand.

I set off slowly, taking giant steps. I felt as if I was flying. Boing! Boing! Like a cartoon character or an imaginary man on the moon. It was impossible not to lose balance as I gained momentum. At the bottom I fell hard on my chest and lay there, quite winded. Eliza and Jonathan bent over me in alarm.

'She can't talk.'

'Perhaps she's hurt her heart.'

'Will she die?'

'No, look, she's trying to breathe.'

I tried to smile reassuringly, but I did feel a shock. After a few minutes I sat up and croaked, 'See? Not dead, just had the wind knocked out of my sails.'

We were all quite cheerful as we set off home.

As we passed the Mooneys' cottage we could smell the usual delicious chips frying. Eliza said, 'I'll just go and see if Wilma's doing anything interesting,' and Jonathan added, 'Perhaps I'll go and play with Raymond for a while.' I grinned and said I'd tell Mother they wouldn't be long. Her concert hour was not quite up, anyway.

As I was taking off my raincoat in the hall I could hear the wireless turned up to full volume playing Spanish-sounding classical music. Was it *Capriccio Italienne*? I went towards the living room and was about to open the glass door when I stopped and stared. Mother was dancing in a rather passionate, sensual way, swirling her long silk scarf about her like a partner. She was quite self-absorbed and didn't notice I was watching. The table was set for afternoon tea, with biscuits, a plate of sandwiches and two cups and saucers. Suddenly there was a loud knock at the front door. I fled down the passage and hid in the kitchen. If it was Uncle Martin, I didn't want to meet him. The music was turned off abruptly and Mother went to open the door. I peered out the window and saw Reverend Marsden standing on the doorstep in dripping motorcycle gear. He looked at Mother appealingly and she ushered him in. Neither of them said a word.

I listened while he took off his wet things in the hall. Still nothing was said. This seemed odd. Mother hadn't told us we were expecting him.

After a few minutes my curiosity got the better of me and I crept down the passage to peer in through the glass door. They were sitting on the sofa by the fire talking; at least, Mother was talking and Reverend Marsden was listening with rapt attention. His wet silk scarf was draped over the back of the sofa with steam rising from it. It seemed very intimate, just the two of them, and I had a sudden urge to burst in on them. Instead I strained to hear what they were saying.

Mother had her back to me so I couldn't make out much at all, but then Reverend Marsden leaned back, stretched and said quite loudly, 'You know, I'd have gone mad in this town if it wasn't for you.'

'Oh. Why?' She looked pleased.

He stood up and crossed to the bookshelf. 'Because you have the finest collection of moral scientists in the district.' He turned round and gave her a wicked smile.

'Moral scientists? I thought they were philosophers.' Mother was smiling too. She understood the game.

'They are, but at Cambridge we called the subject

Moral Sciences. Made the theologians feel less guilty about it.'

Mother laughed. She looked quite young and pretty, partly because she was still flushed from her wild dancing. 'Did you always want to be a theologian?' she asked.

'No.' He turned back to the books and seemed to change the subject deliberately. '*Enfranchisement of Women* by Harriet Taylor Mill. *On the Subjection of Women* by John Stuart Mill. Very progressive stuff.'

'They belonged to my mother. She was rather keen on women's rights.'

'A wise woman. You've read these essays?'

'They're a bit earnest for me. I'm saving them for Anna.'

'I admire Anna,' said Reverend Marsden, looking up from the book. He sounded sincere. I felt hot with pleasure. I would read those essays immediately.

Mother watched Reverend Marsden closely. 'Yes, she's very capable. Do you know, she can even fix spoutings?' They both laughed. Then there was a little pause in which they looked at each other seriously.

At last Mother said, 'I'll bring the tea.' She stood up and began to walk towards the glass door. I fled on tiptoe down the passage and bounded silently upstairs to my room. My heart was beating high up near my throat. I felt a mixture of delight that Reverend Marsden admired me and fury that Mother had flirted with him.

I sat down on my hard bed and stared at myself in the mirror. I looked a mess. My hair was damp and straggly. I hated its coppery colour, the fact that it crinkled up and curled when it was wet. My nose was the wrong shape. I wished it would turn up cutely like the film star Debbie

Reynolds'. For months after I'd seen her in *Singin' in the Rain* I'd tried going to sleep with my finger pushed hard up against the point to make it grow into a snub nose, but it hadn't worked at all. My pointed nose helped to give me the family's look of arrogance. There was no escaping it. My shoulders were too broad, my limbs too long and I walked very straight with my head held high. 'She thinks she's a queen,' someone had whispered behind my back at the school bus stop. It was all I could do not to hunch my shoulders immediately and hang my head down. I would have to learn to toss my hair flirtatiously and laugh at the boys' dirty jokes too. Then maybe I'd feel normal. At fourteen I was already taller than Charlotte. She had grown into a perfectly formed, dainty young woman and I was a female Amazon.

Just then I heard Reverend Marsden's motorbike revving. I looked out the window and there to my horror was Mother climbing onto the bike behind him. She was carrying a small bag and wearing the scarf she'd been dancing with. She clutched him tightly round the waist and then they drove off, both with scarves flying flamboyantly behind them. I ran downstairs and there on the kitchen door was a note. *Dear Big Children, Have gone with Reverend Marsden to visit poor Mrs Bartrop who has nothing for the new baby. Back by five. Help yourselves to some afternoon tea. Love, M.*

'How selfish! How thoughtless!' I ranted to myself. 'She's thirty-seven, he's twenty-seven, not even ordained as a minister yet. I bet she forced him to take her. I bet she said' – and here I imitated Mother behaving like an outrageous coquette – ' "Oh, Albert, let's just pop over to see poor Mrs Thingummy, er Bartrop – what a dreadful name. We'll take her some baby clothes and you can fix up a date for the Christening. Shall we, hmmm? Oh, do say yes, you gorgeous man, and don't let's talk about Anna any more. She's a child, remember, an extremely ugly one!" ' With this I burst into tears.

I went and finished *Tess of the D'Urbervilles* and pretended I was crying about that. Then I stoked up the fire and gobbled all the leftover sandwiches and biscuits from Mother's afternoon tea. When she came in just before five she looked shamelessly cheerful.

'Why that sullen look?' she asked me.

'People might talk.'

She threw back her head and laughed. 'Oh, Anna. Darling, don't be silly.' She came across to where I was hunched in the rocking chair and stroked my hair. Then she said quietly, 'Let them. I'm a free spirit. What do I care what people say?'

I can't imagine anyone not caring what people say about them. Sometimes I pretend it doesn't bother me, like the time I overheard that sneering remark at the bus stop, 'She thinks she's a queen.' I was genuinely shocked to hear that. I'd never thought anything of the kind. But then I had to ask myself, 'Do I?' Not a queen, but someone different. Someone who's not going to spend the rest of her life here in this little seaside town doing what everyone else does? I do think that. I'd rather die than be miserable and fighting against my boring life like Mother is. Was that what the girl at the bus stop saw? My ambition? I'll have to be more careful. People don't like to see that you have plans to be different from them, otherwise they'll make things very unpleasant for you, even possibly destroy you. I wish I could warn Mother to pretend to be ordinary to protect herself but she'd only make a joke of it.

Charlotte, I know, is pretending to be ordinary at present. She's given up the plan to go to Europe and study to be an opera singer. She's seems to be quite enjoying playing a flirty gondolier's girlfriend in an amateur comic opera and going out with Dougie Devlin, although I'm sure it's only temporary.

Mrs Mooney has almost finished making Charlotte's dress. To keep it clean while she's sewing, Mrs Mooney wraps the whole dress up in a large piece of white silk. She carries the bundle all over the shabby old cottage and, incredibly, the dress doesn't get a speck of dirt on it. Charlotte let me watch her try it on the other night and I must say it looked amazing. The only problem is that the skirt is so full and heavy that it will have to be supported by something stronger than rope petticoats. Mrs Mooney says it really needs a wire frame – but then Charlotte wouldn't be able to sit down and would have to walk to the ball. Dougie had a brilliant idea. He said he could weld a metal frame under the skirt and Charlotte could ride the fifteen miles to Geronga standing up in the back of the timber yard truck. He could park the truck around the back of the Palais, put down a ramp like those used for cattle, help Charlotte alight in secret, walk her down the back lane to the front door and there she could make a splendid entrance. No one would ever know she'd had to be transported like a prize bull. Apart from curtsying to the Lady Mayoress, there would be no need for her to bend over at all for the rest of the evening. Dougie really is a genius.

If anyone had suggested to Charlotte a few weeks ago

that she might arrive at the most glamorous social event of the year in a timber truck, she would have bitten their heads off, but now she thinks it's all a bit of an adventure. Dougie seems to have had a very soothing effect on her. I hope she isn't mean enough to drop him right after the ball, but I wouldn't put it past her.

Last Friday I had some bad news about the ballet shoes. The shop refused to take only a deposit and let me pay them off over time. I still have almost three weeks to get the shoes before Mrs Krantz puts another girl into the troupe. I will just have to wait until Mother is in a good mood and ask her if I can borrow the money from the child endowment account. I can work on weekends for Mr Devlin and pay her back gradually, though I'm not sure what I'll say if she asks how I'm earning the money.

chapter eleven

I can hardly believe what Charlotte's just done. I'm so angry with her I dare not go to her room and confront her or I might throttle her.

She has broken the date to go to the ball with Dougie. I saw him this afternoon at the timber yard and he looked just dreadful. I think he'd been crying. How could she do such a thing? They've been practising the dances together at the Palais every Saturday afternoon with the other debutantes and their partners for weeks now, and Dougie has spent hours welding the special hoop for Charlotte's dress. He's besotted with her and she's treated him like dirt. She reminds me of Mother, who treats Mr Devlin in much the same way. In fact, this is all partly Mother's fault.

Last Sunday afternoon Mother, Charlotte and I were invited to the Lorimers' for afternoon tea. Mrs Lorimer always comes to Mother's soirees and brings her two tone-deaf daughters, Joan and Shirley, who are also Mother's piano pupils, so we weren't really surprised at the invitation but I did wonder why Charlotte and I had been included. Perhaps they wanted us as company for Joan and Shirley.

Mr Lorimer is the local real estate agent. He drives the

latest model car, a rather flashy electric-blue Ford Cus-
tomline, which is the only one in the district. Their house
is a large, brand-new triple-fronted cream brick 'villa'
with no trees or shrubs at all, just lots of concrete, which
I think is really ugly.

The reason for our being invited soon became obvious.
Mr Lorimer's younger brother, Max, was staying with
them. Max is a stockbroker who lives in Melbourne. He
looked about forty, as old as Uncle Martin, when he was
introduced, but apparently he's only thirty-three. Max is
tall and thin with a protruding Adam's apple and a rather
loud, nervous laugh that reminded me of a horse whinny-
ing. He has quick, anxious movements and his eyes dart
everywhere as if he's afraid of missing something. I did
not find him at all attractive.

As soon as he saw Charlotte his face lit up and he
ignored the rest of us. He passed the scones and pikelets
only to her and after a few minutes of rather hesitant conversation he asked if she'd like to take a look at his
'machine'. How rude not to ask anyone else! I'd noticed a
shiny British racing green MG in the driveway and I'd have
loved a proper look at it. After a few minutes we heard the
engine rev and the car backing out of the drive. I was stuck
with Joan and Shirley, who wanted to show me boring
Butterick dress patterns. I tried to look interested, while
Mother did her best with Mr and Mrs Lorimer.

Mrs Lorimer explained rather unconvincingly that she
thought it would be nice for Max to meet some young
local people while he was here and that as he was interested in music and had once played the saxophone in a
dance band, she'd immediately thought of Charlotte, who
sang so beautifully at the soirees.

As soon as Charlotte returned about half an hour later, we said we had to be going as we'd left Eliza and Jonathan alone in the house.

On the way home Charlotte said to Mother, in a doubtful voice, 'Max is a divorcé.'

'Well, so am I, dear,' Mother replied nonchalantly. 'That doesn't make him a leper.'

I'm sure that had something to do with Charlotte's decision to go out with Max.

He didn't waste much time. The very next evening unsubtle Max showed up in his MG to take Charlotte out to dinner at the Merlin Heads Hotel. As she flounced down the steps in one of Mother's remade dresses and some high-heeled shoes borrowed from Beverley, she did look very pretty. She waved at me cheerfully as if she had no conscience whatsoever.

I thought that she'd be bored with old Max after one evening, and just hoped that Dougie didn't see her driving off.

It was just before midnight when Charlotte came home. I was still awake reading and when she saw the light she came into my room.

'You're rather late,' I said.

'It was a dinner dance. There was a band, so we stayed till the end,' she said dreamily.

'Is he a good dancer?'

'Very.'

My heart sank.

'So you enjoyed yourself, then?'

'Yes. I felt very grown up.' Charlotte twirled in front of my mirror.

'What did you talk about?'

'Oh, life. We drank a bottle or two of Porphyry Pearl.'

'What's that?'

'A sparkling wine. A bit like champagne. Max says we'll have champagne next time.'

'You're going out with him *again*?' I asked in dismay.

'Yes, Anna. I might even marry him!' She gave another twirl.

'You're tipsy. You must be. Or absolutely mad.'

'I told you I'd find someone rich. And Max is rich!'

'Has he asked you to marry him?'

'Of course not, silly. This is our first date.'

'Did he kiss you?'

'I wouldn't let him. Not on the first date.'

'I don't suppose he liked that.'

'He understood perfectly. Max is a gentleman,' Charlotte said airily.

I giggled. 'A rather elderly gentleman.'

'Anna, you're such a child.'

'Well, he is. And what about Dougie?' I asked indignantly.

Charlotte sighed. 'Yes, I can't very well take Dougie to the ball now I'm going out with Max.'

'So you're just going to dump him! Don't you care about his feelings?'

'I'm sorry about his precious *feelings*, Anna. Look, I'm really tired. I think I'll go to bed.'

'Well, I think that's pathetic. I think *you're* pathetic!' I said angrily. 'Dougie really loves you, you know.'

'Oh, Anna, he doesn't. He's got a bit of a crush on me, that's all. He'll get over it.'

I knew more about Dougie's hopes than Charlotte did but I certainly didn't intend to flatter her by telling her about them now. 'And what if Max doesn't propose, eh? What if he's got another girlfriend in Melbourne?'

'He hasn't. He told me. He vowed that I'm the only girl he's ever wanted since his marriage broke up.'

'And why did it break up?'

'They were incompatible. She was ambitious, cold, and only after his money.'

I nearly fell out of bed laughing. 'And you're not?'

'Good night, Anna.'

Charlotte has been out with Max Lorimer almost every night this week. Usually they go to Geronga to dinner or the pictures. Once they went to the drive-in but they came home early because it was too cold in the MG with the hood back.

'Why didn't Max put the hood up?' I asked.

'It's jammed.'

'Why doesn't he get it fixed if he's so rich?'

Charlotte refused to answer. I think she wishes she hadn't told me quite so much about Max the night she was tipsy.

Anyway, Max is going home to Melbourne next week. Unfortunately he's coming back on weekends to see Charlotte and to rehearse with her and the other debutantes for the ball, which isn't until two weeks before Christmas, so I suppose that means he'll be hanging around here for more than two months.

Dougie has been very noble and given Charlotte the metal hoop for her dress even though he's no longer her partner, but I've no idea how she'll get to the ball without his truck.

I'm so fed up with Charlotte that I don't even try to

be tactful about her blighted future as a singer any more.

'If you do marry Max and he leaves you like he left his first wife, how will you carry on your singing lessons without a job to support yourself?' I boldly inquired as we sat shelling peas together the other evening.

'Ex-husbands are obliged to provide some support for their divorced partners if they need it. Max is already doing that for Wendy.'

'Well, he's better than some,' I said, wishing that Mother hadn't 'lost touch' with our father quite so willingly. 'But wouldn't you feel ashamed to accept money from someone you no longer loved?'

'Not at all.'

'Charlotte, there's no need for you to marry anyone just so you can have singing lessons, you know,' I said. I was eager to tell her about something I'd just found out at school that day. 'You could apply for a teaching bursary from the Education Department, go to Teachers College where they pay you, and then you could afford to pay for the lessons yourself!'

I had been quite excited by this discovery and intended to apply for a bursary myself in a couple of years. I had been waiting to tell Charlotte the good news about how she too could be financially independent.

She gave me a look of pity. 'Teaching might be all right for you, Anna, but I intend to have a real career.'

'But it *would* be a real career. You could teach music for a few years and learn to be a fine singer at the same time! Then you could leave teaching and just be a singer.'

She gave me an exasperated look. 'I couldn't bear to teach, even for a month. You know I have no patience.'

'Well, you might just have to learn some!' Suddenly I felt furious with her arrogance and self-centredness. 'How dare you plan to run away and marry the first rich man who comes along! How dare you go off and leave me here to take care of Mother all by myself! And Eliza and Jonathan too. I can't do it alone, Charlotte, and why should I? I have to go to school while you loll around all day in your room pretending to be a great singer. Then when I come home I have to look after the little ones and see to the animals and settle Mother's moods instead of doing my homework because you have to go out to rehearsal. I've had enough!'

Charlotte stared back at me in shock. 'But I thought you liked doing all that. You're so good at it. I'm not. The little ones love your stories. Mother calms down when you bring her cups of tea and listen to her woes. And as I just said, I have absolutely no patience . . .'

'Well, get some, please. I need your help. The accounts are in a shocking state. I have to go through them all and see what can be done. Mother's given up. I don't think she's even paying off the house any more. She keeps saying we'll just have to sell it. And then where would we go? Don't answer that! I know where *you'd* go, but think of the rest of us. It's only two more years before I can get a teaching bursary and earn enough money to save us. Charlotte, you could get a bursary now if you applied. You did very well in your leaving certificate.'

'No! I'll never be a teacher. But all right, I'll help with the little ones so you can start work on the accounts. Will that do?'

I nodded. 'It would help.'

'Tonight. I can do it tonight because Max is busy working on his car.'

This weekend Max is not coming to Skinners Bluff. He's suggested to Charlotte that she come to Melbourne and stay in his South Yarra flat instead. He's told her she can have the guest bedroom, and that it will all be perfectly respectable. Of course she is delighted, even though it means they'll have to miss dancing practice for the ball. Max says he doesn't need to practise anyway. Charlotte's told Mother that she's going to her friend Beverley's place for the weekend.

'There's just one problem, Anna,' she confided in me. 'I don't have the money for the train fare. Could you lend me some?'

'Charlotte, I'm sorry.' I explained about the ballet shoes and how short of time I was. She didn't look convinced. 'Why not ask Max for the fare?'

'I couldn't do that. I do have some pride.'

'Well, if he's going to marry you he shouldn't mind at all.'

'I don't *know* that he's going to marry me,' she said crossly.

'What? He hasn't even asked yet?' I pretended to be shocked. 'But you've hardly been out of each other's sight.'

Charlotte sighed. 'Look, the real reason I want to go to Melbourne so urgently is not to see Max but because I have an interview at the Conservatorium of Music. It's a sort of audition, to see if I'm good enough to get in. I know I can't afford to go there but at least I can find out whether or not I'm acceptable. I'm just staying at Max's because I've nowhere else to go.'

I wasn't totally convinced about that last part. 'I'm glad you've got an audition. That's great. Maybe you could get a scholarship!' I said enthusiastically.

She looked hopeful. 'Maybe.'

'What are you going to sing?' I said, testing her to see if she was genuine.

'Three pieces. Tessa's song from *The Gondoliers*, some German lieder, and "Donde lieta usci" from Act Three of *La Bohème* by Puccini.'

'Oh,' I said. I'd overheard her practising the German songs and she'd been playing the aria from *La Bohème* over and over on the little gramophone she'd borrowed from Mrs Mooney and singing along with it. It is a very good recording, made only this year by Maria Callas. Mother had sold her little antique writing desk to buy us all decent birthday presents this year, and Charlotte's had been the new Callas recording.

I nodded, then said, 'I'm sorry I can't lend you the train fare. Haven't you saved any money at all?'

'There's a bit left over from last Christmas but I need that to have my hair set before the ball.'

'Mrs Mooney can do your hair for nothing. She's a genius.'

'I didn't think of that.' She brightened up. 'Thanks, Anna, I'll use the hair money for the train.'

I was fast asleep on Saturday night when something crashed against my window. A seagull? I sat bolt upright, staring at the glass. It hadn't broken. I switched on the light and moved cautiously towards the window. As I carefully opened it a husky voice below called, 'Anna, it's all right. It's me, Dougie.' I stared down and saw him standing on the pathway with a girl wrapped in a blanket. It was Charlotte.

As dawn came up over the sea, Charlotte sat on my bed with a hot cup of cocoa and told me the whole sad story.

She had taken the train up to Melbourne early in the morning as she'd planned and had her audition at the Conservatorium. She thought it had gone rather well. The director had particularly liked Tessa's song but he thought the other pieces were perhaps a bit ambitious for such a young voice, although he'd complimented her on attempting such difficult work. He then asked who had coached her in the Puccini aria and when she said Maria Callas he was astonished. Charlotte had laughed then and confessed that she'd only imitated Callas's latest recording. The director had been impressed. She had then been interviewed by a panel of teaching staff, who seemed very favourably inclined towards her, but at the end of the interview she discovered that she'd need to matriculate before being eligible for the Conservatorium, and there were absolutely no scholarships to cover tuition. She was very depressed about this, and told the director that although she could study for her matriculation at night, she couldn't possibly afford the Conservatorium fees. He asked whether she had considered applying for a teaching bursary because, with her singing talent and good marks in the leaving certificate, he was sure she would be accepted to train as a music teacher. She had said she would think about it.

'I felt so disappointed, Anna. I took the tram to South Yarra in a sort of daze and walked about in the Botanic Gardens opposite Max's flat for an hour or so until he came home,' she said. 'He was very kind to me. He said it didn't matter about the stupid Conservatorium not having any scholarships. He put his arm around me, gave me a glass of champagne and tried to make a joke of it.'

'Did he ask you to marry him?'

'No.' Charlotte looked shamefaced. 'Foolishly I'd imagined that he might. It would have been the perfect time to do it. He said we'd go out to dinner and then to a club, which we did. We drank rather a lot. He kept insisting I drink more and more sweet wine, but it was making my head ache, and then he said, "It's late. Let's go home to bed." Earlier he'd shown me the little spare bedroom which was to be mine for the night, and I'd been very touched that he'd gone to all that trouble, even putting flowers in a vase for me. But when we got back to the flat he said, "Don't be silly. That was only a joke. Tonight, my love, you're going to sleep with me."

'I just laughed and said no, I wasn't, because I wasn't his wife or even his fiancée, and I wanted to wait until I was really in love before I slept with anyone.'

She paused and looked as if she might cry. 'And then he became very angry. I had no idea he could change personality like that. He said that when I accepted his invitation to stay the weekend, it of course meant that we would sleep together. Didn't I know anything? He called me a cock-teaser and all sorts of other filthy names. He was like a monster, wrestling me, but I fought back. I was terrified . . .'

'Oh, Charlotte.' I put both arms around her and began to cry in sympathy. 'How did you get away?'

'I just ran. Out into the street. In my flimsy little dress with no shoes on! I ran and ran down the road. I'd left everything back in the flat – my coat, overnight bag, money, handbag, shoes – but there was no way I was going back there to face that . . . rapist.'

'But he didn't . . .'

'No, no, he didn't, because I ran away before he could. I scratched him rather badly and he ripped my dress. It was horrible.'

'But how did you get home like that, with no money and no shoes?'

Charlotte smiled triumphantly between her tears. 'I had the return train ticket in the pocket of my dress. No money. Just the ticket. And I walked to the station. It took hours.'

'In your stockings? To Spencer Street Station?'

I pulled back the blanket she was still wrapped in and saw her bruised and bloody feet. 'Oh, Charlotte. Let me bathe them. I'll get some Dettol.'

'They're all right. Let me tell you the rest first. I sat in the ladies' waiting room at the station, huddled up in the cold. I thought I'd have to sleep there all night because the last train had gone, but it hadn't! Remember that late-night train we used to call "the drunk's train" which leaves at about eleven thirty? Well, I caught that! I was thrilled. One of the drunks was kind enough to lend me his coat and I slept all the way to Geronga, for almost two hours.'

'But how did you get to Skinners Bluff?'

'Well, I thought I'd have to spend the night at the bus stop waiting for the six a.m., but then I thought, there is one person in the world who might rescue me.'

'So you rang Dougie? At two a.m.?'

'I did. And he answered. I asked him to forgive me for being such a complete and utter fool and told him that I'd learned a hard lesson and that I'd never hurt him again.'

'And he came with a blanket? How romantic.'

'No, he just happened to have one in the truck, which was lucky. I was freezing.'

'Charlotte, you did mean it, about never hurting him again, didn't you?' I asked anxiously.

'Of course. He's very sweet. I really do like him a lot.' She smiled as if she meant it. Then she looked at me and said in a puzzled, disappointed voice, 'I don't think I could marry someone just for their money, you know. I thought I could, but I'm not as tough as I imagined. I just couldn't bear to sleep with someone I didn't love even if they were King Midas.'

I think she knew how glad I was to hear it.

Charlotte and I have been much more like real sisters since her awful experience with Max. He had the nerve to deliver her belongings back here the very next day. She looked very pale when she heard his car and begged me to go and send him away. I said I'd be pleased to. I took her things from him with icy politeness. He could see I knew just what had happened, and yet he still had the nerve to pretend to be sorry.

'Please tell your sister that I didn't mean to upset her. I'd had a few too many drinks. I drove around the streets of South Yarra looking for her for hours.'

'Then I'm very glad you didn't find her. She doesn't wish to see you again, Mr Lorimer.'

As I turned to walk away up the path he said, 'How did she find her way home?'

'She's a very resourceful young lady.' I glared at him. 'And you are not the gentleman you pretend to be. Don't *ever* come here again!'

My heart was pounding with rage as I tramped up the path with Charlotte's clothes, handbag and shoes. If he'd stayed another minute I might have hurled a rock at him.

As I heard the MG roar off I realised with shock that I had behaved just like Mother would have if she'd known what had happened to Charlotte.

chapter twelve

I'm feeling much more hopeful about our future lately. It's two and a half months until Christmas, and we seem to be almost like a normal family. Charlotte is being unusually tolerant of everyone, Mother has had no fits of rage or despair, and the accounts, when I checked them, showed that we weren't in such dire financial straits as I'd imagined. If we could just find a way of making about two pounds a week extra I feel sure we could manage to make the payments the bank requires so that we can all stay together in The Tower House.

I have persuaded Mother to make an appointment to see the bank manager and ask him to extend the loan. She has promised to do it before the end of the month.

I have several ideas about how to make the extra money we need. One is to sell the goats' milk. Mother has been saying for ages that we could sell it to the Children's Hospital, but instead she gives any milk we don't use to the O'Neill family who have three children suffering from asthma. We don't like goats' milk much so we wouldn't miss it and the O'Neills will just have to pay for it.

Another idea is to sell a few more valuable pieces of

furniture, but Mother hates parting with the family heir-looms which came all the way from Ireland, and there aren't many fine pieces left. She wants to keep as much as possible to leave to us when she dies, so perhaps that's not such a good option.

The last idea is that I could work on a more regular basis at the Devlins' timber yard on weekends. Mother would have to agree to it, of course, and this might take some persuasion.

I've been working there quite a bit lately and have saved over half the money I need for my ballet shoes. Still, it's less than two weeks before I'm due to present them to Mrs Krantz so I'm hoping for a miracle.

Apart from my lack of ballet shoes, our situation is far from hopeless. I said a little prayer of thanks to God last night, even though I'm not sure I totally believe in him.

Tom and Sarah are home from boarding school this week-end and we're all meeting at the Merlin River for a picnic lunch today. I love picnics, even though this one will be slightly embarrassing for me, having to face Uncle Martin for the first time after telling him that he was one of the most selfish people I'd ever met. I've decided to be pleas-ant and polite to him but nothing more. If he tries to jolly me up or uses his famous sarcasm, I'll just withdraw with dignity.

Mother is very excited this Sunday morning, hurling things into the picnic basket with gay abandon and singing a rather rollicking sea shanty, 'What Shall We Do with the Drunken Sailor?', which is not her usual style. I hope it doesn't mean she intends to drink too much wine. She almost never drinks but she's recently discovered some dusty bottles in the cellar which I think must be the ones left by Aunt Ingeborg and Aunt Hedda all those years ago. They should almost be very fine wines by now. I notice she's polished one up and put aside two crystal glasses. Not very practical for a picnic.

Even Charlotte has decided to grace us with her presence on this family occasion. She's been so much nicer to us all since that dreaded evening with Max Lorimer. Fortunately he doesn't seem to visit his relatives in Skinners Bluff any more. Dougie has completely forgiven her and they went to dancing practice on Saturday afternoon, just like they used to, although they still have to keep it a secret from Mother. I've noticed that Charlotte's much more affectionate to Dougie now, and he is very tender towards her.

Charlotte is pleased about the picnic because she gets on well with Uncle Martin and Aunt Ursula, although she thinks Tom's 'too wild' and Sarah is 'smutty'. I like Tom a lot and I enjoy Sarah's company although she is far more knowledgeable about sexual matters than I am and sometimes, when she tells dirty jokes, I'm ashamed to say I don't get them.

We set off walking towards the river, pushing the cream wicker pram full of rugs and beach paraphernalia – buckets, spades, towels, umbrella and the picnic basket. Charlotte refused to walk with us, as she thinks the pram makes us look like a family of hobos. It's quite a nice pram and except for the huge dark-blue barrel of homemade ice-cream sticking up where the baby's head should be, you might believe we had a real baby in there. This ice-cream is Mother's 'great contribution' to all picnics. She makes it herself and it takes days to prepare. First you have to bash up ice and saltpetre in a hessian bag with a mallet. Then you mix the ice-cream from a secret blend of gelatin, cream, nutmeg, sugar and vanilla (once she added rose petals but they tasted so awful we've objected ever since). Then it has to set and the barrel is sealed. Once the barrel is opened you must eat the rich ice-cream immediately or it turns back into a glutinous mess. We often return from picnics feeling sick from having eaten too much of it but today Tom and Sarah will help us to get through it.

As we approached the river we began to smell tea-tree and honeysuckle. At this time of year a silvery-white clematis climbs the trees and covers the fallen logs. It smells of honey and makes great dress-ups. When I was younger I would tear off long strands of it and wind them round my head and body, pretending to be a wild nymph bride.

We pushed the pram along the river track until it got bogged in the mud and then we pulled it, Jonathan and I pretending to be horses in harness and Eliza running behind with a whip of clematis. Mother followed, looking elegant as usual, swishing her parasol at the flies. Charlotte was further back, gazing dreamily about her and stopping to trail her hands in the creek whenever our progress was so slow that she was in danger of catching up to us – not that there was anyone about to think she might belong to us.

We turned the bend in the river and there was the picnic party, already seated under the tea-tree with folding tables set for lunch. Their smart maroon Humber was parked in the shade. We waved and called out excitedly to our cousins, who waved back with less enthusiasm.

Suddenly I felt cross. Our small expedition must have looked bedraggled and comical to them, and we were late. I could tell they'd been talking about that. We were hot and tired and our ice-cream was melting, and they were cool and rested, sipping their drinks under the trees. Why hadn't they offered to come and collect us in their big car? It was only an extra three miles. We were the poor relations and they enjoyed seeing us pulling our pramload of possessions through the black mud in the heat. I broadened my smile and waved at them joyfully. I would show them that if they pitied us we simply didn't care.

Polite hugs and kisses were exchanged and Aunt Ursula bustled about unloading their lunch baskets from the boot of the car. We stood about, looking and feeling awkward. Uncle Martin and Mother were the only two who seemed to be completely enjoying themselves. They threw back their heads and laughed together at almost nothing. They seemed delighted with each other's company and didn't notice how ill at ease the rest of us were. Jonathan and Eliza grabbed their buckets and spades and dashed off to find crabs, and Tom began collecting wood for the fire we'd light in the evening, tearing whole dead trees apart with his bare hands. Sarah grasped my arm and hauled me aside to tell me about her latest adventure with the boy she is currently mad about, and Charlotte, rolling her eyes at the infantile things that amused the rest of us, began rather primly to help Aunt Ursula unpack their picnic lunch. I watched apprehensively as their perfect picnic was displayed and wondered what our Mother would have to offer, apart from the melted ice-cream. Aunt Ursula had corned beef and lettuce sandwiches neatly packaged in greaseproof paper, a cold egg and bacon pie, a homemade sponge cake, chocolate crackles, scones with cream and jam, lemon cordial, a thermos of tea and mandarins. All this was neatly laid out on two card tables on a green and cream chequered table-cloth, with cutlery, paper napkins and cardboard plates and cups. Our mother flung open her picnic basket to reveal her contribution – a loaf of wholemeal bread, a wedge of old cheese, several artistic-looking bunches of sour grapes, some flowers, a bottle of wine and two crystal glasses. I gasped.

Uncle Martin held the picnic basket aloft. 'A jug of wine, a loaf of bread and thou . . . the perfect picnic!' He laughed loudly, then opened the wine with a flourish and poured some into the two crystal glasses, one for Mother and one for himself. He toasted her and avoided Aunt Ursula's gaze. She doesn't drink.

'Katharine, this wine is brilliant!' he said in surprise.

'Thank you,' said Mother and, peeping over the rim of her glass, she added demurely, 'Unfortunately the grapes didn't come from our vines.'

Aunt Ursula turned to Mother and said with tight lips, 'Did you bring anything for the children to drink, Katharine?'

'Lord, I forgot!'

'Let them drink brine!' said Uncle Martin and they both burst out laughing. 'No, really. They have a choice. Wine. Or wine,' he said, like a character in some English comedy.

They laughed again. Then, still smiling but slightly irritated, he turned to Aunt Ursula. 'Give them some of our cordial.'

Mother, sensing the need for escape, stood up and said charmingly to Martin, 'Take me for a walk.'

He gave a mock bow, put on his white straw hat, offered his arm and they set off along the sand, Mother twirling her parasol. They made an elegant couple. When they had gone about twenty paces, Uncle Martin turned and gave Aunt Ursula a little apologetic wave. She stared after them with a bitter smile, then flung a large piece of cheesecloth over the lunch to protect it from flies and plopped down on a deckchair with the latest *McCalls* magazine.

Charlotte, who loves foreign magazines, peered at it longingly, which must have irritated Aunt Ursula, because after a minute or two she said, 'Charlotte dear, it's rude to read over other people's shoulders. If you wait until I've finished this, I'll lend it to you.'

'Oh, really? Thank you, Aunt Ursula!' Charlotte said with such gratitude that I felt sick. I suddenly remembered one of the most embarrassing moments of my life.

I was about six and had been staying the night with Sarah at their holiday house at Merlin Heads. Next morning, because Uncle Martin had the car, Aunt Ursula said she would take me the three miles home to Skinners Bluff on her bicycle. I sat on the little seat behind her. Aunt Ursula had been in a hurry to set off so I was still eating my breakfast, a large slice of toast covered in butter and thick blackberry jam. As we were crossing the Merlin Heads Bridge, we hit a headwind. Aunt Ursula stood up on the bike to push harder. I looked happily out at the waves, and rested my toast on Aunt Ursula's seat, which was padded with white lambswool. To my horror she suddenly sat down! What could I do? The damage was done.

After a few minutes I thought I should confess. 'Aunt Ursula!' I yelled above the wind. 'You're sitting on my toast.'

'What's that, dear? I can't hear. Tell me later.'

Later, there was no need to say a thing. Aunt Ursula's cream slacks were ruined and the lambswool padding on her seat had to be thrown away. I looked sadly at my poor crushed toast.

'Why didn't you tell me, Anna?' asked Aunt Ursula with the same tightly controlled irritation as she had just spoken to Charlotte.

As it seemed that lunch would be postponed until Uncle Martin and Mother returned, and Sarah had no more to tell me about the Grammar boy she had a crush on, I decided to take myself off for a walk along the sand. I could see Mother and Uncle Martin up ahead, still arm in arm, laughing and talking intimately. When they reached the little river path they turned up into the tea-tree to avoid the mud. I skulked along behind, trailing them. When they disappeared into the bush, I followed.

Now I could hear them reciting lines from Sheridan's *The Rivals*. An Irish play, of course. On the rare occasions when we're all together at family dinners these two love to perform little scenes from plays by Sheridan, Goldsmith or Wilde.

'Objection! Let him object if he dare! No, no, Mrs Malaprop, Jack knows that the least demur puts me in a frenzy directly,' said Uncle Martin, playing pompous Sir Anthony Absolute. 'My process has always been very simple – in their younger days, 'twas "Jack, do this"; – if he demur'd – I'd knock him down – and if he grumbled at that – I always sent him out of the room.'

'Aye, and the properest way, o' my conscience! – nothing is so conciliatory to young people as severity . . .' said Mother, playing self-satisfied Mrs Malaprop. Then they both burst out laughing.

It occurred to me that they were very like the two characters they were playing and they couldn't have been happier if they'd been a pair of actors performing this wordy old farce on stage in London or Dublin a hundred years ago.

I hadn't planned to spy on them but there I was, hunched behind thick bushes watching as they sat all alone in a clearing. Now they had stopped play acting and Mother was perched on a low bough in the shade while Uncle Martin sat on the grass at her feet.

'I shouldn't, of course,' Mother said.

'Take it!'

'You always were a bad influence.' She was teasing, amused, a bit coquettish.

'Think of the parties.'

'At the house of a bedridden old lady who hates noise?' She laughed.

'You'll be free one day a week. I'll come and take you out. You'll be living in the middle of town. I'll take you to dinner at the club, to the Law Society Ball, the art gallery, concerts . . .'

'And what about Ursula? Will she come too?'

Uncle Martin seemed to be considering this. 'I don't think so. She'll be far too busy. Bottling quinces.' They both laughed. Then there was silence.

'She doesn't like me, your Ursula. She never has.' Mother said thoughtfully.

'Oh, come on, she doesn't mind you.'

'She thinks I'm . . . fickle. A flirt.'

'Well, you are,' Uncle Martin said affectionately. 'Look at that poor young parson. Hangs around you like a lap dog. What are you trying to do? Make him ride his Norton off the bluff?'

'I like him. We have the same interests.'

Uncle Martin snorted in disgust.

'Music, philanthropy, and Moral Sciences,' said Mother playfully. 'Nothing carnal. Not at all what you think.'

He turned to her, looking concerned. '*Don't* make him fall in love with you, Kate. If you take that job, I'll introduce you to men far more interesting than Reverend Marsden.'

Mother smiled, turned her head away and said dreamily, 'Perhaps it's too late.'

From my hiding place I beamed a look of pure hatred at Mother. Uncle Martin just gave her a look of exasperation.

'If I do take that job,' she said, glancing back towards the picnic group, 'I'll really miss them.'

'Naturally. You're their mother.'

She shrugged. 'Well, I'll miss the children too. But I meant the people. The people in our township. The halt, the maimed and the blind. Those who get bashed up by drunken spouses, the deserted young mothers with not a penny in the bank to feed the baby.' She paused, noticed that Uncle Martin was not sympathetic, so she added a touch of ridicule. 'The mental cripples crying out for Schubert, the people who cut themselves trying to bite the top off a beer bottle and need someone to mop up the blood.'

'Katharine, for God's sake.' He waved her to silence. 'I know where it comes from, this Lady Bountiful stuff.'

'It's all right for you with your law firm and your amusing friends and your good wife at home to look after things,' she said defensively. 'But I'm bored cross-eyed! I have to do something. People admire me in this "seaside backwater" you so despise.'

'No more than they pretended to admire our mother,' he said like a flash. This hurt her as he had intended it to. 'Get out while you can, Kate. Accept the challenge. I'm offering you an escape.'

'Blast you!' She got up and stalked off, walking back towards the picnickers. He followed, smiling. Suddenly she turned to him as if appealing for help and said, 'Anna is becoming appalling.'

'I agree,' he said sympathetically.

'And the little ones need . . . some sort of father figure.'

He nodded.

I caught my breath. *I* was appalling? I, who was doing my utmost to keep the family together and the house from being sold and my mother from being put away in a lunatic asylum? How could they see me as nothing more than a troublesome child? I felt cut to the quick.

chapter thirteen

*F*or years now I have realised that Uncle Martin is a bit mad. This, I have always been told, is partly because he is Anglo-Irish and partly because he suffered so much as a prisoner of the Japanese in Burma. He was an officer and whenever one of his men displeased the guards, he would be punished. He was beaten and tortured on many occasions, although he never mentions it, and three times he was taken away to be executed. Each time – by some miracle, Mother says – he managed to escape death, either by talking his way out of it, or because fate intervened. The third time he was standing blindfolded in a pit waiting to be shot when word came through that the allies had won the war. He was extremely lucky but he must also have been very tough to survive those years. For that reason he thinks other people, including his own children, should be taught to be tough too.

Ever since they were small, Sarah and Tom have been given 'endurance tests'. Whenever I went to stay with them I would be given the tests too. When we were five, Sarah and I were told to see how long we could hold our heads underwater in the bath without coming up for air. Sarah was much better at it than I was, and I could tell that she and Uncle Martin thought I was weak. Then he would give us the 'ear torture'. He would stand behind us and press his thumbs hard into the hollows at the base of our ears. If we screamed, he had won – we were weak. Tom was given much tougher tests, and was constantly covered in cuts and scratches. He and Uncle Martin went out stalking at night. Tom was fearless, but one day he called his father's bluff. He told Uncle Martin that he was going to paddle his canoe through 'the rip', a notoriously dangerous stretch of ocean where the waves are mountainous. Several quite large sailing vessels have been wrecked there. Uncle Martin was forced to forbid it.

So on the afternoon of the picnic when Uncle Martin proposed a 'toughening-up' game for Eliza and Jonathan, I was on the alert.

In among the tea-tree by the river grows a gorse bush which has bright-yellow flowers and sharp, green thorns. A large gorse bush is about the size of a small car, and it was this size bush that Uncle Martin chose for the game. He demonstrated. Standing at a distance of about twenty yards he ran downhill towards the bush at full-pelt. Leaping into the middle of it, he yelled, 'This is the life for me!' He sank down to his shoulders and, grinning from ear to ear, shook his head about to show there were no ill effects. As he climbed out he began picking the thorns out of his clothing and smoothing down his ruffled hair. He beamed up at Jonathan and Eliza. Jonathan shrank back.

'Right you are, Eliza. You go first,' he commanded.

She hesitated.

'Oh, come on, are you a man or a mouse?' he teased.

'Sarah used to do this when she was half your age. Have some guts, girl! Ready, steady, go!'

Eliza, keen to get it over with, ran as hard as she could, leapt into the bush and disappeared completely.

I ran forward to help her out but Uncle Martin signalled me to go back. Mother looked on anxiously. Perhaps this was not quite what she'd had in mind when she told Martin the children needed a father figure. Aunt Ursula and Sarah seemed amused. Tom and Charlotte had made themselves scarce.

After a minute or so Eliza emerged slowly. She had several nasty red scratches on her face and bare arms but she was bravely refusing to cry. Defying Uncle Martin, I ran forward to help her climb out.

'Good girl! No tears. What's a few prickles?' bellowed Uncle Martin. 'Now, Jonathan's turn. Get ready, get steady and go!'

Jonathan ran forward but swerved off just before he reached the bush. He put his hand to his head and staggered up a small sandhill where he leaned forward and vomited into the marram grass. Uncle Martin turned away in disgust.

Tom, who had been secretly observing the toughening ritual from behind a rock on the cliff above, suddenly leapt down, landing close to Jonathan. He walked across and bent over him, putting his hand on his shoulder to comfort him. I marched up to Uncle Martin and gave him what I hoped was a look of controlled anger. He just shrugged and then wandered over to Jonathan, motioning to Tom to leave him alone. Then he sat down beside Jon and offered him his perfectly laundered white silk handkerchief. Thankfully the game was over.

Later in the day, when the shadows grew longer, Tom lit the fire. We all sat around it, watching the blaze.

I'd been rather quiet all afternoon, trying to decide whether to become truly 'appalling' and give Mother and Uncle Martin something to really complain about or to give up on the whole stupid family and take myself off to live at the YWCA in Geronga. I had a school friend who lived there and earned her keep by doing housework, but she was two years older than me and an orphan.

Sarah asked why I was so quiet and serious today and I had to think of something, so I said, 'I've promised my ballet teacher that I'll bring new shoes to class by Monday week but I haven't been able to save the money yet and I'm afraid she'll throw me out of the troupe.'

Sarah looked shocked. 'But why doesn't Aunt Katharine give you – ?' She stopped short in embarrassment. 'Describe the shoes you need.'

I did.

'Your troubles are over,' she said grandly. 'I have a pair of ballet shoes I never use because after three lessons I decided I simply hated it. They're a half-size too small but you can stretch them. Also, they're black, not white, but at least you could wear them for rehearsals.'

I grabbed her with both arms and gave her a huge hug.

'You haff saved my bacon! Zat gives me much more time to save for ze white shoes I *must* haff for ze concert!' I said, imitating Mrs Krantz.

We both burst out laughing, and I was relieved to be able to joke about Mrs Krantz who had been terrorising me for weeks and weeks.

Later Tom and I climbed up the cliff to watch the sun go down. We sat on a rocky ledge and stared at the great orange ball sinking into the sea. I thought of my father and wondered if he'd ever flown into a sunset as beautiful as this one.

Directly below us the picnic party was finishing the last of the cake and ice-cream and drinking hot thermos tea. The campfire had relaxed them and they were chatting and laughing happily.

I have always admired Tom but now that he seems almost a man I feel a bit in awe of him. He is only two years older than I am but much taller, broader and more confident. Yet he is still relaxed and friendly. Sometimes when kids go away to boarding school they come back a bit stuck-up. Their accents change and they look down on people they used to like. But Tom hasn't changed a bit.

'When we were little, Sarah and I had to climb rocky cliffs in bare feet,' he said. 'All part of the "toughening-up" ritual.' He smiled apologetically, as if offering some explanation of Uncle Martin's odd behaviour earlier.

'Stupid,' I said.

'In a way.' He paused and then added with a touch of pride, 'Dad was twice decorated, you know. Won two medals for bravery.'

'Yes, I've heard the stories.'

We stared at the last tip of the sun sinking into the horizon.

'My dad wasn't decorated for bravery,' I said, 'I don't think he even left Australia. He was in the air force, stationed in Townsville for the whole war. Mother says he was a coward.'

Tom shook his head adamantly. 'He flew bombers all over the Pacific. He crashed up near New Guinea and took three days to walk out. He was no coward. I admired Uncle Frank.'

'Did you?' I was surprised. I'd never heard anyone in our family say anything good about my father.

Tom nodded enthusiastically. 'Whenever he came home on leave he used to take me shooting rabbits. He used to bring this fantastic chocolate back with him, and cartons of real orange juice that he'd got from the American canteens and –'

'Tom, do you know why he left us?' I cut in.

Tom considered. 'No. Maybe because he felt guilty.'

'Guilty?' I said, puzzled.

'That might be why he sent you all those presents.'

I stared at him. What presents? Was he joking?

'He's been sending them for years. Dad told me,' Tom said, realising too late he'd told me something that he shouldn't have.

As soon as the others were out of the way that evening and I had Mother to myself, I confronted her.

'Presents?' she said wearily. 'Yes, he did. Every year. Silly things like walking dolls and electric train sets. Never any books or records. I sent them back for the first three years, but he kept on sending them so I packed the lot up and gave them to St Augustine's Orphanage.'

I was outraged. 'But they were ours! Eliza would *love* a walking doll. Jonathan's never had a train set. Charlotte thinks he doesn't care about us at all. I'd love *anything* from my father. How could you do such a thing?'

Perhaps I had expected her to deny it. Somehow her nonchalance made me angrier. She explained it all to me as if I wasn't very bright. 'He sent presents to win your affection. It was a cheap trick. He should have been sending money for the things we really needed – food, house payments, roof repairs.' She sighed, then looked at me sadly. 'We have to sell the house, Anna. I'm sorry. It sucks up money like a giant sponge. Do you know what Uncle Martin calls it? Frank's Folly and the Viking Raider's Revenge.'

'He's a liar!' I said with passion. 'Why do you let him call our father stupid names?'

She seemed surprised at my outburst. Why couldn't she understand me? I turned to her and said as gently as I could, 'Look, you married for love, so why did our father leave us? We need him.'

Mother said quietly, 'We don't need him, Anna. I thought we did but I made a mistake.' Then she became angry. 'He was weak. Your father was weak!' She paused, regained control and said softly, 'Don't mention him again – ever.'

That night, telling Eliza and Jonathan the story of The Brave Airman, I added some new bits. 'The airman was strong, not weak. Before the war he worked hard, building things. He had brown, sinewy hands and he laughed a lot. After he had gone away his wife hid all the photographs of him. Every one.'

'Why did she do that?' Eliza asked.

'She was afraid they would make her cry.'

'Tell us about when he came home from the war,' said Jonathan.

'Well, there was a grand party with fireworks and champagne and streamers. The lovers were reunited in their beautiful house on the cliff by the sea. And the children were dressed in their best clothes and allowed to stay up all night to join in the dancing and feasting with all the neighbours who were invited too.'

'Even the Mooneys?' Eliza said in disbelief.

'Yes, all the Mooneys, even Ernie because he had decided never to be drunk again, and the Devlins, and lots more.'

'And did Dougie Devlin come with Charlotte in her new ball gown?' Eliza asked.

'Shhh,' said Jonathan. 'I want to hear about the tower.'

'The brave airman told his wife that he had a surprise. He was going to build a tower on their house so they could sit in it together and watch the sunset. He had planned the tower many times while flying over the sea. "If ever I have to go away on a journey," he told his wife, "you must keep this Tower House safe until I return." '

'I love that story,' Eliza sighed. 'Tell us some more. I want to know the end.'

'I haven't made it up yet,' I said as I tucked her in.

'I bet it's a bad end,' said Jonathan.

'It is not, Jonathan!' she cried.

'How can the wife keep The Tower House safe when it's falling down and she's got no money to fix it, stupid? I bet the airman has a crash and gets killed.'

'He doesn't! He does *not*, does he, Anna?'

'No, of course not. He just goes away for a long time.'

'Why?' Eliza sounded hurt and cross. 'Why does he go away and leave his wife and children all by themselves?'

I kissed her goodnight and then Jonathan too. 'There's a very good reason, but you'll have to wait for the next episode to hear it.'

'Awwgh!'

'How does the wife stop from selling The Tower House?' asked Jonathan.

'You'll see,' I said mysteriously, and turned out the light.

I had no idea how she did.

But on my way home from the school bus stop the following afternoon, I passed Cathken Guesthouse which was being repainted ready for the summer holidays. Suddenly I had a brilliant thought.

chapter fourteen

'*A* guesthouse!' I said.

'What?' said Mother. She was lying on a wicker sofa on the balcony reading a book of poetry by Yeats. Mother never reads magazines like normal women. She says they are frivolous. The sea was crashing on the rocks below so I thought she hadn't heard me.

'A guesthouse. We could turn this place into a guesthouse,' I said excitedly. 'Like Cathken. It's big enough. People are always wanting to stay with us, even when we hardly know them. Make them pay. Turn it into a guesthouse. We could do it!'

To my astonishment she didn't say no.

That evening we began planning the grand event that was to save our house from being sold. Everyone was enthusiastic, even Charlotte. We sat around the big oak dining table and made lists of tasks to be done. I seemed to be in charge of the operation, which I didn't mind at all. Mother was there, but kept jumping up to rearrange flowers in a vase on the mantelpiece or to look for some book she'd mislaid on the bookshelf. Whenever we made suggestions, however, she would turn around to listen.

She seemed bemused by the idea of the guesthouse. I think it appealed to her as a novelty rather than as a practical means of solving our financial problems.

'We'll need three more breakfast trays,' I said, adding them to the list.

'I'll carry them in,' said Eliza quickly. 'Can I carry them in?'

'Yes, that's one of your jobs,' I said, ticking it off. 'Jonathan can be in charge of wood for the stove and the open fires and organising croquet teams on the lawn.'

'Teams?' Jonathan looked a bit shocked. 'How many guests are we having?'

'Only six to begin with, but we'll build up.'

'What if they don't want to play croquet?' Eliza asked.

'People in guesthouses *always* play croquet,' I said breezily. I had read somewhere that this was so.

'You said on the lawn. What lawn?' Jonathan asked.

'On the grass,' I said, irritated. 'We'll cut it.'

'But it's got bumps in it. Hills,' Eliza pointed out.

'Shhh!' said Charlotte. 'You said we would start with six guests, but we only have two spare double rooms.'

'I'm afraid you'll have to move into my room and I'll move back in with Eliza and Jon,' I said as tactfully as possible. 'It'll only be temporary. We'll try to get single people. There are four spare single rooms.'

'The ones hanging over the cliff? But they're appalling! Who'd sleep in them?' asked Charlotte.

'We'll paint them,' I said. 'Anyone with a sense of adventure would love those rooms.'

'People with suicidal tendencies might.' Charlotte shook her head. 'I'm not at all sure that I want to move out of my room.'

'Well, if you don't the whole plan is hopeless. We need a minimum of six guests to make the guesthouse pay, and most people prefer a double room.'

'I suppose so.' Charlotte sounded resigned. 'I suppose you're right.'

'How will we afford to buy all the food?' asked Jonathan. 'We can't give the guests scrambled eggs and silver beet every meal!'

'We'll open an account with the butcher. And one with the grocer and the fruit shop. Lots of accounts,' I said with more confidence than I felt. 'Buy now. Pay later. Guesthouses always have accounts.'

Jonathan nodded but he looked uneasy.

'Now, let's draft a notice for the *Geronga Advertiser*. It's important to get it in for next Saturday, October nineteenth,' I said, amazed that Mother had allowed the guesthouse plan to proceed so far.

'Mention how close we are to the beach. How many minutes does it take to get there?' said Mother. Then she laughed and, entering into the spirit of things, cried out, 'Run, Jonathan! Run and find out!'

Jonathan jumped up enthusiastically. 'Time me. I'll wave when I get there.' He dashed out of the room.

We watched as he ran full-pelt down the sandy track to the beach. When he reached the dunes he turned and waved. 'Two and a half minutes,' said Mother, checking her watch.

Jonathan began running back. He arrived panting, perspiring and red in the face. He collapsed onto a chair. 'Five minutes, twenty seconds the round trip,' Mother declared. Then she turned to me. 'Say a three-minute stroll to the beach.' I wrote it down.

Mother has been surprisingly encouraging about the guesthouse. I think she's almost as excited about it as we are. Last night I stood outside the dining-room door and overheard her telling Reverend Marsden about it. (I no longer have a crush on him. Any man who can allow himself to be besotted by a woman ten years older than himself is not worth bothering about.)

'Guest towels, twelve; bath towels, fourteen; single bed sheets, sixteen,' he read from the inventory I'd prepared, and then, looking admiringly up at Mother, said, 'Katharine, you're amazing. Are you really going to do it?'

She nodded and then, much to my surprise, gave the credit to me. 'It was Anna's idea. It just might work. Why not give it a try?'

She started stacking the linen. 'We've got piles of this stuff. Old but good. Did you know I ran a sort of nursery school here during the war? There were ten women and babies sleeping here some nights. The women came in from their farms to work in the munitions factory and I provided them with a place to stay and looked after their children while they worked. I only did it for a few months. It was exhausting!'

'You're amazing, Katharine. Optimistic, energetic and quite uncrushable.'

'Capricious, foolish and impossible with money,' she corrected playfully.

'Who says that?'

'My father did, when he was alive. And now my older brother does.'

'They don't know anything about you,' said Reverend Marsden protectively.

They gazed at each other affectionately. I couldn't

stand it. I burst in carrying a pile of clean towels and dumped them beside the linen. Then I dashed out again, but not before I'd overheard Mother saying to him, *sotto voce*, 'I think you have an admirer.'

I decided to have my revenge. Some of the spoutings on our house are rusted and broken. I've tried to fix them but the worst ones need professional attention. If it rains hard while the guests are here, the spoutings will just break away and water will flood into the house. So I asked Mr Devlin, who is an expert on such things, to come and look at them. (Of course I hoped he would be kind enough to do more than look.) I arranged for him to come while Mother was out.

I was up the ladder helping him replace the worst section of broken spouting by handing him the nails when, to my horror, I saw Mother walking briskly towards the house in her best hat and coat. Why wasn't she at the Musical Society meeting? Had it been cancelled? I panicked. 'Mr Devlin, could we finish this another time, do you think?' I said, nodding at Mother, who had now almost reached the front gate. He chuckled, shook his head and hammered more loudly, so that Mother looked up and saw us. She stopped and stared in disbelief. Then she marched up the garden path and stood glowering beneath us.

'What are you doing on my roof, Jack Devlin?' she said accusingly.

'Spouting's rusted through, Kate,' he replied cheerfully. 'It's all right. No charge.'

'I don't want your charity!' she said angrily.

'Suit yourself. Half the job's finished. Next time I'll send a bill.'

He grinned at me and in spite of my embarrassment I felt triumphant.

Charlotte and I have painted the four single rooms she calls the Suicide Cells and they've come up quite well. They each have a small balcony overlooking either the sea or the Merlin River. Those facing the river get glorious sunsets. Mrs Mooney made some frilly curtains out of her 'oddments' basket, and we have used linen sheets as bedspreads. Charlotte suggested we dye them to break the monotony of white, so we bought a royal-blue dye and soaked them for a day in the bath. Unfortunately the dye came off on our hands and arms and I had to go to school looking like a plague victim. Luckily my school blouse has long sleeves and I kept my gloves on as much as possible, pretending my fingers had chilblains.

We must remember not to call these rooms the Suicide Cells in front of the guests. I have put that on the list.

On Monday I had to go and see Mrs Krantz. I was dreading it because what with painting rooms every afternoon after school I haven't had a minute to work in the timber yard and earn that money for the ballet shoes. Mrs Krantz stared at me and shook her head. Then she looked at the blue dye on my wrists, sighed and said, 'Vell, Anna, you disappoint me but ze shoes you haff in rehearsal from your cousin are satisfactory for a few more weeks. But by Tuesday ze fifth of November, when we move into ze theatre, you *must* haff proper shoes, or you will be out! Understood?'

I thanked her and dashed out of the room before I did something embarrassing like giving her a kiss or bursting into tears of gratitude.

While I was cleaning up the house ready for guests I went into the attic to look for some spare chairs. Mother has forbidden us to go up there because she says the roof is in danger of collapsing, but I had a good look at it and I don't think it is. Perhaps Mother has other reasons for not wanting us prying about up there. She keeps the attic locked but I know that the key is kept in the top drawer of the chiffonier. The only access to the attic is by way of a ladder that swings down from the roof on a cord and the light doesn't work so you have to take a torch. I went up there nevertheless.

Inside the attic everything is dusty, like a sad memory of happier times. There's a rack of old clothes hanging like ghosts – a blue evening dress of Mother's and some expensive-looking children's clothes that must have been ours. There are little girls' velvet frocks with lace collars and smocking, a boy's sailor suit and cap and, most surprising of all, my father's airman's uniform. I put my face close to it but it didn't smell of him, just of dust.

There were framed photographs of us as little children, and of mother looking young and beautiful. I couldn't find one of our father, although I searched and searched. I found a transparent cellophane box of old letters neatly tied with different-coloured ribbons and sealed with wax but I didn't like to open them. Perhaps one day I will. I also found my mother's satin wedding dress. It was in a cardboard box, covered in layers of blue tissue paper. I lifted it out and held it up against me. Then I put on the bridal veil. I looked in the dusty full-length mirror and smiled at myself. It was eerie. Although I'm taller and broader than Mother, I did look rather like the photographs of her as a bride.

I also found my first Girl Guide uniform, which brought back disturbing memories. I was just eleven when I went on my first Guide camp which was held in mountainous bush beyond Healesville. I was very excited and determined to do well. In spite of being so young, I'd just been made a patrol leader. There were about a hundred Guides from all over Victoria on the camp. After a day of learning to tie knots, building rope bridges across fast-flowing streams and cooking our own food we'd sing songs round the campfire and do acts to amuse each other. On the second night of camp I had stuffed a pillow down my front and performed an unflattering imitation of the District Commissioner, the most intimidating woman in the whole organisation who had visited us briefly the day we arrived. Although she was huge and old she still wore the girlish short blue uniform with beret and lanyard as we did, which seemed funny to us. The act had been loudly applauded by the other guides and I was feeling rather pleased with myself. But next morning, as I was passing the tent of a city group, I overheard their patrol leader giving them a pep talk. 'Guides, we have to show an example to the other girls here because we are St Mary's.' This was followed by some clapping. 'As a Catholic company it is our duty to show those Protestants the way. They are all going to hell, whether they think they can tie knots or bake damper better than we can or not. They poke fun at our leaders. They have no respect. So we, the Girl Guides of St Mary's, should set them a good example.' More applause. 'We are in a state of grace and they are show-off sinners. Doomed. Let's show them we are the chosen ones. Let's get out there and do it!'

I was astonished. It had never occurred to me that Catholics might think *they* were superior. Like Mother, I hadn't spent much time worrying about it. And how could they think that my light-hearted impersonation was showing off? I felt indignant. What did they mean by 'being in a state of grace'? And why did they think we were all going to hell? Was this why Uncle Martin some-times ranted in front of us about Catholic corruption?

I thought of bursting into the St Mary's tent to tell them what I thought but I was feeling rather sick. I retreated to the tent I was sharing with three other girls and lay down. Perhaps it was the baked beans and sausages we'd had for breakfast. The others were all out doing field work and I felt guilty that I wasn't helping, showing the Catholics who was better. But I didn't care. By late afternoon I was moan-ing. Rain was pouring down and the others had gone to the mess hut for indoor activities. I got up and staggered to the open latrines. To my horror I urinated blood. Was it pos-sible I'd caught something from Marlene Barry, my school friend whose mother had been in hospital for years with TB? They didn't know her mother had it until she coughed up blood. Now the blood was running down my legs, ruin-ing my Guide socks, and the pain in my stomach made me gasp. I went back to the tent and crawled into my sleeping bag. The best thing to do in the face of difficulty was not to show weakness, Mother had taught us. I must not panic or whine, but cope. If I went to sleep, the pain and blood might stop.

When I woke up it was dark. The rain had stopped but there was a leak in the tent which had made a puddle on my sleeping bag. Water was seeping through to my stom-ach. I was cold and wet and when I tried to get up I felt the nauseating stickiness of blood between my legs. I was so frightened and miserable I began to cry. Soon there was a torch beam and the voices of my friends coming back from the mess hall. 'Anna, we've been looking everywhere for you! We saved you some dinner. Look! It's Irish stew, prunes and custard.'

I turned my head away. 'I'm sick. Sorry. Just leave me.' I covered my face to hide the tears and hoped they'd leave before they smelt the sticky blood.

They didn't say a word. They'd never seen me like this.

'Please, just go away,' I repeated.

The pain was coming in waves. Sometimes it was so bad I groaned out loud.

'We'll get Salty,' they suggested and scurried off to find her. I didn't care what they did. Soon the guide captain appeared. Her name was Elwyn Salt. She sat down beside me and began to ask me questions about how I was feeling. She was young, in her twenties, very sensible and patient. The more patient she was the more I could not stop crying.

'Let me take a look down there,' she suggested after a while.

'No, no, it's too disgusting.'

'Can you walk?'

'I don't know. It's caked all over me.'

'Anna, do you know what menstruation is?'

'Yes, I have a book about it.'

'A book? Has no one ever explained it to you? Your mother?'

'Yes, she gave me the book. About plants and animals reproducing.' I had never been very interested in that book, with its black and white drawings of stamen. There was only one interesting photograph of a little naked boy piddling. It was a statue in Brussels.

'Anna, I'm going to help you get up.'

'But I'm filthy!' I wailed. 'I've used up all the pants and all the hankies in my pack but it's still seeping through.'

'If you lean on me I'll help you to walk to the care-taker's house where you can have a bath.'

On this rugged camp we'd been expected to wash in the icy river.

'Really? A hot bath?'

'Yes. I'll light the chip heater. Can you manage to walk that far? We can wash your things in the trough up there and dry them by the fire. Here, put this blanket around you and lean on my shoulder. I'll get you some aspirin for the cramps and show you how to put on a belt and pad.'

Now I was crying with gratitude. That kind young woman seemed to understand how proud I was as well as how humiliated by my ignorance and defensive of the mother who had not bothered to explain what my first period could be like. Perhaps Mother hadn't expected it to start so soon. Perhaps she thought Charlotte would explain the finer details. But at that time in our lives Charlotte rarely spoke to me. Mother couldn't have known that. I didn't want anyone to blame her.

On the bus a few days later, on the way back home from camp, one of the girls in my patrol said, 'Guess what I found out?'

'What?'

'Salty's a Catholic!'

The others tittered. Some of them started chanting,

'Catholic dogs, Jump like frogs, In and out the water logs.'

'Shut up!' I said. 'I don't care if she's Catholic, Buddhist or Jehovah's Witness. Salty's a saint.'

As I folded the Guide uniform and put it back into its box in the attic I wondered whatever happened to Salty.

There were lots of other boxes and some old toys, a high-chair and a dusty bassinette. I wondered why Mother hadn't given the bassinette and high-chair to 'poor little Mrs Thingummy' for her baby. Perhaps she's forgotten we have them. I didn't find any chairs for our guests, though, so after about twenty minutes I crept very quietly down the ladder and gently swung it back up against the ceiling. I can't wait to go to that attic again.

chapter fifteen

*W*ell, the grand day is here. Friday October twenty-
fifth, 1954. Our first guests are about to arrive.
I have never seen The Tower House looking so beautiful.
There are flowers in every room, even the bathrooms, and
the wooden floors and panelled walls are gleaming. The
silver on the chiffonier has been polished (I always
thought it might have been brass, it was so tarnished!), all
the cobwebs have disappeared, the salt has been cleaned
off the windows and the house smells of honeysuckle,
beeswax and freshly baked scones.

We are all dressed very neatly, with hair brushed and
fingernails cleaned, waiting. Mother is wearing her 'housecoat', which is long and elegant, and her hair is swept up
in a tidy bun, not all wispy and trailing as it usually is.

We are to have almost a full house by this evening –
Miss Eunice Crooks, a spinster from Geronga, is arriving
on the bus this afternoon, Dr Pettigrew and her two
adult sons, Archie and Mervyn, are also coming from
Geronga, and Mr and Mrs Rawlins are driving all the
way from Ballarat.

When the guests arrive they will be served afternoon

tea in the sunroom. (I hope they don't all arrive at once because we only have one silver teapot.) Then Charlotte will show them over the garden and escort them to the beach, if that is what they would like. We hope they will be back in time to see the sun set over the river and watch the flocks of black swans flying off towards Lake Connewarre. Mother can tell them about the swans' migration habits while I set the table for dinner.

We had a rehearsal for the first dinner last night and everything worked really well. The table was set with a linen cloth, silver candlesticks and a bowl of climbing wild daisies from our garden. I dressed in a black skirt, a frilly white apron and a cap (made most cleverly by Mrs Mooney from a lace handkerchief) and practised serving warm water instead of soup to Eliza and Charlotte to see if I could do it without spilling a drop. I could. We imagined the atmosphere might be a little tense on the first night so we thought some lively background music on Mrs Mooney's gramophone would be useful. Charlotte suggested *The Gondoliers* but I thought some Strauss waltzes would be better. Mother offered to play some Schubert, but then we all realised she would be too busy in the kitchen.

We are to have a three-course dinner tonight. Mother's been working very hard. Pumpkin soup to begin with, followed by *coq au vin* with mashed potato and brussels sprouts and then baked apples stuffed with dates, cinnamon and brown sugar and served with cream. The guests will be offered a glass of sherry before dinner and a glass or two of wine with the meal. We can't really afford wine, Mother says, but as this is our very first night as a guesthouse, there is some cause for celebration. Thank heavens for the great-aunts and their vineyard on the Margaret River.

I wonder if the guests will expect to dress for dinner. Mother says they won't. Charlotte thinks they will if we set them an example. I had to remind her that the family will *not* be sitting down to dinner with the guests. Everyone but me will be in the kitchen helping and I will be the waitress.

'They're here!' Jonathan dashed in from the balcony where he'd been keeping watch.

'Who? Which ones?'

'An old couple. The man looks bald and a bit fattish and the woman is small, like a mouse.'

'A mouse?' said Eliza in disbelief.

'You know, greyish and sort of scared.'

'The Rawlins,' I said. 'It must be. Do they have much luggage?'

'Two big cases.'

'Heavens! They're only here for the weekend. We'd better go and help them.' Jonathan and I dashed out the front door.

When we staggered in with the cases the whole family was waiting to welcome the guests. They looked surprised to see so many children. Mother introduced herself graciously.

'I'm Katharine Danielssen. You must be Mr and Mrs Rawlins. Welcome to our Tower House.'

'This is the guesthouse?' Mrs Rawlins said uncertainly, sniffing her little pink nose from side to side. Jonathan's description was perfect.

'It certainly is. And these are my children, Charlotte, Anna, Jonathan and Eliza.' We each shook hands and smiled sincerely into their eyes as we had been taught to do since we were very young.

Mr Rawlins seemed charmed. Then he gave us all a shrewd look. 'Family business, eh?'

'Yes indeed. I couldn't manage for a minute without my young assistants.' Mother gave her sweetest smile.

Charlotte and I exchanged looks. Mother was already well into her role as overly gracious hostess.

Jonathan and I showed the Rawlins to their double room. It had the most character of any of the guest rooms, but I could see that it was not to their taste. I proudly showed them the antique washbasin that folded out from the wall and a carefully concealed trapdoor with a narrow hatchway that led to the floor below.

'Oooh, nasty!' cried Mrs Rawlins. 'You could fall down there and break your neck.'

I smiled and said reassuringly, 'Best to keep it closed then, Mrs Rawlins. This room was furnished with things salvaged from the shipwreck of the *Ibis*. It went down thirty years ago, just out there.' I pointed to the wild ocean outside the window. 'You can still see bits of it sticking up when the tide is low.'

'Worth a few pennies, a view like this,' said Mr Rawlins. 'Did you ever think of pulling the old place down and putting up a modern block of flats?'

I must have looked horrified because he added quickly, 'Don't mind me. Just my little joke.'

Mother had overheard this crass remark. She put her head round the door and said imperiously, 'People either love or hate this house, Mr Rawlins. *We* love it.'

Jonathan and I exchanged a quick glance of admiration at Mother's well-timed put down.

The dinner went splendidly. Even better than the rehearsal. The guests were so pleased with everything – the food, the atmosphere and particularly the wine. I'm afraid they drank more than the two bottles we had allotted, but then it is their first night here. And they liked the food so much they almost all had second helpings.

'Anna, please give my compliments to the chef,' said Dr Pettigrew. 'I haven't had *coq au vin* like this since I was in the south of France, oooh, it must be ten years ago.'

I like Dr Pettigrew. She is very tall and impressive and wears a fine tweed suit with flat-heeled brogues and has her grey hair tied in a no-nonsense bun at the back. I can just imagine her giving orders in the hospital, and perhaps flinging a stethoscope across the room if it hadn't been cleaned properly by the orderly, but she also seems kind, as if she would really listen if you had a problem.

Her sons, Arch and Mervyn, are twins, about twenty years old, and quite entertaining. They're not at all handsome; in fact, rather chunky – almost fat. They look like Tweedledum and Tweedledee, but they make jokes and laugh a lot.

Mr Rawlins is a bit sly and, I have to say, greedy. When he thinks I'm not looking he scrapes the last of the mashed potato from the dish onto his plate and then says to his wife, 'Like some potato, Mavis? Oh, goodness, none left. Could you get some more of that scrumptious potato for the table, Anna dear? And I'll have some more gravy while you're there.'

Mrs Rawlins knows what he's up to, and gives little giggles into her napkin.

Miss Crooks is a spinster who lives alone. She is middle-aged and seems very shy but is anxious to make friends. She keeps passing things to the others and doesn't eat very much at all herself. She speaks softly and smiles apologetically almost all the time. She is stick-thin, with frizzy permed hair and rather sad blue eyes. I think I overheard her tell the others she was a corsetière. Then she blushed. Mrs Rawlins was rude enough to giggle.

I swirled into the kitchen from the dining room with the last tray of dirty plates balanced above my head like a professional waitress and said, 'Congratulations! They loved it!'

'But they've eaten every scrap! There's not a crumb left for any of us,' wailed Eliza, who was standing on a chair so that she could reach the sink, washing knives and forks.

The kitchen was in chaos. Every plate, saucepan and cooking utensil had been used. Dirty dishes were stacked everywhere, on the bench, table and floor, and Mother was bent over the stove feeding more wood into the fire to heat water for the next load of washing-up. She looked hot and tired and there was a smudge of black soot on her forehead. I felt like hugging her and wiping her brow but I didn't.

Jonathan staggered in with a bucket of split wood and began to stack it around the stove.

'Where's Charlotte?' I asked.

'Gone to get changed so she can sing for the guests,' said Mother, her head still bent low over the stove.

'And tomorrow night I'm going to recite "The King's Breakfast" for the guests,' Eliza announced. 'But first I'm going to hide some of the dessert before those greedy pigs eat it all. It's crème caramel tomorrow, isn't it, Mummy?'

'Hmmm?' Mother looked up vaguely. She really did look awful.

We could hear a hush as Charlotte entered the dining room. The guests were now sitting comfortably around the fire in armchairs with their coffee. I had told them that there would be a short 'item of entertainment'.

'Maybe I'll do my recitation tonight after all,' said Eliza quickly, and jumped off the chair.

'But you're in a mess!' I protested. 'Wait till tomorrow.'

'No, please. Let me change and do it now. Oh, please!' She couldn't bear to be upstaged.

I sighed. 'All right. Come quickly and I'll do your hair.'

Poor Mother and Jonathan were left with the washing-up.

Eliza made her entrance just as the last of the applause for Charlotte's 'Oh, My Beloved Father' was finishing. The audience said 'Ahhh!' as she walked confidently up to take Charlotte's place. (I think Charlotte had been considering an encore, but Eliza soon put a stop to that.) She looked very pretty in her one and only frilly white dress with a wide blue sash and her long blonde curls brushed and tied with a matching blue ribbon.

'I will now recite for you "The King's Breakfast" by A. A. Milne,' said Eliza, gazing around at the small circle of admirers and bestowing a sweet smile upon each of them. She completely stole poor Charlotte's thunder. Charlotte was obliged to sit down in the front row and endure Eliza's whole performance, which must have been painful for her. I sat beside her as moral support.

Eliza was most dramatic and very good at doing the voices of different characters. She changed from imperious queen to timid dairymaid to sleepy, deep-voiced cow to outraged king and back again with no trouble at all. The audience listened in fascination. When the recitation was over Eliza curtsied graciously to loud applause.

After this Arch and Mervyn leapt up. 'What about a lively duet on the piano, eh, Merv?'

'Don't mind if I do, old chap.'

To my horror they opened Mother's Steinway and began belting out 'Chopsticks'. I prayed that she wouldn't make a sudden entrance and order them to 'Stop abusing the instrument!' as she often did to her pupils. As soon as they'd finished I dashed back to the kitchen.

'The guests seemed to like our spontaneous little soiree. It would be wonderful if you would play for them one evening, perhaps before dinner,' I said tactfully. Mother just sighed.

I hurried back to the dining room with a fresh pot of coffee. The guests were sitting by the fire, chatting like old friends. Charlotte was impressing Arch and Mervyn with some tale of her accomplishments. Eliza was snuggling up close to Eunice Crooks and Jonathan was sitting next to Dr Pettigrew, showing her his camera. I overheard him say gravely, 'It belonged to my dad. He was killed in the war.'

'Oh, my dear, I'm so sorry to hear that,' she said sincerely.

'He was a hero. He won two medals for bravery.'

'Did he really?' She sounded impressed.

'Yes. He shot down masses of Jap planes,' he continued enthusiastically. 'When he came home on leave he used to train me, make me jump into gorse bushes until I was bleeding, but I never cried. Not once.'

Dr Pettigrew looked at him strangely. She seemed to realise he was fantasising but was too tactful to say so. 'And do you have a film club at school, Jonathan?'

'No, I just have to teach myself how to make films.'

'That's a pity. One of my patients has a son about your age who goes to a school with a film club.'

'Really,' he said eagerly. 'I didn't think there were any schools in the world like that. Where is it?'

'Near Geronga. It's a boarding school called Mount Enderby.'

'Oh, it's probably outrageously expensive,' he said sadly.

Outrageously expensive was one of Mother's expressions.

'Well, yes, I would say that it probably is,' Dr Pettigrew said with a smile.

Back in the kitchen I helped Mother stack away saucepans and wipe down benches. I prattled on excitedly, trying to keep her spirits up. 'I like Arch and Mervyn, and Dr Pettigrew is really kind. She was chatting to Jonathan as if he was an equal, and she *appreciates* everything, not like Mrs Rawlins. She's a whinger, and she eats more than anyone, except Mr Rawlins. Eunice Crooks is frightened of the Rawlins. She's head of the ladies' underwear department and she –'

'Anna, don't chatter on and on. My head is splitting,' Mother said. She did look pale.

'Sit down. I'll get you a Relaxatab.' I got one of her pills from the packet in the cupboard and brought it to her with a glass of water. She gulped it down and flopped into a chair.

'Now that we're making money from the guesthouse it will be worth my while keeping that appointment I've been postponing.'

I looked at her blankly.

'I'm seeing the bank manager tomorrow.'

I nodded gravely.

chapter sixteen

'Well?' I had run fast all the way home from the butcher's where I'd had the great pleasure of paying our account two days before it was due, and I was completely out of breath. 'What did he say?'

Mother was still dressed in her good plaid coat and hat. She slowly took off her gloves, sat down in the wicker chair by the stove and re-enacted the interview.

First she was herself, charming, gracious and vulnerable. 'You've already been far too kind to me, Mr McLaren. I don't know how I'd have managed without you. The guesthouse is doing extremely well, but I don't expect you to keep on extending the loan. Why on earth should you?'

Then she became the bank manager, self-important, middle-aged, with a paunch. She spoke with some severity. 'Well, the fact is, it's not up to me this time, Mrs Danielssen. It's head office in Melbourne. They've decided to sell your property. There's not much I can do about it. I'm sorry.'

As herself again, she began to weep very quietly. 'Mr McLaren, I don't blame you for an instant.' She looked up with a pleading expression. 'You have been a true friend to me and my children. More than anyone I know.' She smiled bravely through her tears.

She stood up, as the bank manager again. 'Mrs Danielssen, I should not be doing this, but I cannot stand by and watch a fine, brave lady like yourself turned out of her home with her dependents. I can't do it. I'm going to make a special recommendation to head office that they extend the loan for another six months.'

I leapt in the air. I could hardly believe it. 'You put a spell on him!'

'Perhaps,' said Mother, smiling. 'He's sending his aunt to stay at our guesthouse.'

We both burst out laughing.

'Uncle Martin will be furious,' I said.

We laughed again. I felt deliriously happy. I grabbed Mother's hands and said excitedly, 'Teach me! Why don't you teach me?'

'What?'

'How to put a spell on a man.'

Mother gave me a surprised, disapproving stare. I suddenly felt quite foolish and dropped her hands at once.

The following Saturday Mother was cooking bacon and eggs for the guests' breakfast. The kitchen was in a mess. I hurried in from the dining room carrying a tray of dirty plates. Then I took down from the shelf a small pile of letters I'd been saving as a surprise.

'Look! Five more people want to book in next week-end. Charlotte can move into the children's room with us, which will free up my old room and –'

'No, Anna,' Mother said wearily.

'But it's only for the weekend. I can do everything

except cook. We need the money. Dr Pettigrew and Eunice Crooks want to come back a second time.' I held out one letter to her proudly. 'And this one's from the bank manager's aunt.'

'No.' She shook her head and waved the letter away. 'I feel like a rat trapped in this wretched kitchen. My hair's full of grease.'

'Mother, Monday's the last day I've got to bring that money for the shoes.'

'Shoes?'

'Ballet shoes for the concert. Could I borrow the money from the child endowment account? I've saved one pound, fourteen shillings, but if I don't bring the other one pound, thirteen and six, they'll put another girl in to take my place. They're already making our dresses and we're dancing on the stage at the Regent Theatre.'

'I told you we need that money for school books and uniforms. We simply cannot afford ballet shoes!'

On Monday morning it was wild and wet. I was riding my bike to the school bus stop, pushing hard against a headwind. Red mud from the road splashed up on my bare legs. My eyes streamed in the wind and my vision blurred. The sound of the wind dissolved into an orchestra playing *Moments Musicaux*. I saw myself dancing on the stage at the Regent, the prima ballerina in a long white tulle dress and bare feet. All the other dancers wore short dresses and white satin toe shoes. I tried to stand on pointe without shoes but I kept stumbling. My toes were bleeding. People in the front row began to laugh and point at me. Suddenly someone in the audience stood up. He began striding down the aisle in the middle of the performance.

He came right to the stage and held a package out to me. It was a pair of shocking-pink satin toe shoes, more beautiful than any of the others. I sat down quietly on stage and put them on. Then I stood up and began to dance superbly. The audience was clapping wildly, and the brave airman, my father, stood and watched too, applauding me.

Today at school I did something rather odd. It wasn't an ideal solution to the problem but I'm desperate so I took the risk. I borrowed one pound, thirteen and sixpence from the social services jar in our form teacher's desk. She won't notice it's gone because I am the social services representative and I know she never checks the money until the end of each month. By then I'll have earned enough to put the money back and no one will be any the wiser.

As I was riding my bike home this afternoon, with a box balanced under my arm, who should pull up beside me but Mr Devlin and Dougie in the timber truck.

'Hullo there, young Anna!'

'Hullo, Mr Devlin. Hullo, Dougie.'

'Watcha got in the box? Chickens?'

I shook my head, a bit embarrassed.

'Look, I'm sorry I haven't been over to help unload much lately.'

'That's all right. Your mum's not keen on you working as a builder's labourer.'

'It's not that. It's just that we've been really busy with the guesthouse. Would it be all right if I came and worked for you next Saturday after lunch?'

'I'll give you a job anytime,' Mr Devlin replied, then they both waved and drove off.

I looked at the battered truck and wondered what

Mother would say when she found out Charlotte was going to her coming-out ball in the back of it.

I crept inside quietly to hide the box which contained my precious ballet shoes. But first I couldn't resist taking them out for a look. They were made of softest, white leather with silky satin ribbons and were wrapped in pink tissue paper. I rubbed one shoe against my cheek, smelling the leather and letting the ribbons trail down my neck. 'Anna Pavlova', I dared to whisper to my reflection in the mirror. At my ballet rehearsal tomorrow I would show Mrs Krantz that I had kept my word.

As I came out of my bedroom I heard Mother in the bathroom, singing. I peeped through the louvre window and there she was, soaking in the old-fashioned lions-feet tub, almost completely submerged in bubbles. Foam was frothing over the top of the bath and floating to the floor like snow. Mother's fair hair was wound into a knot on top of her head but strands of it hung down in the water. She hummed as she stretched out one shapely leg and lathered it admiringly. She looked a bit like a pin-up girl on a calendar and she knew it. I giggled to myself and was just going upstairs when there was a loud knock on the front door.

'Blast!' said Mother. 'Who on earth . . . ?'

The knock came again, louder, and I darted out of sight while she scrambled out of the bath.

Ten minutes later Uncle Martin was sitting at the dining-room table in his business suit with Mother opposite him in her cream candlewick dressing-gown wearing a towel wound elegantly round her wet head like a turban.

'I can't believe you're *doing* this,' he shouted.

'Well, I'm making money,' she replied rather smugly.

'It's illegal!'

'So is selling apples by the side of the road, but a lot of the farmers around here do it.'

'You have to get a licence to run a guesthouse, Katharine. Did you know that?'

'I suspected you might.' She didn't sound particularly worried.

'You have to have proper fire escapes and kitchens and staff. What if the guests were all burnt to a crisp in their beds?'

'If they were, we would be too. So what would it matter?' She smiled at him sweetly. 'Look, Martin, I'm not completely feckless. We only take six guests at a time. They know this isn't a proper guesthouse, but they don't seem to care.' She thrust a handful of letters at him. 'At first they only wanted to book for weekends, but now some are coming mid-week as well. We've got a waiting list!'

'I can't believe this.' He shuffled the letters in shock.

Mother was enjoying herself. 'I'm afraid I won't be able to accept your kind offer of that job looking after the wealthy bedridden gentlewoman, Martin. I've found a better challenge. I'm not going to sell the house. I'm going to turn it into an *Hôtel Extraordinaire.*'

'And what does your bank manager have to say?'

'I've started paying him back already. He's agreed to be very, very patient.'

'I'm glad to hear it. And when you collapse in a heap with bouts of weeping and migraine headaches, as you most certainly will, don't expect me to come to your rescue. You're on your own, Katharine. If you won't play by the rules —'

'Play by what rules? Yours!' she shouted. 'All my life I've played by your rules. Or father's. "Don't study to be a concert pianist – come home to us and we'll give you a fine inheritance. Don't marry the man you love or we'll take away that inheritance."' Then she said quietly, 'You've always tried to crush me. Well, it's no use. I'm uncrushable.'

Uncle Martin stared at her coldly.

I vowed to myself at that moment that I would love and support my Mother no matter what, but just three days later I broke that vow.

It was a school holiday. To celebrate I had spent the whole morning riding Grayling for wealthy Mrs Armitage. She lives alone, except for the housekeeper, in a large house at Merlin Heads. She keeps a number of horses in stables behind the house. Her three daughters used to ride them, but now they've gone away to university and bought sports cars and lost interest in horses completely. This she confided to me in disgust one afternoon as I mucked out the stables. Mrs Armitage is well known in the district as 'horsy'. She once rode in shows all over the state and won rosettes for jumping and dressage. Her daughters did too. She has told me that she's keeping Grayling for her grand-children. I can just imagine them appearing in their tiny hard hats and tailored jodhpurs shouting imperiously in baby-voice imitations of Mrs Armitage. Perhaps then I will be dismissed as voluntary groom and stablehand and my wild gallops on the hard sand will be over. Sometimes I lie awake at night willing this not to happen. Perhaps Grayling will die of old age before the grandchildren appear, or maybe they'll be allergic to horsehair or prefer motorbikes.

In the meantime I gratefully ride my old bike every Friday afternoon the three miles to Mrs Armitage's property, where I clean the riding tackle, muck out the stables and spend one to three hours, depending on his mood, chasing Grayling round a hundred-acre paddock, so that I can ride him home and put him safely in the tiny paddock close to The Tower House where I can see him from my bedroom window and ride him all weekend. Sometimes, after hours of trying to catch the wily old thing, I'm so furious that when I finally put my hand on his quivering rump, I feel like beating him to death, but of course I don't. Mother, who rode horses in her youth, says that if you learn to manage horses, you can manage anything else in life.

Mrs Armitage pays a Hungarian dressage expert named Lazlo to exercise the other three horses, which are very valuable. Sometimes I bump into him when I'm feeding and grooming Grayling. He doesn't say much to me, but occasionally he'll ask me to hold one horse while he saddles another. He treats me a bit like a stablehand, which amuses me, because Mrs Armitage treats him like one. Lazlo swaggers about arrogantly and speaks with such a heavy European accent that it's hard to understand what he's saying. 'Horpen you bortom!' he shouted at me when I was practising dressage in the small paddock behind the stables one morning. I didn't know he was watching. I blushed. Was he saying what I thought he was? I tried 'opening my bottom' and it worked. My shoulders dropped, my hands relaxed and my seat improved instantly. In spite of being crude, Lazlo must know what he's talking about.

Mrs Armitage isn't exactly tactful in her instructions to me, either. As I was riding out the gate, she yelled, 'Maind his mouth, gel. And keep him orf the bitumen!'

I waved my riding crop and nodded politely. She treats everyone as if they're an imbecile, so there's no point in feeling hurt. I've been riding Grayling for years now and I'd never take him on a hard road or harm his poor old mouth.

In exchange for feeding, cleaning, grooming and shoeing him, I'm allowed to ride Grayling every weekend. The shoes take all my Christmas and birthday money and I have to go into debt to buy the chaff and lucerne hay Mrs Armitage insists I feed him when he's stabled in bad weather. 'The meanest dowager in Christendom,' Mother calls her, but I don't mind. I'll never be able to afford a horse of my own.

As we made out way home slowly after a gallop I saw a motorbike parked in the sandhills. Odd. Someone had pushed it up a small rise and stood it in the shade under a clump of tea-tree. There was nobody about, so I dismounted to have a better look. The motorbike was a Norton – Reverend Marsden's Norton. I tied Grayling to a bough and went to investigate.

What I saw over the next hillock took me by complete surprise. I flattened myself on the sand and watched them from behind thick tufts of marram grass. Two people were having a picnic, all spread out on a tartan rug. It was a sheltered little glade and they seemed very comfortable. The picnic basket was open and I recognised the plates and glasses. The man had just opened a bottle of wine and was holding something behind his back, hiding it from the woman. It was none other than Reverend Marsden and Mother.

'What is it?' she cried in a girlish voice.

'Guess.'

'Goose-liver pâté? Truffles?'

'Stilton. I've got Stilton!'

'You haven't!' said Mother with delight. 'My favourite. But where did you get it, Albert?'

'Aha.'

She held out her hand and he gave her the cheese. She sniffed it. 'Superb!'

They smiled at each other and sipped their wine. I crawled so close I could almost smell the putrid Stilton. They were sitting some distance apart and talking quite formally.

'Why did you become a vicar?' Mother asked him directly.

'To please my father, I suppose. He's a bishop.'

— 'You'd rather have been a philosopher?'

'Or an eternal student.' He looked out into the distance, then back at her. He gave her his most charming smile. 'I liked Cambridge. I enjoyed myself immensely. Played cricket, drank too much, wrote bad poetry for student magazines. I thought I might stay there forever, become a classics tutor – but I didn't do nearly well enough for that. Got a third, in fact. It was shattering for my father, so I decided to make it up to him.'

'But that's a dreadful reason to become a minister of religion!'

'It's not the only reason,' he said seriously.

'I'm sorry. I didn't mean to imply that you . . .'

'Had no faith? I do have doubts. What about you, Katharine? Are you a believer?'

'When I was a young woman. Not so much now.'

He was smiling again. 'Is that a challenge?'

She laughed. 'Not at all.' Then she said almost sternly, 'Why did you come to this backwater?'

'I love the sea.'

'You weren't running away from someone?'

'Who?'

'I don't know.'

They smiled at each other as if they had shared their thoughts for a hundred years. Then Mother stood up. Reverend Marsden gazed at her admiringly. He seemed to be wondering what she might do next. She paused as if she wasn't quite sure either. She looked young and full of vitality with her hair blowing in the wind. She threw her arms wide as if embracing the landscape.

'A toast to the sea!' she cried, raising her glass. She gulped down the wine and hurled the crystal glass away into the sandhills. Then she raced off down the hill towards the sea.

Reverend Marsden watched for a few seconds, then, wrapping the tartan rug round his shoulders like a cape, he leapt off the sandhill and chased her, catching up to her by the edge of the water.

They kissed very gently at first, and then more urgently.

I couldn't bear it and turned my head away.

As I rode home I felt furious with both of them. Mother is not only mad but dangerous to others. What if Reverend Marsden's father, the bishop, had caught his son kissing a married woman? What would any of the local girls who imagine themselves to be in love with him think? His name would be mud. His career would be finished. And who did Mother think she was? Anna Karenina? Some romantic heroine who could lead any man by the nose to fall in love with her? But unlike poor Anna, she was not in love with him, just playing games. How could she be so cruel?

She might be brilliantly useful at charming old bank managers, but surely she should leave young men of God alone!

Perhaps they would end up rolling around naked in the sand dunes like that grotesque couple I had seen a few weeks ago. I covered my face with one hand and let out a cry of disgust at the very thought of it.

Why did my mother do such things? To shock people? To upset them? I vowed to put a stop to her behaviour.

As I rode home through the sandhills I wondered how I was going to face Reverend Marsden at church. Perhaps I would follow Charlotte's example and refuse to go at all, but Mother relies on me to take Jonathan and Eliza. When I asked her a few years ago why she didn't take them herself, she explained that she'd once been a devout Christian but was feeling pagan lately so it would be hypo-critical of her to go. I didn't argue with her, although I thought it was hardly logical to send your children to church when you were a non-believer.

So every Sunday morning at twenty to eleven Jonathan, Eliza and I trudge up the red mud hill which is called, much too grandly, Presidents Avenue, towards the church. If the mud is thick we wear rubber boots and carry our good shoes in a string bag that we hide in the vestibule. We have to walk carefully, sliding our boots through the mud like skis for fear of splattering the backs of our legs or, worse still, covering the backs of our clothes with it. Once Eliza's pleated cream skirt had been a mass of red spots and she'd giggled and said it had measles, but I'd been ashamed and made sure we all sat in the back pew and waited until everyone else had filed out before we did so that people wouldn't see.

If the bell stops ringing before we reach the corner of Presidents Avenue we know we're going to be late. Then we have to run for it, past the sign pointing to St Peter's Church of England which has two bullet holes in it (the locals say that Warren Devlin shot the sign – because he's a Catholic as well as a larrikin), past the bushy land with the air-raid shelters full of yellow water in it (no children are allowed to go into that bush since Jenny Kelly nearly drowned in an air-raid shelter a year ago, but no one had volunteered to fill them in), through the barbed-wire fence and into the churchyard.

If we are late, as we often are, it's best to wait until the singing starts before we creep in because the flywire door has a terrible creak. Once we came in during the catechism and the door made such a noise that two dozen heads had turned to stare in disapproval.

It isn't always easy dealing with Eliza and Jonathan in church. Eliza gets the giggles about almost anything and when she does she cannot stop. Jonathan sets her off by whispering something as he kneels beside her on the hassock. She starts to shake all over until she's almost choking and the tears are running down her face. Once I tried to stop her by whispering, 'Think of something sad: Jesus on the cross,' at which she exploded with a shriek of laughter and simultaneously wet her pants. I still blush at the memory.

In spite of these difficulties I quite enjoy going to church. Up until now I've really looked forward to hearing Reverend Marsden preach. Because he isn't yet ordained, he only does it about once a month, so as I creep into church I feel quite excited, wondering if this will be one of his Sundays.

But it was a great relief on the following Sunday to find that Reverend Marsden was not in the pulpit. Reverend Taylor was preaching instead. He is old with a mop of white hair, but quite tall and impressive with a loud, dramatic voice. When I first took Eliza to church she asked if he was God. I didn't concentrate on what Reverend Taylor was saying but watched the two old Miss Mastertons instead. They are twins who have been coming to church for as long as anyone can remember. The one in green plays the organ and the one in red turns the pages for her. Even their hats, feathers and gloves are red or green. As the church is so small it is possible to observe their every emotion. They behave as if they are the only people there, whispering to each other, screwing up their faces in laughter or disapproval, and even kicking out at each other under their long skirts. They have shrivelled old faces like walnuts and hands like claws. When I was younger I thought they were at least a hundred years old and probably witches. When the service is over the Miss Mastertons never stay to chat like the other parishioners. They scurry off into the thick bush behind the church, one fluttering behind the other along the narrow track like two garish old parrots. The track leads to their secret home deep in the bush that no one has visited, not even Reverend Taylor. There's a rumour that the Miss Mastertons have a mad brother locked up in the loft and that is why they never invite anyone to visit.

St Peters is a tiny church made of dark wood with a lot of polished brass and stained glass. The window I always find myself staring at is the one which shows a black swan pecking blood from her breast to feed her young. The swan looks graceful in self-sacrifice, leaning in towards the young birds who have greedy, gaping pink mouths and no grace at all. This stained-glass picture has always reminded me of my mother and us.

But on this morning the church window looked different. Now that I knew what Mother was really like, how selfish and manipulative, how clever at making poor young Anglican ministers fall in love with her, something odd had happened to the graceful swan. It had transformed into an eagle, its claws all bloody as it gnawed on a foolish dead crow. For the first time I noticed that the black crow was wearing motorcycle goggles and a long white silk scarf, and I started to giggle. Eliza stared at me in disbelief.

chapter seventeen

*W*hen I got home from school today there was a dreadful letter on the kitchen table. Mother had it open and was sitting waiting for me. I had a premonition of bad news as soon as I saw the school crest on the envelope. As Mother read it aloud I sat opposite her with tears streaming down my face.

She concluded, '. . . so I intend to make an example of Anna in front of the whole school at assembly next Monday morning. I should also inform you that as a further punishment I am considering suspending your daughter from the school. Yours faithfully, Marcia Hooper, Headmistress.'

'I was going to put it back. They never count it before the end of the month,' I sobbed. 'I was going to earn it and put it back.'

Mother nodded and said sympathetically, 'It was very foolish of you, Anna.'

'I know, I know, but I can't be suspended. I'll miss too much work, and I won't do well enough in the exams to get a preliminary teaching bursary which is worth fifty pounds and would pay for all my books and uniform for two years. Oh, if Miss Hooper stands me up in front of the whole school and tells them what I did, I'll just die!'

I put my head down on the table and howled.

Next morning promptly at nine Mother strode into Miss Hooper's office. She sat down opposite the head-mistress and stared at her arrogantly. I stood meekly beside her, wishing the floor would open up and swallow me. I had begged Mother not to come to the school but she had calmly dressed herself in her most intimidating outfit – tweed coat, black hat and leather gloves – caught the school bus with me and marched us into the hallowed office.

Our headmistress is tall and unflinching. She has fine white hair, eyes that bore into your soul and a voice that can immobilise the bravest girl at fifty paces. Recently she called an assembly because one girl had dropped her tram ticket in the gutter. The girl was given a humiliating lecture about littering in front of all of us and told to go back and pick up the ticket. Among the whole five hun-dred girls there was not one titter.

Mother didn't give Miss Hooper a chance to humiliate her. She began in dulcet tones, 'I would have thought, Miss Hooper, that a woman of your experience, a leader in society, would have had more compassion, a better understanding of this situation.' Here she indicated me by inclining her head. 'Have you ever had cause to find fault with Anna before?'

Miss Hooper was about to reply but apparently the question was rhetorical. Mother disregarded her.

'Never! She has been a model student, judging from her school reports. Words like excellent, capable, sensi-tive, inquiring and helpful. Would they have been used if the child was a menace? I don't think so. It is a shock to me, Miss Hooper, to discover that you intend to humiliate Anna in front of some hundreds of her peers simply because she has erred on one occasion.'

'Ah, but –' Miss Hooper tried to interject.

'And err she certainly did,' Mother continued. 'Whether or not she intended to replace the money is immaterial. She still committed a crime. She did so because she was desperate to represent the school in the ballet performance and did not want to upset me by asking for money that she knew I did not have to buy ballet shoes. She has apologised to you and her form teacher for the theft, and the money has been replaced. I think it would be the height of callousness and bad taste for you to carry the matter any further. I absolutely forbid you to suspend Anna. You should consider yourself fortunate to have a girl of her calibre at the school,' said Mother with cool deliberation. She stood up and offered her hand. 'Good morning, Miss Hooper.' Then she turned and left with a dignified flourish. I hurried in her wake, not daring to look at Miss Hooper, who seemed to have been struck dumb.

This evening, I'm ashamed to say, I re-enacted Mother's interview with the headmistress for the amusement of Jonathan, Eliza and Charlotte in the children's bedroom.

'I absolutely forbid you to suspend Anna. Good morning, Miss Hooper.' They all fell about laughing, even Charlotte. When Mother appeared in the doorway and saw what was happening she looked shyly pleased.

'Tonight I thought we might have our own little dinner party in here after the mid-week guests are fed. No one will find us in here,' she said quietly.

This was a special treat. Even Charlotte said she could

take some time off from learning Tessa to have dinner with us and skipped off singing.

'When a merry maiden marries,
Sorrow goes and pleasure tarries,
Every sound becomes a song,
All is right and nothing's wrong.'

'Is Tessa a very soppy character?' Eliza asked me.

I said I thought she might be.

That Tuesday evening we only had four guests and as soon as their dinner was cleared away we set up our own little special dinner on a card table in the children's bedroom. Mother spread it with a cloth and set a candelabra in the centre. We had a bottle of wine for a treat, and some leftovers from the guests of rabbit pie with onions, potatoes, pumpkin and beans followed by a delicious plum sago pudding with cream.

'Uncle Martin would call this "sheer indulgence",' I said, finishing off the last drop of my only glass of wine.

'Yes he would,' said Mother, who'd had three glasses. 'He's such a wet blanket!'

The others stared. They'd never heard Mother criticise Uncle Martin before.

'We've eaten tomorrow night's pudding tonight. Poor guests!' she said, and we all laughed.

Eliza leapt up suddenly. 'Let's have charades!'

We cleared the things off the table quickly. Mother was most enthusiastic and began miming the first syllable. She transformed herself into a rather arrogant person, sticking out her chest and giving silent orders, marching up and down delivering lectures. She is very funny when she acts and we were all laughing so much we could hardly concentrate on guessing what she was supposed to be.

'Martin!' yelled Jonathan.

Mother shook her head and mimed a diminished version of the same ludicrous person.

'Little Martin!' shouted Eliza.

Mother shook her head again and continued her unflattering impersonation of what had to be our uncle. We laughed until we almost cried. She had his gestures exactly right. We hadn't realised she thought of him as such a pompous ass.

'Marty!' tried Jonathan.

'Mart!' said Charlotte.

Mother nodded vigorously and started on the second syllable. She mimed, rather poignantly, the word 'tear'.

I knew what it was straight away but I waited, hoping one of the little ones would guess it.

'Crying!' said Eliza.

'Teardrop. Tear!' yelled Jonathan.

Mother nodded, then mimed the final syllable. She became a character discovering the difference between fake and real jewellery. I guessed the syllable was 'real' and the whole word was 'material'. Eliza was bursting to get it right, her face contorted into horrible grimaces.

'Diamond? Ring? Jewel!' she cried.

'Fake!' yelled Jonathan.

Mother indicated that he was getting close.

'Real!' yelled Charlotte. 'Material.'

Mother nodded vigorously. I gave Charlotte a look of pure disgust. She shrugged.

We'd all been jumping up and down shrieking for so long that we hadn't noticed Reverend Marsden standing watching by the door. He was staring in admiration at Mother. Eliza scowled at him. She knew that his presence signalled the end of our intimate family game. The others seemed resentful too. Mother suddenly became very self-conscious, brushing back her tousled hair and straightening her clothes. She was excited. I felt angry and embarrassed and turned away, busying myself tidying up the dishes.

'I'm sorry. I knocked but I couldn't make myself heard,' he said in his sickeningly charming way. 'You were all having too much fun. I've interrupted.'

'No, no, you haven't. Just silly games. Charlotte and Anna, clear all this mess away quickly. Eliza and Jonathan, you should've been in bed ages ago.'

'But you said I could do the next charade, Mummy. You promised,' Eliza pleaded.

'Into bed!'

As the little ones went silently to do as they were told, Reverend Marsden moved across to Mother's side and, producing a bulky parcel, said intimately, 'I brought you some white elephants.'

Mother looked puzzled. 'For the stall. At the flower show.'

Mother laughed. 'The flower show! I almost forgot. Come into the dining room, Albert. We'll sort them out there.' She squeezed his arm playfully. 'Like some coffee?'

It was all too sickening to bear.

That night I stayed up late to write a very important letter. I had to think hard before writing the first sentence. It began: *Dear Reverend Marsden, This is not an easy letter for me to write . . .*

I put down my pen and wondered if it would be better to write in a more formal style, rather like the letter Mr Darcy wrote to Elizabeth Bennet. 'Be not alarmed,

183

madam, on receiving this letter by the apprehension of its containing . . . etc.'

But the fact was I did want to alarm him and I didn't want him to think I was just mimicking Jane Austen for a joke.

It would be better to write in the style of an affectionate younger sister. So I began a second letter.

Dear Albert,

I do hope you won't mind my calling you by your Christian name. The fact is that I have always wished for an older brother and if that wish were to come true I could not think of a better choice than yourself. Having said that, I must proceed to more serious matters.

During the past few months I have observed that your attentions to my mother, Katharine, have become more than just those of a considerate clergyman.

As you might have noticed, my mother is an attractive and lonely woman. Her talent for music and her intelligence are both a bit wasted in this small town. When she met you, an intelligent, handsome man, naturally she was pleased. But my mother is not always rational. Some people regard her as eccentric. I do not know whether I agree with this, but I do know that she is easily bored and will take risks to distract herself.

Forgive me, Albert, if I tell you that I think you are one of those risks.

I must also say that I think you are risking your own reputation in this town full of gossips by continuing the sort of relationship you have at present with my mother.

This has been a very difficult letter for me to write.

Please do not disregard it or think badly of me.

Yours very sincerely,
Anna Danielssen

I posted the letter on my way to school next morning. The following week there were no visits from Reverend Marsden to The Tower House.

It has been a chaotic week for the whole family because we've been preparing for the annual flower show held by the Royal Institute for the Blind. Mother is their patron. It is always held in our garden, which is large enough for all the paraphernalia of pet parades and cake stalls. We have a lot of big shady trees that also provide shelter if it rains, and we usually decorate the sunken garage as a fortune-teller's cave. Mother used to dress up as a gypsy and, staring into our goldfish bowl camouflaged by spooky lights, she would tell shocking stories about what would happen to people. This year Charlotte has agreed to be the fortune-teller. My job is usually to organise the children to parade with their pets and their decorated prams and bicycles. The Ladies Guild takes charge of cakes, preserves, vegetables, flowers, white elephants and serving afternoon tea on the lawn. Now that we have croquet sticks and balls, Jonathan is going to organise a game of croquet. Eliza is running the Lucky Threepenny Dip this year and has spent hours wrapping up tiny presents to be hidden in a tin tub of sawdust. The weekend guests have been invited to come along and join in too, of course.

While Mother was making her traditional opening speech I had strangely mixed feelings. She looked very elegant in a wide straw hat with daisies round the brim and a plain white linen suit. Her clothes may be old but they always look good. She spoke well. People in the crowd were listening attentively and smiling and applauding her. I felt two completely opposite emotions – pride in having a mother who opened up her garden to the public to raise money for a worthy cause and hatred for her being a collector of admirers who were men. Always men.

I looked at Reverend Marsden watching her shyly from the crowd (he wasn't beaming as he would normally have been so perhaps my letter had had some effect), and the bank manager and even the strange-looking Polish man who kissed her hand when she brought a jug of lemon juice to him and his gang of road workers in the sun a few months ago. They all had the same hopeless look of adoration on their silly faces. It made me feel sick.

I'm quite ashamed of feeling like this and would hate anyone to know about it.

Mother was standing on a little dais made of packing cases covered with crêpe paper. 'I know that many of you intend to contribute generously to this very worthy appeal. Here is the box into which you may put your donations, ladies and gentlemen,' she said, holding up a cardboard box. 'And just to start the ball rolling, I am going to donate ten pounds.'

There was loud applause and murmurs of 'So generous!' and 'What a fine gesture!' Reverend Marsden came forward to place a smaller note in the box and other people followed his example. The bank manager and the Polish road worker were among the first.

Mother thanked each contributor charmingly, then was helped down from the dais by Reverend Marsden. She took his arm as they strolled off into the stalls of homemade cakes, vegetables, fruit and flowers. They made an attractive couple. I noticed Mrs Barry and Mrs Hill watching them with interest, then putting their heads together to gossip. Other people turned their heads to stare as well. I followed at a distance, scowling.

When I caught up I overheard Reverend Marsden saying, 'It was a brilliant idea to give that money. Far too generous of you.'

Mother laughed girlishly. 'Not at all.'

Then he gave her an intimate look and said, 'Katharine, there's something I've been meaning to talk to you about. Can we meet somewhere?'

'Of course, Albert.'

'Tomorrow?' He seemed flustered. She nodded. 'The Grange at four o'clock?'

'I'll be there.'

They parted then, exchanging affectionate glances, and Mother walked on, smiling radiantly to herself, nodding to acquaintances as if she were royalty.

When she was out of the crowd I marched up to her, looking furious. 'How could you?'

'Anna, you're becoming rather tediously moralistic.' She obviously thought I was referring to her intimate promenade with Reverend Marsden.

I said self-righteously, 'I've got every right to be. We just can't afford it.'

'Oh, I see,' she said, realising her mistake.

'We were doing really well when we started the guest-house, but we're not any more. The butcher rang again this morning, wanting his seven pounds, twelve and six. The phone's about to be cut off, and Mrs Rawlins keeps asking when that new radiator we promised her is coming. We've got a pile of bills that we haven't yet paid, and you give ten pounds away!'

'Anna, how dare you lecture me!' Mother said with

controlled anger. 'You've become an insufferable little bore.'

I was struck silent by this insult and felt close to tears. Suddenly Mr Devlin appeared, carrying a huge pumpkin. I was relieved to see him but Mother gave him an icy look.

He raised his hat to us. 'Good afternoon, ladies. You'll notice I did it again this year.' He proudly turned the pumpkin around to show a royal-blue 'First' card attached to it.

'Congratulations,' I said. 'It's bigger than last year's.'

'Anna, I'll make you a present of it,' he said magnanimously and plonked it in my arms.

'Hey, thanks, Mr Devlin! We'll make soup out of it for weeks. I'll bring you some over.'

He grinned and said, 'No, you won't bring it over. I'll come and get it. I've been promising to fix the other half of that rusted spouting on your west side for weeks. You be home later on today, Kate?'

Mother recoiled and said coldly, 'I don't remember inviting you to fix my roof.'

'You didn't, Kate. Anna did. Says you damn near drown when it rains.'

'Whatever the state of the roof, Jack Devlin, I'm not asking you to touch it.'

Mr Devlin said quietly, 'I'm doing it for free. I know you're not flush.' They stared hard at each other. 'Frank was a mate of mine.'

'How dare you!' Mother said angrily. She turned and walked away. I gave Mr Devlin a look of embarrassed apology and followed Mother.

When I caught up with her I asked, 'Why are you always so rude to him? You treat him like dirt.'

'He is dirt,' she said, still furious. 'He and his whole wretched family.'

'Why? What have they ever done to you?'

Mother darted a look at me as if she might tell what they'd done but then thought better of it. I wondered how she'd react when she heard that Charlotte was going to the Lady Mayoress's Ball with Dougie Devlin in the back of the timber truck!

Just then Jonathan rushed up, pushing his old bike which was decorated with red, blue and yellow crêpe paper threaded through the spokes. 'Quick, Mum, come and watch. The best decorated vehicle's just about to be judged!'

'All right, all right.' She didn't like being called 'Mum'. She pointed to a small boy with a decorated goat on a leash and said imperiously, 'Will you get that animal off the flower bed, please!'

I raced off to organise the pet parade. Storm clouds were gathering and I wanted to get it over with before the rain started. There was a wider assortment of pets than usual – cats, dogs, ponies, goats, a mouse in a cage, a blue-tongue lizard, a turtle, a lamb and a piglet. I collected all the competitors together and explained how they were to parade slowly in a circle, one behind the other in front of the judges. Pets were to be judged on their appearance and obedience. There was also a prize for the most unusual pet.

As I was marshalling the competitors I noticed a tall, good-looking boy watching. He smiled at me and came over. He wasn't a local. I'd never seen him before.

He nodded at the children lining up with their pets. 'I think the pig should win.'

I nodded shyly.

'But the bantam wearing a bonnet in the doll's pram might beat it,' he added.

'It won't,' I said.

'Oh, why's that?'

'It belongs to my sister and my mother's the judge.'

'Ah, I see.' He smiled. 'Can't have nepotism.'

I smiled back, embarrassed. I didn't know the meaning of the word.

'I'd better go and help cover the stalls before the rain starts,' I said.

'Need any assistance?'

'No, it's all right, thanks.'

He walked along beside me anyway. 'I believe your family runs a guesthouse here.'

'Yes, that's right.'

'My family is looking for a place to stay in the school holidays.'

I felt happy all of a sudden. He was well mannered, had a good sense of humour and was quite handsome. I had a hopeful feeling that he liked me too. I look older than fourteen, which is lucky because he must have been at least eighteen. We introduced ourselves, shook hands and he promised to call by in a week or so to talk to Mother about accommodation for his family.

The rain held off until the flower show was over but by nightfall it was teeming down. The guests huddled by the fire, discussing the afternoon. They all seemed to think it had been a great success. Mr and Mrs Rawlins had correctly guessed the weight of a fruit cake and had won it as a prize. After dinner they cut the cake and offered us all a slice, which is certainly generous behaviour for them.

Mr Rawlins ate four slices to our one, but still, we think the Rawlins' manners have improved since they became regular weekend guests. The other regular guest is Eunice Crooks, the spinster corsetière. We're all very fond of Eunice, who isn't so timid now she knows us better, and even makes jokes. She's promised to fit me with a proper brassiere if I go to her department in Bright and Hitch-cocks. I can't quite afford one yet, which I think Eunice suspects, so she doesn't mind when I make weak excuses.

Dr Pettigrew is back this weekend, although this time she hasn't brought Arch and Mervyn with her, so it's a bit like a family reunion.

One of the new guests is the bank manager's aunt, Miss Morant. She is elderly and has to be helped up the stairs. She's a little deaf and short-sighted and needs two hot-water bottles at night. She also uses a chamber pot, which is rather disgusting. I always thought they were mainly for decoration. I must say I haven't volunteered to empty it. I imagined that she emptied it herself when none of us were looking but early this morning I noticed Mother doing it. Poor Mother! Apart from being frail and a bit helpless Miss Morant is a sweet old lady. She smells of baby powder and her skin is as dry as parchment. Yesterday she gave me a little lecture. 'You must promise me, Anna, that when you grow into a woman you will never paint your nails red. Blood-red talons excite the male passion, you know.' I promised faithfully and then went up to my room and had a great giggle. I must add the 'Femme Fatale with Red Talons' to the group of women I sometimes dress up as.

We all went to bed early because it had been such an exhausting day.

I didn't sleep for long and woke suddenly. A storm was

raging. The lightning was blinding and seemed very close. I counted the seconds between each flash of lightning and the rumble of thunder. Four seconds. Three. Rain was lashing my windows. It seemed colder than usual. I put out one hand to touch the glass and found it wet. I leapt out of bed and turned on the light. Water was dripping down inside my window and making a puddle on the floor. I grabbed my dressing-gown and ran downstairs. What a sight! Water was pouring down the west wall like a stream. The carpet was a sodden mess but – worst of all – the grand piano stood open and rain splashed steadily onto the keys. Mother's most precious possession was almost certainly ruined.

chapter eighteen

*F*or a few seconds I just stared in horror at the piano and then I rushed forward to try and push it away from the leaking roof. It was heavy and I had to brace myself against the wet wall but I managed to move it a few yards. Then I raced to the bathroom for towels to mop up the water, and to the kitchen for buckets, saucepans, baking dishes, vases – anything to catch the wretched endless stream.

'Oh, God!' said Charlotte, coming downstairs in her night-gown and staring at Mother's piano. 'Has she seen it?'

'She hasn't woken.'

'Lucky. She must have taken some Relaxatabs.' Charlotte examined the piano closely and tried a few notes. It did not sound tuneful. 'God, what will we do?'

'Surely it can be fixed.'

Charlotte shook her head. 'It's soaked. It would cost a fortune. Oh, God. It's been in her family for generations.' She looked up at the ceiling angrily. 'Why didn't Mr Devlin finish replacing that spouting?'

'She wouldn't let him.'

'Why ever not?'

'She despises him.' I shrugged. 'It's something to do with our father.'

Charlotte appeared thoughtful. 'They were friends, apparently, our father and Jack Devlin. Dougie told me.' She sighed. 'Well, she's cut her own throat this time. What a nightmare!'

Charlotte helped me push the oak table, chairs and chiffonier away from the wall and roll up the carpet. We emptied the buckets and saucepans that were filling up and replaced them under the drips. Then we made a cup of tea and ate a piece of Mr and Mrs Rawlins' fruitcake which was still on the sideboard. We sat and stared at the raindrops falling – plink, plunk, plonk – into the dozen or so containers. Charlotte started to conduct them like an orchestra. I began to laugh. It was too dreadful to take seriously. We thought we were laughing quietly but suddenly there was Mother standing behind us. She leaned against the opposite wall, looking miserably at the devastation. Her eyes rested on the piano for a second, then she looked quickly away. I felt deeply sorry for her. 'We've done all we can,' I said softly. 'I'm sure the piano can be fixed.'

Mother said nothing.

'I'll get Mr Devlin to come over first thing tomorrow. As soon as the spouting's mended we'll clean up this mess and put everything back where it belongs. The carpet will soon dry out. The guests can have breakfast in the sunroom.'

Mother nodded vaguely, then she turned and walked back to her room. I looked at Charlotte.

'At least she didn't say no about Mr Devlin.'

Mother slept late next morning.

While Mr Devlin was hammering on the roof I tried to

speak privately to him, but because Dougie and Warren were helping, it wasn't easy. As I passed him a different hammer I said, trying to sound casual, 'I didn't know you were a mate of my father's.' But he evaded me, calling out, 'Pass me those four-inch nails, will you, Warren!'

Charlotte took advantage of Mother's absence to invite the Devlins into the kitchen for tea and crumpets when they'd finished the job. Dougie kept looking nervously at the door to see if Mother was coming. He doesn't want to offend her too much before he takes Charlotte to the ball, I suppose. Charlotte was very relaxed and even flirted with Dougie in front of his brother and father, which made him blush. Warren didn't say much at all. He seemed rather shy for a bodgie.

When I served the guests breakfast in the sunroom they were all quite cheerful despite the inconvenience of having no dining table. They balanced trays on their knees and chatted excitedly about the storm. Luckily none of their rooms had sprung leaks.

Dr Pettigrew was concerned about the mess in the dining room and offered to help us tidy it up but I said we could manage.

'The piano was insured, dear, wasn't it?' she asked me directly.

'Oh, yes,' I lied and then blushed almost as brightly as Dougie does.

I served the guests lunch in the sunroom too. The rain had stopped and there was a glorious rainbow above the sea. After lunch, when most of the guests had gone off for their walks and Miss Morant was settled on the sofa with her murder mystery, I tapped on Mother's door. She was awake and sitting up in bed staring out the window. She looked very pale. I brought in a tray of lunch and laid it gently on her lap. She smiled and patted my hand but didn't make a move to eat anything.

'Why wasn't the piano insured?' I asked quietly.

'Because, like everything else, I let it lapse.' She shook her head as if she couldn't believe her own stupidity. 'Oh, what a failure I am! What a failure as a mother!' She hung her head, then looked up at me with tears in her eyes. 'Charlotte should have had the money for singing lessons. You should have had those ballet shoes.'

I was amazed. I hadn't thought she cared.

'Sometimes I think I'm not fit to live,' she said softly.

'Oh, Mummy, you are, you are! Don't say that, please. We're all right, really. Charlotte is thinking of accepting a teaching bursary and I was too tall for the ballet anyway.'

What I said wasn't strictly true but she nodded as if it was a comfort to her. 'Did you manage their lunch all right?'

'Yes, they had pearl barley broth, tuna salad, fruit, cheese and biscuits. It was easy. They're all being so kind and sympathetic about the damage. Mr Rawlins helped me lug the carpets onto the balcony and they're drying in the sun.'

'Did you give them the Stilton?'

'Yes.'

'I was saving that!' said Mother with a deep sigh.

She pushed the tray aside and began to get out of bed. She staggered and leaned against the wall, her hand to her head. 'I'm just so weary,' she sighed, 'and soon I've got to go and meet Reverend Marsden.'

'What? But you're not well. Please don't get up.'

'I never break appointments.' She straightened herself, with an effort. 'How's the roof?'

'Fixed,' I said sullenly. 'No charge.'

Mother nodded, as if she expected as much. 'I don't want you visiting the Devlins again, Anna.'

'Why on earth not?'

'I forbid you to go there,' she said emphatically.

I turned my face up to the ceiling as if I might have 'a good scream' but then thought better of it. Instead I turned defiantly to face Mother for a second, then stormed out of her room. What a brilliant manipulator she was.

She *had* been a bad mother and yet she'd shocked me into denying it by telling the truth about herself. Charlotte would never have fallen for such a trick. She still blamed Mother for not being able to afford singing lessons whereas I just blamed myself for growing too tall for the ballet. Actually it had been much more humiliating than that.

On Tuesday, November the fifth, as I had promised Mrs Krantz, I had triumphantly appeared at rehearsal with my brand new ballet shoes. Mrs Krantz had hurriedly taken me aside before I could take my place onstage with the other dancers. 'Anna, I must tell you some not too pleasant news,' she said. 'I haff already promised your place in the troupe to one of my private students. I am sorry, Anna. It isn't so much that you had the wronk shoes or were beingk too tall. It's just that this girl has had lessons for many years and is so much better than you.'

I couldn't speak.

'You understand me, dear? We all haff different talents.'

I nodded dumbly. 'But why didn't you tell me before, Mrs Krantz?' I whispered.

'I did not want to hurt your feelingks. You were so determined. You had such a nice feelingk for the music. One day you might become a different kind of dancer.'

'What kind of dancer?' I didn't know any other kind.

Mrs Krantz waved her arms about wildly. 'More free. A primitive dancer. Modern. Not so classical. For taller, strongker girls.'

I felt as if she'd described me as an ape.

At least the ballet shoes that had never been worn could be taken back to the shop for a full refund. I returned them that afternoon. My eyes were so red and swollen that the shopkeeper asked if I had the flu. Next morning I returned the money to the social service jar, but it was too late. The theft had been discovered and the letter that threatened my punishment had already been written. After Mother's expedition to see Miss Hooper I was forgiven. This was a comfort, but it hardly made up for my humiliation about the ballet.

Charlotte was at home on Sunday afternoon and I thought it was time she gave me the help she'd promised a few weeks ago. Mother's behaviour was getting too much for me. Charlotte was the oldest. Why shouldn't she share the responsibility for Mother's outrageous love affair?

I ran up to Charlotte's room, which is one of the Suicide Cell rooms now that the guests have taken over her old room, and knocked loudly. I could hear her singing.

'And oh my darling, oh my pet,
Whatever else you may forget,
In yonder isle beyond the sea,
Do not forget you married me.'

Then she called out crossly, 'Who is it?'

'Me. Anna.'

She opened the door a crack. 'Is it urgent? I'm really busy.'

I nodded and she let me in. Her new room, although smaller, was just as messy as the old one had been. In the middle of the chaos stood her music stand with *The Gondoliers* propped open at Tessa's song.

'Anna, now that you've interrupted, you couldn't sing Gianetta for me in this duet, could you? It's not hard. Beverley couldn't rehearse this afternoon.'

'Later I'll try if you like but, Charlotte, right now I need your help.'

I sat her down and explained.

Half an hour later we were both neatly dressed and hurrying towards The Grange tea rooms.

'What if she's there already?' Charlotte asked.

'No chance. She takes ages to do her make-up and "grooming" as she calls it. You know that. Besides, she'd never get there too early because she hates to be kept waiting.'

The Grange is very popular, particularly on Sunday afternoons. It's a rather grand tea room, with potted palms and a large-bosomed pianist who plays old favourites and occasionally, in a quavering soprano, sings 'Vilia' and 'You Are My Heart's Delight'. We guessed that Mother would sit as far away as possible from this travesty of a musician, so we asked for a table close to the piano and behind one of the largest potted palms. We politely ordered one pot of tea with two cups and said that as we had just finished a large Sunday roast we did not feel we could manage cakes or scones just yet. Perhaps later. The elderly waitress looked sceptical.

After about eight minutes Mother appeared looking pale but attractive in suit, hat and gloves. The waitress seemed to know her and showed her immediately to a pleasant table in the corner furthest from us. The table was set for three, which seemed to annoy Mother. She argued with the waitress, who seemed to be insisting that Reverend Marsden had made the booking for three.

We hid our faces in our menus. 'We couldn't afford one passionfruit pavlova, I suppose,' said Charlotte wistfully.

'Not a chance.'

'What do we do if she sees us?'

'Pretend we're amazed by the coincidence.'

'What are we supposed to be doing here?'

'Meeting a friend who didn't turn up.'

'At The Grange? Come on. How old is this friend?'

'Ancient. She's an old lady friend of yours. She's in *The Gondoliers*!' I said, suddenly inspired.

'She plays Inez, the foster mother who mixed up the king and the gondoliers at birth!' said Charlotte, getting into the mood of things.

'And she's a dear friend of the very same lady pianist who plays once a week at The Grange, whom she hasn't seen for years and years.'

We giggled helplessly and the elderly waitress glared at us.

'Shhh. We'll get thrown out. He's here!' I whispered.

'Who's that he's with?' We stared at Reverend Marsden standing politely at the reception desk waiting to be shown to his table. Beside him stood a tall, willowy young woman with long fair hair and the expression of an angel.

'I've no idea. She's not from round here.'

'She's beautiful.'

'Poor Mother,' I said.

'Oh, really,' Charlotte said in disgust. 'I do think

you've been imagining this whole thing. What would Reverend Marsden see in Mother? She's thirty-seven!'

'I told you. They were kissing, passionately.'

'Erk!'

Reverend Marsden had waved at Mother sitting alone at her table and now, leaving the young woman waiting by the desk, he hurried eagerly towards her.

Mother looked disconcerted and Reverend Marsden seemed nervous. He looked apologetic, sat down opposite her and handed her a sheet of paper. It seemed to be something grave, for as soon as she had read it and handed it back they both looked awkward and unhappy. After a minute he returned to the desk and ushered the other woman towards the table. As he introduced them we watched Mother's face closely. She seemed to be grief-stricken. The young woman, by contrast, was quite at ease. She held out her hand serenely and smiled warmly, deferring politely to the older woman. Then Mother said something that made the young woman give Reverend Marsden a bemused, questioning look. He smiled and appeared to be trying to cover up some misunderstanding by paying Mother compliments.

Mother looked pale and said nothing.

The young couple sat side by side, the woman looking happy and relaxed. After a few minutes she leant her head on Reverend Marsden's shoulder and began absent-mindedly patting his hand.

'Perhaps it's his sister,' I whispered.

Charlotte slowly shook her head. 'No, it isn't. Look!'

The angelic young woman was holding out her left hand rather demurely for Mother to admire a ring – her engagement ring.

chapter nineteen

On Sunday night I thought I heard a woman weeping.
I sat up in bed. There was silence. Perhaps I'd dreamt
it. The moon was full and its light streamed white and
ghostly through my window.

Then the weeping began again. It was terrible. Like a
lament.

I leapt out of bed and ran to Mother's room. Thankfully the weekend guests had all left and Eliza and
Jonathan's room was too far away for them to hear the
plaintive sound.

I stood outside the room for a few minutes, aching to
rush in and comfort her but knowing that she wouldn't
appreciate it. Well-bred people do not burden others, particularly children, with their private miseries. She had
taught us that.

Suddenly I flattened myself against the wall. Mother
was coming out. The door opened and I stood concealed
behind it. The weeping had dwindled to sniffing. She
walked to the chiffonier in the dining room, opened the
top drawer and took out a key. Then she went towards the
attic, reached up, pulled down the ladder and began to

climb it. I watched as she unlocked the attic door and went in. There was a faint beam of torchlight coming from the attic.

I couldn't resist following. Stealthily I climbed the ladder and went into the attic. Mother was bent over some papers in a cellophane box on the floor. She looked up, startled, when she saw me.

'Why did you write that letter?' she asked very softly.

'I had to,' I said, trying to sound gentle, but the words came out sounding matter-of-fact. 'People were gossiping. I wanted to protect you.'

Mother stared at me.

Then she stood up angrily. 'What are you doing here? You know it's forbidden to come up here.'

I left quietly. I felt like crying myself.

Next morning I got up very early and went riding before school. It was low tide. The beach was wide and the sand was hard. There was no one in sight. I urged Grayling into a gallop, leaning forward on his neck. Water splashed up from the wet sand. I lifted my head up and shrieked at the sky, 'Damn you, Frank! Where are you?'

It was pretty stupid but it made me feel better.

Suddenly Grayling shied at a large lump of seaweed and I was thrown off. As I fell a stream of images flashed through my mind – the grotesque naked couple on the sand, Mother threatening Ernie Mooney with the poker, Eliza blurting out the story of my crush on Reverend Marsden and Mother weeping on her bed in the moonlight as if her heart would break. As I landed with a thud on the wet sand it was almost a relief because the images stopped. I lay still. Grayling cantered over me and off along the beach, dragging his reins. After a few seconds I tried to get up but fell back in pain. Grayling was headed for home at Merlin Heads. I just hoped he wouldn't trip on the reins and break a leg.

'Blast!' I said to myself. I got up and hobbled along the beach after him. I suspected there was a graze on my thigh where the wretched pony had trodden on me. Now I'd miss the bus and be hours late for school. Mrs Armitage would be furious if Grayling came home without a rider and would probably forbid me to borrow him ever again. I felt like an utter fool. My thigh ached. When I undid my jodhpurs to look there was a bloody patch spreading from the top of my leg down towards the knee. I limped on, head down against the wind.

Suddenly in the distance I saw two horses coming towards me. The big black one had a rider but the small grey was being led. As he came closer I recognised Dougie Devlin on Black Jack, leading Grayling.

He looked concerned. 'You all right, Anna?'

'Yes thanks,' I felt embarrassed about falling off. 'He shied at some kelp.'

I tried to mount Grayling but my leg was too painful to lift to the stirrup.

'Hang on. I'll give you a leg up.' Dougie dismounted and hoisted me up. I sprang into the saddle with a little cry of pain.

'You sure you should ride him?'

'Yes, yes, I'm fine. It's just a graze. Thanks.'

We rode back together towards Skinners Bluff.

'Your dad was a good rider,' Dougie said.

'I didn't know.' I must have looked surprised.

'He used to ride this fella, Black Jack. With Thel. She had a mare called Trixie.'

'Your sister, Thelma? The nurse?'

'Yeah. She's over in London now, working in one of the big hospitals.'

'My dad's somewhere in Europe. We've lost touch. He moves around a lot.'

Dougie looked disapproving when I said this. 'Is that what your mother told you?' He suddenly urged Black Jack into a canter as if he didn't want to talk any more.

I cantered alongside him. Conversation was impossible now that the horses' hooves were smacking hard on the wet sand.

'Dougie, can you stop a minute?' I gasped.

'You all right?'

My thigh was hurting but I said, 'Yes, fine.' We slowed the horses and he waited until I plucked up the courage to blurt out, 'Do you know where my dad is?'

Dougie hesitated. 'He writes to you, doesn't he?'

'No.'

'Well, he used to write.'

'When?'

'I dunno. When you were younger.'

'He's never written to me,' I said adamantly. 'Not once in my whole life.'

Dougie avoided a reply by urging Black Jack into a fast canter.

That night, when Mother was asleep, I took the key to the attic, pulled down the ladder and climbed it. I had brought a torch.

There on the floor, where Mother had left it, stood the box of papers. The seal had been broken and it was only loosely closed. Inside were perhaps a dozen piles of letters, each one tied with a different coloured ribbon. They mostly seemed to be addressed to Mother and almost all were in the same handwriting.

I opened the first one on the pile. This was certainly a love letter. Was it from our father? I couldn't tell because it had no date and no signature. It was just signed '*Your Beloved*'.

I hurriedly sorted through the other letters, searching for one that was addressed to me or Charlotte, or to Jonathan or Eliza. At the very bottom of the pile I found a package tied with thin brown velvet ribbon. On the top were birthday cards to Charlotte and me from Uncle Martin and Aunt Ursula and even some from our maternal grandmother who died when we were small. Underneath these were three yellowing envelopes in the same handwriting addressed to me. I drew a sharp breath, but didn't allow myself to open them. Beneath these were more letters, addressed to my sisters and brother. I clasped my three letters close to my chest for a minute then slipped them into my pocket. I neatly packed the other letters back in the box, closed it and crept backwards down the ladder.

I took two days to read and reread the letters from my father before confronting Mother. She had been unhappy and ill, spending much of the time in bed, and I hadn't wanted to make her more miserable. Sometimes she would get up in the middle of the night and I'd hear her playing the piano, which was still not perfectly in tune. We'd hired the best man they had to come from Geronga Music Store to inspect the damage, and he'd done a reasonable job of tuning it, but Mother didn't play her beloved Schubert any more, just mournful pieces by Ravel. I did feel sorry for her, but by Wednesday I could wait no longer.

I went into her room in the early morning, bringing her a cup of tea. She was lying still with the blinds drawn against the sun.

'Why didn't you tell me he was living in Townsville?'

'What?' she said faintly.

'My father. Frank. You told me he was overseas. Somewhere in Europe. You told me we'd lost touch.'

She put one hand up to her forehead. 'Go away, Anna. I've got a migraine. I can hardly see.'

'You lied to me. Why?' I held out one of the envelopes. 'This letter's only three years old. He wanted to see me! To show me the rainforest and the islands, the places he loves. Why didn't you give it to me?' I was pleading, close to tears.

'To protect you. He's no good.'

'Why is he no good?' I was determined to know. 'Why do you hate him?' There was silence. Then, on an impulse, I said, 'Is it because he went riding with Thelma Devlin, or what?'

Mother sat up suddenly. She was enraged. 'Get out of here, you little viper!'

Never had she spoken to me in such a way before. I ran from the room in tears.

I ran to the kitchen. There was the guests' breakfast all laid out ready to serve. 'Damned if I'm going to do it,' I muttered.

Charlotte was away, staying with Beverley, so I burst into Eliza and Jonathan's room. It had been transformed into a movie set. There was a miniature jungle of trees and a number of ferocious wild stuffed animals. Tarzan, a brown doll in a leopard skin, was suspended by a thread, about to leap into a ravine. Jonathan was poised ready to shoot the scene and Eliza was holding the spotlight.

'You two will have to serve breakfast today,' I announced.

'I can't! I'm filming!' said Jonathan, as if I was mad.

'I can't. I'm the assistant,' said Eliza.

'Well, don't then. Tell Mother I've gone out.'

'Aren't you going to school today, Anna?'

'No, I'm not, but you two get ready. It's late.'

'I've got a bad cold,' said Jonathan.

'So have I, Anna,' Eliza whined.

'Well, stay home, then. What do I care?'

They exchanged puzzled looks and continued filming.

At the timber yard I was relieved to see Dougie unloading a truck on his own. It was a big job and he was glad of my help. I put a lot of energy into carrying planks and stacking them neatly in a corner by the peppercorn tree. Dougie asked me about the leg. 'Much better, thanks. I don't think I'll be scarred for life.'

Before he could get on to the inevitable topic of Charlotte, I asked him casually if his father was still in touch with mine. Dougie said he didn't think so, but he'd probably know where to find him. Feeling very excited, I was just about to rush inside and ask Mr Devlin to give me the latest address, when Dougie said in his laconic way, 'Dad's up the Murray fishing. I reckon you'll have to hold your horses till he gets back.'

'When's that?'

'In two weeks.'

'Two weeks!'

Dougie grinned. 'Don't worry. Frank won't run away.'

He could see how thrilled I was about the possibility of making contact with my dad, and I could tell he was pleased for me.

Just then his younger brother screeched into the yard in a battered old red sports car. He swerved close to us and pulled up in a cloud of dust.

'Jeez, Warren. You got it going?' Dougie said admiringly.

'Yeah. Found some more parts at the tip. You comin' for a burn?'

'Righto,' I said. I wasn't sure that he was inviting me but I was feeling elated after the news about my father.

Dougie looked at me in a concerned, protective way. 'Don't go fast, Warren,' he said.

I hesitated. 'Aren't you coming?'

'Gotta finish unloading.' He walked back towards the truck, then turned and called out, 'Keep your head down when you go down the main street.'

He must have realised that if the gossips saw me in a car with the town larrikin they'd pass the news on to Mother who would throw a fit.

Once we were out on the open road I popped my head up. It was a fine, sunny day. Blue-green ocean was speeding past on one side and yellow paddocks on the other. What a blend of smells – salt water and ripe grain! I'd never been in a sports car before. It was exciting. My hair streamed out behind me. I stood up and let out a yell of sheer exuberance. Warren Devlin grinned up at me. You could see why he loved driving fast cars. He wasn't such a bad chap after all. This was thrilling. Even better than galloping Grayling along the beach at low tide.

After about ten minutes he slowed down and pulled off the road into a secluded sandy inlet. I gave him a questioning look.

'What are we doing?' I asked.

'Going for a swim.'

'I haven't brought my togs.'

Warren grinned cheekily. 'Swim in your skin like me.' He got out of the car and started taking off his shirt.

'No,' I said. I waited. 'Would you take me home, please?'

Warren stared at me unpleasantly. 'Wouldn't your mother like to know you went skinny dipping with Warren Devlin?'

I felt confused and embarrassed. 'It's not that, it's . . .'

He got back into the car and leaned towards me. 'Your mother thinks she's pretty good, doesn't she?' He put his arm along the back of the seat and flicked my hair menacingly. 'You think you're pretty good too, don't ya?'

I pulled away from him, shaking my head. He lunged at me, grabbing both shoulders, and tried to kiss me. I struck him on the chest and then pushed him to the other side of the car. He sat there staring at me for a few seconds. Then he got out and walked around to my side of the car. My heart was beating hard. Was he going to try to force me? Suddenly he stuck his head in through the window so it was close to mine and yelled, 'Your mum's a snob! Your dad couldn't stand her!'

I was shaking with rage and fear. 'Drive me home, do you hear!' I shouted.

Half an hour later, walking up the steps to The Tower House, I was still shaking. How could I have been such a fool? Warren was a well-known lout around town and a hater of our family. Why on earth did I invite myself to go alone in a car with him? I must have been mad. And how could he possibly know what our father thought of our mother? He'd made it up just to infuriate me. I had shouted just like Mother would have shouted at a creature she despised.

Imperiously. Yet to my astonishment he had done what I ordered and driven me home. I began to giggle with relief.

I could smell something rather delicious cooking in the kitchen. Jonathan, Eliza and her great friend Jenny were making toffee. There was a dreadful mess. When I came in Eliza said, 'Where have you been? Mummy's been locked in her room all afternoon and she won't come out. The guests had to carry their own lunch to the table.'

'We finished the film!' Jonathan said triumphantly.

'But Tarzan got broken,' said Eliza, licking the spoon.

'There's someone waiting to see you in the dining room,' said Jonathan.

'Who?'

'A man,' said Eliza.

When I walked into the dining room I was surprised to see the good-looking young man I'd met at the flower show, standing admiring our family portraits. He was wearing more formal clothing than last time – a tweed jacket, moleskin trousers, leather boots and a shirt and tie – so he looked much older.

He turned to me and smiled. 'Who won the pet parade?'

'Oh, I think it was . . . the turtle.'

We both laughed.

'Anna, isn't it?' he asked.

I nodded.

'Michael Cameron.' We shook hands, even though we'd already introduced ourselves the first time we met. He probably thought I'd forgotten his name and wanted to save me the embarrassment of having to ask what it was. He had the knack of being very polite and making you feel relaxed at the same time.

'I'm staying at Skinners Bluff for a few days studying for

exams with friends from school. I hope you don't mind that I dropped in.'

I shook my head. 'You go to school?' I asked in disbelief.

'My final year. Next year I go to the Institute to study wool classing. Then I'll work at home on the property.'

'You have a sheep station?' I was impressed.

He smiled. 'A farm, really. We run mainly sheep and a few cattle, up near Ballarat.' He gestured at the dining room. 'This is a terrific house. It feels like a ship.'

I nodded, pleased that he liked it.

'My family is still looking for a place to stay in December. I don't suppose you could squeeze us in.'

We exchanged conspiratorial smiles.

Before going to bed that night I stood in my room in front of the long mirror smiling to myself and thinking of Michael. I closed my eyes, hugged myself and said in his deep, charming voice, 'I don't suppose you could squeeze us in.'

A few days later I noticed those Polish men were working on the road outside our place again. They were still wearing knotted handkerchiefs on their heads even though it wasn't particularly hot. They don't seem to mind that they look ridiculous.

The one who had kissed Mother's hand a few months ago was leaning on his shovel chatting to her over the gate while the others did all the work.

That evening I was trying to catch up on some neglected study in the kitchen where it's warm when Mother came in and sat down at the table opposite me. She seemed in the mood for a chat.

'It's awful. I'm behind in nearly every subject. I might even fail the exams,' I said, hoping she'd take the hint and leave me in peace.

'People in our family usually make their mark whether they pass their examinations or not,' she said airily.

I looked at her in disbelief. I thought I would let this arrogant remark pass and get on with my work but I couldn't.

'Some people around here think you're a bit of a snob.'

'Do they indeed?' She sounded amused.

'Was my father a snob?'

Mother pretended not to hear. 'Do you know, I met a man today who is a superb violinist.' She is brilliant at changing the subject when it's not to her liking. 'Superb, and yet he is forced to work breaking stones on the road so his hands are covered in calluses.'

'Who?'

'His name is George Milandowska. He studied with some of the finest musicians in Europe. He's just arrived in this country and he's living in a one-bedroom shack in a holiday camp with his wife and three children. It's disgraceful.'

I nodded sympathetically. 'A lot of New Australian kids at school are living like that.'

'But *they* are not musicians.' Mother paused and looked at me steadily as if daring me to object. 'I've invited the Milandowskas to come and live with us.'

'What! Here?'

'They can have all the spare bedrooms and the kitchen and living room downstairs. We don't need them.'

'But where will the guests sleep?'

'After this weekend I'm finished with guests. Far too

exhausting. The Milandowskas move in on Sunday, the day the last guests leave.'

I stared at her in shock. 'But the Camerons are arriving next week. Michael's family. Father, mother, two sons and a daughter. You met the parents. You liked them. They love the house. They've paid a huge deposit and they want to stay a whole month.'

'Give them back their wretched deposit.'

'I can't,' I cried. 'I've promised them.'

'Give it back.'

'I can't give it back! I've already used it to pay some of the bills.'

'Anna, you're not telling me the truth.'

'I am! When you were ill I had to pay the worst bills. The butcher, telephone, and the man who came to try and fix the piano.'

'What a charlatan he was!'

'No, he did a good job. You said so!'

She sighed. 'Perhaps. I'm sorry about the Camerons, Anna. We'll just have to borrow the money from Uncle Martin and give them back their deposit. The Milandowskas can't afford to pay rent.'

'No!' I said vehemently. 'I haven't done all this work and nearly failed my exams and given up the ballet club just so we can go back to leaning on Uncle Martin! We can manage on our own. Don't you see that? Just a few more bills to pay and we're out of debt. We can save this house we all love. We've nearly done it!'

Mother stared at me strangely. 'Anna, I don't love this house. I did once, but it's exhausted me. It's a mad house.' She paused, then she continued softly, almost as if she was talking to herself. 'I know why you're struggling to

214

keep it. For a father you don't even know, a phantom. You think he'll appear like some hero and save us. He won't.'

Mother hardly seemed to care whether I listened to her or not. She was speaking her thoughts aloud and there was some truth in what she was saying, which I found frightening. She muttered, 'He'll never come back. He used this house to punish me, left it as a burden to break my spirit, but I won't be broken. I won't.'

I nodded gravely.

Farewelling the guests we'd grown fond of over the past four weeks was quite painful. The Rawlins, Dr Pettigrew and Eunice Crooks were the last to leave. We all went down to the road to wave them off. Even Mother came, although she stayed in the background.

I looked back at her standing alone in the wind, her hair blowing and her face drawn and thin, and I thought, if only our father would come back and look after her! I can't do it. I can't.

'Anna, love, now don't forget,' said Eunice, waking me from my daydream. 'Come and see me when you need that bra.'

'Thanks, Eunice, I will. Second floor beside the lingerie.'

She hugged me. The Rawlins hugged us all too.

Then Dr Pettigrew took me aside and said seriously, 'Anna, your mother seems very low-spirited. I'm concerned for her and for you. The responsibility for a family is a lot to ask of a fourteen-year-old, however capable she may be. This is the telephone number at my consulting rooms in case you should ever need it.'

I felt deeply grateful but I couldn't speak. I put my

head down to hide the tears. Crying, that's all I seem to be doing these days.

Then the guests jumped into their cars and drove off slowly, with much tooting and waving out the window.

As they reached the end of our red muddy road their smart cars passed a small battered truck headed in the opposite direction. It was loaded with beds, carpets, chairs, brooms, buckets and pots and pans. On the top of the load perched three scowling children. It was the Milandowskas.

chapter twenty

*W*ell, Mother has really dropped her bundle this time. Apart from the child endowment of a few shillings a week, there is no money at all coming in. Music lessons have finished for the year and the Milandowskas not only pay no rent but they don't even pay for the electricity they use, which is a substantial amount. All because George Milandowska is an 'artist'.

Mr Devlin is still away on his fishing trip so I can't get my father's address to write to him for help.

It is now less than a month to Christmas, when I said I would make a decision about whether to fight on to keep us all together or give up. I must admit that I'm not feeling optimistic about the future.

One of the worst things about Mother's decision to become a philanthropist is that I will never be able to face Michael Cameron again. He is one of the most decent, charming young men I've ever met and now he must think our family is completely unreliable and, as Charlotte would say, 'totally unhinged'. Mother wrote the Camerons the briefest letter, hardly apologising at all for cancelling their four-week holiday. She simply said that due to a change in circumstances the guesthouse would no longer be operating. Uncle Martin, of course, was delighted to lend her the money to return their deposit, and gave her a brotherly lecture about taking on 'hare-brained schemes', after which I heard them both laughing! If I ever meet Michael Cameron in the street or anywhere else by accident, I will just die of shame.

My cousin Sarah is home from school this weekend. She phoned to say that as she was 'at a loose end' she'd ride her bike over from their holiday house at Merlin Heads to visit me. She said she had a book that I'd find very interesting. Sarah's not much of a reader so I wondered what it could be.

We stood side by side in my bedroom, staring down at what had once been the guests' croquet lawn. Now it was almost completely covered with washing lines from which hung a great number of snow-white sheets, pillowcases and shirts. Mrs Milandowska, almost hidden in the billowing sheets, was pegging out the last items, a row of ugly brown stockings. She was a stout woman in her thirties, with a long blonde plait wound round and round her head. She was singing snatches of a Polish song as she worked.

'Why does she have so much washing?' Sarah asked.

'She does it for other people.'

'She's running a laundry? On your property? That's a bit rich.'

I nodded. 'There's never enough hot water left for our showers, but I suppose it's hard to find another job when you don't speak English.'

Sarah shrugged with disapproval. 'Dad says Aunt Katharine's gone soft in the head, letting the whole lot of them live here for nothing. They're only Balts, for goodness' sake.'

'They're not so bad,' I said defensively. 'At least Mother's doing something for them. No one else in the district seems to give a damn.' I felt quite cross with Sarah. 'Where's the book?'

She produced a thick black volume from her bag and laid it proudly on the bed. It was called the *Ladies' Home Journal* and had paper markers sticking out of various pages. Sarah opened it at one spot and showed me a medical illustration of the male body. It was in colour, with fold-out organs – very graphic and a bit shocking.

Sarah turned to another page and read aloud, 'The penis, when erect, measures six to nine inches.' She looked up to gauge my reaction. I tried to look blank. 'During intercourse it is placed inside the woman's vagina, and semen, a thick white substance containing spermatozoa, is emitted.'

'How revolting!' I said.

'You've had absolutely no experience of sex, have you?' she said with satisfaction.

I shook my head.

'I'll tell you a secret.' She paused dramatically. 'I have felt semen.'

'When?' I said, shocked, but trying not to be.

'When we were coming home from England on the *Orsova* last Christmas.'

'Last Christmas?' That was almost a year ago. How could Sarah have had a sexual experience at fourteen?

'Yes. We had this Italian steward called Giacomo with white skin and black hair,' she said with relish. 'He looked as if he never shaved. His beard was sort of blue under the skin, just waiting to burst out.'

I pulled a face. He sounded disgusting.

'One day I was lying down in my cabin when he came in to clean. He looked at me for a long time and smiled in an odd sort of way and then he locked the door. I was so excited I could hardly breathe.'

I stared at her curiously.

'He came and sat on my bed and just looked at me for a while and then he sort of pounced.'

'Pounced?'

'Yes, it was as if he'd lost all control. He fell on top of me and kissed me really hard with his tongue halfway down my throat. I thought I was going to choke, and he sort of massaged my breasts and groaned.'

'Why didn't you scream?' I said in alarm. 'Why didn't you kick him?'

Sarah looked at me as if I was a simpleton. 'Because I didn't want to.' She paused. I thought she wasn't going to bother continuing the story. 'And then he started rubbing himself against me, up and down and up and down and groaning, "Madonna, madonna mia".'

I shook my head but didn't dare ask why.

'And then, all of a sudden, I felt this warm sticky stuff on my leg.'

'You might have got pregnant!'

'It was on my leg, Anna.'

'What did it look like?'

'Clag. Just like the Clag we use at school. White and thick but sort of runnier.'

'Errrk!' I covered my eyes with both hands.

'Well, it was an experience,' said Sarah, sounding superior. 'It happens to every woman.'

'It's never going to happen to me,' I said adamantly.

Then my curiosity got the better of me. 'Did you let him do it again?'

Sarah shook her head. 'I think he got a bit panicky. He kept coming up to me in the corridors saying, "You no tell Papa. You Mama she not like what we play in cabin." '

'What we play?' I started to laugh. Sarah did too. We laughed and laughed.

'Hey!' I said at last. 'I've got something to read to you.'

I took down from my bookcase a small black book and opened it at a marked place.

'The Bible?' said Sarah, disappointed.

'Yes, listen.' I read: 'Thy breasts are like two young roes that are twins, thy belly is as a sack of wheat, thy navel is a golden goblet. We have a little sister and she hath no breasts: what shall we do for our sister?'

'Show me!' Sarah grabbed the bible and read it for herself.

'It's the Song of Solomon. They're full of that sort of thing,' I said knowingly.

Sarah flicked through the pages. 'But it's all about women. Where's the stuff about men?'

I grabbed the bible back from her, opened it at random and, parodying the biblical style, I recited, 'Thy penis is as a dangling flower that is limp.'

She leaned over my shoulder and continued, 'Thy balls are like two hard-boiled eggs that are twins.'

We both exploded with laughter. We laughed until we were helpless.

It crossed my mind that if Reverend Marsden could see me now he would not admire me any more, but even this sobering thought did not make me stop laughing.

Mother has decided to give the Milandowskas English lessons. Every evening after dinner they all troop upstairs and sit around our dining-room table with pencils and paper, chanting sentences while Mother corrects their pronunciation. Mrs Milandowska, who's been working hard at the washtub all day, finds it hard to concentrate, but George, her husband, seems really keen and the three children, Con, Leo and Danka, who are eleven, nine and seven, seem, to my amazement, to quite enjoy it. I must say I find these regular lessons an intrusion. The Milandowskas seem to feel they've become part of the family. Sometimes they don't even wait until we've finished eating before they come charging upstairs and take their places at the table. Mother doesn't seem to mind at all.

I was finishing off the dishes in the kitchen one evening while Mother was articulating clearly and slowly, 'This is a pencil. This is paper.' The Milandowskas repeated whatever she said in unison.

'I am writing on the paper.' I peeped through the servery and saw that Mrs Milandowska was not writing on the paper. She had fallen asleep.

'George, Mrs Milandowska is tired,' said Mother in the same maddeningly correct English. 'I think she should go to bed.'

'Yes, Katharine. I think so you are right.' George got up to help his wife.

'Yes, Katharine. I think you are right. Not "so you are right",' Mother corrected.

'I think you are right,' George repeated obediently.

Just then Eliza came into the dining room in her pyjamas. She looked worried. 'Mummy, can you please ask Danka to give back my doll?'

Danka clutched the doll tighter and scowled at Eliza.

'Don't be selfish, Eliza. Danka does not have as many dolls as you have,' said Mother slowly and clearly, so the Milandowskas could understand.

'But she's had Matilda for three days. I'll give her another doll, but Matilda's my favourite.' Eliza looked distressed.

Mother shooed her away. 'We'll talk about it later.'

The Milandowskas packed up their pencils and paper and went off downstairs, Danka still clutching Matilda.

Later that evening I was studying for my exams in the kitchen when I heard George come back upstairs. Mother had just made coffee and had apparently invited him to listen to a concert on the ABC with her. As John Cargher introduced the Beethoven Violin Concerto I looked through the servery and could see them leaning back on the sofa exchanging smiles. They seemed to enjoy each other's company. George has actually been quite useful because he knows about pianos and has helped to tune Mother's damaged Steinway so that it's almost back to normal. I think he's hoping that in return Mother, with her great influence in Skinners Bluff, will be able to find him a job in the shire office so that he won't have to dig roads all day. In the meantime George and Mother have started practising violin and piano pieces together.

About an hour later there was a knock on the door. It was late for visitors. I listened while Mother went to open it. It was Reverend Marsden! I strained to hear their conversation.

'Will you forgive me?' There was a pause. 'I've behaved extremely badly towards you. Genevieve has been my fiancée for some months but I enjoyed your company so much I . . . Please, Katharine, can we talk?'

I couldn't hear Mother's reply but Reverend Marsden was ushered inside.

I rushed to look through the servery into the dining room, concealing myself by bending low. Reverend Marsden, holding a small bunch of flowers, was unpleasantly surprised to see a strange man sitting on the very sofa that he had often shared with Mother. George was sipping coffee and looking rather smug.

'George, this is Reverend Marsden, the local vicar who helps me with fundraising and borrows my books,' she said coldly. 'Reverend Marsden, this is George Milandowska, a very fine violinist who'll be staying with us for some time, I hope.' She gave George an admiring, affectionate glance. 'He's inspiring me to new heights of performance.'

George stood up and the two men shook hands. George was taller and better built than Reverend Marsden. For the first time I noticed how young and immature he looked.

'Katharine is a fine musician,' said George sincerely, 'and a wonderful teacher of English.'

'George learns very fast. He's hoping to become a clerk in the shire office,' Mother said proudly.

'Many thank yous to Katharine. She found for me the job.'

Mother refrained, for once, from correcting his English. She was enjoying Reverend Marsden's discomfort too much.

'Won't you stay for coffee, Reverend?'

'Ah, ah, no, thank you. I have to prepare a sermon and

I have a confirmation class . . . ah, to prepare for as well. Thank you. Ah, goodbye.' He left in confusion, still holding the flowers.

George got the job in the shire offices. Today was his first day. I watched from my bedroom window while he climbed down the steps to the laundry to say goodbye to his wife. She emerged in a cloud of steam from the copper, looking tired, although it was only eight in the morning. He looked very smart in his suit, white shirt and tie and seemed pleased with himself. He gave her a quick kiss and went back up towards the gate. She looked after him with a mixture of pride and apprehension.

Meanwhile Mother had decided to escort Con, Leo and Danka to their new school, Skinners Bluff State Primary. Eliza and Jonathan were not happy about the idea. 'Please persuade her not to come to our school, Anna,' begged Eliza. 'The kids think she's a loony. She might even make a speech!'

'Why would she do that?'

'It's the last week of school and there'll be an assembly,' said Jonathan. 'She wants the Milandowskas to be introduced properly before the holidays so they won't be scared to come to school on their own next year. She thinks Mr Barton doesn't respect New Australians and he won't tell the kids to respect them either, so she just might make a speech.'

As my school had given us a few days off to study for exams, I offered to escort Con, Leo and Danka to their new school instead of Mother. When she agreed, Eliza and Jonathan were delighted, but as we set off out the gate she suddenly changed her mind. Eliza signalled desperately to me not to desert them so I traipsed along as well. We were a comical little procession, led by Mother striding along in her flowing scarf holding Danka by the hand. Danka looked most peculiar in her very short dress, woollen stockings and large white chiffon hair ribbon. Next came Con and Leo, leaping about in their short leather pants, their shaved heads bobbing up and down like coconuts. Last came Eliza, Jonathan and me, looking as conservative as possible.

We arrived at the school just as the whistle was blown for assembly. The children hurried to line up in front of the flagpole from which the Australian flag fluttered.

Mother had a word to the headmaster, Mr Barton, who was standing in front of the students. He nodded to her and then, to our dismay, she stayed standing beside him, with Con, Leo and Danka in front of her. Jonathan and Eliza hurried in embarrassment to line up with the others and I waited in the background under a gum tree, trying to look as if I wasn't there.

The assembled school of fifty pupils stood to attention.

'I love God and my country, I'll honour the flag, serve the Queen,' they droned, 'and cheerfully obey my parents, teachers and the laws.'

Mr Barton drew himself up importantly, puffing out his chest.

'Boys, *salute*!' he commanded.

They did so very smartly.

'Stand at – *ease*!'

The children obeyed.

'Today, girls and boys, we have some new pupils from Poland.' He deliberately pronounced it Poe Land, which made some of the children titter. Mother was right. He had no respect for foreigners. 'All right, settle down,' he said, smirking at his own joke. 'Mrs Danielssen, who I'm sure you all know . . .' he paused and there were a few more titters, 'has kindly brought the new pupils along, and now she's going to say a few words about them.'

Mother stepped forward. 'Thank you, Mr Barton,' she said pleasantly, ignoring his rudeness. 'Good morning, girls and boys.' She cast her eyes over the assembled group and demanded their attention. Not until she had it did she begin. 'The Milandowska family has had a very different life from yours and mine,' she began conversationally, indicating Con, Leo and Danka. 'They have suffered. They were prisoners of war. Some of you have fathers who were taken prisoner, but have any of you been prisoners? No. Have any of you been separated from your parents?' The youngest children shook their heads. 'Have any of you been thrown into camps with barbed wire around them, left to cry alone in the cold, half-starved for years?' There was a shocked silence. 'I don't think so. We are very lucky people. The war barely touched us. That is why it is our privilege to look after people like Con, Leo and Danka. We are not going to tease them,' she said sternly. 'We are going to welcome them and help them to become fine New Australians. Thank you.'

Some of the children actually applauded. Eliza, I noticed, blushed pink with pleasure. As the younger children marched off to their classroom, Eliza took Danka by the hand.

The school has doubled in size since I was a pupil and there are now two classrooms, one for grades three to eight and the other for the infants. The infants' teacher is a strict old lady with white hair named Miss McGilray. As I passed their classroom I heard her screech, 'What are we, girls and boys?'

'Workers, Miss McGilray!' they shouted back in unison.

'That's right! Tell me again. I didn't quite hear.'

'Workers, Miss McGilray!' they screamed even louder.

'And what are we going to do right now?'

'Work, Miss McGilray. Work, work, work!'

'Then get to it, get to it. Let's see this lovely work!' Through the window I saw her racing along the aisles whacking the three-foot blackboard ruler down hard on each desk. No wonder Eliza had warned Danka a few days ago that their teacher was really a witch.

It was now early December and the weather was getting warmer. I was determined to enjoy the first day of my study vacation and had planned to go for a walk by myself on the beach before starting work to think about my future. When I say my future I really mean Mother's future. She seems calmer now that she's got her way about the Milandowskas moving in, and she's not so tired because there are no guests. Also, she's enjoying the company of George as a musical soulmate as well as someone who admires her and allows himself to be bossed around. What concerns me is that she seems to have completely forgotten about money.

I'm afraid that Mother has lost all interest in getting us out of debt. I don't think she's even continued to pay the mortgage on the house. Usually a few weeks before Christmas she sells a piece of furniture to pay for our presents and get rid of the most urgent bills, but this year there isn't much furniture left, just the oak table, the balloon-backed chairs and the chiffonier, and she hasn't even rung the antique dealer (I know because he rang here the other day and inquired in his oily voice if my mother had 'any of her beautiful pieces she could perhaps bear to part with'. I said I'd ask her but I haven't yet. She gets depressed when she has to sell the family heirlooms, so she's letting the finances slide into the abyss.) I honestly think she believes Uncle Martin will take pity on her and support us all when things come crashing down around our ears, and I couldn't bear to depend on Uncle Martin for anything. I needed to walk on the beach and think of an alternative.

But before I could get out the gate Charlotte beckoned me into her room and whispered that she needed to tell me something urgently. 'Look, the ball is in less than two weeks, right?'

'Right,' I said, although I had forgotten about it, what with all the other drama.

'Mother still doesn't know that I'm going with Dougie, or even that I'm going at all. I told her I didn't want to be bothered with making my debut and she didn't seem to mind. She thinks I'm too busy with *The Gondoliers*. I've told her that I have a rehearsal on the night of the ball.'

'But you'll be getting dressed here, won't you?'

'No, at Mrs Mooney's. Then Dougie will bring the truck round to her back gate. That's where I need your help.'

'Sure. Do you want me to help you get up the ramp?'

'Well, yes, that would be good, but there's another problem.' To my surprise, Charlotte blushed. 'You know how I always get awfully nervous before I go onstage to sing and have to go the lav quite often . . .'

My mouth fell open. 'Oh, no. You can't bend!'

'Exactly.'

'But what can I do?'

'Come with me in the truck and bring some jam tins.'

'What! But how . . . ?'

'Oh, Anna, don't be dumb. Use your imagination,' said Charlotte crossly. 'The trip to Geronga takes about half an hour. I'll certainly need to pee at least twice in that time and the only way I can do it is if you . . . help.'

'But how do I lift up the dress? It's rigid.'

'You don't. You crawl underneath,' said Charlotte, trying to be patient.

'What if you need to go while you're at the ball? Do I have to follow you around the dance floor with a string bag full of IXL tins?'

'No, you idiot! I won't need to pee once I get there. It's just the anticipation before I arrive. Lots of performers have weak bladders before the show. Don't you know anything?'

I started to laugh. Suddenly it seemed the funniest thing I'd ever heard. I rolled on the floor.

'And don't breathe a word about this to anyone!' hissed Charlotte, which only made me laugh all the more.

chapter twenty-one

$\mathcal{I}$ studied for my English and History exams all day
and got so involved that I even forgot to have
lunch. I do enjoy learning things. Sometimes I think I'd
be perfectly happy living alone on an island with books.
Then in the late afternoon I went for a ride on my bike
to get some fresh air. I passed the primary school, where
classes had finished for the day. The playground was
deserted except for a group of older boys standing
around a rusty incinerator bin. Muffled yells seemed to
be coming from inside the bin which was the size of a
large oven. Suddenly a small girl darted out from behind
the school tank where she'd been hiding and ran towards
me. It was Wilma Mooney, and her face looked like a
frightened rabbit's. 'The kids are in the bin and they're
gunna set fire to it!' she shrieked in terror. Then she
raced back behind the tank. I leapt off the bike, grabbed
a large stick and ran across the schoolyard towards the
group around the incinerator. The boys, who were intent
on what they were doing, didn't see me coming. One of
them jumped on the lid and did a sort of war dance.
Another one put his head close to the incinerator and

yelled, 'We were very lucky people. We weren't half starved in the war, so have some crusts!' He lifted the lid a fraction and shoved some rubbish into the bin. The screams grew louder.

'Yeah!' yelled another boy, pushing more rubbish under the lid. 'Have some banana peel and a bit of squashed cake!' They all laughed. They took it in turns to hold the lid down. Whoever was inside thumped desperately.

'The war barely touched us. Well, my dad got wounded, see. How about we show them what war's really like, eh, Maxie?'

'Yeah! Give us the matches and we'll burn the little buggers!'

'Hey!' I yelled. Three of the boys saw me coming and ran off, but the two biggest who were holding down the lid didn't notice until I was almost upon them. I swung the stick high and whacked it across their backs. They jumped off the incinerator. I hurled the lid away. Two heads emerged slowly, covered in filth – Jonathan and Eliza. I hauled the children out, almost crying with anger. Then I lunged ferociously at the two boys, belting them with my stick.

'Get them, Anna! Get Lennie and Maxie!' yelled Eliza.

I chased after them, whacking into them as I ran.

'Stop!' yelled one. 'We was only kidding.'

'It was a joke. We weren't really gunna light it. Leave us alone, Danielssen!'

After another couple of whacks I let them run off and came back to comfort Eliza and Jonathan.

'Don't tell Mummy, Anna,' said Eliza, picking squashed banana out of her hair.

'Why not?'

'She might come up to the school again,' she said gravely.

I nodded in agreement.

Early next morning Con and Leo Milandowska were running madly round the garden in their pyjamas, yelling. Danka, in her nightgown, was chasing after them. I looked down from my bedroom window, wondering what the commotion was about. Then I saw that the boys had taken Matilda, Eliza's doll, away from Danka and were throwing it from one to the other like a football. I hurried to put on my dressing-gown and go to the rescue, but it was too late. Con hurled the doll to Leo and it landed hard on a rock, its china face smashing into pieces. From behind Danka, Eliza appeared in her nightgown and began to pummel Con with both fists. Danka laughed. Con pushed Eliza away. Jonathan, who'd been watching from the balcony of his room, hurled a boot at Con and hit him between the shoulder blades. There was a howl of pain from Con, who looked furiously up at our rooms to see who had injured him. Jonathan had bobbed down, so he assumed it was me. Carrying the boot inside as evidence, he went sobbing to his parents.

Life with the Milandowskas was not proving to be harmonious.

After she finished school that day, I took Eliza to the Doo Duck Inn to try to cheer her up and bought her a double-header ice-cream cone, one side strawberry, the other vanilla. She'd never had a double-header before.

As we sat in the booth licking our ice-creams I leant across to wipe the tears off her cheeks. 'Feel a bit better now?'

'Mmm. But the doll's hospital couldn't fix faces, could they?' She looked down at poor Matilda.

'Well, there'd still be a few little cracks, I suppose. Maybe Matilda could get a new face.'

'No. No, I'd rather keep the old one with the cracks,' she said bravely.

As we came out the door of the Doo Duck Inn I noticed that across the road on the vacant block there was an array of tents and coloured booths being erected, with a flapping sign that said 'Holiday Carnival'. A jukebox inside one of the booths was playing rock and roll music.

Eliza and I walked across the road to have a look. Suddenly a voice called, 'Hullo, Anna!'

I turned and saw Michael Cameron slowly riding by on a bicycle. I stood stock-still. There was nowhere to run and hide. He was wearing shorts and a T-shirt and looked much younger than last time we met. My heart seemed to freeze in my chest.

'Oh, hullo,' I said breathlessly. 'I thought you'd gone back to the country.'

He wheeled around and pulled up in front of us.

'No, we were lucky. The family got a cancellation at Cathken Guesthouse. We're here until New Year.' He smiled and nodded reassuringly as if he understood that I was feeling mortified.

'That's wonderful,' I said, grinning foolishly, and then I started hiccupping loudly.

Eliza stared at me as if I'd gone mad.

Michael didn't seem to notice. He nodded towards the carnival.

'I was going to take a look at this tonight. Would you like to come along, Anna?'

'Oh, all right,' I tried to sound casual, but I was too excited. 'That'd be all right.'

'I'll come and pick you up. At seven?'

I nodded. Michael waved and rode off.

'Is he your boyfriend, Anna?' said Eliza, agog. 'I didn't know you had a boyfriend.'

'He's not,' I said, flustered. 'He's just a friend.' And then I muttered, 'It's a wonder he's even talking to me.'

When I got home I stood for a long time in front of the mirror in my long, silky dressing-gown, trying out poses. I wrapped it tightly round me so that my breasts stood out, then turned side on to get the full effect. In the background I could hear a violin concerto on the wireless. It sounded like Paganini. I began to swirl gently to the music. Then I let the dressing-gown fall open to my waist and watched my breasts moving as I danced. It was not a sexual dance, I told myself, just a romantic one.

I didn't have any fashionable clothes to wear to the carnival – no full skirt with a rope petticoat underneath and pretty cardigan that buttoned up the back like most girls wear nowadays – so I wore my jodhpurs and a cast-off jumper of Charlotte's. It was deep purple, a colour I like, and quite tight, with wide sleeves that taper in at the wrist, a style that's still almost in fashion, so, apart from the jodhpurs, I felt rather smart.

As I was dressing I looked out the window and saw Jonathan sitting on a rock by himself in the garden, staring down at Mrs Milandowska's long line of washing. It was almost as if he was willing it to disappear.

I had told Mother I was going to the carnival with the Camerons and, as she'd met Michael and his family and quite liked them, she didn't object. I neglected to say it was just Michael and I who were going. When he arrived on his bike I was down at the gate waiting.

We walked along, with him wheeling the bike. He talked about his family and I tactfully did not mention mine.

Michael is very interested in facts. He told me that the proportion of Australia's unionised workforce had reached sixty-two per cent and that John Landy had not just broken one world record when he ran the mile in three minutes, fifty-eight seconds, but two, because he had also run fifteen hundred metres in three minutes, forty-one point eight seconds.

I tried hard to think of some facts I knew which might interest him, but apart from Rising Fast winning the Melbourne Cup this year and 'Gelignite' Jack Murray winning the Redex round-Australia car trial, which I felt sure he would know already, I couldn't think of any, so I just listened.

It was getting dark by the time we arrived at the carnival. There were strings of coloured lights draped all over the booths and hanging between the tents and trees. It looked like fairyland. Lots of people were crowding around the stalls and shooting galleries. There was a merry-go-round and a flying boat machine for young children to ride on. I felt a pang of guilt that Jonathan and Eliza had not been invited too. I decided to work in the timber yard on Saturday so I could take them the following week.

Suddenly I noticed the chairoplane. It was a very fast machine that flew around high overhead. The chairs were made of tractor seats on long chains attached to a central pole. People were screaming as they flew out almost parallel with the top of the pole.

'Let's go on that. Are you game?' said Michael.

I nodded.

It was both scary and exciting once we gathered speed. My chair was on the inside of Michael's so he flew out even further than I did. If you bucked in your seat you could make it zig zag and almost crash into the person in front. When we were going at full speed, our eyes and hair streaming, it really did feel like flying. Suddenly Michael eased his chair close to mine and took my hand. I was so excited I could hardly bear to look at him. We flew side by side, hand in hand for the whole second half of the ride.

We had two more rides on the chairoplane holding hands while people down below stared up at us. (I was rather glad I didn't have a rope petticoat and a full skirt after all.) I wondered if there was anyone I knew in the crowd but we were going too fast to see. Michael didn't seem to mind that everyone could see us holding hands in public. I just felt weak with happiness.

When we got off we were quite giddy and staggered about laughing and pretending to fall over. Michael bought me a Coke and then we went off to try our luck at the shooting gallery. I went out after three shots but Michael was very good and actually shot enough ducks to win a prize. There were lots of stuffed toys to choose from. He asked me to choose one I'd like. I chose a little green fluffy dog with a sad face. As we were making our way back through the crowd I was walking ahead when two bodgies in ripple-soled shoes and stovepipe pants pushed against me on purpose. Michael suddenly appeared from behind and put one arm out to hold them back and the other around me protectively. He gave the bodgies a look that seemed to make them shrivel, because they just put their heads down and mooched off into the crowd. Not a word was spoken. 'Thanks,' I said. I do admire that kind of strength in a man.

We had to pay to go into the tent where Bill Haley and the Comets music was playing. Inside there was a huge jukebox and teenagers were dancing, some of them jiving. The girls in full skirts and rope petticoats looked the best. You have to be short, with a tiny waist, fairly big breasts and high-heeled shoes to look fashionable, so at first I thought I'd just watch. But the music was so loud and exciting we couldn't bear to stand still. Michael started tapping his feet and then he held out his arms and I just drifted into them and we were dancing! I'd never jived before in my life and I loved it. It helped that Michael knew when to push my hand so that I'd spin around and then, before I could fall over or crash into someone, he'd catch my hand again and steady me. It was wonderful, much more exciting than ballet. We watched the expert couples who were mostly bodgies and widgies, and picked up a few moves. 'Nice' girls aren't supposed to jive, I know, but somehow I didn't care. It was terrific fun. We danced to 'Crazy Man Crazy' and 'Shake, Rattle and Roll' and they played a new number called 'Rock around the Clock'. I'd never heard it before but we joined in yelling along to the music with everyone else, 'One, two, three o'clock, four o'clock rock . . .'

When the song finished Michael pulled me into a huge hug.

It was the most wonderful night of my life.

I walked into the kitchen at ten o'clock that night to find Mother, Charlotte and Eliza sitting at the table looking very worried.

'Where on earth have you been?' said Mother.

'To the carnival with Michael. I told you I was going.'

'Yes, but why are you so late? It's after ten.'

'It's exactly ten. I told you I'd be home by ten.'

'Jonathan's run away!' said Eliza, looking upset.

'What!'

'He did a dreadful thing to Mrs Milandowska's washing and now he's run away.' Eliza looked as if she was about to cry. 'He told me he was never coming back.'

'What did he do?'

'He put a big dollop of red mud on every one of Mrs Milandowska's snow-white sheets and on every shirt and every stocking she had on the whole clothes line,' Eliza said gravely.

I started to grin.

'He did it on purpose. He told me.'

I laughed out loud. I couldn't help it. I was feeling too happy and relaxed to take anything very seriously. Eliza looked shocked at first, but then she started to laugh too. So did Charlotte. Mother was furious.

'How dare you laugh! That poor woman works herself almost to death and when her day's work is ruined you laugh? Tomorrow you can all spend the whole day rewashing her sheets and shirts and stockings for her!'

There was a short silence in which we three tried to look sorry, and then I asked seriously, 'How long has Jonathan been gone?'

'Hours,' said Mother.

'Where have you looked?'

'All over the house, the Mooneys' . . .' Charlotte said.

'The beach? Have you looked there?'

'It's too dark. He'd be frightened,' said Eliza.

I took the torch, put on my raincoat and set off down the hill. The wind had whipped up and it was beginning to rain. I tramped over the sandhills, calling 'Jonathan!' It was a very dark night. I was heading for the giant sand dune. The tide was high so it was hard walking along the boggy beach and there were rocks jutting out into the sea that I had to climb over. Every few minutes I'd stop, cup my hands to my mouth and yell, 'Jonathan!' I hoped he might see the torchlight even if he couldn't hear my voice above the wind.

When I reached the huge sand dune I stood at the bottom and peered up. It looked eerie by torchlight, with gusts of sand blowing across its pale expanse.

'Dear God,' I whispered, 'if you let me find him, I'll believe in you for the rest of my life, and I'll never think one rotten thought about her again. Please, God, let me find him.'

Then I turned and started the steep climb up the dune. It took longer than I expected, and I was breathless by the time I reached the top. My eyes were becoming used to the dark now. I flopped on the sand and yelled 'Jonathan!' Silence.

What if he'd fallen off one of those rocks and been washed out to sea? He hadn't taken a torch. It would be easy to miss your footing on a night like this.

I was just about to give up and trudge home to get help from Dougie Devlin or the police when I heard an odd sound like a cough. Behind me there was a clump of tea-tree. I stumbled towards it. The torch beam picked out what looked like a canvas sheet flapping in the wind. 'Jonathan!' I ran forward, lifted the flap of the one-man tent, and there he was, curled up in a sleeping bag.

'I'm not coming home,' he said croakily.

'I need you, Jonathan. I need you to help me.'

'I hate them. I hate George and Mrs Milandowska and Danka and Con and Leo. All of them!'

'I know, but I need you to help me find our dad.'

'We haven't got a dad.'

'We have. I'll show you his letters.'

'He's dead!'

'He isn't. I'll prove it to you.'

When we reached The Tower House it was after midnight. The lights were still blazing. The others seemed to have gone to bed. Mother was sitting at the piano playing a mournful piece. She looked haunted. We stood quietly by the door for a few minutes but she didn't notice us. Gently I pushed Jonathan, still carrying his bedraggled little tent, towards her. She hugged him. Tears of relief streamed down her face.

chapter twenty-two

As the next day was a Wednesday and Charlotte had to go to town for rehearsals, Jonathan, Eliza and I were left to rewash Mrs Milandowska's sheets. By eight a.m. they were already bubbling in the copper. I was prodding and stirring them with a long wooden pole. Jonathan and Eliza were feeding the rinsed sheets through a manual wringer and catching them in a wicker basket, ready to be hung on the line. With steam completely enveloping us, we felt like experts, moving in unison and pretending to be some efficient industrial machine.

'We could go into business,' I said cheerfully.

'Once we get rid of the Milandowskas,' said Jonathan.

He picked up the heavy basket of wet sheets and struggled with it towards the laundry door. Con appeared in the doorway, blocking his way and looking amused. He pointed a finger at Jonathan, jeered and then ran off. Danka popped her head round the door and stuck out her tongue at Eliza.

'Cheeky brats,' I said. 'I don't care if they did lose all their possessions in Cracow.'

'Anna!' Eliza looked shocked.

I helped Jonathan carry the basket to the clothes line and we began pegging out the sheets. Con and Danka kept running around us, ducking in and out under the line and getting in our way. We ignored them. When Mrs Milandowska appeared they ran off. She approached us and stood watching. She smiled, pointed at the washing and said, 'Goot children. Thet is goot!'

We smiled back.

When she had gone Jonathan said, 'When are you going to show me those letters?'

'Tonight. When George comes upstairs for their little soirée.' Using a peg as a bow I imitated George playing the violin as if his life depended on it. Jonathan grinned.

'Now, both of you, hurry off to school. I've got study to do.'

That evening after dinner I kept watch from the servery in the kitchen to see when it was safe to take Jonathan to the attic. Mother and George had been engrossed in playing the andante movement of a Schubert piano trio for some time. It was a tender, yearning piece which Mother played with feeling but I didn't think that George played very well at all. He kept stopping and making mistakes but Mother was very patient. Once they'd finished, Mother would make coffee and, as it was a fine night, I thought they'd probably take it out onto the balcony and we could get past them to the attic without being seen.

When they finished playing George stayed very still. The piece seemed to have awoken painful memories.

He turned to Mother. 'The last time I play this I am a prisoner. I play it to the German officers. Afterwards we are sent to a labour camp near the city. We march each day from the camp to the city. There are many beatings from the guards. I have a mark . . .'

He drew back his shirt and showed her a scar about six inches long on his chest. He gently placed Mother's hand on it. They stared at each other sorrowfully. Then she removed her hand.

'Your life will be much happier now, George,' she said softly.

'Katharine, I am sure of it.'

They looked at each other again and for a terrible moment I thought they would certainly embrace, but suddenly Mother turned and walked quickly away. 'I'll get the coffee,' she said.

I unlocked the attic door and we made our way inside. The torch made a faint beam of light in the gloom. Jonathan followed close behind me and stared around in wonder. Everything looked so musty and covered in cobwebs.

'There's my rocking horse!' he said excitedly. 'Mummy told me it was sold.'

'Shhh. She'll hear us!'

He poked about in silence, discovering pieces of clothing he recognised, books and a box of ancient tin soldiers.

'Why does she keep it all locked up?' he whispered.

'It's her past life. She comes up here sometimes.'

He looked hurt. 'I loved that rocking horse.'

'Here they are!' I shone the torch into the box of letters tied with ribbon, took a small pile out and untied them.

'Don't! She'll know,' said Jonathan, alarmed.

'Don't you want to find out what he wrote to us?'

He nodded uncertainly. I looked at the postmark on the top of the first letter, and read aloud, 'Townsville,

244

September, 1943. That's too early.' I flicked through the letters. 'Here's one dated 1947.'

'That's the year Eliza was born,' he whispered.

I opened the letter and began to read. It was written to Mother. 'He says he's put a lot of money in her bank account. He wants to come home and restore the house. This house. It isn't finished yet and he wants to make it safe for Anna to . . . "Please let me see the children, Katharine. If you are determined not to have me back, at least let me visit them. I have never seen my own baby daughter. Can you imagine what that feels like?"'

'Who? Eliza? Why hadn't he ever seen her?' said Jonathan.

We stared at each other like explorers, half afraid of what we were discovering.

'Mummy said he ran away and left us,' he said. 'She said he couldn't care less about us.'

'It's not true, is it?' I said, hurriedly retying most of the letters but keeping about a dozen aside.

One had slipped onto the floor. 'Hey, this one's addressed to you!' said Jonathan excitedly.

'Look at the big print. I must have been too young to read properly.'

I opened the letter quickly and began to read it. Tears trickled down my cheeks. Jonathan passed me his hand-kerchief. I took it but did not wipe them away. I just kept reading.

Later that evening, I couldn't stop thinking about those letters. Even though it was late I ran down the road towards the Devlins'. There was a light burning in the kitchen so I knew someone must still be up. Please, God, let Mr Devlin be home from his fishing trip, I prayed.

As I ran into the yard I saw his utility. 'Thank you, God. You little beauty!'

I knocked on the back door and Mr Devlin opened it. It was almost as if he was expecting me. I beamed at him and he ushered me in without a word. Inside a cosy fire was burning. The Devlins' is a messy, welcoming sort of house. The remnants of a meal were still on the table – three tin plates full of fish bones and leftover chips and three empty beer bottles. On the floor were piles of old newspapers, fishing tackle, rods, boots and coats. Two large dogs lay by the hearth. Smoky Dawson was playing on the wireless. Luckily Dougie and Warren were out so I could talk to Mr Devlin privately. He ushered me over towards one of the armchairs by the fire and offered me a glass of lemonade. I sipped it absent-mindedly.

'Mr Devlin, I've just read a letter my father wrote to me years ago. It was very affectionate but I never got it.'

He nodded slowly, keeping his face lowered.

'There are others too, written to my brother and sisters. None of us has ever been given a letter from our father, although we would have loved them. Jonathan believed he was dead! For some reason Mother has kept the letters from us and I thought you might understand why. You're the only person I know who was a friend of his. Please, can you tell me where our father is?'

Mr Devlin sat down in the armchair on the other side of the fire and looked at me gravely.

'Seven years ago I made a promise, Anna.'

'What promise?'

'To your mother. That I'd never talk to you about your father. Never answer any questions. Never mention him.'

'But why? Why won't anyone talk about my father?'

'He hurt your mother very much.' Mr Devlin looked hard at me to see if I knew any details and, concluding that I didn't, he said decisively, 'but that's in the past. He's been punished enough, I reckon, and you deserve a few answers too. Ask what you like.'

He held out both hands with the palms facing up, inviting me to speak. Suddenly I felt scared. 'Go on,' he said encouragingly. 'Ask away.'

I couldn't say anything. Jack Devlin was my father's friend and I knew he'd tell the truth about him. I wasn't sure that I wanted to hear it.

'Was my father a coward?' I blurted out.

Mr Devlin narrowed his eyes. 'No, Anna. He was ill.'

'What sort of ill?'

'Nerves. He had nightmares after the crash. They sent him home early. He was in a bad way. He spent months in hospital in Melbourne. He was a sensitive chap and the war did a lot of damage to his nerves.'

'But he recovered?'

'Well, they sent him home from hospital but he still had the nightmares. Some nights he'd come over here for a few beers and tell me about them. Shocking.'

'He was a drunk?'

'No, Anna, he wasn't.' He said this with conviction.

'So what was the reason their marriage broke up?'

Mr Devlin began slowly. 'Kate never forgave him for being sent home early from the war. It was sort of a disgrace. Well, you know your Uncle Martin, what a hero he is. Two medals for bravery. Kate thought your dad was weak compared to him. Your uncle didn't help matters. He made up nicknames for your father. The Viking

Raider, the Norse Avenger and Eric the Red. Sarcastic bastard. I never liked your uncle much.'

I was surprised. I'd never heard Mr Devlin say a bad word about anyone. 'I might be prejudiced, of course. He worships the royal family and he hates Irish Catholics. Eight hundred years we suffered under the likes of your Uncle Martin. Do you know much about Irish history, Anna?'

'Not much. I know the potato famine was a disaster and the British didn't help.'

'And the Devlins suffered along with the other millions in that famine while the Fitzsimons raised the rents.' He looked angry for a few seconds and then smiled and said, 'Ah, but I'm getting off the track. Ask me about your dad.'

There was a pause and then I took the plunge. 'Did Thelma have anything to do with the marriage break-up?'

He smiled, remembering his daughter with affection. 'Thel was young. She liked your dad. Admired him. Listened to his stories. He was a handsome fellow too. She knew he hadn't been getting on well with Kate ever since he came back. It happened to a lot of ex-servicemen. War changed them. One night after he'd been over here telling stories Thel invited him to stay.'

'With her?'

'It shouldn't have happened but it did. Kate found out and that was it. She threw him out. Refused to let him back inside the house.'

'She would've been hurt.'

'She was. We weren't exactly in her class neither.'

'And Frank was . . . more like you?'

'He was well educated but he wanted to work for me,' said Mr Devlin proudly.

'Building houses?' I asked enthusiastically.

'He would've been good.'

'She wouldn't have liked that.'

'No, she didn't like it,' he said bitterly.

'So where did my father go when she . . . threw him out?'

'He rented a shack near the Merlin River. Used to take you up there, play with you for hours building sandcastles.'

'And making dams and houses for crabs! I remember that, but why did he go away?' I asked in desperation. 'Why did he leave us?'

'Kate decided to punish him. She got a court order to stop him seeing any of you.'

'How could she do that?'

'It wasn't hard. He'd left the marital home. Deserted her, according to the law. Thel was named as the scarlet woman.' He narrowed his eyes and said bitterly, 'I over-heard your uncle telling your mother Thelma was a Catholic slut, and I nearly flattened him. It was all pretty ugly.' He paused. 'So Thel went to England and your dad went up north.'

I felt shocked but I wanted to know more. 'He went to Townsville. The letters were from Townsville. Do you know if he's still there?'

Mr Devlin nodded. 'Still in Townsville. He was there for part of the war. Seemed to like the place.'

'Who does he live with now?' I felt scared again. He probably had a new family.

'As far as I know he's alone.'

'You've got his address, Mr Devlin?' I asked eagerly.

'Yeah.' He wrote something on a piece of paper and handed it to me. 'I reckon he'd like to hear from you, young Anna.' He winked. 'You're a bit of a chip off the old block.'

I ran all the way home feeling elated. I had found my

father and he was like me! In looks? In personality? It didn't matter which, as long as we were similar. I had never felt close to Mother. We had always clashed. Perhaps that was why we clashed, because I reminded her of our father. Suddenly everything began to make sense. I would write to my father, ask him to send me the train fare and I would travel to Townsville this very school holidays to meet him. Who knows, he might invite me to live up there, I fantasised as I ran up the path to the front door, and Jonathan and Eliza could live there too, even Charlotte if she stopped disapproving of him.

I pushed open the door and crept down the hall as the lights were all off and I didn't want to wake Mother.

As I passed the dining room I saw that a lamp had been left on in the corner and I was just going to turn it off when I heard voices and saw in the dim light two people sitting on the sofa. I drew back and listened.

'You think it is easy to leave a wife and children? Carola and I, we spend many years in prison apart from our children,' said George huskily. 'Now we find a good life together. You think I want to break up my family, Katharine?'

'No, George, I don't. Of course I don't.'

'But it's too late. I love you, Katharine! Of course I will leave them. I have already told Carola. What else can I do? I am in love with you.'

'George, you are not in love with me. We have just been friends,' said Mother firmly and kindly, 'and now I think you should go back downstairs to your family. Good night.'

That night I stayed up late writing to my father. I told him how happy I was that Mr Devlin had told me he was living in Townsville and not overseas as we children had been led to believe. I didn't say that Mother had deliberately lied to us because I wanted him to think well of her. I said that we all missed him very much and would love to see him soon. I told him how Jonathan and I had found some of his old letters in the attic and had been very moved by them. I said that Mother was finding it increasingly difficult to cope on her own. I didn't go into details as I didn't want to alarm him or frighten him off. I told him how much we all loved The Tower House and how grateful we were to him for doing it up and building the tower. Then I just wrote little bits of personal news about each one of us which I thought he might want to hear.

At the very end I said:

What I have been avoiding asking until now is whether you would consider coming back to live with us so that you could be the father we all need so badly. I feel sure that you and Mother could overcome your differences, as I know that you both loved each other very much at one time. I hope you do not feel that I am asking too much. It is just a suggestion, but one that I hope you will consider very seriously.

Your loving daughter,
Anna Danielssen

Early next morning on the way to school I posted the letter. I thought it would probably take three days to get to Townsville. With any luck I should have a reply by early next week. I could hardly contain my excitement.

chapter twenty-three

*M*other was in one of her wildly cheerful moods this afternoon when I got home from school so I didn't mind that she forgot to ask me about my exams. Her eyes were shining, she had picked a huge bunch of blue and white agapanthus from the garden which she was arranging in her favourite cornflower-blue jug and she was singing a skittish folksong.

'It was on a Monday morning that I beheld my darling,
She looked so sweet and charming in every high degree,
She looked so sweet and charming o,
A washing of her linen o,
Dashing away with the smoothing iron,
She stole my heart away.'

For one mad moment I thought my father must have got my letter overnight and telephoned her to say he loved her deeply and was coming home immediately, but it wasn't that.

'Anna, you will not believe this, but I have been offered a job,' she announced proudly.

I stared at her in disbelief. 'Really?'

She took a typed letter from the pocket of her housecoat and tossed it to me. The address at the top read Mount

Enderby Grammar School. This is an Anglican boarding school just outside Geronga which I would love to go to if we had the money because the students learn dancing, acting, music and horse riding as well as the usual subjects.

'A teaching job?' I asked doubtfully. Mother had no formal qualifications.

'Just piano to private students, and I'd also be required to organise a concert or two. What do you think of that?' She beamed at me.

'It's wonderful, but when did you apply for this job? I haven't heard anything about it.'

'Ah, I've been keeping it a secret.' She patted the cushion next to her. 'Sit here and I'll tell you all about it. The headmistress, Miss Hawthorn, is a friend of Reverend Taylor from St Peter's here in Skinners Bluff.'

I nodded. Reverend Taylor, the old white-haired vicar who looks a bit like God, sometimes comes to Mother's soirees.

'He noticed the advertisement in the local paper about a month ago and suggested to Miss Hawthorn that I would be an excellent piano teacher and also told her that I gave little concerts for the local people. She called me in for an interview at the school. Quite an informal interview; we laughed a lot and ate rather too many cream cakes. We did like each other. She was very keen on the idea of me organising soirees at the school, and now she has formally offered me the job, commencing early next year.'

'Oh, Mummy, you're a genius! A genius! A proper job! I can't believe it. This will solve all our money problems!' I leaped up and hugged her.

She pushed me gently but firmly away. 'I'm not sure that I will take this job, Anna.'

'What! Why ever not?'

'It's a very responsible position. I'd have to travel to the school almost every day of the week, and when the end of year concert was on, I'd probably have to rehearse with the students on weekends.'

'But it's not far to travel on the bus. Less than half an hour. I do it every day. We'd all help at home. We'd be so proud of you having a real job, and we'd be wealthy!' I was jumping on the spot with excitement.

'I don't know. I'm thrilled to be offered the job, Anna, but I really don't think it's for me.'

'Oh, please don't say that! It's a gift from heaven. Reverend Taylor probably pulled all kinds of strings to help you get it. He knows how broke we are.'

Mother's smile faded. 'Yes, he does, which is another reason I feel loath to accept it. I don't want charity.'

'It isn't charity. The headmistress liked you. You said so, and it's a bloody good job!'

'That's enough, Anna. If I took that job I'd be a kind of servant to the school.'

'Everyone who takes a job is a kind of servant. What's wrong with that?' I shook my head. 'Look, if you'd just swallow your pride you could keep this family together,' I was pleading. 'You could do it!'

'I'd rather you didn't mention this offer to the others, Anna.' Mother took the letter, put it back in her pocket and walked out of the room.

I felt like shaking her till her head fell off.

On Friday morning I was waiting at the school bus stop when I overheard a group of older girls from my school talking.

'Last day, thank God.'

'Lucky you. I've gotta come back next year. Gotta get me Intermediate.'

'Not me. I couldn't stand it. I've got a job in Woolworth's.'

The girl who had to stay on at school suddenly noticed me. 'Oooh, look who's listening in. The Balt lover.'

'Balt lover?' I said in confusion.

'She doesn't know what you mean, Shirl,' said the other girl sarcastically.

They moved towards me and closed in on either side menacingly.

'She thinks she's better than us because her mother's the famous Mrs Danielssen who gives to the poor,' said Shirl, so close that specks of her saliva hit my cheek. 'Your mum's a stuck-up prig, Danielssen!'

'Yeah, and that's not all she is!'

'Judy and I know something about her that even you don't know.'

'What are you talking about?' I tried to sound calm although my heart was beating wildly. The girls were talking loudly and others had turned to watch. I wished some of my own friends would appear but none of them got on at this stop.

'What are you talking about?' mimicked Judy, exaggerating my tone in a superior manner. She looked around to check that all the others at the bus stop were listening and then announced in a voice that was almost a shout, 'What we're talking about, Danielssen, is that your mother sleeps with Balts!'

There was laughter from some of the schoolkids and a shocked silence from the others.

I raised my hand and lunged towards Judy, but before I could reach her Shirl wrenched my school hat down over my eyes. I heard more laughter. Shirl jerked the hat back up and slapped me hard on the face. I reeled back in shock.

I was still upset when I got home from school that afternoon. I'd had to go straight into a full day of exams so I hadn't had time to think much about it until then. I hadn't reported the attack at the bus stop to any teacher because I didn't want to be questioned about the reason for it. All I knew was that I'd been utterly humiliated in front of other girls from my school and I felt like dying. I would think of a way to get back at Shirl, but first I had to confront Mother.

As I climbed the steps that pass the Milandowskas' downstairs apartment I heard sobbing. I looked through the window of their bedroom and saw Mrs Milandowska lying on the double bed crying. She seemed half demented. Every few seconds she would jump up, go to the open wardrobe and rip bits off the sleeves of her husband's immaculate white shirts which were hanging in a row. Then she would fling herself back on the bed and continue her sobs. I watched for a few minutes and then carried on up the steps to our kitchen.

Mother was banging saucepans about, preparing dinner. She seemed agitated. It would have been impossible for her not to hear the sobbing downstairs.

'Why is Mrs Milandowska so upset?' I asked, trying to control my anger.

Mother looked up at me quickly, like a bird alert to danger. 'How should I know? She's an over-emotional European. A frustrated peasant.'

'I thought you liked her.' I was tight-lipped with rage.

'I never liked her. I felt sorry for her.'

'Do you feel sorry for George?'

'Of course,' she said lightly.

I flared up. 'Why don't you ever tell the truth?'

'Don't be impertinent!'

'You don't feel sorry for them. You use them. You think they're pathetic so you play games with their lives.'

I paused. I wanted to say, 'You flirt with George until he's convinced that you love him and he tells his wife he's leaving and then you say to the poor idiot that you're just good friends!' But I didn't say that. Instead I said, 'You play games with everyone's lives. Mine. Eliza's. Jonathan's. Reverend Marsden's. Our father's. Everyone's but Charlotte's because she's too smart for you.'

'What on earth are you talking about?'

'You lied to us. Our father did love us! You never told us that. You let us think he didn't care, but I know he loved us. I've read his letters.'

There was a pause. The atmosphere was like ice. We stared at each other. Then the self-control she had taught me triumphed over my emotion and I said calmly, 'I think the Milandowskas should go.'

'I've already asked them to leave,' she said, equally calm. 'George is not such a fine musician as he led me to believe.'

'And *that's* the reason you asked them to leave?'

'Not entirely. As you might have noticed there is some friction between our two families.'

'So where are they going?' I knew it was impossible to find a house to rent in Skinners Bluff so close to Christmas.

'I've arranged accommodation for them in a holiday flat near the beach. It's not large, but the children will be able to walk to school from there and George won't have to change his job,' she said matter-of-factly, 'And, Anna, I'd like those letters back please.'

'I've put them back. Except for mine. I'm keeping those.'

I was about to walk out of the room when I remembered something. 'Did you accept that job at Mount Enderby Grammar?'

'No. I turned it down.'

'Fantastic,' I said grimly. 'I would have expected you to have more courage.'

I was feeling quite defeated as I climbed the stairs to my little salt-caked room to study. It's rare for me to feel so hopeless.

That evening, just before bedtime, I found Eliza sitting on the floor of her bedroom in semi-darkness, clutching one of her soft toys and crying quietly. I squatted down beside her and put an arm round her shoulder.

'What is it?' I asked gently.

'Jenny's mum won't let her come here any more,' she sobbed.

'Why?'

'Because Mother's having an affair.' The sobs grew louder. 'Jenny's my best friend after Wilma. First I wasn't allowed to play with Wilma because she's too common and now I'm not allowed to play with Jenny because of the stupid affair. I haven't got any friends left!' She turned to face me. 'What's an affair, Anna?'

'It's nothing,' I hugged her and then pulled her up to sit on my knee. 'It's sort of like having a crush on someone. Tell Jenny's mum it's only gossip anyway. It isn't true.' I became indignant for Eliza's benefit. 'Our mother would never do such a thing!'

She brightened up instantly and became indignant too. 'No, she wouldn't, would she!'

The Milandowskas left early the next morning. It was Saturday and I watched from the balcony as the last of their belongings were packed back up on the battered truck. Eliza and Jonathan came and stood beside me. Mrs Milandowska looked dignified and distant. She didn't turn around to look back at our house but sat quietly in the front seat of the truck, staring straight ahead. Con, Leo and Danka, sitting up on top of the load of furniture, turned and waved to us and called goodbye. They seemed quite sorry to be leaving. Although we didn't share their sorrow, we waved and called back. We even smiled at them. George looked dreadful. As he walked around the truck checking that the load was tied on securely, he stumbled and bumped into things. He looked like a big broken doll. He kept turning to look back at our house, hoping to see Mother at one of the windows, but she didn't appear. The truck drove away. After it had gone I saw Mother standing alone on one of the smaller balconies, staring out to sea. Her face was wracked with grief.

She went to her room to lie down. A few hours later I opened her door and looked in. She was lying with her face to the wall but she wasn't asleep.

'Would you like a cup of tea?' I asked softly.

She turned slowly towards me and her face was streaked with tears. She put out her hand and beckoned me to come closer. I sat on the bed and took her hand.

'You didn't like him, I know that,' she said, 'but I want you to understand something . . . he was very like your father.'

I didn't want to have George Milandowska compared to my father. 'You don't have to tell me about it.'

'But he was!' She seemed determined that I should hear. 'I want you to know. I want you to know why I was . . . fond of him.'

'Try and sleep. The doctor says you have to get some sleep. I've brought the tablets.'

Our doctor had visited her earlier in the week because she had complained of being unable to sleep at nights.

I took two sleeping tablets from the bottle and put them beside her glass of water. Then I picked up the bottle and was leaving the room with it when she gestured for me to come back.

'Leave them there,' she said firmly.

'He said only two.'

'Leave them!'

I waited for an instant, considered arguing and then, resentfully, I put the full bottle down beside her.

'He was nothing like my father,' I said with scarcely controlled anger. 'He was just a Balt like all the others. Why do you always . . . romanticise everything?'

'At first I thought he was an artist. A fine musician. I am so lonely for someone to share my . . . music with, Anna.'

'He worked as a coffin maker in Cracow and played the violin in a cheap café at nights. Con told me,' I said brutally.

Mother turned away from me then. She said in a very small voice, 'I've been foolish. You're very wise, Anna. Sometimes I feel as if you are the mother and I'm your child.' Her body shook as she wept silently. I wanted to hug her but I couldn't quite bring myself to do it. There was too much resentment. I wanted to shout, 'I don't want to be your mother. I need a mother of my own,' but I didn't. I felt sad to see her so vulnerable. I covered her gently with the tartan rug.

'I'll bring you some tea.'

'How is she?' Michael asked next morning on the beach.

'Still the same. I wish she'd get better.'

'What did the doctor say?'

'Can't find a thing wrong with her. She just lies there looking pale. She cries a lot. She doesn't eat or sleep much. She's lost interest in everything since . . . I've given up.' Suddenly I felt angry. 'I wish she had a husband to look after her.'

Michael and I had just had a swim and were lying on our towels sunbaking. I lifted my head and a stream of water dripped out of my nose. I laughed, embarrassed.

'Only sea water,' he said. 'Mine's worse.' He shook his wet, curly head from side to side like a dog, but no water streamed out.

'Very polite nose,' I said.

Michael makes me feel so relaxed I can say almost anything to him. Silly things like that, or serious things.

'So now that school's broken up, when do you get your exam results?' he asked.

'They'll come in the post in a few days' time, I suppose.'

'You don't sound too worried about them.'

'Well, I am. If I don't do well enough to get a preliminary teaching bursary that will pay for the next two years' school books and uniforms, I might have to leave and work in Woolworth's,' I said seriously.

'Which department would you like?' he asked, straight-faced.

'In Woolworth's? Lollies. I'd like to be the girl in the pink and white cap who gives out bags of broken chocolates free to schoolkids every Friday afternoon.'

We both laughed. He had the knack of changing my bad moods in an instant.

'Still no reply from your father?'

I shook my head. 'Maybe he's changed his address.'

'If he has, the post office will send your letter on,' Michael said. 'About your mother. It sounds to me as if she's suffering from depression.'

That afternoon I took the *Ladies' Home Journal* that Sarah had kindly left for me to study sex from its hiding place under my bed and looked up 'Depression'.

Depression, according to this heavy black medical book, was also known as 'involutional melancholia'. It was an emotional state of mind that made the patient feel gloomy and inadequate. Depression could be so severe that the patient lost touch with reality and had to be treated as insane or 'psychotic'. I read that some depressive behaviour was more frequent in women than in men and that shock treatment was often used if the patient was severely depressed.

I put the book down to think. Surely she wouldn't need shock treatment. I'd heard horror stories about people in lunatic asylums being forced to undergo electric shock treatment. They had to be restrained in straitjackets and, if not protected, they could bite off their own tongues. Afterwards some of them became mute and unmoving, like vegetables.

Certainly Mother was gloomy, and felt inadequate and withdrawn, and she did seem to have lost touch with reality because she kept falling in love with hopeless men and imagining they were like my father. I wished there was someone who could advise me what to do. The local doctor had never even mentioned depression. He thought Mother was just 'run-down' and needed sleep. I remembered what I'd overheard her saying to Uncle Martin about her 'bouts of melancholy'. I wanted to ask him for advice but hesitated, for fear of having him move in and take over our lives.

That evening I was preparing a dinner of boiled eggs and toast on the wood stove while Eliza sat at the kitchen table humming contentedly. There was a mess of toys, books, food and clothing all over the kitchen. It was rather cosy by candlelight with the wood fire crackling. Jonathan came in with Mother's tray and put it down on the sink.

'Did she eat anything?' I asked, without turning around.

'Only the dry toast.'

'I like having no electricity,' said Eliza, spreading thick cheese and Vegemite on her toast, 'and I love this Velveeta cheese. Better than that smelly old Stilton stuff.'

'Did she say anything?' I asked Jonathan.

'She asked when Uncle Martin was coming.'

'Never!' said Eliza. 'Are we getting the water cut off too?'

'No, the rates have been paid,' I said hastily.

'Is Uncle Martin coming?' Jonathan asked me.

'Yes, I'm afraid so.'

There was a knock at the door. We exchanged anxious looks. Uncle Martin never knocks and we weren't expecting anyone else.

'Anna, it's only me, love,' called Mrs Mooney.

I opened the door. We were all pleased to see her. She came in carrying a steaming bowl covered with a doily. She looked about her and we realised with shame that although she'd been a regular guest at Mother's soirees, she'd never been invited into our kitchen, the intimate part of the house. I guessed that she only felt secure about coming here now because Mother was out of the way.

'I brought some chicken broth for your mum,' she said, putting the bowl on the table. It smelt delicious. 'Lights gone out, have they?'

'Yes, we got the final notice a week ago,' I explained.

'Ah.' Mrs Mooney understood completely. 'Never mind. If any of yous want a bath, come over to my place.'

'Thanks, Mrs Mooney.'

I must have sounded very grateful because she patted me on the arm and said kindly, 'You managing everything all right on your own, Anna? Charlotte's not much help, what with rehearsals for the ball and that darn comic opera.'

'Yes, yes, we're fine, thanks. Uncle Martin keeps asking us all to come and stay with him but we're all right.'

'Oooh, I forgot. Did you see that picture of Reverend Marsden and his fiancée in the paper?' She produced a newspaper cutting from her apron pocket. 'Genevieve. Lovely name. Pity your mum was too sick to go the engagement afternoon tea. He invited all the parish. Gee, she's a lovely looking girl, isn't she?' She peered over my shoulder at the photo. 'Too good looking to go and be a missionary in China, Ernie says, but that's what she wants to do.' She laughed. 'Good job those Balts left, Anna. Smelly lot. Cooking up all that garlic and cabbage.' She wrinkled her nose in disgust. 'Your mum's so good to people, though, isn't she? That's how she makes herself sick, I reckon.' She suddenly beamed. 'Oh, some real good news we got today. Ernie's got a job on the Kiewa Scheme. Hydro-electricity. Got to live up there in the mountains for weeks at a time with a hut full of Balts, but it's good money. Ernie's on top of the world! Leaves tomorrow morning –'

Mrs Mooney suddenly froze. Mother was standing in the doorway in her dressing-gown, staring at her with contempt.

'I, I just brought you over a bit of soup, Mrs Danielssen,' she stuttered nervously.

'Thank you. I've already eaten,' said Mother arrogantly.

'That's all right,' said Mrs Mooney, trying to sound cheerful. 'Keep it for tomorrow. It's good broth.' She removed the doily and showed the soup to Mother. 'Build your strength up.'

'I don't want it,' said Mother adamantly.

Mrs Mooney looked hurt and began backing out of the kitchen with her little bowl. 'I'll be off then. Bye bye, kids.'

'I don't want that woman here again,' said Mother, almost before she had closed the door behind her. Then she asked me pathetically, 'When is Martin coming?'

'Soon.'

Mother turned vaguely as if she wasn't quite sure where she was. I motioned to Jonathan and Eliza, who leapt up, took an arm each and guided her slowly back to her bedroom. I stared after her sadly. I would run down to Mrs Mooney's place and apologise later. She'd never seen Mother in one of her black moods. Mother was usually more careful about hiding them from everyone but us.

Uncle Martin arrived about an hour later and, while

he was in with Mother, Sarah and I sat together on the sofa chatting. I feel much more equal to Sarah than I did a few weeks ago. She spent a long time telling me all the latest developments about her romance with the Grammar boy, Gareth. (He had 'felt her up' after the school dance and she'd encouraged him to go further, but unfortunately the school bus had come early and his housemaster had surprised them in the bushes and given Gareth a detention.) Then she asked me about Michael.

I felt rather shy about discussing him with anyone, even Sarah, who tells me everything.

'Eighteen! Gareth's not even sixteen. He must be quite experienced!' she exclaimed.

'He's not. I mean, it isn't like that.'

'Has he kissed you?' she interrogated.

I blushed. 'No, but we've sort of hugged.'

Sarah rolled her eyes in disgust.

Luckily Uncle Martin came out of Mother's room right at that moment. He closed the door quickly but I could still hear Mother crying. Sarah and I both looked up gravely.

'Sarah, would you mind getting my briefcase from the car?' he asked her.

Sarah seemed to understand that he wanted to speak to me alone and went off obediently.

'She's got depression, hasn't she?' I said.

Uncle Martin sat down beside me. 'Depression? Well, I don't really know, Anna. Perhaps she has. It's a depressing sort of life she leads. She's a sensitive woman. She deserves something better.'

I wished he would try and take this seriously. 'Depression is a real condition, Uncle Martin. I read about it in a medical book. She's got all the symptoms.'

'Has she?' He sounded vaguely interested.

'Yes. It makes her say things she doesn't mean.'

Suddenly he was alert. 'What sort of things?'

'She feels guilty about everything. Once she said she had no right to live.'

'She should go into hospital for a rest. At once.' He was brusque, trying to hide his feelings. 'She's very run-down after trying to turn this place into a guesthouse. Ridiculous notion. I'll be over here first thing tomorrow. Don't worry, Anna.' He patted my hand inexpertly. 'She's just having one of her bouts of melancholy.'

'Uncle Martin, what will happen to us if she goes into hospital? Shall we stay here? We'd be quite all right.'

'You'll stay with us, of course.'

'But what about the house? The goats and bantams need looking after and the garden and . . .'

'The house is going to be auctioned, Anna. Just after Christmas. Didn't your mother tell you? The sign will be up on the front gate before you're awake tomorrow morning.'

chapter twenty-four

$\mathcal{I}$t was very early morning. Patches of pink sunrise still flecked the sky. I had just come back from a fast ride on the beach and was rubbing the sweat off Grayling with a towel. As I rubbed I sniffed because it was still cold and I was close to tears. I stared resentfully at the large AUCTION sign attached to the gate of The Tower House.

Michael rode up on his bike, propped it against the fence, and we both stared at the sign. He'd been the first person I'd rung last night as soon as Uncle Martin told me the bad news.

'Whoever buys it will pull it down and build a revolting block of holiday flats. I just know they will,' I said angrily.

Then I gave a sort of gurgle and sobs came bursting out. Michael put his arms around me. He was wearing a cream woollen jumper and I tried not to get it damp. Michael passed me his handkerchief and when I'd stopped sniffing I looked up and saw that Grayling was staring at me with his ears cocked as if he knew something sad was happening.

'Anna!' Eliza was standing at the back door in her dressing-gown, looking down at us. She seemed a bit embarrassed, as if she'd had to wait until Michael had finished holding me before she could call out. 'Come and have some toast. I made cinnamon for Mummy, but she won't wake up.'

Michael and I hurried up the steps.

Mother was lying absolutely still in bed with her eyes closed.

She was paler than usual. I shook her a little and said firmly, 'Katharine, wake up!' I pretended to be the matron at her boarding school. If she was shamming she'd probably start to laugh. She didn't move. 'Please, Mother, please wake up!' I felt her pulse. It was very weak. I sent Eliza out and then I whispered to Michael, 'I let her keep the pills. It's all my fault.' The bottle I had left by the bed was gone. We searched under the bedcovers and the bed, and found it, empty, under her pillow.

To my surprise I did everything that had to be done quite calmly. I sent Eliza to wake Jonathan and told them both to get dressed. Then I rang the ambulance service and our local doctor, explaining that it seemed Mother had taken an overdose of sleeping pills and was unconscious. They both said they would be at the house as soon as possible. I rang Charlotte at Beverley's place and told her to come home. Last of all I rang Uncle Martin. For someone so cold and well bred he sounded quite emotional. He said he would be there in a few minutes. I said, 'Please drive carefully,' which surprised me. He asked if there was anyone with me besides Eliza and Jonathan and I said there was Michael.

'Good,' he replied.

Mother was being carried out on a stretcher by the ambulancemen when Uncle Martin arrived. He looked quite dishevelled, with his hair sticking up and his shirt hanging out. His eyes were red, as if he'd been crying. The sight of him so lacking in composure alarmed Eliza and she began to cry. We were all afraid that Mother might be going to die. When I gave the empty bottle to the doctor who'd prescribed the pills, he just shook his head. He said he'd ring me as soon as there was any news, and went off in the ambulance to the hospital with Mother. Uncle Martin grabbed her hand as she was carried down the steep path and walked alongside her, wiping his eyes. He said he would go to the hospital but that we should stay home by the phone and wait for news.

When the ambulance had driven off with its bell clanging, Eliza turned to me and said, 'Couldn't she just cough those pills out like Snow White did with the poison apple?'

'I hope so.'

'If she does, do we still have to go and stay with Uncle Martin?' Eliza persisted. 'I hate Uncle Martin.'

'It's just for a little while.'

'I'd rather go to Uncle Martin's than St Augustine's Orphanage,' Jonathan said quietly.

'What?' I said, shocked. 'Whoever suggested that?'

'Mother did. She said that if she got really sick and Uncle Martin wouldn't have us, Eliza and I would have to go to St Augustine's.'

Eliza's mouth fell open in disbelief.

I tried to make a joke of it. 'I'm sure she didn't mean it. She was just unwell, Jon. You know how she gets.'

'You wouldn't let her put us in the orphanage, would you, Anna?' Eliza looked as if she was about to cry.

'Of course I wouldn't,' I laughed. 'Don't even think about it.'

We all went into the kitchen and Michael made pancakes covered in golden syrup which Jonathan and Eliza ate in their fingers. The children seemed surprised that I wasn't hungry.

After they'd eaten as many pancakes as they could I asked Eliza to go and feed the bantams and Jonathan to let the goats out and tether them to their stakes in the bottom garden where they keep the grass down. I wanted to keep them both busy.

While I sat with my eyes glued to the phone, willing it to ring, Michael took my hand. 'I've never seen her look so pale,' I kept saying. 'How could she say such a thing to Jonathan? She must have been desperate.'

'You were right to tell him she didn't mean it,' he said comfortingly.

Suddenly there was a yell from the garden. Eliza came panting into the kitchen. 'Tabitha's gone and tied Jonathan all up and he can't get away!' she announced.

I leapt up to go to the rescue but Michael said, 'I'll go. You stay by the phone.'

'She's a very clever goat,' Eliza explained to Michael as she took his hand and skipped out the door. 'Do you know what she does? She waits until you're hammering in the stake and then, very quietly, she runs round and round you on her chain and before you know it she's tied you to the stake!'

I stared at the phone. It did not ring.

Ten minutes later Michael came back with Eliza and Jonathan.

'That big FOR SALE sign on our house looks dreadful,' said Eliza. 'I hope they take it down soon.'

'As if anyone would want to buy this place!' said

Jonathan. 'You should hear what people call it,' he told Michael.

The phone rang. I sprang towards it. I felt as if I was moving in slow motion and it would stop ringing before I could reach it. 'Yes?' It was our doctor. I listened carefully. The others watched me in silence. 'Oh, is she? Thank you.' Tears of relief streamed down my face. 'Thanks, Dr McAuliffe. Thank you.'

'She coughed them out!' yelled Eliza. 'Didn't she, Anna?'

'Well, sort of.' I didn't think I'd mention the stomach pump.

'Just like Snow White. I knew she would!'

I was laughing with happiness and hugging them all. 'She's going to be all right, but she'll have to stay in hospital for a little while under observation.'

'Awwwgh! So we still have to go to Uncle Martin's,' Eliza moaned.

'Yes.'

'I wish you were coming with us, Anna,' said Jonathan.

'I'll be there in a few days' time.'

'Are you sleeping in The Tower House all by yourself?'

'No, I'm staying with the Mooneys.'

'Lucky pig!' Eliza said.

That afternoon I went to visit Mother in the Geronga Hospital. Michael drove me there in his family's big black Ford. He said he'd wait for me outside. We parked under a shady gum tree and he took out a book and put on his reading glasses. I laughed because he suddenly looked so learned. He was reading *Pears Cyclopaedia*. 'No wonder you know so many facts,' I said.

'Got to do something to impress you,' he replied with a grin.

I smiled because I knew this wasn't true. He learns facts because he loves them. I couldn't care less about them. In fact, I sometimes get a little bored when he recites statistics on weather and athletes, but I would never hurt his feelings by saying so. He is such a gentleman and so very kind. I think I must be a little bit in love with him. Even wearing glasses he looks handsome.

I have only been a patient in hospital once in my life, but as I hurried along the corridors searching for Mother's room, the memory of it flooded back to me. Perhaps it was the smell of disinfectant or the polished linoleum or the clang of sterile bedpans.

I was five when I caught scarlet fever and had to be admitted to the Infectious Diseases section of the public hospital. The children's ward was long and full of crying. We weren't allowed any visitors because scarlet fever was contagious and very dangerous. Several children had died of it.

Every afternoon at about two o'clock Mother would come to the footpath outside the hospital with Charlotte to wave to me. I was allowed to stand at the window. Our ward was on the fourth floor so it was hard to talk to people so far below, but Charlotte had a loud voice and she would shout jokes to me. I could never hear them properly but I'd always laugh at the end. Mother delivered an ice-cream to me every day but I didn't always get it. The nurses thought it was unfair to the children whose parents didn't bring them ice-creams, so they shared them around. I didn't tell Mother this.

We ate food that had almost no taste – runny porridge,

lumpy custard and rice pudding – from the same bowls every meal. They were made of enamel that had chipped away and when we all ate at once our spoons scraped horribly. Even today if I hear the sound of a spoon scraping an enamel plate I feel like crying. It is such a lonely sound. I stayed in the isolation ward for five weeks.

I found Mother's room at last and knocked gently. A soft voice called out, 'Come in.' She was sitting up in bed with a tray of lunch that seemed, to my surprise, to be almost all eaten.

Mother looked much less pale. Her hair was brushed, she wore some lipstick and the sun was shining through her open window. I placed the small bunch of blue wildflowers I had gathered that morning on her tray and said, 'Pincushions. Your favourite. I know we're not supposed to pick them, but I thought it wouldn't matter just this once.'

She smiled. She seemed different. In better spirits. More serene. Rather vague.

'They're lovely, darling.'

'Are you feeling better?'

'Yes. Much better, thank you.'

I felt a surge of relief. Perhaps our doctor was right. All she needed was rest, and, I thought sadly, to get away from us and The Tower House.

I put the flowers in a vase and filled it with water. 'Charlotte sends her love. She's coming in to see you later this afternoon, and Uncle Martin's bringing Jonathan and Eliza in tomorrow.'

Mother nodded and smiled.

'Did you say Charlotte is coming tomorrow?'

'No, later this afternoon. Uncle Martin is bringing the little ones tomorrow.'

274

'Ah, I see.' She looked surprised at her own forgetfulness. 'I hope the little ones weren't too upset . . .'

'They're all right. I'm glad you're feeling better because I wanted to tell you something,' I said, before I lost the courage to do so. 'I've written to our father. I've asked him to come back to us.'

Mother's face suddenly changed. Her whole body became agitated. 'No, Anna. No.'

'I know you don't like talking about him, and that you had a horrible time bringing us all up by yourself, but please, I really need to know. Why did you tell us that he didn't want to see us any more?'

'I didn't want you to be hurt,' she said softly, 'as I was hurt.'

'But we felt like orphans. Jonathan told people our father was dead!'

'It was better that way. I didn't need him,' she said coldly.

'We needed him! Didn't you think of us?' I tried to sound reasonable and sympathetic. 'Look, I know about Thelma. It must have been awful for you.'

She looked quickly away, stared out the window and said nothing. Then she said almost to herself, 'Why did he do it? To humiliate me?'

'It was a mistake. He loved you. Read the letters!' I produced the small pile I'd been concealing in my bag. 'He asked you to forgive him.'

'I couldn't,' she said definitely. 'It was too public. Everyone knew. They sniggered at me. At my bloated belly, because they knew he'd been with her.' She paused and then, half-smiling, said, 'I still loved him, you see.' Then came another lightning change of mood. 'But he humiliated me! So I punished him. I forbade him to see you children.'

'But that was punishing us!'

Mother nodded and said very quietly, 'And he punished me by leaving me alone in poverty in the wretched, crumbling Tower House. My albatross. I hated it!'

I was confused. 'If you hated it so much why did you pretend you wanted to save it?'

'You wanted to save it, Anna. You're like him. Determined to do what you want.'

'What I want?' I was suddenly furious. 'What about you? You tried to leave us! To die. You don't want us. You never have. All you care about is your music and your "good works" and your games with men.' I took a breath and then said vehemently, 'Why did you have us if you didn't want us?'

Mother looked at me calmly and said, 'I think you almost hate me.'

'I don't!' I felt desperate to make her understand. 'But I'm scared I'll get like you if I stay living with you. You play with people's feelings. You make men fall in love with you and half the time you don't even want them. Like George, and Reverend Marsden. It's just a game.'

'You're growing up, I see,' Mother said coldly. 'You're jealous of me, Anna.'

I was so shocked I almost laughed. 'Jealous? Of you? I'd hate to be like you. I don't care how beautiful you are. I'd never seduce a younger man in the sandhills, kiss him passionately when he was engaged to someone else!'

Mother stared at me in silence. She realised what I'd seen. Then, in a rage, she shouted, 'Get out! I don't want you! Go to your father! I don't want to see you ever again!'

I stared at her in shock. I hadn't meant to cause such anger. I moved towards her, hoping to calm her down, but she picked up the vase of pincushions and hurled it at my head. I ducked down and it smashed against the wall, scattering slender blue flowers all over the floor.

'Hypocrite!' said Mother in a low, threatening voice that chilled me. 'You little hypocrite.'

'What are you saying?'

'Don't you remember?'

'Remember what?'

'It was you who sent him away. You!'

I felt afraid. She was forcing me to remember something very painful.

'No,' I murmured. 'I don't remember.'

'You were six. It happened in the dining room at night,' she prompted.

The memory was coming back. There was a dreadful sound of weeping that went on and on. Mother was lying on the sofa and I stood beside her in my nightgown shouting at someone. I was very angry although I was so small. I couldn't stop myself. I was shouting at my father to leave the house and never come back. He wouldn't go. I shouted that we didn't love him any more, and other things.

'He made you weep,' I said brokenly. 'You were always weeping.' The memory of what I had shouted at him was very painful.

'You sent him away and he never came back. I would have forgiven him.'

I shook my head angrily. 'You wouldn't! You'd never have forgiven him. You were going to walk into the sea.'

'What?' Mother whispered.

277

'You told me, "If he doesn't go away, I will walk into the sea." '

'I would never have said that to a child of your age.'

'You did.' I spoke calmly, telling her what I had told my father when I was six, repeating the dreadful words that made him leave the house. 'I said that if he didn't go away you'd walk into the sea and the water would cover you all over till you couldn't breathe. He cried when I said that. He said he was sorry. I didn't like him crying. He was useless!' I said vehemently. 'I told him I hated him, and then he went.' There was a long pause as I realised what I had just admitted to myself. 'I said I hated him, but it wasn't true. It wasn't true!' Tears streamed down my face.

Mother stretched out one hand towards me in consolation and said, 'You were always a strong girl, even when you were little. Unlike Charlotte you took responsibility. I needed you, Anna. I still need you.'

'I don't want you to need me!' I said and rushed from the room.

Michael saw my tear-stained face but tactfully didn't ask questions. He probably guessed I'd had a row with Mother. I felt like telling him the truth and saying, 'Look, you might think I'm a sweet young girl but really I'm a monster. I say things that upset my mother so much she throws vases at me. I'm the one who told my father to leave home. I'm the reason we've all grown up believing he didn't love us. Don't waste your time being nice to me, Michael. I can't control my anger and I don't deserve a thing.'

But I didn't say that. I just stared out the window at the cows grazing and the orchards passing by and let Michael

278

pass me bits of Cadbury's Dairy Milk Chocolate until we were nearly at Skinners Bluff and then I said, 'Would you mind dropping me off at the Devlins', please?'

Michael looked hurt, as if he wondered why I couldn't bear to talk to him and yet I'd happily pay a social call on some neighbours. I felt sorry to have hurt him but I just couldn't explain. There was a hard lump in my throat that wouldn't let me speak. I wouldn't have blamed him if he decided never to see me again, but as I was getting out of the car he said in a subdued voice, 'See you Friday night, then.'

I'd almost forgotten about the Lady Mayoress's Debutante Ball, to which Dougie was escorting Charlotte and Michael and I had agreed to play supporting roles.

'Yes, see you then.' I tried to smile. 'Thanks for the lift.'

As I was running into the Devlins' place I thought how casual and offhand I must have sounded, as if he meant nothing to me. I hated myself for treating him like that. He must think I'm a heartless, immature schoolgirl. I suppose in a way I am.

When I knocked on the Devlins' back door I could hear hillbilly music playing on the wireless. Mr Devlin opened the door and ushered me in. Dougie and Warren were dismantling a motorbike on the carpet. They'd put newspaper underneath to stop grease dripping, but it wasn't quite adequate. Tools lay about all over the floor and two dogs were finishing off the remains of some fish and chips wrapped in newspaper. Mr Devlin apologised for the mess and after I'd said hello to Dougie and Warren (Warren was still a bit sullen towards me because of that awful day I'd gone for a ride in his car), we went into the kitchen.

Mr Devlin must have noticed I'd been crying because

he said, 'Lemonade, young Anna? Second thoughts, what about a shandy?'

He took two bottles from the ice chest and poured us both a mixture in tall glasses. I'd never had a shandy before. It was quite pleasant.

After he'd asked about Mother and I'd told him that she seemed much better, he said, 'I'm glad you called in. I've got something to show you.'

He produced a telegram from his pocket and held it up, grinning.

'For me?'

'I was just going to bring it over to you.'

'From . . . my father?'

'I reckon he thought it might get to you quicker if he sent it care of me.' He winked.

'You wrote to him?'

'Same time as you. He only got our letters yesterday.'

I felt like hugging him. 'Oh, Mr Devlin, thank you! I just had a funny feeling when my father didn't write back to me that he might contact you instead.'

I ripped open the telegram.

Mr Devlin waited while I read it several times. Then I took a deep breath and read it aloud to him.

'SORRY CAN'T COME BACK TO LIVE WITH YOU BUT WHY DON'T YOU COME TO TOWNSVILLE FOR CHRISTMAS STOP YOU ARE WELCOME TO STAY WITH ME AS LONG AS YOU LIKE STOP LETTER AND TRAIN FARE FOLLOWING STOP GIVE MY LOVE TO CHARLOTTE, JONATHAN AND ELIZA AND MUCH LOVE TO YOU STOP FROM YOUR FATHER FRANK DANIELSSEN.'

chapter twenty-five

The first thing I did after leaving the Devlins' was to race to Cathken Guesthouse to show Michael the telegram. I hoped he'd forgive my bad behaviour in the car when he saw how happy I was. It was late afternoon and the guests were mostly out at the beach or playing tennis. As I hurried along the verandah towards the rooms his family was staying in I saw him waiting for a game by the side of the tennis court with an attractive girl a bit older than me. They were standing side by side, both wearing whites, and she was throwing her head back to laugh at something he'd just said. Suddenly he put one arm around her waist. Someone was taking a photograph. I didn't wait to see who it was. I felt sick with jealousy. I turned and went quickly back the way I had come. He'd found someone much more suitable than I could ever be. How could I have imagined he liked me?

I heard footsteps running along the verandah behind me. 'Anna, wait!' He grabbed me from behind and swung me round to face him. The girl was puffing along behind him. 'I'd like you to meet my sister, Jennifer.' I put out my hand to shake hers, smiling far too widely. She must have thought I was an imbecile.

After we'd chatted for a few minutes Jennifer said she had to go back because the court was free. She seemed to sense that Michael and I wanted to be alone together. 'I'll play with Dennis if you want to sit this one out,' she said casually. She had the same good manners as Michael.

When she'd gone I said excitedly, 'I've got something to show you.' He nodded and we walked along the veran- dah towards the garden where there was a little stone seat under an archway of pale-yellow climbing roses that had gone a bit dry because of the heat. We sat down and I passed Michael the telegram. He must have read it several times because he held on to it for a long time.

'He sounds as if he really wants to see you,' he said. 'Are you disappointed he's not coming down here?'

I shook my head. 'No, I'd rather go to Townsville.'

'Alone?'

I laughed because he looked so worried. 'I'll be all right. It only takes four days by train, Mr Devlin said. He told me my father builds houses up there, weird ones, out of natural materials like mud and river stones and whole great trees.' I laughed again. 'I wonder who'd live in them.'

'We might,' said Michael, and then he kissed me.

Afterwards I tried to remember what I'd felt. Not surprise. No surprise at all. Just happiness. Happiness flowing through me as if this was what I'd been waiting for all my life and now it had come, and then I felt quite separate, like some spirit looking down on the two young people sitting on the stone seat under the dried yellow roses gently kissing.

After the kiss Michael and I walked back along the

verandah holding hands. He said that he'd better go and play tennis with Jennifer as he'd promised, and I said I'd better get back to Mrs Mooney's where Charlotte would be waiting for me.

I walked there in a daze of happiness. My life was changing, becoming wonderful. I had found my father, who'd invited me to come and stay for as long as I liked, and Michael had just kissed me.

Would I tell Charlotte about all this? About our father, yes. But about Michael, not just yet.

Charlotte and I had been given permission by Uncle Martin to stay at the Mooneys' for the next week until he and Aunt Ursula could arrange accommodation for us at their house in Geronga.

What with Sarah and Tom home from boarding school, Eliza and Jonathan moving in, and Mother about to take over the guest room as soon as she comes out of hospital, their house would be unusually full.

We were delighted to be staying at the Mooneys', even though their cottage was tiny and we'd have to share a springless bed on the verandah under a mosquito net, because it meant we could go to the ball without being caught. Mrs Mooney, of course, knew all about it, and it was she who'd suggested, about a week ago, that as I'd agreed to travel to Geronga in the back of the truck with Charlotte, I might as well go to the ball as well!

I hadn't even considered this. What would I wear? Who would be my partner? Would I be able to dance as well as the other guests? Wouldn't someone realise I was only fourteen and throw me out? How could I afford to buy a ticket?

Mrs Mooney had found a solution to all of these problems.

'I've got a lovely emerald-green gown that would fit you perfectly if I let the hem down,' she told me. 'I only wore it twice, just before I met Ernie. I was going to sell it but it's got sentimental value. Michael will be your partner and pay for the tickets – sheep farmers can afford it. Charlotte can teach you the steps of the foxtrot and waltz, and the rest are easy. You'll pick them up. You've been a ballet dancer.'

'But won't I look too young?'

Mrs Mooney had laughed. 'Not when I've finished with you. The dress will make you look sixteen. The green will match your eyes and look wonderful with your red hair, and with a bit of rouge and lipstick, some green drop earrings and some high-heeled shoes I just happen to have and your hair done up in a French roll, you'll look eighteen at least!' She was even more excited about me going to the ball than I was.

She was right about Michael. He agreed to be my partner and then offered to pay for our tickets even before he was asked, which was very thoughtful of him. He seemed quite pleased to be invited with Charlotte and Dougie. They'd met once or twice at the beach and we'd all sunbaked together. I'd asked Michael what he thought of Dougie and he'd said he was a decent chap who worked hard and was already doing very well in the timber and building business. They'd discussed engines, which was a bit boring for Charlotte and me. From what I'd overheard, Michael could pull motorbikes to bits and put them together again just as well as Dougie could. He also said he used one to round up sheep on his property, which was a bit disappointing. I'd always imagined him riding a horse.

At least Michael and Dougie would have things to talk about when they sat up front together in the truck on the way to the ball while I 'assisted' Charlotte in the back. Of course our partners knew nothing about the real reason I was travelling in the back. They thought I was just keeping Charlotte company.

When I got to Mrs Mooney's I took Charlotte out on the verandah to show her the telegram. After she'd read it she just said, 'I suppose it would be all right to meet him, but it's an awfully long way to travel. What if you don't like each other?'

'Charlotte! Of course we'll like each other. I gave you his letters. He loves us, all of us.'

She shrugged. 'He hasn't even seen us for eight years. He'll probably think we've grown up like Mother and find us intolerable. He might at least offer to travel down here and meet us all, instead of expecting you to go there alone. What if you get kidnapped on the train?'

I laughed. 'I'm not an idiot. I won't talk to strange men,' I said mockingly. 'It'll be an adventure. Anyway, I'd love to see the tropics where he lives and see the houses he builds . . .' I broke off, hoping I didn't sound too much like Mother, talking about 'adventure'. I realised Charlotte was probably hurt that he hadn't invited her to travel north as well. 'Why don't you come with me? I'm sure he'd send you the fare if you wanted to come. He'd love to see you, Charlotte!'

'I don't think so. He didn't have much time for me when I was nine. We'd have even less in common now.'

'But you said you hardly remembered him. What do you remember?' I said, hungry for details.

'A big man with a loud voice. Arguments. Mother getting upset. Me going into my room and singing loudly to drown out the noise.'

'Weren't there any good times? Didn't he take you places? To the beach?'

'I hated the beach when I was young. Didn't like getting sand all over me, getting sunburnt, those awful picnics. I hated salt water, those awful murky rock pools where we were supposed to dive in and see if we could touch the bottom. Full of slimy kelp.' She shuddered.

I had learned to swim in one of those pools.

'Well,' I said sadly, 'I suppose we're just different. I can't believe you don't have one nice memory of our father.'

I waited hopefully and after a few seconds Charlotte said, 'He used to take us to the Fitzroy Gardens in Melbourne. Do you remember that?'

I shook my head. 'I must've been too young.'

'He was on leave. It was before he was posted overseas, so you would've been two and I'd have been five. He'd meet the train from Geronga and Mother would hand us over and then go off to a concert by herself and he'd take us to the gardens. Once, when he met the train, I remember him saying, "The baby's shoes are dirty." You were the baby. And Mother got that fiery look in her eye and then said absolutely coldly, "You try running through red mud at six in the morning to catch the bus to Geronga in white shoes," and that was that. They didn't talk much.'

'And what did we do in the Fitzroy Gardens?' I asked eagerly.

'Ran across the lawns screaming while he chased us,

286

visited Captain Cook's Cottage, gaped at the Fairytree, leaned over the fence to look at the miniature Tudor village of Stratford-upon-Avon, where Shakespeare lived, and tried to catch carp in the ponds.'

'Did he let us do that? It's against the law.'

'He didn't seem to mind. He caught one in his hand once and held it up to show us. He asked you if you'd like to have fishy in a dishy for lunch. You said very seriously, "No thank you very much. I'd prefer a meat pie without any sauce," and for some reason he thought that was hilarious. He laughed his head off and gave you a big hug. You were always serious and spoke correctly, even then.'

'I wish I could remember him better,' I said. 'Was he good looking as well as charming?'

'Tall like you and fair like me and, yes, I suppose he was, though I always thought he was too hairy.'

'How do you mean?'

'You know, hairy arms and legs and chest. Hairy.'

'I'm hairy on the arms and legs, but it's fair hair. Does it matter?' I asked anxiously.

'I think you should shave it off before the ball.'

'Really?' I looked at my arms in dismay. 'Wouldn't the hair just grow thicker if I did that?'

'Yes, of course. You'll have to keep doing it. It's part of being a well-groomed woman.' Charlotte gave me a superior look. 'Fortunately I don't have your problem.'

I made a pledge to leave my limbs hairy and risk being poorly groomed, at least until after I'd met my father.

'Didn't we go to see films with him sometimes?' I asked Charlotte. 'I have a vague memory of films about animals. Badgers and hedgehogs and squirrels hibernating in hedges.'

She groaned. 'Mother was the one who took us to those. She thought these "educational" films would elevate our minds because they were English, not Australian.'

I laughed. 'When I was six what do you think she took me to see for my birthday?' Charlotte continued indignantly. '*Bambi*? No! *The Great Mr Handel*, a dreary thing about nothing but one man playing the piano. I grew up believing all films were long, educational and incredibly boring!'

'You must admit, though, she's an original sort of mother,' I said affectionately. I seemed to have forgiven Mother everything, now that I'd found my father.

Charlotte shrugged and didn't seem inclined to say anything else, so I listened to the sound of the waves for a minute and then I said, 'Will you really be happy living with Uncle Martin and Aunt Ursula?'

'Oh, it will be all right for a while. At least there'll be some order after the chaos.' I felt hurt that she hadn't said she'd miss me. 'Anyway, who knows what might happen in the future?'

'You don't feel sad about selling The Tower House?'

'Not much.' When I looked away she said crossly, 'Anna, you know it was a disaster.'

I thought I'd better change the subject before I got angry or cried.

'Are you excited about the ball?'

'Yes.' Her eyes lit up. 'I'm glad you're coming too. With Michael. Of course you'll only be watching us dance a lot of the time, but you'll get a chance to have a go at it later in the evening. I must say that Mother's timing for that hysterical act couldn't have been better. She's safely in hospital for at least three more days and we won't have to creep around deceiving her like we thought we would.'

'How was she this afternoon?'

'Fine! She thrives on a bit of drama and attention. There are messages and flowers and visitors galore. She loves it.'

'Come on. You don't think she took those pills just to get attention, Charlotte. She wanted to die!'

'Well, why didn't she?'

I stared at my sister in disbelief.

'Because fortunately we got her to hospital in time to have her stomach pumped. If I hadn't gone riding early and Eliza hadn't brought her breakfast in bed . . .'

'I know. I wasn't there! I should have been there to help and I wasn't. If I had been there I'd probably have slept in till ten and she'd have died. You, as usual, were the responsible daughter who found her and saved her life. Well, that's all going to change now. You can stop being the martyr of the family. Uncle Martin has been dying to look after Mother for years. Let him!'

'But he'll crush her. Break her spirit. Don't you see that?'

Charlotte shrugged. 'Never! They just enjoy arguing. They're Anglo-Irish. They love it!'

'But Mother's ideas are so different from Uncle Martin's. He's mean and she's generous . . .'

'He's being pretty generous inviting us all to come and live with him.'

'I don't think that will work for long,' I said. 'Aunt Ursula will get fed up and put her foot down.'

'Well, it's the only solution in the short term,' said Charlotte decisively.

'Mother and Uncle Martin do seem to like each other's company,' I said doubtfully, 'but I'm not sure that she should live with him. He's a bully.'

'And she's a drama queen. Well matched.'

'What will you do? You won't be able to stand by and watch them fighting.'

'I won't be there for long,' said Charlotte. 'Something is sure to turn up . . .'

'. . . as Mr Micawber would say,' we said in unison. Then we laughed. A foolish family joke. I felt sad because soon we'd be a family no longer.

I must have looked mournful because Charlotte jumped up and gave me a hug, which was not like her. 'Now, come and we'll practise the foxtrot,' she said.

Mrs Mooney had set up the wind-up gramophone on the verandah and we turned it up loudly so we could dance right down one end and back.

The Mooneys came out on the verandah to watch and some of them joined in. We did the foxtrot, the Pride of Erin and then the waltz to 'Irene Goodnight'.

I wondered if Mrs Mooney was missing Ernie. I couldn't imagine that she would. She seemed much more girlish and light-hearted since he'd gone away to work on the Kiewa Scheme, but while we were dancing to 'Irene Goodnight' she said quite sadly, 'This is his favourite song.'

When Charlotte and I were in bed on the verandah that night under the green mosquito net, listening to the pounding of the surf, I said, 'Won't you really miss The Tower House?'

She didn't reply and I thought she must be asleep.

'I will miss it, Anna, but not as much as you.'

I felt grateful to her for saying that.

'Do you have our father's address?' she asked then.

'Of course,' I said eagerly. Maybe she'd changed her mind and was going to ask him for the train fare to Townsville. 'He'd love to hear from you.'

'I might send a telegram.'

'A letter takes less than a week.'

'It's more urgent than that.'

'What is? What do you need to know?'

'Shhh. Let's get to sleep.'

'No, tell me.'

'Shhh.'

chapter twenty-six

'*O*h, we should take a photo!' said Mrs Mooney.

Charlotte and I were both dressed and ready to be loaded into the truck.

'There'll be plenty taken at the ball,' said Charlotte.

'But only of the debutantes. I'd love a photo of Anna too. She looks like Scarlett O'Hara in *Gone with the Wind*!'

I blushed. I'd been amazed at the change in my appearance caused by Mrs Mooney's gown, make-up, hairdo, shoes and shimmering earrings. She'd been like a fairy godmother transforming Cinderella ready for the ball.

'I'm glad we decided to scrap the French roll,' said Mrs Mooney, fussing with my hair. 'Having it all free and flowing is much lovelier.'

Charlotte pulled a face at me behind Mrs Mooney's back. She was feeling miffed that she, the debutante, was getting less attention than I was. 'The ugly duckling turns into a swan,' she cooed.

I laughed. 'Thank you.'

The little Mooneys all crowded round, making noises of admiration. They said Charlotte was the most beautiful lady they had ever seen, and she did look superb. Her skin was peachy and her hair had been curled so that it fell in bunches of pale gold down her back and almost touched the low neckline of her dress. The dress was white silk with a tiny waist and a wide, wide skirt so that when she danced she would look like a fine china doll in a mass of swirling silk. She wore silver shoes, white gloves to the elbow and a necklace of pearls, which had been Mother's gift for her seventeenth birthday. They had belonged to Great-grandmother Fitzsimons.

'Here they are!' shouted Raymond as the truck backed into the Mooneys' overgrown driveway. 'Here's the boys!'

The children all ran out to meet Dougie and Michael, and Mrs Mooney yelled at them to look out or they'd get squashed under the wheels. Didn't they know it was Friday the thirteenth?

Dougie and Michael leapt down from the front seat and came striding towards the verandah to meet us. They looked wonderfully handsome in their dinner suits and bow ties. Mrs Mooney had lit two hurricane lamps and placed them on either side of Charlotte and me so that we were spotlit as we stood waiting. She'd told us not to move until the boys had got a good look at us. This romantic little trick worked well because we could tell that Dougie and Michael were impressed. Dougie was speechless and Michael said, 'Anna, you look like a princess.'

'No, no, I'm Scarlett O'Hara!' I said and twirled my imaginary fan.

Charlotte gave me a withering look and said, 'Have you got everything we need?'

I understood and grabbed my ancient handbag from the hook I'd hung it on just inside the door.

'You can't take that bag, Anna!' said Mrs Mooney in dismay.

'It's all right, I'll leave it in the truck,' I said with a smile. We were off down the driveway on our partners' arms, with all four Mooney children whooping along beside us. Dougie leapt up and let the ramp down with a clatter. He had lined it with a strip of red carpet.

The little Mooneys cheered.

Dougie and Michael each took one of Charlotte's arms and guided her slowly up the ramp. Next it was my turn. I gave Mrs Mooney a hug. 'Thank you for making me beautiful,' I whispered. Then I was standing beside Charlotte, waving down at them all, and the boys were locking us in.

As we drove out of the bumpy drive we lurched to one side and both squealed with surprise. We steadied ourselves by holding on to the leather straps hanging from the roof.

'Oh no!' said Charlotte.

'What?'

'Quick. Get a jam tin!'

'Not already?'

'Yes!'

I grabbed my handbag and produced one of Mother's tall crystal wine glasses wrapped in tissue paper.

'Oh, Anna, you idiot.'

'It's much more refined than a jam tin,' I said proudly.

'But it's too small!'

I looked at the glass in disbelief. 'I can empty it.'

'Where?'

I looked around and it was true, there was nowhere to empty a wine glass of unwanted liquid.

'Quick! Get it ready!'

I lifted her gown and crawled underneath. The skirt was so wide that there was quite a lot of room to move down there. It was like being inside a birdcage. I pulled down her pants and held the glass in place. To my relief, she only half filled it. I hitched her pants back up and carefully crawled out, balancing the wine glass.

'Thanks,' said Charlotte. 'Now, think of a way to get rid of it.'

I walked first along one side of the bouncing truck and then along the other, examining every square inch for an opening through which I might dispose of the liquid. There was none. It was hard to balance the glass as we hurtled along.

'Hurry up!' said Charlotte.

I looked at her, aghast. 'Not again?'

'I told you to bring jam tins!'

'Hold it!' I thrust the glass at her and bent down to examine the floor. It was rather dark. I ran my hands over the rough surface searching for a hole or a crack. We could see the boys' heads through the small window of the driver's cabin. Suddenly Michael turned to look back. He saw Charlotte holding the half-full wine glass and nudged Dougie, who also looked.

'Oh, God,' wailed Charlotte. 'What are you doing down there, Anna? Be quick. I'm in agony.'

She'll just have to wet her pants, I thought crossly, and then the whole night will be ruined. Suddenly my hand touched air. 'A hole!' I said. 'Give me the glass.' I poured the warm liquid into the space and darted back under her gown.

'Just in time,' she sighed, and almost filled the glass in seconds.

I disposed of the contents and wiped the offensive glass with tissue paper. 'I presume that will be the last time Madam will require her champagne glass this evening,' I said rather crossly.

My hair was all messy, as if Scarlett had crawled backwards through a thorn bush. Charlotte looked at it and burst out laughing, then shrieked, 'Don't make me laugh, Anna! It'll happen again.'

'Thank God I was born with a normal bladder,' I said.

'It's nerves. Just nerves. I'll be fine as soon as I get there.'

'Just don't drink a drop at the ball,' I told her.

There was no further use for the wine glass in the last stages of our journey so I put it back in my handbag. Mother would have been scandalised if she'd known what we'd used her favourite crystal for, I thought, with a little smile.

I brushed my hair, shoved the brush back in my bag as well, hung it on a hook and prepared to alight.

Dougie had parked the truck in a back lane so there was no danger of anyone seeing us walking down the ramp. As we were walking arm in arm towards the Palais, Dougie said to Charlotte, 'I didn't know you had smuggled champagne on board my truck.'

To which Charlotte replied without a flicker of guilt, 'I drink a glass before every important occasion. It helps to calm my nerves.'

We could hear the wonderful sound of a big band playing. As we walked in through the tall wooden doors and showed our tickets there was a flood of light from the dance floor. Couples were gliding around elegantly under a glittering ball that revolved from the ceiling. Michael squeezed my arm.

'You should just see your eyes. They're like stars,' he said. It was the most exciting place I had ever been in.

We were shown to our table, number 23. It was decorated with pine branches and red and silver balls because it was only two weeks before Christmas. There were two other couples already seated. Charlotte and Dougie knew them because they had been rehearsing together for months. They introduced Michael and me. The girls were at least seventeen, but neither of them seemed to notice how young I was.

Charlotte, of course, could not sit down so we all went to the bar for a drink. Michael bought me a lemon squash. He had a beer because he was eighteen and Dougie, who was twenty-one, had one too. I watched Charlotte anxiously to see if she would gulp her lemon squash but she only sipped it.

Fortunately the debutantes' ceremony started quite soon. There were twelve couples. Michael and I went upstairs to the gallery so we could get a better view of the dancing. They had to perform the foxtrot, the Pride of Erin, the waltz and a strange dance called the Valetta. Then they were to walk gracefully down a flight of stairs and curtsy to the Lady Mayoress.

All the debutantes wore white dresses with long white gloves. The dresses were all different, made of tulle, organza, satin and lace, but none of them was anywhere near as elaborate as Charlotte's. She danced better than the other girls too. I thought she stood out like a queen.

At the end of each dance the audience applauded the debutantes, who swirled on in perfect formation to begin the next one. The Valetta was particularly graceful, with the dancers holding their arms above their heads and passing from one partner to the next. I thought I would love to try that. Michael and I leaned our elbows on the edge of the balcony and gazed down at the dancers in admiration. I realised I would have to wait three whole years to be old enough to make my debut.

When the debutantes had all curtsied to the Lady Mayoress, their partners led them back onto the dance floor and the band broke into loud swing music. The formal part of the evening was over. Michael caught me by the hand and we raced down the stairs to join in.

I had only danced with Michael once before, and this was very different. He was a good dancer – though not as good as Dougie, I noticed, when he asked me to dance later that evening. The foxtrot was quite difficult. Michael and I both kept missing steps and saying 'Sorry' when we trod on each other's toes, but by the time the band broke into a waltz we had relaxed. He held me tightly and swirled me expertly, so that I could lean back and look up at the high, ornate ceiling of the Palais and still not crash into the other dancers.

We danced for a long time and then went to join the others. The debutantes were relaxing. One girl actually flopped down on the floor with her legs spread out, which didn't look particularly graceful. 'What an ordeal!' she groaned. 'I'm glad that's over.'

Her partner brought her a drink with lots of mint, cucumber and slices of orange in it, and she gulped the lot down. 'Aghhh! That's better. Pimm's Number One!' She held out her glass for another.

Michael and Dougie asked Charlotte and me if we'd like to try a Pimm's. We said we would. It certainly looked healthy, but when I tasted mine it was bitter and seemed rather alcoholic, so we sipped our drinks cautiously.

We danced every dance, partly because Charlotte had to keep upright. I would occasionally look at her questioningly to see if she needed my assistance, but she always turned away nonchalantly, so I assumed she was all right.

When I danced with Dougie she danced with Michael. I don't think she thought much of his dancing because she came back quickly to reclaim Dougie from me after the first five minutes.

During the progressive barn dance I had the chance to meet other partners. Some of them were quite old men with beery breath who were inclined to fumble and stagger, but most were young and pleasant. One young man mistook me for someone else and kept saying, 'Glenise, I wish you wouldn't give me the cold shoulder. I really like you, you know.' I tried to explain that I wasn't Glenise but he just kept saying, 'God, you're a tease.' I was glad to get back to Michael.

We had supper of cold chicken and salad, jelly, trifle and cream. Charlotte pretended she wasn't hungry and didn't want to sit down. I stood up after a few minutes to keep her company and brought her a small glass of cordial. I could see she looked hot and must be thirsty. The debutante who had flopped down on the floor and drunk rather a lot was having a little sleep. Her mouth was open and saliva trickled down one side. Her partner didn't seem worried. 'She'll wake up in time for the photos,' he said.

After supper the band seemed to go wild. They played a wonderful number called 'Golden Wedding', which had a clarinet solo. Everyone leapt onto the dance floor as soon as it started. It was a compelling sort of dance that made you feel like showing off and making up all sorts of steps that weren't part of the dance. I had never enjoyed myself so much.

The evening went far too quickly. When it was almost midnight the lights came up in the Palais and the Master of Ceremonies announced from the platform that it was time for the highlight – the choosing of the Belle of the Ball. The Belle would be judged on her deportment, dancing and dress.

I looked down at the poor debutante who was still on the floor and snoring. Michael and I exchanged glances. We didn't think she would win.

Most of the other debutantes and a lot of other dancers took to the floor. Michael and I sat and watched. There were some excellent dancers and some elaborate dresses of all colours. As well as the usual dances, these couples had to demonstrate that they could do the tango, which looked very difficult indeed.

After about ten minutes the music stopped and the Master of Ceremonies announced that the Lady Mayoress had made her choice. It had been a very difficult one because of the charm and talent of so many young ladies, but she had finally reached a decision. The Belle of the Ball was Miss Charlotte Danielssen.

chapter twenty-seven

*A*ll four of us were crammed into the cabin of the truck and laughing madly. Charlotte had decided it was silly for her to stand up in her ball gown all the way home so she'd taken it off. It hung from one of the leather straps dangling from the ceiling in the back of the truck like a discarded ballerina. 'Poor Belle!' said Charlotte, looking back at the dress, and we all laughed even more.

Charlotte was wearing her long white petticoat, which was quite modest really, and looked like a nightgown. She was sitting very close to Dougie, practically on the gear stick. I was sitting on Michael's knee, which I think we both liked. We'd been humming 'Golden Wedding', or, rather, making the sounds of the different instruments, as we drove along. Suddenly Dougie pulled the truck up and parked by the side of the road.

He turned to Charlotte and said seriously, 'Shall we tell them?'

She looked rather shy and said, 'I don't see why not.'

'Charlotte and I are engaged to be married,' said Dougie, beaming proudly. He picked up her left hand, which she'd been carefully concealing ever since we left the Palais, and held it up so we could see the diamond ring. 'I proposed to her weeks ago but she only said yes tonight.'

'Oh, Charlotte!' I was flabbergasted. 'What will Mother say?'

'It doesn't matter what she says,' said Charlotte serenely.

'But you're under eighteen. You need her permission.'

'I need the permission of one parent, and I received that today. By telegram.'

'From our father?'

'Precisely.'

I hugged her tightly, kissed both cheeks and then hugged Dougie too. Michael grasped his hand and said, 'Congratulations!' and then he kissed Charlotte. 'I'm very happy for you.'

'We need a toast!' said Dougie and produced a bottle of bright-red liquor from under the dashboard. 'Cherry brandy. I've been saving this. Unfortunately I don't have glasses. Wait a minute! You naughty girls were scoffing champagne back there in a very posh glass. Where is it?'

'No!' we both screamed and started laughing hysterically.

Michael and Dougie looked baffled.

'We prefer to drink brandy out of the bottle,' I explained, still laughing.

'Oh, well. *We* can use the glass then,' said Dougie sensibly, and was just about to get out of the truck and search for the glass in the back when we both yelled, 'No, no!'

'All right, we'll all drink out of the bottle,' said the ever-obliging Dougie.

I had never tasted anything as delicious as cherry

brandy. We only had three gulps each and half the bottle was gone.

Dougie said he wouldn't have any more because he didn't want to smash us all up before the wedding.

'When are you getting married?' I asked. 'I'd like to be a bridesmaid.' The cherry brandy had made me feel bold enough to say that sort of thing.

'As soon as possible,' said Charlotte, 'and then we're going to London.'

'So you can study singing?'

'Of course.'

I looked anxiously at Dougie. Did he know what he was in for? A lifetime of serving a would-be prima donna?

He seemed aware of my concern and said reassuringly, 'We'll stay with my sister, Thelma, until we can find a flat of our own. I've got a job lined up for myself in the hospital where she works. Orderly, at first, than maybe ambulance driver. Thel says there are plenty of jobs. Dad's going to keep the business going here until I get back. Charlotte can start studying as soon as we get there.'

'We might go to Italy first,' said Charlotte.

'For the honeymoon,' said Dougie happily.

'I could visit La Scala in Milan.'

'We could see the Colosseum and St Peter's Basilica.'

I suddenly remembered that Dougie was a Catholic. Uncle Martin would go crazy.

'And the Opera House in Rome,' said Charlotte.

I sighed. It sounded unbelievable. I wondered what Mother would think.

Charlotte didn't come home that night. I waited, wide awake on the Mooneys' verandah in our springless bed, listening for her until it was almost light. Not that I was worried. I suppose when you're engaged it isn't unusual to spend the odd night with your husband-to-be, though I think I'd rather wait until the wedding night. I just wished she would come home so we could talk. I felt so happy for her and for Dougie. He's exactly the sort of person I'd like to have had as a brother and now he was going to be my brother-in-law. Of course I'd also have to put up with Warren! Still, I might be able to have sisterly talks with him and help him to behave a bit better towards girls. My mind was whirling, full of thoughts. Dougie had hinted to me once in the timber yard when I complimented him on working so hard that he was saving up for something special. He must have been saving for years to buy Charlotte that diamond ring. And the boat fares to London! I wondered if they were going on the P & O or the Orient Line. Uncle Martin would be livid. Eventually, when the first birds began to sing, I fell asleep. I had a horrible dream about Mother being given shock treatment. I seemed to have turned into Mother because I could feel all the pain that was going through her body and someone was gripping my arm, holding me down as I struggled to escape. Suddenly I woke up.

Mrs Mooney was shaking me by the arm. 'Anna, love, are you all right?' She handed me a cup of tea. 'You were tossing and turning and muttering away in your sleep.' She laughed. 'It's nearly eleven o'clock. Hey, look at this!' She thrust a copy of the *Geronga Advertiser* at me, showing me the front page. There was a picture of Charlotte and Dougie with a headline saying *Local Beauty Belle of Ball*.

Mrs Mooney put her finger to her lips and laughed wickedly.

'Now the cat's out of the bag there'll be trouble with your mum, I bet! Still, she might forgive Charlotte if she sees that lovely picture of the both of them. Belle of the Ball, eh? Fancy that . . .'

'It was your dress that did it, Mrs Mooney.'

'Aw, sure. It was your beautiful sister. Where is she, by the way?'

I looked around vaguely, feeling embarrassed.

'You don't have to tell me,' she said with a wink.

I thought I'd better wait for Charlotte to tell Mrs Mooney the news of her engagement. In the meantime I dressed quickly and ran up to The Tower House to ring Uncle Martin.

I asked him about Mother and he assured me she'd been much better when he visited her last night. 'But she will need to stay in hospital for some weeks for further treatment,' he added.

'Weeks? What sort of treatment?'

He was evasive. 'Special treatment. She's already had some. It has helped her a great deal.'

'Shock treatment?' I asked, feeling frightened. 'You didn't let them give her shock treatment, did you?'

'It's the latest thing for people in her condition,' he said crossly, as if I was making a fuss about nothing. 'She's behaving much better already, although she's only had one mild dose. You saw the difference when you visited her. She was eating, sleeping well and, thank goodness, no longer feeling such guilt.'

'But it will change her as a person, Uncle Martin. Break her spirit!'

'Don't be silly, Anna. The doctors know what they're doing. They're going to give her a course of shock treatment, gradually increasing the frequency and the intensity of the doses until she is well.'

'Well? Until she no longer fights back and does exactly what you tell her, you mean. Until she no longer has a mind of her own and you have her where you want her, living under your roof like some dumb decoration. Until she turns into a vegetable!'

'Stop being hysterical, Anna.'

'Please don't let them give her any more, Uncle Martin. Just wait,' I tried to sound calm. 'Wait until I can get a second opinion. Will you do that?'

He seemed amused. 'You're arranging a second opinion?'

'Yes. Will you promise to stop the shock treatment until I can do that?'

'The treatment is resuming on Monday. She's having it three times a week. As her next of kin I've given my permission.'

'Then I'll get the second opinion before Monday.'

I hung up and rushed to my bedroom to find the card I had carefully put away in the drawer of my desk. Then I dialled and waited.

'Neurology. Dr Pettigrew's rooms,' said the receptionist.

'My name is Anna Danielssen. May I speak to Dr Pettigrew, please?'

'She is with a patient at present. Would you like to make an appointment?'

'No, I'm a friend of hers. She said I should call if I needed advice, and I do need it now, rather urgently.'

'What is your number, please?'

I gave her the number and then asked how long before Dr Pettigrew might call back.

The receptionist said rather brusquely that the doctor's consulting hours finished at midday on Saturdays, and that Dr Pettigrew went straight to the hospital after that. I didn't hold out much hope that I would hear from her.

I thought I would hang around by the phone until midday, at least, but after just a few minutes it rang. I felt so grateful to hear Dr Pettigrew's kind, competent voice that I poured out the whole story of Mother's overdose and hospitalisation and the course of shock treatment that would increase in frequency and intensity over a period of weeks. In one way I hoped she would say just what Uncle Martin had said, that my fears were unnecessary, and it was all perfectly safe. But she didn't say that. She asked questions about the name of the hospital Mother was in, the names of the doctors treating her and how many times shock treatment had already been given.

'You realise, Anna, that as your mother already has a doctor I can't interfere with the treatment he has prescribed and your uncle has agreed to. That would not be ethical.'

'But do you think shock treatment is safe for Mother, Dr Pettigrew?' I asked anxiously.

'In my opinion, it isn't safe for anyone, Anna. We don't know enough about it yet to be giving it to patients, even in a mild form, let alone in increasing amounts.'

'So it's dangerous?'

There was a pause. 'There are a number of doctors who like the sound of shock treatment. As your uncle said, it is the latest thing, but it may not be the wisest thing.'

'Will Mother be all right? She's only had one mild dose so far.'

'It is unlikely that she will have suffered any serious damage, Anna, but I will go and visit her this afternoon; as a friend, you understand, not as a doctor.'

'Oh, thank you, Dr Pettigrew, and will you speak to Uncle Martin, please?' I begged. I rattled off his phone number.

'I will contact your uncle after I've visited your mother. If he doesn't agree, I have no power to change your mother's treatment, but I will do my best and it will all be quite ethical.' She laughed, because she knew I would be worried about that side of things. I laughed too. What a wonderful woman! If only she was Mother's next of kin instead of Uncle Martin. I was afraid it would be a battle, even for her, to change his mind about the shock treatment.

I raced back down the hill to Mrs Mooney's place where Charlotte was poring over her picture in the newspaper.

'Uncle Martin hasn't seen it yet,' I said cheerfully. 'I rang him to ask about Mother and he didn't even mention it.'

Charlotte looked up and nodded. She didn't look particularly happy for a Belle of the Ball who had just become engaged.

When I reached out to take her hand to admire the diamond ring, she snatched it away. 'Have you told Mrs Mooney yet?' I whispered.

She shook her head. 'Anna, I need to talk to you. Let's go for a walk.'

She called to Mrs Mooney that we were going to the

beach for an hour or so and strode off before one of the little Mooneys could ask to come with us.

Charlotte said nothing until we reached the sandhills. 'Here will do.' She stretched herself out on the warm sand out of the wind and out of sight of other people. I lay down beside her and waited for her to speak but she just picked at the marram grass. The round, spiky balls we called blowaways were just starting to detach themselves from the grass. Soon they would go hurtling along the beach at amazing speeds like cartwheels in the wind. When we were young we used to chase them.

'I'm pregnant,' said Charlotte in a small, tight voice.

'Oh,' I said, shocked. 'Are you sure?'

'I saw a doctor this morning. A doctor who doesn't know our family. I'm about eight weeks.'

'Eight weeks. Is it Dougie's?'

'Of course it is. I've never slept with anyone else.'

'Oh, I thought perhaps . . . You were going out with Max . . .'

'I didn't sleep with him!' she said in disgust. 'I told you that.'

'Well, what's the great problem? You're already engaged to Dougie. Couldn't you just speed up the wedding?'

'That's just the point. I don't want to.'

'Don't want to get married?'

'I don't think so.'

'You love Dougie, don't you?'

'I don't know,' she said miserably.

'But last night you were so certain! All those plans to go to London, to La Scala . . .'

'Last night I didn't know about being pregnant, did I?

I couldn't go anywhere with a baby,' Charlotte said. 'I just feel trapped!'

'Ah.' I thought hard. 'Couldn't you delay the plans to go to London and study? Do it a year or so later, after the baby?'

Charlotte shook her head adamantly. 'I'd never do it. My career would be over. Dougie told me last night he's bought a block of land right here in Skinners Bluff. He wants to build us a house. Just the thought of that makes me want to run away. I think I've made a terrible mistake, Anna.' She looked at me steadily. 'I'm going to get rid of it.'

'What, the baby?' I was shocked. 'But it's very dangerous – and it's illegal.'

'I know. I'll need your help. Will you help me?'

I shook my head in despair. 'Poor Dougie. What does he think?'

'He doesn't know.'

'But, you can't do that! It's his baby too.'

'I know, I know. He'll be very upset, but it's not his life that will be finished. It's mine! You've seen those local girls who get married at eighteen and have three screaming kids before they're twenty-one.'

'Why didn't you think of that before you got pregnant?' I said indignantly.

'Anna, I didn't mean to get pregnant. It was an accident.'

I had read about birth control in the *Ladies' Home Journal*. 'Did you use the rhythm method?'

'No, of course not. That's unreliable and only for strict Catholics. Dougie's not strict. He uses rubbers.'

I blinked. My sister and Dougie were much more worldly than I'd imagined.

'Sometimes they break,' she said flatly.

'Oh.' I waited. 'Does Dougie know?'

'Yes, he came with me to the doctor. He's overjoyed.' Charlotte started to cry. I put both arms around her. 'What a mess!' she sobbed. 'My life is ruined before I'm eighteen.'

'We'll think of something,' I said comfortingly. 'Perhaps you could have it adopted.'

'No! I don't want to have it! I want to get rid of it. Please, Anna, you've got to help me find an abortionist.'

Just the very sound of that word made me shiver.

chapter twenty-eight

I hoped that if we left it for a few days Charlotte might change her mind about getting rid of the baby.

I had read in a Sunday newspaper about a woman dying because she trusted a 'backyard' abortionist. Apparently the operation cost a lot, even though it was often performed badly and left women unable to have any more babies. No self-respecting doctor would agree to do it because it was against the law.

I suggested we ask Mrs Mooney for advice, but Charlotte didn't want anyone except me to know in case they tried to talk her out of it.

'If you don't marry Dougie, how will you get to London to study?' I asked her as we walked back along the beach.

'I won't be able to go to London. I'm resigned to that,' she said sadly. 'But once I get this abortion over, I'll apply for a teaching bursary and go to Melbourne. At least I'll be able to pay for my own singing lessons then.'

'Oh, Charlotte!' She had decided to be independent. Suddenly I felt very proud of her. 'Look, don't worry. I think I know someone who'll help us.'

As soon as we got back to Mrs Mooney's place I raced

up to The Tower House and rang Uncle Martin. I said that Dr Pettigrew, a neurologist Mother had met through the guesthouse, was going to phone him later in the afternoon. I pleaded with him to listen to her. He was angry that I had dared to interfere in Mother's 'case', as he kept calling it, but I persisted. I tried to remain calm and sensible and even lied a bit, saying finally, 'I know you have Mother's best interests at heart, Uncle Martin. You've been so wonderfully good to her, but think how terrible you'd feel if the shock treatment did destroy her mind. There are alternatives, and all Dr Pettigrew wants to do is explain them to you.'

After this he said grumpily that he would listen to 'the woman' if she called before he went out to his club for the evening.

I felt sure that Dr Pettigrew would ring me that afternoon as soon as she'd seen Mother, but she did better than that. She rang and said she'd like to call in to see me at The Tower House that evening.

'Oh, and Charlotte's here too,' I said quickly. 'Would you like to see her as well?' She said that it would be a good idea for us both to hear about Mother's condition.

I felt guilty about the possibility of burdening her with the problems of two members of our family in one day, but I believed she would know an abortionist who wasn't dangerous, if there was one to be found anywhere. I was determined to help poor Charlotte go through with her ordeal, even though I felt sorry for Dougie, so I was rather taken aback when Dr Pettigrew said, 'Your Uncle Martin will be coming with me to talk to you both.'

I explained to Charlotte that we'd have to wait to talk to Dr Pettigrew about the abortion.

'Well, I can't wait long. I hate deceiving Dougie. He doesn't know why I'm so miserable. When it's all over I'll tell him I had a miscarriage and then, very gently, I'll break the engagement.'

'Oh, Charlotte, do you have to break it so soon? Dougie will be shattered. Couldn't you just stay engaged until you go to Melbourne next year?'

'No, Anna. Don't you see? I'd probably have to sleep with him again if we were still engaged. He would certainly want to, and then the whole mess would begin all over again.'

'Isn't there any contraceptive that's completely safe?'

'None at all. Ask your friend Dr Pettigrew.'

I shook my head. I didn't want to ask for any more free advice. 'Well, someone should invent something. It's an awful predicament for women.' I thought I would reread *Essays on Sex Equality* by John Stuart Mill and Harriet Taylor Mill, a book I had been dipping into ever since Reverend Marsden had remarked casually to Mother that I would appreciate it. I didn't remember anything in the book about the importance of reliable contraception for women, but there was one piece of advice about marriage that I had thought was worth remembering: before she married, a woman should determine whether marriage was to be a relationship between two equals or between a superior and an inferior, a protector and a dependent. Then all her other problems would be easily solved.

I supposed that it was no use reciting this to Charlotte because her marriage to Dougie would have been a mixture. Charlotte would have regarded herself as intellectually superior to Dougie and yet she'd have been dependent on him as her protector. I didn't see why it couldn't have worked quite well like that. I'm sure Dougie wouldn't have minded, but now it was all too late.

That evening after we'd helped Mrs Mooney make a meal and bath the younger children, we hurried up to The Tower House to meet Dr Pettigrew and Uncle Martin. I noticed that Charlotte had taken off her engagement ring on our way back from the beach and hadn't worn it since.

The electricity was still off so we lit candles in the dining room and put fresh daisies in a vase on the oak table, which looked quite atmospheric. I lit the primus to heat water for coffee and Charlotte found a packet of vanilla wafer biscuits Mother had been saving for guests. We set the table with plates and coffee cups and waited.

It was one of the last times we would sit together in that dining room, I realised. I felt sad and looked across at Charlotte to see if she was feeling the same, but she just looked distracted. She had more urgent things to worry about.

Uncle Martin arrived a few minutes earlier than Dr Pettigrew. He'd obviously forgotten about our electricity being cut off and looked flustered. It would be embarrassing for him to let Mother's doctor friend see that he had been too mean to offer his sister the money to re-connect it.

He asked if we were all right with Mrs Mooney, which we assured him we were, and said that a room in his house would be ready for us to share by next Wednesday. We thanked him politely.

He said rather proudly that the big guest room was being prepared for Mother and that when she came out of hospital her clothes, furniture, paintings, and even her properly repaired piano, would be there waiting for her.

We nodded and smiled and Charlotte thanked him but I couldn't bring myself to say anything.

He then told us that Tom was going to take Jonathan to Melbourne on the train so that he could attend his first meeting of the Victorian Filmmakers Club and that Sarah was teaching Eliza to knit. I felt very grateful to Tom, but Charlotte and I raised our eyebrows at each other at the thought of Eliza sitting still knitting with only Sarah for an audience.

When Dr Pettigrew came she shook hands with us all and with great tact made no comment on the fact that the lights had gone out. When we were all settled with coffee she thanked us for making the time to meet – although she was obviously much busier than any of us, I thought.

She said that during the four weekends she had stayed at our guesthouse she had admired Mother very much. She could see, from a professional point of view, that Mother was under enormous strain and needed a rest. 'Perhaps, as a doctor, I should have intervened. I could have offered her a few weeks at a nursing home. I thought of doing that,' she said, 'but Mrs Danielssen is a very proud woman and I could see that she was determined to try and support her family and keep them together under one roof. I think it's disgraceful that there's no government assistance for women supporting families on their own as she has been doing for so many years.' She looked hard at all of us. 'I'm sure you're all aware of just what a strain those years must have been for her.'

Uncle Martin, for once, did not butt in and take over.

'I saw your mother today,' she said, turning to us, 'and I feel sure that with a few weeks of complete rest she will recover. In my opinion she does not need shock treatment but compassionate nursing and peace of mind. Electro-convulsive therapy is administered to the most severely disturbed patients in large mental hospitals in the United States and Britain, and it is also becoming very fashionable here. It is a means of managing unruly patients for whom other treatments are not available or have not worked.'

'What kind of patients?' I asked.

'Patients suffering from delusional depression, endogenous melancholic depression, acute mania and schizophrenia. Your mother has none of these. In my opinion she is suffering from a mild neurotic depression for which shock therapy would not be effective.'

'Surely the risk of suicide is a clear indication that shock treatment should be a consideration, Dr Pettigrew,' Uncle Martin objected.

'When it is not manageable by other means, perhaps. Your sister tells me, Mr Fitzsimons, that she has been taking no antidepressant medication whatsoever. Were you aware of that?'

'I never pry into my sister's medicine cabinet,' he said with a slight sneer.

'But you have been aware of her depression for many years.'

He shrugged. 'She manages her own affairs. I am not my sister's keeper.'

'She takes Relaxatabs quite often,' I said, trying to be helpful.

'They are a mild muscle relaxant, Anna, nothing more.' Dr Pettigrew turned to Uncle Martin. 'Studies have shown that shock therapy doesn't stop people killing themselves, Mr Fitzsimons. I hear from Katharine's doctors that you have agreed to her having a course of twelve treatments. Have you discussed this with her?'

'She is in no condition to make decisions about her own health at present,' he blustered, 'and I really don't think you should discuss such private matters in front of the children.'

Dr Pettigrew smiled in a peculiar way. 'They are hardly children, Mr Fitzsimons. As you must surely be aware, Anna has been taking responsibility for this family for some years.'

I blushed.

'And Charlotte has been a great help lately,' I added quickly.

'What are the side effects of shock treatment?' Charlotte asked, anxious to demonstrate her new-found helpfulness.

'Loss of memory, disorientation, headaches that can last for hours, heart attacks, strokes, and some patients have been known to die.'

'There is absolutely no need to alarm the girls like that!' Uncle Martin protested.

'They are family. They have a right to know the facts,' said Dr Pettigrew evenly.

'When I visited Mother I noticed she was vague,' Charlotte said. 'She'd forgotten that I was coming and for a minute she didn't seem to know who I was. Dr Pettigrew, what exactly happens when shock treatment is given?'

'Oh, Charlotte, don't be morbid!' said Uncle Martin.

'The patient is strapped to the treatment table, given some sodium pentothal and a muscle relaxant, and then electrodes are applied. A resistance reading of the patient is taken and the voltage and shock duration set. Patients generally receive a one- or four-second electrical charge to the brain, which causes an epileptic-like seizure for thirty to ninety seconds. A mouth guard is inserted into the patient's mouth to stop damage to the tongue and teeth. Sometimes shock treatment causes apnoea, a temporary loss of breathing, and artificial respiration is necessary. The patient remains unconscious for about five minutes after treatment.'

Charlotte gasped. 'And Mother has already been through this?' She glared at Uncle Martin. 'How could you agree to it? You didn't tell us what it was like!'

'Unless your uncle agrees to let me take over her case and try alternative treatment, your mother will have the next shock treatment on Monday,' said Dr Pettigrew calmly.

'Out of the question!' said Charlotte.

'What sort of alternative treatment, Dr Pettigrew?' I asked.

'There is a new antidepressant drug called lithium, which was only discovered recently in America. I would recommend that your mother take lithium tablets and have a few weeks' complete rest in the small private hospital in Geronga at which I am a consultant. The cost would be covered by medical and . . . other benefits.'

'That's a wonderful idea!' said Charlotte. 'She's our mother and I vote to keep her sane and unharmed with Dr Pettigrew.' She turned to me.

'So do I.'

Dr Pettigrew looked to Uncle Martin. 'And you, Mr Fitzsimons. What is your opinion?'

He threw up his hands in a dramatic gesture. 'Do what you want with her. Take over her case and good luck to you. I wash my hands of the whole affair!' Then he picked up his briefcase and walked out.

When he was out of hearing, Charlotte and I hugged each other with joy. Not only were we delighted to have Dr Pettigrew taking over our mother's treatment but we could now ask her the other vitally important question.

chapter twenty-nine

*D*r Pettigrew sat with us at the oak table by candle-light and gave Charlotte quite a lecture. I was surprised. What had I expected? That she would be like some fairy godmother who could wave a wand of wisdom over our dilemma, presenting us with the name of a kind and reliable abortionist who would charge us nothing and insist on protecting our privacy? I suppose, quite fool-ishly, I had thought that.

Instead Dr Pettigrew sat there like a headmistress cross-examining Charlotte. Why did she want to terminate her pregnancy? Didn't she love her fiancé? Surely she should discuss the matter with him before making this important decision. A termination could be medically harmful. It was illegal and expensive. Charlotte should think very carefully before deciding to go ahead with it. Had she con-sidered adoption?

Charlotte was adamant that she did not want to do anything but have the abortion as soon as possible.

Dr Pettigrew sighed and said that Charlotte was a strong-minded young woman and she would like to be able to help her but it was difficult. She could not be directly involved. The most she could do was seek advice from colleagues on the name of a safe abortionist in Melbourne and pass this on to Charlotte, who must be careful never to reveal where the name had come from. Finding a safe abortionist might take some time. Charlotte would have to arrange her own transport, finance and after care. It was obvious she wanted Charlotte to change her mind and have the baby. My disappointment was overwhelming.

After she had given Charlotte a final brief lecture on considering the feelings of others, Dr Pettigrew recommended she use a contraceptive device called a Dutch cap instead of rubbers in future. Charlotte said grimly that she did not intend to be sexually active for a long, long time.

Dr Pettigrew looked at me, smiled and said, 'And what do you think of all this, Anna?'

'Me?' I was unprepared to think anything. 'I'm very grateful to have learned so much,' I said honestly.

At which Dr Pettigrew laughed and patted my arm affectionately. 'Let's hope the contraceptive pill they are experimenting with is available before you become sexually active.'

As soon as Dr Pettigrew had gone Charlotte exploded. 'How dare she! What an unbearable woman! Giving me lectures on morality! I wouldn't use the name of her wretched abortionist if she paid me!' She stalked up and down the room, looking furious. 'And anyway, how on earth am I supposed to raise the money? It's about a hundred pounds!'

'We could sell the chiffonier,' I suggested. 'Mother said it would go to me when The Tower House was sold. She's giving you the oak table, and the chairs are to be

322

divided between Eliza and Jonathan. The chiffonier
would be easiest to sell. I could ring the antique dealer
first thing in the morning. He's been trying to get hold of
it for years.'

'Mother would ask why you sold it.'

'I could say I needed it for the train fare to Townsville.'

'It belonged to her mother.'

'Yes, she'd be upset.'

'And you love the chiffonier, Anna.'

I looked at her gratefully. 'But the abortion's more
important.'

'Listen! I have an idea,' said Charlotte, suddenly
excited. 'Would you mind waiting upstairs while I make
a private phone call?'

I went to my room, feeling uneasy. Charlotte was
desperate enough to do something foolish. After a few
minutes I crept down and sat at the top of the stairs,
straining to overhear her conversation. She seemed to be
explaining that it was a friend who needed the abortion.
I couldn't hear much more. I went back to my room and
stared out at the dark ocean. After a few minutes the
phone rang and I heard her talking again. I waited and
soon Charlotte called out, 'Anna, come down! It's all
fixed.'

The abortion had been arranged to take place in a
Melbourne surgery the day after tomorrow. I was to
travel with Charlotte by train, to sit in the waiting room
for about half an hour and then, when the nurse gave me
the signal, meet Charlotte in the lane behind the surgery
where a taxi would be waiting to take us both back to the
station.

Charlotte had been assured by whoever she spoke to

on the phone that she'd be well enough to travel by public transport after the operation. The doctor would instruct her on what to do if there was excessive bleeding or cramps. Charlotte was to rest in bed for a few days afterwards and, if the bleeding and cramps continued after that, she was to get in touch with her local doctor. We weren't to know the name of the doctor performing the operation or to reveal his address to anyone.

'But how much will it cost?' I asked her.

'All taken care of,' she said mysteriously. 'Ask me no questions, Anna, and I'll tell you no lies.'

'But how do you know this doctor is a safe one? Wouldn't it be better to wait until Dr Pettigrew contacts us with the name she promised?'

'If I waited for her, I'd be too far gone to even have an abortion! Couldn't you tell she was stalling? So much for Dr Morality. We don't need her.' She laughed with relief.

There wasn't much to laugh at on the train journey home from Melbourne on Monday. Charlotte sat hunched in a corner by the window and winced every time the train jolted, which was often. She didn't say much about the operation. When I asked what had happened she just said, 'I lay on a table. He asked me to count up to ten, said I had a nice accent and then I went out to it.'

'And what then?'

'I woke up feeling a bit sick. He was gone. The nurse gave me a cup of tea, but before I'd had time to drink more than a few sips she was hustling me out the side door to the lane where you were waiting in the taxi.'

'Oh. Does it hurt much?'

'The cramps come and go. Aghhh! There's one.'

'At least you don't feel like vomiting any more.'

'No, the nausea was caused by the anaesthetic, I suppose.'

'Will you be all right to walk to the bus when we get to Geronga?'

'I think so. Just hope I don't bleed on the seat.'

'Oh, Charlotte, I'm so sorry about all this.'

'Gruesome, isn't it?' She tried to smile. 'Who'd be a woman?'

I wondered how Dougie would take the news of the 'miscarriage'. He was away helping a friend finish his house at Cape Conroy for a few days, which was fortunate. When he came home Charlotte should feel better and then she'd have to tell him.

I had explained to Mother and Uncle Martin that I was spending Monday in Geronga watching Charlotte rehearse for *The Gondoliers*. We were going to tell Dougie the miscarriage had happened after rehearsal and I had rushed Charlotte to the nearest doctor who had given her a curette and told her to rest in bed. We just hoped he wouldn't try to contact this mythical doctor.

It was all very complicated, this unpleasant deception. We'd told no one at all, not even Mrs Mooney, who believed that Uncle Martin had agreed we could stay together in The Tower House instead of with her. Fortunately she had no phone so it wasn't easy for Uncle Martin to check up on us.

By the time we reached home on Monday afternoon Charlotte was very pale. I heated water on the primus for her to wash in and then she went straight to bed. She slept for an hour or so. I kept looking in to see if she was all right.

At about six p.m. I warmed up some stew Mrs Mooney had given us and brought it in to her. She was curled up like a foetus and when she opened her eyes I could see that she'd been crying.

I handed her the stew and sat on the end of the bed. The sun was going down and there was a golden glow all over the room which made Charlotte's hair look like a halo.

'Do you think I'm wicked?' she asked softly.

I shook my head. 'I think you're brave.'

'Would you have done the same?'

'If I wasn't sure I loved the man, I wouldn't want his baby . . . but then, I can't imagine making love to him in the first place.' I said this carefully because but I didn't want to hurt her feelings.

'You're so lucky,' she said. 'You've always known exactly what you feel. I wanted to love Dougie and some-times I was sure I did. Like the first time we made love, and on the night of the ball, and the night he rescued me from the station . . .'

'The night you escaped from rotten Max,' I said grimly.

'Don't be too hard on Max,' said Charlotte surpris-ingly. 'I suppose I was pretty naive to think I could spend a whole weekend in his guest room when he's such a man of the world.'

And suddenly, like a bolt of lightning, I knew who had arranged the abortion.

'It was Max who helped you, wasn't it?'

'Yes. I told him it was for a friend but he didn't believe me for an instant. He guessed it was Dougie's because he knew we'd been going out together before I met him, and he was surprisingly decent. He said the doctor was a friend who owed him a favour and there'd be no charge. He said he owed me that at least, and he sent the money for our train fares and the taxi. He wrote to me a while ago, apologising for that awful night. Did I tell you?'

'No.' I was stunned.

'I'm not the slightest bit interested in Max, Anna. Don't think that. I just think it was decent of him to do me that favour, don't you?'

I shrugged. I was speechless.

'The problem now is Dougie. As soon as he told me he'd bought that block of land I realised I didn't love him enough to want to live with him forever in a house he'd built himself in a boring place like Skinners Bluff. Is that a dreadful thing to say?'

'Well, I think if you said it to Dougie he'd be very hurt indeed.'

'I won't say it to *him*.'

'But he'll guess it, won't he?'

She was silent. 'I don't know what I'm going to say to him. Help me, will you. I've got to think of something to say before tomorrow.'

That night I dreamed that Dougie had fallen down a deep well. Charlotte was dancing on the lid, singing Tessa's song in a frilly skirt with white stockings but instead of smiling and flirting as her character is supposed to, she was crying. I was trying to persuade her to get off the lid so I could throw a rope down and pull Dougie out, but she couldn't hear or wouldn't listen. He was drowning.

Next morning I brought Charlotte a cup of tea with toast and honey in bed. She was sitting up, smiling, and looked much better. She said that she'd already been out on the balcony looking at the sunrise and felt that her life was starting all over again.

'I think you should tell Dougie the absolute truth – about the abortion, not wanting to live in this town, not being sure if you love him, everything!' I said. 'It might be cruel but it's fair.'

'But he'll hate me!'

'Then you'll just have to put up with being hated.'

'Anna, you're a very hard little person,' she said with narrowed eyes.

This hurt me very much.

'And you should give back that engagement ring immediately,' I said. 'I happen to know that he saved for it for over a year.'

chapter thirty

$\mathcal{I}$ got dressed, left Charlotte in bed, and took the bus into Geronga to visit Mother. She had been moved from the public hospital to the small private one recommended by Dr Pettigrew. It was really just a large old Victorian house, a pleasant place with a garden, lawns, big shady trees and a verandah all around. We sat together under a gigantic fig tree. Mother looked happy, even pretty. She talked a lot about Dr Pettigrew, whom she saw every day and admired a great deal.

'I shouldn't tell you this, I suppose, but that generous woman has arranged for me to stay here for a whole month free of charge if I want to. Mind you, I don't think I'll need that long. I'm feeling so much better I may even be home by tomorrow! Dr Pettigrew has connections all over the place, serves on boards, that sort of thing. I would have liked you to become a doctor, Anna. I can just imagine you as a competent Dr Pettigrew.'

I laughed but I was pleased.

'I feel so ashamed that there isn't enough money for you to go to university. All your teachers tell me you should go.'

'Don't worry about me not doing medicine.' I smiled. 'I'd probably faint at the first sight of blood.'

She nodded. 'No, you never liked blood. You know these antidepressant tablets are working very well! I feel really quite cheerful. I astonish myself.' She laughed.

We chatted on without any strain for ten minutes or so and I was careful not to mention our father, as Dr Pettigrew had advised me not to. 'Will you be happy to live at Uncle Martin's when you leave hospital?' I asked.

'Well, dear, that is something I haven't decided yet.'

'Where else will you go?'

'There is a possibility, depending on how well I am, that I will take a job!' She looked positively delighted.

I was wary, remembering her last job offer.

Mother seemed to read my thoughts. 'I had a visit from Reverend Taylor a few days ago, and he told me that his good friend, Miss Hawthorn, had been completely understanding about my decision not to accept the job at her school. It was not the right time for me then, but now I feel so much better, things have changed.'

'Hasn't the job already been taken?'

'Well, not exactly. Miss Hawthorn has offered me an even better position. She has asked me to be a house mistress and help look after the boarders. I'd be a music teacher too, of course. Being a house mistress would mean that I'd have my own flat at the school and wouldn't have to travel there each day.'

'That would be much better,' I said, trying not to sound too enthusiastic in case Mother decided against taking this job as well.

'It would be, yes. It's a wonderful school. Very arty. I think I'd enjoy the atmosphere.'

'I'm sure you would.'

'The only problem is that I won't be able to take all of you children with me, just Eliza and Jonathan. It's a live-in job, you see. They'll allow two children but that's the limit. Charlotte told me a few days ago she plans to go to Melbourne Teachers College and study music part time, and that just leaves you,' she finished awkwardly. 'I know you don't like Uncle Martin much, Anna, but he's generously offered to have you stay, just for a year or two until I can earn enough money to put a deposit on a small house. We could even find one near the old house in Skinners Bluff if you like.'

'Oh, don't think about me. I'll be fine wherever I go,' I said quickly to hide the hurt at being the only one in the family she'd decided to dump on Uncle Martin.

'The flat is quite large so there'd be room for you and Charlotte to come and stay on weekends occasionally. What do you think?'

'Where would Eliza and Jonathan go to school?'

'There! They would be taken on as Grammar School students and would pay no tuition fees as long as I was there. They'd live in the flat with me. It's a wonderful opportunity for them to have the sort of education I can't afford to give them. Miss Hawthorn is very keen to have me because she's heard from Reverend Taylor about my soirees and the garden parties I used to give and the guesthouse, all that nonsense, and she thinks I might be a fine organiser of school concerts!'

'Well, you would be,' I said loyally, although I knew how exhausted she'd become. I was still feeling numbed by the news that Mother was considering living somewhere without me.

'Of course I wouldn't have to organise the concerts all by myself. Miss Hawthorn says I would have several assistants.'

'You've seen Miss Hawthorn again?' I asked in surprise.

'Yes, she came here to visit me. She's a charming woman, very strong, very kind. Not unlike Dr Pettigrew. I feel as though I've been adopted by two fairy god-mothers, in tweed suits and orthopaedic brogues!' Mother threw back her head and laughed merrily.

'But wouldn't you have to stay at the school a long time to educate Eliza and Jonathan?' I asked. 'Eliza won't finish school for another ten years!'

'Well, yes, if they wanted me, I don't see why I shouldn't stay on that long. Miss Hawthorn says she'd like me to think of this as a new career. I must say I feel flat-tered, as I have no formal teacher training.' Mother's eyes were shining. 'Jonathan is quite excited. Apparently they have a film club at the school.'

'You've already told the others?' I felt doubly hurt. 'It all sounds rather definite.'

'Well, it isn't, of course. Not yet, but Dr Pettigrew thinks I'm making such good progress that I could be ready to start the job in February when the new school year begins.'

'So we won't need a little house for the family at Skinners Bluff after all?'

'Oh, yes. We could still buy a cottage and all meet there for holidays,' Mother said. 'Wouldn't that be fun?'

'Ah, yes, for holidays.'

Our family was about to break up into pieces and Mother didn't care at all. For the first time in our lives we had no family home and little hope of ever getting another. I felt a lump forming in my throat and the need to get away fast. I looked at my watch and said, 'Oh, the bus! I'll have to dash. See you tomorrow!' and blew her a kiss as I ran across the lawn with tears streaming down my face.

On Wednesday evening we all sat round the table at Uncle Martin's place for Mother's welcome home from hospital dinner. It was odd to see our beloved dining table in Uncle Martin's house and to have to sit on our own balloon-backed chairs in such a modern room. Our furniture didn't seem to fit in at all. This was to be an extremely formal dinner in honour of our furniture, apparently. There were three different wine glasses for everyone, even the children. The linen was stiffly starched, the silver polished, and there was a mass of cutlery and serving dishes on the chiffonier. On this special occasion Aunt Ursula had even hired a maid in a white cap and apron to serve each one of us individually. It could hardly have been less formal if we'd been at Government House.

Mother sat at one end of the long table and Uncle Martin at the other. We were all there – Tom and Sarah, Aunt Ursula, Charlotte, Jonathan, Eliza and me. Uncle Martin suddenly tapped his glass for attention and then stood up.

'I would like to propose a toast to someone who has, in her usual manner, broken all the rules, and even defied the laws of medicine, to make a splendid and sudden recovery. To Katharine!' He said it rather pompously, but with some genuine affection.

We dutifully raised our glasses. 'To Katharine.'

'Welcome home, Katharine,' Uncle Martin continued,

'and this is your home now. Even though you've capriciously gone and found yourself a job at Mount Enderby Grammar School and are taking Jonathan and Eliza away with you, I'm sure we'll see a lot of you three in school holidays – and of Charlotte when she comes home from college, of course. That only leaves orphan Anna here with us on a full-time basis,' he chuckled, 'and I'm sure she'll be pleased to see you all here when you visit for holidays. Welcome all of you, Katharine, Eliza, Jonathan, Charlotte and Anna!'

There were well-bred murmurs of 'Thank you, Uncle Martin' from around the table. He looked pleased and sat down. I stood up.

'Thank you, Uncle Martin, but I won't be needing you to provide me with a home,' I said.

There was a deathly hush. Everyone stared at me.

'Sit down, Anna,' Mother said quietly.

'I'm going to Townsville to live with my father.'

There was a commotion at the table. For eight years no one had mentioned our father, let alone thought of him as someone who might invite one of us to go and live with him.

'Do as your mother says, Anna,' said Uncle Martin firmly. 'Sit down at once.'

I remained standing.

'Charlotte and I have both had telegrams and letters from our father in the last few weeks which were very affectionate and reassuring. Jonathan and Eliza, he would like you to know that he loves you very much and hopes to see you both soon. I won't be leaving you forever, so don't worry that you'll never see me again, but I feel it's time that one of us went to spend some time with the

father who says he has never stopped loving any of us.'
I smiled at the two young ones and sat down. They
looked pleased. Then they turned towards Mother to see
what her reaction would be. We were all expecting her to
be fiery, but she seemed to be absorbed in her dinner and
went on eating.

I suddenly realised that she was relieved I was going
away, that Uncle Martin was relieved he didn't have to
provide me with a home, and that my sisters and brother
were relieved I was going because now they wouldn't
have to watch me struggling to keep The Tower House
which was a losing battle and had exhausted us all. I
realised with shock that I was the only one in the family
who had wanted to keep us all together and I felt very
much alone.

I stepped back, pushed in my chair politely, said,
'Excuse me,' and left the room.

As soon as I was out of sight I ran to the guest room
that now belonged to Mother. Huge dry sobs came bursting out. I flung myself down on the bed and wept. After
a few minutes I pulled myself together and put my head
up to look around. Uncle Martin had set a nice trap.
Mother's new room, although it was only for school holidays, was large and light with a balcony overlooking the
garden. Her paintings and furniture had been moved in,
even the piano, and her clothes hung in the wardrobe.
I angrily brushed away the tears and went to the window
to look out.

Soon I heard Mother's footsteps. She came across to
where I was standing and said quietly, 'Anna, I understand why you want to go. I'm sorry that I haven't been a
better mother all these years.'

I shook my head. 'It's not that. I just have to meet him. See what he's like. He's my father, you see, but I'm afraid to leave you . . .'

'You mustn't worry about me. I'll be happy here in the school holidays, with my music and Martin and the children . . .'

'But not me! You won't be happy with me. I upset you. I fight you. It's true, isn't it?'

Mother nodded calmly. 'Sometimes the child has to wound the parent deeply before they can live together as adults. Did you know that?'

I didn't. Her words were like a revelation.

Then she took off her long silk scarf, the one she had used as a dancing partner, the one she had worn on the back of the motorbike with Reverend Marsden, her favourite scarf, and gently wound it round my neck.

'For you.'

Tears streamed down my face. 'I do love you, even though I wound you,' I said.

'And I love you.'

I couldn't ever remember having heard my Mother say those words before. I sat on the floor at her feet while she sat on the bed and stroked my hair. I couldn't move or stop crying. 'You said once that you thought I almost hated you. It isn't true.'

'I know that, Anna, and I'm sorry that I said such a foolish thing. Can you forgive me?'

I nodded. 'Do you really not mind that I'm going away?'

'I'll miss you very much, but I know you have to go. You need to make up your own mind about your father. You're intelligent enough to do that. I'm not afraid for you,' she said. 'You're much stronger than me. You can fly by yourself.'

'Really? Do you think so?' I turned my face up to her. She nodded. She looked proud of me.

'And what about you? Are you really well enough to do this job at the school?'

'I believe so, and if I'm not, I'll come back and live here. It won't be ideal but I'll manage. You don't have to stay here and save me.'

'Thank you,' I said and she hugged me.

A great load had suddenly been lifted from my shoulders, and it made me feel bold.

'Mother, I've been reading a lot about the Irish race lately. I didn't realise how ignorant I was about our history. I'm beginning to understand why this family loves jokes, stories, danger, and why they're as arrogant, moody and mad as they are. It's just like you said. Imagine growing up in a country you thought of as your own and being surrounded by people who hated you!'

Mother stared at me in surprise. She nodded, encouraging me to go on.

'I feel ashamed that Anglo-Irish Protestants like the Fitzsimons persecuted Irish Catholics like the Devlins for eight hundred years,' I said. 'There isn't a lot I can do about that, but I understand now why you feel shame that comes out as anger whenever you meet Mr Devlin.'

Mother looked at me in astonishment. She was speechless.

'I discovered one rather odd thing about our family,' I continued. 'When I looked up Great-great Grandfather – the one who was supposed to have supported the Emancipation Bill of 1825 and helped, by losing his seat in

County Clare, to get the first Catholic into parliament, I found that it wasn't a Fitzsimons who'd done that at all, but a Fitzgerald! Did you know?'

Poor Mother. I expected her to look shocked that she'd been deluded all these years. But she only smiled at me and said, 'Ah, dear me, Anna. But it makes a fine story, wouldn't you agree?'

'There was nothing about Great-great-grandfather riding his horse into parliament either,' I said.

'I don't suppose they bothered recording such acts of exhibitionism,' she replied seriously. Then she turned to me with a wicked smile. I smiled back.

At last I was beginning to understand her.

And then, as was her habit, she deftly changed the subject.

'Now, about that holiday cottage. I really do want to buy one, just as soon as I save up some money,' she said enthusiastically. 'It will be just for us, for our family. You must come down from Townsville and help me choose it.'

'I'd like to.'

'And then we can leave Uncle Martin in peace.'

I nodded. I think she meant it.

chapter thirty-one

The night before I left for Townsville Mrs Mooney gave me a spontaneous little farewell party on her verandah, just with her children, Eliza and Jonathan, Charlotte and Michael. It was sad that Dougie wasn't there but he hasn't wanted to see Charlotte since she told him the truth about the abortion and returned the ring. He's been away working on his friend's house and has lost a lot of weight, his father told me, because he's been too upset to eat. It is just as well Charlotte is leaving to live in a hostel at College early next year.

Charlotte is disappointed that I'm not staying until the opening of *The Gondoliers* but I want to be in Townsville with my father by Christmas Eve. I think she understands that. It will be the first time in my life I've ever been away from the family and The Tower House for Christmas. It's odd that the others don't seem to mind spending Christmas at Uncle Martin's. Jonathan even said he was quite looking forward to it because Tom is giving him his old canoe and teaching him to paddle it, and Eliza said she loved reading all Sarah's comics (we were never allowed comics at home), and Aunt Ursula was teaching her to bake butterfly cakes, which Mother always said were too fiddly to bother with.

Because of missing Christmas with the family it was particularly touching that Mrs Mooney gave me the farewell party. She had a Christmas tree on the verandah and we all danced to the gramophone and ate homemade sausage rolls and drank lemonade. Mrs Mooney made a sponge cake with a palm tree and a crocodile on it. I was just about to cut it when, to my surprise, the mystery guest I'd been told was coming arrived. It was Reverend Marsden on his motorbike. He hadn't brought Genevieve because she was back in Melbourne. I was quite glad about that. He looked just as dashing as he had four months ago when he'd surprised me that afternoon on the cliff. He'd brought a farewell present of a beautifully bound copy of Tolstoy's *Anna Karenina* which he thought might keep me busy all the way to Townsville. It had 853 pages. I wondered how he knew this was one of my favourite books. I'd borrowed it from the Geronga Public Library three times. On the inside cover he had written, *For another Anna, Tolstoy's most perfect work, Best wishes, Albert Marsden, December 1954.* He seemed to have forgiven me for writing that letter about Mother, and I secretly forgave him for daring to flirt with her. When he danced with me on the verandah I whispered, 'I promise not to throw myself under the train on the way to Townsville,' and he threw back his head and laughed loudly. I told him about Mother's new job and he seemed pleased and asked to be remembered to her. He congratulated me on passing my exams and winning a preliminary bursary, and I asked when he and Genevieve were going to China to be missionaries. He looked surprised and said that must have been a local rumour because they'd never planned to go any further than Arnhem Land. We laughed about that.

Just before Reverend Marsden left, when Michael and I were dancing, he asked us if we'd like a ride on the back of his motorbike. Michael said that I should have the ride as he had ridden one before, but Reverend Marsden said it was a big bike and all three could fit on if we wanted to. So we jumped aboard with me sandwiched in the middle and had a most exhilarating ride along the winding road by the beach. It should have been like my dream come true. At last I'd been able to hug Albert Marsden's black leather jacket and snuggle my head in his neck and at the same time I had Michael clinging to me tightly, but somehow it just seemed like a crazy ride and great fun. Nothing more.

He took the others for a ride then waved to us all and rode off. 'He's not what you'd call the usual kind of reverend,' said Mrs Mooney as he disappeared round a bend.

When the party broke up I gave all the Mooneys hugs and promised to write regularly to Mrs Mooney and send the little Mooneys postcards with pictures of real crocodiles.

Michael drove us all back to Uncle Martin's. It was a bit emotional saying goodbye to Eliza and Jonathan that night, but I had to do it then because I was leaving early in the morning before they'd be awake.

I sat in the middle of Eliza's new bed with an arm around each one of them and told them that I wasn't going to Townsville forever.

'Well, how long then?' asked Jonathan.

'I don't know. A year or two, perhaps. It depends on whether our father and I get on well together.'

'What if you don't?' asked Eliza. 'What if he's like Ernie Mooney and belts people?'

I laughed. 'I don't think he'll do that.'

'Anyway, you're too big to belt. You could run away,' Eliza said.

'If you don't like him, just send us a telegram and one of us will come and bring you home,' said Jonathan seriously.

'I really think it's going to be all right,' I told them, 'and as soon as I get to know him I'll see if we can both come down to visit you so you can get to know him too.'

'How will you know what he looks like when he comes to meet you at the station?' asked Jonathan anxiously.

'He wrote that he'd be wearing a big hat and a smile.'

Eliza laughed but Jonathan looked worried. 'It's hot up there. I bet everyone wears a hat and a smile.'

'Promise you'll bring him down here to meet us very soon,' Eliza pleaded.

'As soon as I possibly can, and I'll send you a photo of him and I'll write lots of letters.' I hugged them both. 'You'll have a great time at your new school. You're lucky to be going to such a good one, and Mother is so proud of getting the job that she'll be happy too.'

'The uniform's quite nice,' Eliza said. 'We wear straw hats with ribbons hanging down.'

Jonathan grinned. 'There really is a film club, Anna.'

'I know, and, Eliza, you'll be able to act in real plays, with professional lighting and costumes and sound effects.'

Eliza beamed. 'Miss Hawthorn says they're doing *The Magic Pudding* as a musical next year.'

'You can be the pudding!' teased Jonathan.

She leaned over and whacked him.

'You should audition for the pudding. It's the best part,' I said.

After I'd kissed them both goodnight Charlotte came in and hugged me very tightly, which is not like her. Then she whispered that she'd tell Jonathan and Eliza a goodnight story so that I could say a last goodbye to Michael. I knew that would be sad.

We sat in the car that he'd borrowed from his family for the evening and at first we couldn't think of anything to say. He kissed me gently on the cheek and said, 'I'll miss you, Anna.'

I said, 'Me too,' but I felt rather hollow and disappointed inside.

Then he grinned at me in a lopsided, questioning way as if I'd done something funny but rather bad.

'You didn't tell me you were only fourteen.'

'You didn't ask.' I felt indignant. 'Who told you how old I was?'

'Dougie.'

'Dougie! When?'

'The night of the ball. He said, "I know she seems older but she's still just a kid so look after her."'

'A kid?' I felt myself going red with shame. 'Do you think I'm just a kid?'

'No, I don't. Dougie was just trying to protect you.'

'From who?'

'Me, I suppose.'

'Did he need to?' I turned to look at him.

'Perhaps.' He kissed me again, properly on the lips this time, which was wonderful. The kiss lasted a long time. I had visions of rolling over and over with Michael down the giant sandhill and landing on top of him at the bottom and just going on kissing forever. When the kiss was over he whispered, 'Come back to me, won't you?'

I nodded and then said, 'Don't come to the station.'

'Why not?'

'I've got to fly by myself.'

I think he understood.

It is very early in the morning on Friday, December the twentieth, the day of my departure. I have packed everything I need for the trip into one medium-sized suitcase and I'm standing in front of The Tower House waving goodbye to Uncle Martin. In twenty minutes Mr Devlin is coming to drive me to the station in Geronga where I'll catch a train to Melbourne and then another one to Townsville.

When Mr Devlin said that he would like to drive me to the station, I felt pleased. After all, if it wasn't for him I might never have found my father. I'm grateful that he's been my father's loyal friend for so many years.

I am here to have one last look at The Tower House. Uncle Martin has driven off quickly because he seems to understand that I want to be alone here.

The sun is about to rise. I stare out to sea. Clouds float like battleships in the pale-grey sky, the trees are black silhouettes and the waves are dark quivering humps, and up it comes! A ball of gold above a steel-grey sea. Now its rays are spreading and flecking the clouds golden. The sky is turning pale blue and the dunes are touched with pink. The sun rises quickly, transforming earth, sea and sky, bathing them in glorious orange light. Birds cry out to greet the new day.

I turn and walk up the path to The Tower House. I unlock the door with the key that nobody knows I still have. The house is empty and it echoes when I walk on the bare floor, but it still feels like our home. Our albatross. It looks rather shabby without the dining table, chairs and chiffonier. There are nail holes in the wall where the family portraits used to hang. I wander through the rooms and stand staring out to sea from each of the salt-stained windows. I open and close the trapdoor and the wash-basin salvaged from the wreck of the *Ibis* and slide my hands along the smooth wooden banisters.

Then I climb the winding stairs to my bedroom beneath the tower. It looks odd without my bed. I think of the dreams I had here, the plans I made and the secrets I acted out in front of the mirror.

I climb up to the tower, the 'unsafe' tower that my father built. As I stand looking out I can see the whole district – the ocean, the Merlin River, the hills and every house in Skinners Bluff. It is splendid. I know why my father built this tower. From here one could fly. I try to memorise every detail of this view because in four days' time I will describe it to him, and I will give him the key as a present.

I climb down carefully and take a last look at the big dining room where I've eaten every Christmas dinner of my life, where we decorated a pine tree each Christmas Eve and sang carols round the piano, and where on Christmas mornings, even during the war when there was nothing to buy, my mother managed to stuff our stockings full.

I look down from the big front window. The garden looks neglected already. Leaves have blown all over the stone steps. There is no bleating from the goats or clucking from the bantams. They have gone to the market to be sold. Grayling has gone back to Mrs Armitage's. I suppose the grandchildren will get him after all.

I pick up my case and carry it down the path to the gate. I do not look at the AUCTION sign and feel grateful that I won't be here to see our house sold in a few days' time.

Now the sun has climbed higher and the sky is all rosy. I can see Mr Devlin's truck coming round the bend.

I feel panicky all of a sudden. Have I made the right decision? I have lost The Tower House but how can I leave my family? And Michael? Did anyone ask me to go? Not one of them. It is I who feel like a misfit. It is I who decided to go. I couldn't fulfil the most important dream of my life, so I feel like a failure who should leave.

Am I angry because somebody trod on my dreams? Yes, I am, to be honest, but other people have had their dreams trodden on. Mother. Charlotte. Dougie Devlin. We will recover. We will think up new dreams. I will miss my family. Oh, yes, I'll miss them, but I must go in search of new dreams now.

I sigh with relief. The panic has gone. I smile and wave at Mr Devlin who is turning the truck round.

I pull Mother's scarf from my pocket, look at it critically, give it a swish and put it round my neck. Then I hold my head high, close my eyes and whisper, 'Please, God, please make my father like me.'

Tanglewood

KRISTIN WILLIAMSON

On a Queensland beach in 1962 Meg, Virginia and Sally plan their lives and make a pact to build a place in the bush where they can meet once a year. Twenty-five years later, nothing is as they imagined it would be. Meg, an investigative journalist, is distressed by her childlessness, Virginia has fled her artist lover to set up a commune in far north Queensland, and Sally has been left by the husband she has devoted over twenty years to.

But their love and friendship survive, and it is to Tanglewood, the house they dreamt of, that they go to gather the strength to take them into the future.

'A compelling novel conceived in the turbulent waters at the interface of life and art.' Peter Carey

*'*Tanglewood *loops through four decades as it tells the story of three women learning to claim their place in the world . . . often wry and sardonic, always absorbing.'* Glenda Adams

'Does for Australian readers what Marilyn French did for American readers.' Veronica Sen, *Canberra Times*

THE JACARANDA YEARS

KRISTIN WILLIAMSON

Meg, Sally and Virginia share a special friendship begun at university in the early 1960s. Idealistic, talented and ambitious, thirty years on they lead very different lives.

Meg, editor of a radical independent newspaper, is confronted by an angry young woman from her past who is determined to make her suffer.

Sally juggles the demands of a family with her promising writing career, realising that she must sell the old home as a final break with her estranged husband. But can she let go?

Virginia, struggling to maintain her dream of an art gallery in the rainforest, finds an unexpected and very special love.

Witty, sad, lively and familiar, *The Jacaranda Years* reflects on the wisdom and the freedom of the middle years.

'Williamson writes knowingly and frankly about key issues that have touched Australian society in the past three decades.'
Sydney Morning Herald